Alexander Tille

Yule and Christmas

Their Place in the Germanic Year

Alexander Tille

Yule and Christmas
Their Place in the Germanic Year

ISBN/EAN: 9783337378950

Printed in Europe, USA, Canada, Australia, Japan

Cover: Foto ©Andreas Hilbeck / pixelio.de

More available books at **www.hansebooks.com**

·YULE AND CHRISTMAS·

THEIR·PLACE IN THE GERMANIC YEAR

BY

ALEXANDER TILLE, PH.D.

LECTURER IN GERMAN LANGUAGE AND LITERATURE IN THE UNIVERSITY OF GLASGOW

DAVID NUTT, 270-271 STRAND, LONDON

1899

PREFACE

This book treats of the problems connected with the Germanic year—the three-score-day tide of Yule, the Germanic adoption of the Roman calendar, and the introduction of the festival of Christ's Nativity into a part of the German year, which till then had apparently been without a festivity. It traces the revolution brought about by these events, in custom, belief, and legend up to the fourteenth century. By that time, the Author believes, most of the fundamental features which go towards the making of modern Christmas had already come to have their centre in the 25th day of December.

Five chapters of the present book—but somewhat shortened—appear simultaneously in the *Proceedings of the Glasgow Archæological Society*.

ALEXANDER TILLE.

2 STRATHMORE GARDENS, HILLHEAD,
GLASGOW, *March*, 1899.

CONTENTS

YULE AND CHRISTMAS:

CHAPTER I.

THE GERMANIC YEAR.

THE oldest descriptive remark on the mode in which the Germanics divided their year is exactly eighteen hundred years old. It is found in the *Germania* of Tacitus, which, in all probability, was written A.D. 98, and runs thus: "They do not divide the year into so many seasons as we do. Only winter, spring, and summer have a name and a meaning among them; the name of autumn they know as little as its gifts."[1] It plainly means that the Germans of the first century of our era divided their year into three seasons, the names of which cannot, of course, have exactly corresponded to the Latin terms, *hiems*, *ver*, and *aestas*, each covering a quarter of a year. This statement has been assailed from various sides, and for various reasons, even Jacob Grimm expressing his belief that it was based on some misconception by Tacitus.[2] He understood Tacitus to refer solely to the meaning of the words, and remarked that the Romans did not use

---

[1] *Germania*, chap. xxvi., "Unde annum quoque ipsum non in totidem digerunt species: hiems et ver et aestas intellectum et vocabula habent; autumni perinde nomen et bona ignorantur."

[2] *Deutsche Mythologie*, p. 717.

A

the name of *autumnus* for the harvest of grain, but for the gathering of fruit, vintage, and after-math, things which were at that time unknown to the Germans.   But such a view is scarcely tenable.   For Tacitus speaks decidedly of the seasons as such, and in the case of *autumnus*, at the non-existence of which the Romans might wonder, he makes an explanatory and rather melancholy observation.   In course of time, on a closer study of the questions connected with the Germanic partition of the year, extensive material has been discovered which undoubtedly goes to support Tacitus. Grimm himself lived to collect part of it, and to admit that he had been wrong.[1]

Another scholar has told us that he knows better than Tacitus, and that the ancient Germans had the word *herbst*, with the meaning " time of fruits." But that word seems to have meant originally, just like English *harvest*, the act of reaping the ripe grain and fruits, and not the time of their ripeness, though it was later used to denote the period of bringing in the harvest.   Considerations of that kind can as little influence our judgment on Tacitus' report as can the fact that we are unable to say exactly which German word he meant to correspond with Latin *ver*, spring; for *spring*, *lent* (German *Lenz*), and *Frühling* are, as is generally admitted, of later growth.

The tri-partition of the Germanic year is an unshakable fact.   It has been preserved for a very long time on legal ground.   The three seasons answer to the three not-ordered law courts, *i.e.*, the three annual legal meetings which were fixed by tradition and not called by special royal ordinance.   This fact is even admitted by Professor Weinhold of Berlin in his book on the German division of the year, who, on the whole, takes the view that the Germanics, just like the Romans, quartered their year according to solstices and equinoxes.[2]   Professor Weinhold, however, there concedes so much as to acknowledge that those law courts were originally held at the beginning of winter, in spring, and about midsummer: whilst later the beginning of winter, midwinter, spring; midwinter, Easter, mid-

---

[1] *Geschichte der deutschen Sprache*, Leipzig, 1848, Vol. I., p. 74.
[2] *Über die deutsche Jahrteilung*, Kiel, 1862, p. 8.

summer; and February, May, autumn, took the place of those terms. Professor Weinhold gives[1] proofs for the several cases. Others agree with him in this proposition. So the greatest German authority on chronology, Grotefend, says:[2] "The tri-partition of the year has been preserved almost exclusively in juridical relations, and there finds its principal application in the so-called *dreidinge, echtendinge, echtendage,* or *etting,* the not-ordered law court of the country, which was held at three terms in the year. The terms vary, though with a general prevalence of midwinter (or beginning of winter), Easter, and midsummer (also the Twelve-nights, Easter, and Pentecost, or St. John's day), the basis of the tri-partition being a division of the year into winter, spring, and summer."

The capitulary of Louis the Pious, of 817, ordains "*in anno tria solummodo generalia placida,*"[3] which, of course, can only be taken as a codification of existing law, and not as a creation of a new jurisdiction. This usage lived on till at least the fifteenth century.[4] The fact of the early existence of three German annual law courts is so generally admitted that it is an exception for any authority to disagree. And even those who disagree have to account for a number of important indisputable facts. So Pfannenschmid,[5] believing that there were four Germanic law assemblies annually, finds it extremely strange that far more frequently only three such assemblies are enumerated, and that the examples of four assemblies are both rarer and later than those of three.

In Anglo-Saxon times the tri-partition of the year was preserved in the mode of paying the wages of female servants, who received a sheep for the feast at the beginning of winter, a measure of beans for the mid-lent dinner (Sunday *Invocavit*), and whey '*on sumera*' (corresponding

---

[1] *Über die deutsche Jahrteilung,* Kiel, 1862, pp. 18, 19.

[2] *Zeitrechnung des deutschen Mittelalters,* 1891, p. 90, *Jahreszeiten.*

[3] Sohm, *Fränkische Reichs- und Gerichtsverfassung,* p. 398.

[4] " 1407 in unsen geheygeden gerichten to Luneborch drie des jares to den eddagen " (Centralarchiv zu Oldenburg), Grotefend, *Zeitrechnung,* II., 2, 194, Hannover und Leipzig, 1898.

[5] *Germanische Erntefeste,* 1878, p. 338.

to Old Icelandic '*at sumri*,' *i.e.*, June 9), which is about July 10.[1] It not only appears from the value of the gifts mentioned that the gift for the winter feast was the largest, but besides the enumeration of the three terms begins with that term, as the old Germanic, and so late as in the eleventh century the economic, year began with it.[2]

In the thirteenth century three terms existed in some districts of Eng-

---

[1] Thorpe's *Ancient Laws*, I., 436, 7, "Rectitudo Ancillae : Uni ancillae VIII. pondia annonae ad victum. I. ovis vel III. denarios, ad hiemale companagium, I. sester fabae ad quadragesimalem convictum. In estate suum hweig vel I. denarium ; Be Wifmonna Metsunge. Dheowan wifmen VIII. pund cornes to mete, I. sceap odhdhe III. peningas to winter-sufle, I. syster beana to lœngten-sufle. hwœig on sumera odhdhe I. pening."

[2] Male servants also received three such gifts a year (*Ibid.*, I., 436, 7: "Omnibus ehtemannis jure competit Natalis firma, et Paschalis sulhæcer, id est, carruce acra, et manipulus Augusti in augmentum jure debiti recti ; Eallum œhte-mannum gebyredh Mid-winter feorm. and Eastor-feorm sulh-æcer. and hœrfest-handful. to-eacan heora nyd-rihte "), though two of the terms for these had, in the eleventh century, shifted to the two Christian festivals, Christmas and Easter, while the third had, in the same direction, moved onwards to August. The payment of shepherds' wages is regulated not so much by an old tri-partition of the year as by the development of sheep during the year (*Ibid.*, I., 438, 9 : " Pastoris ovium rectum est, ut habeat dingiam XII. noctium in Natali Domini, et I. agnum de juventute hornotina, et I. belflis, id est, timpani vellus, et lac gregis sui, VII. noctibus ante equinoctium, et blede, id est, cuppam plenam mesgui de siringia, tota estate ; Sceap-hyrdes riht is that he hæbbe twelf nihta dhingan to Middan-wintra. and I. lamb of geares geogedhe. and I. bel-flys. and his heorde meolc VII. niht œfter emnihtes dœge. and blede fulle hweges odhdhe syringe ealne sumor"), just as the payment of goatherds is (*Ibid.*, I., 438, 9 : " Caprarius convenit lac gregis sui post festum Sancti Martini, et antea pars sua mesgui, et capricum anniculum, si bene custodiat gregem suum ; Be Gât-hyrde. Gât-hyrde gebyredh his heorde meolc ofer Martinus mœsse dœig. and œr dham his dœl hwœges. and I. ticcen of geares geogedhe. gif he his heorde wel begymedh "). The dinners given to the farm servants varied considerably about 1030, being held partly at the two Christian festivals, Christmas and Easter, partly at other times (*Ibid.*, I., p. 440, 1: " In quibusdam locis datur firma Natalis Domini, et firma Paschalis, et firma precum ad congregandas segetes, et gutfirma ad arandum, et firma pratorum fenandorum et hreaccroppum, id est, macoli summitas, et firma ad macolum faciendum. In terra nemorosa, lignum plaustri ; in terra uberi, caput macholi : et alia plurima fuerint a pluribus, quorum hoc viaticum sit, et quod supra diximus ; on sumere [in some !] dheode gebyredh winter-feorm. Easter-feorm. ben-form for ripe. gyt-feorm for yrdhe mœdh-med hreac-mete. œt wudu-lade wœn-treow. œt corn-lade hreac-copp. and fela dhinga de ic getellan ne mœig. Dhis is dheah myngung manna biwiste and eal that ic œr beforan ymberehte ").

land.[1] On German ground it is the very same. To give at least one instance, which covers both the law courts and the terms of payment from the twelfth century : on Jan. 9, 1106, Archbishop Frederick I. of Cologne fixed at 14 solidi the fee to be paid to the provost of Gerresheim on each of the three annual law-days.[2]

However well established these facts are, etymology cannot be adduced in favour of an ancient tri-partition of the Germanic year ; ancient names of three ancient seasons cannot be given ; nay, etymology decidedly points to a dual division.[3] We have, therefore, to accept this as a fact, as well warranted as the tri-partition of the economic year itself. Whilst no other Aryan language possesses the same terms denoting a period of about a hundred and eighty days, all Germanic languages have in common the two words *winter* and *summer*, whilst there is no third season-name to join them. Nay, even more : the word *winter* appears in no Aryan language except the Germanic, all other Aryan languages using for the denomination of the coldest season of the year a word from a root *ghim* (*ghiem*) which means snow or storm (Greek χεῖμα); so that we have Latin *hiems*, Greek χειμών, Old Bulgarian and Zend *zima*, Sanskrit *hêmanta*. We know of no root from which winter might be derived, the derivation from *wind* being excluded on philological grounds. With the word *summer* it is not much different. It appears in all Germanic languages as the name of the warmer half of the year, but exists in no other Aryan language, notwithstanding that words from the same root, though formed by means of other suffixes and having a similar or the same significance, are found in several of them, such as Sanskrit *samâ*, year ; Zend *hama*, summer ; Armenian *amarn*, summer ; Cymric *ham*, *haf*, summer.

---

[1] Nasse, *Über mittelalterliche Feldgemeinschaft in England*, Bonn, 1869, p. 51, Urbarium of the Monastery of Worcester of the thirteenth century, fol. 103[b] : "In hoc manerio sunt 8 virgatae servilis conditionis, quarum quaelibet, si censat, dabit ad quemlibet trium terminorum 12[d] pro omni servitio, ut dicunt."

[2] Kessel, *Der selige Gerrich, Stifter der Abtei Gerresheim*, Düsseldorf, 1877, p. 187.

[3] On the dual division of the original Aryan year, compare O. Schrader, *Die aelteste Zeitteilung des indogermanischen Volkes*, Berlin, Habel, 1878, pp. 11 ss., where the etymological parallels of *hiems* and *ver* are given.

When Hildebrand, in the Old-High-German *Hildebrandslied*, describes his thirty years' wanderings, he says:

"Ih wallôta sumaro enti wintro sehstic ur lante;"[1]

Anglo-Saxon legal language having the same phrase. So the laws of Ine provide that the wife of a ceorl who died, if she has a child, should be given, in addition to VI. shillings, "a cow in summer and an ox in winter";[2] also that a ceorl's close ought to be fenced winter and summer.[3] These two names do not stand alone as the supports of a dual division; there is a number of other phrases which show that the dual division of the year was extremely familiar to the Germanic mind. To denote the whole course of a year, especially in legal language, the terms were used: *im rîse und im lôve*,[4] *im rûwen und im blôten*,[5] and *bî strô ánd bî grase*.[6]

Etymology shows that the dual division of the year was of Aryan home growth; and the very fact that etymology fails as to the tri-partition goes a long way to prove that the tri-partition is of foreign extraction. It certainly is so, and, as far as we can see, it is of Egyptian origin, although it was taken over by the Aryans very early, perhaps even at the time before they divided into self-dependent tribes which evolved idioms of their own. Ewald sums up his investigations as to the division of the Oriental year as follows:[7] "People in those countries of Asia and Africa, according to all evidence, had at first three equal seasons. These were fixed in the most ancient Egyptian almanac, and according to that fact in the hieroglyphic writings, the four months of each of these seasons

---

[1] Braune, *Althochdeutsches Lesebuch*, Halle, 1881, p. 77. A St. Gall document of A.D. 858 mentions two brothers, *Wintar* and *Sumar* (O. Schrader, *Die aelteste Zeitteilung des indogermanischen Volkes*, Berlin, Habel, 1878, p. 18). On the combats between Winter and Summer, compare Uhland's *Volkslieder*. Prof. Max Müller's attempts to show in Greek legends a great number of similar traits seem to me to be rather bold.

[2] *Ancient Laws and Institutes of England* (ed. by Thorpe), London, 1840, I., p. 126, xxxviii.: "cû on sumera. oxan on wintra."

[3] *Ibid.*, p. 126, xv.: "wintres ond sumeres."

[4] Grimm, *Deutsche Rechtsaltertümer*, III., 256, 258.   [5] *Ibid.*, III., 249.

[6] *Ibid.*, III., 31, 62, 130, 190, 223; Grotefend, *Zeitrechnung des deutschen Mittelalters*, I., 77.

[7] *Die Altertümer des Volkes Israel*, 3rd. ed., pp. 455, 456.

being very simply counted as the first, the second, etc."[1] About the earliest Indian year Grimm remarks:[2] "In earliest antiquity the year seems to have been divided into three parts only, the Indians distinguishing either *vasanta*, spring; *grîschma*, summer; and *sarad*, raining time; or, according to the oldest commentator of the Veda: *grischma*, summer; *varscha*, raining time; *hêmanta*, winter; and elsewhere six seasons. The Greeks had ἔαρ, spring; θέρος, summer; χειμών, winter." The early Aryans, like the Orientals in general, subdivided their three large seasons into six smaller, of the duration of about three-score days each. Ewald, after the passage just quoted, goes on to say:[3] "A further step was to divide each of the three seasons into halves and so count six seasons. This habit became law in ancient India, as is shown by Kâlidâsa's *Ritusanhâra*, but it must also have once been prevalent in Syriac and Arabic countries. The proof of this is the fact that, in the Syriac as well as in the Arabic almanac, frequently two subsequent months are distinguished as the first and second of the same 'tide,' and that tide after which they are called is evidently a season. The distinction between a first and second month according to such seasons has, it is true, only effect when the months, at least in principle, are at the same time calculated by means of the solar year. But, as we know, that was the case pretty early."[4]

These very same three-score-day tides are found among the Germanics, Eastern and Western. But the strange fact that no satisfactory Germanic or even Aryan etymology can be given for the oldest names of Germanic three-score-day tides, *Jiuleis* (Gothic), *Lida*, *Hlyda* (Anglo-Saxon), and perhaps *Rheda*, *Hreda* (Anglo-Saxon), and *Hornung*, *Horowune* (German), seems

---

[1] Lepsius, *Chronologie der Aegypter*, I., p. 134.

[2] *Geschichte der deutschen Sprache*, 1848, I., p. 72.   [3] *Ibid.*, p. 456.

[4] O. Schrader is the first to avoid the presupposition that the early Aryans based their partition of the year on a knowledge of the stars. He did so with full consciousness (O. Schrader, *Die aelteste Zeitteilung des indogermanischen Volkes*, Berlin, Habel, 1878, pp. 24), 32, and expressly says that the three roots used for denoting sun in the Aryan languages contain no element referring in any way to time or partition of time, whilst as regards the moon he attributes to her merely a secondary rank in that respect, and remarks that the origin of the months dates from no earlier period than the time when the Aryan tribe had split into several peoples.

to point to the probability that these names, like the institutions they denote, have their origin beyond the world of the Aryan family of languages and nations, and were borrowed from Egyptian and Syriac, or some other Oriental language, together with the six three-score-day tides which formed the course of a year. This probability is enhanced by the fact that Gothic *Jiuleis* in the forms ἰλαῖος, ἰουλαῖος, ἰουλίηος, and ἰούλιος is found to denote the time from Dec. 22 to Jan. 23 in old Cyprus,[1] which can scarcely be ascribed to chance. It is Jacob Grimm's merit to have gathered a number of important facts which show the same habit to have prevailed among several Aryan tribes, including the Germanics.

"Stress is to be laid," says he,[2] "on the connection of two (or even three) subsequent months through the same name, which connection seems to be a relic of an original partition of the whole of the year into six (or four)[3] parts. Thus, among the Anglo-Saxons, there appeared a double *lidha* for the pair June-July, which elsewhere also appears bound together as *brachot-houwot*, or the two *resaille-mois*, and a double *geola*. Thus, in Middle-High-German, there appears a double *ougest*, a double *wintermonat*, (a threefold *herbstmonat*). January and February are even much later singled out as the large and the small *horn*; nay, here and there we find the second of two months presented as the wife of the first, and a *sporkel* followed by a *spörkelsin* and an *ougest* by an *ögstin*. Likewise we find among the Slavs a small and a large *traven*, a small and a large *serpan*, where the small precedes the large one, whilst our small *horning* succeeds the large *horn*. (The Lüneburg Wenden also made a first *wintermonat*, September, precede the other, which was December.) According to Slavic order, however, the small *červen* preceded the large *červenec*. Something similar is found in the Celtic *midu* and *michrundu* for November and December; *ephan*, summer, and *gorephan*, main summer, for June and July.

---

[1] K. Fr. Hermann, *Über Griechische Monatskunde*, Göttingen, 1844, p. 64.
[2] *Geschichte der deutschen Sprache*, 1848, I., 110s.
[3] I put in round brackets what seems to me to be wrong in Grimm's argument. When the meaning of the common heading of two subsequent months was forgotten, and Roman quarters of years had become popular, a third month was sometimes added under the same name, a usage to which the intercalary month may have led.

Even the gipsies, whose month-names are given by Pott (I. 116), style June and July by the cognate names *nutibé* and *nunutibé*; and in Albanese γόστι and γοστοβίοστε for August and November we have the same thing. This coupling is in my eyes a testimony of great age. (The Attic calendar in the leap year added another Ποσειδεών after the first, as the Jews did after their *adar*, a *veadar* or other *adar*.) The Arabic lunar year still shows its months connected in six regular pairs : *rebi el avvel* and *rebi el accher*, *dschemâdi el avvel* and *dschemâdi el accher*, *dsulkade* and *dsulhedsche*. The Syriac year shows a *theschrin* I. and II. and a *khamm* I. and II.; whilst in the Persian and Jewish calendar this coupling has been lost. But it is quite apparent in the division of the Indian year into six parts, each of which embraces two months, most of which have cognate names, viz.: *vasanta*, spring, contains the months *madhu*, mead or honey, and *mâdhava*, honey sweet; *grischma*, summer, contains the months *shukra*, the light one, and *shukhi*, the shining one; *varscha*, the raining tide, contains the months *nabhas*, cloud (Latin *nubes*, Slavic *nebo*, cloudy sky), and *nabhasja*, the cloudy one; *sarad*, sultry tide, contains the months *ischa* and *ûrgha*, the nourishing one; *hêmanta*, winter, contains the months *sahas*, strength, and *sahasja*, the strong one; *sisira*, dew tide, contains the months *tapas*, warmth, and *tapasja*, the warm one. The relation of the names *tapas* and *tapasja*, *nabhas* and *nabhasja*, *sahas* and *sahasja*, *madhu* and *mâdhava* is analogous to *sporkel* and *spörkelsin*, *ougest* and *öugstin*; *gosti* and *gostobieste*, *terwen* and *terwenec*, and the Sanskrit names given here seem to be more popular than the learned ones, which were fixed for the *âditjas*; and through the division of the Indian year into six seasons, the division of the Germanic year into three seasons, which immediately proceeds from it, is justified in a way that must be welcome to us." Further on[1] he says, "A connection between our month-names and the six Indian seasons, and the coupling always of two subsequent months, which proceeds from them, must be acknowledged."[2]

---

[1] *Geschichte der deutschen Sprache*, p. 113.

[2] In Mahâbhârata the six Indian seasons *vasanta, grîsma, varsa, çarad, hemanta,* and *çiçira* are represented as six men who play at golden and silver dice (O. Schrader, *Die aelteste Zeitteilung des indogermanischen Volkes*, Berlin, Habel, 1878, p. 22).

Grimm indicates in a general way the facts that point to an early six-partition of the Germanic year. But since his day so much material bearing upon the point has accumulated, that it is necessary to enumerate the most important items of it. On the Nether-Rhine the division of the year into six tides or periods of sixty days each was known till so late as the fourteenth century, although then it was thought to be antiquated as compared with the new Romano-Christian way of deter-mining seasons. As the starting-point people then, as of old, took one of the three ends of the seasons, July 12, counting from then to September 17, November 11, January 13, March 17, and May 12, by ancient Ger-manic three-score day tides or half seasons. Neither eight weeks nor nine weeks exactly covering these tides, eight weeks and nine weeks were alternately taken. On November 11, therefore, winter began, on March 17 early summer, and on July 12 later summer.[1]

It is rather difficult to say what were the names of these Germanic three-score-day tides, although in German legal and literary documents there occur quite numerous denominations which clearly cover a longer time than a month, and yet neither amount to three nor to four months.

Such are, *e.g.*, *in der brache, in der zwibrache, in der herbstsat,*[2] *in der erne, im houwet, im hanffluchet,*[3] *ze afterhalme und houwe,*[4] *in der bonenarne.*[5] Others are *im brâchet, im wimmot, in der sât, in dem snite, laubbrost,* and *laubrîse,*[6] *haberschnitt,* and *habererndte,* covering August and September, and

---

[1] "Urbarium of the Monastery of St. Victor, Xanten," in the State-Archive, Düsseldorf, under "Stift Xanten," R, No. 8ᵃ, leaf 8ᵃ. The passage was communicated to me, like all the unprinted material referring to the Rhine-country and Tirol, by Dr. Armin Tille of Bonn.   It runs: "Item notandum, quod secundum antiquum modum computandi servicium potest poni per certos terminos infra dictos, scilicet a festo *Margarete* (ubi annus incipit) usque *Lamberti* sunt 9 ebdomade, item a Lamberti usque *Martini* sunt octo ebdomade, item a Martini usque *festum baculi,* quod est octava epiphanie, et sunt 9 ebdomade. Item a festo baculi usque *Gertrudis* sunt 9 ebdomade, item a festo Gertrudis usque ad festum *Pancracii* sunt 8 ebdomade, item a festo Pancracii usque Margarete sunt novem ebdomade et faciunt simul unum annum, scilicet 52 ebdomadas."
[2] Grimm, *Deutsche Rechtsaltertümer,* III., 546.
[3] *Ibid.,* I., 419.   [4] *Ibid.,* I., 673, 679.
[5] Neocorus, II., 75, 426; Weinhold, *Deutsche Jahrteilung,* 1862, p. 13.
[6] Weinhold, *Die deutschen Monatnamen,* Halle, 1869, p. 2.

sometimes even including the time from July 25 to August 1.[1]   To these
lenz (lent, A.S. *lengten*) and *herbst* (harvest) in their medieval senses are to
be added, the latter being on German ground frequently replaced by *augst*
(August), which, however, covers a longer time than August, so that July 25,
St. James's day, can be called *Jacobstag im augst*.[2]   It was out of such words
that the Germanic month-names were formed in the second half-millennium
of our era, after the Roman calendar had become popular among the
Germanics.   So Professor Weinhold[3] seems to be of opinion that *in der erne*
is older than the month-name *ernemânot*; that *im brâchet* and *im höuwet* are
older than *brâchmonat*; and that *höumat* and *im wimmot* are older than
windumemanot: and he expressly states that, according to his belief, *in der
sât* and *in dem snite* have given origin to *sâtmân* and *schnitmonat*, and that
laubbrost and *laubrîse* under our eyes become, by being taken in a narrower
sense, something like month-names.[4]   Beside these words English expressions like *fall*, *backend*, "*houl o' winter*" are to be placed, and perhaps,
also, two other words which later were used to correspond to Latin *ver*
and *autumnus*.   For *ver* the Western Germanics took a root, *lang*, perhaps
connected with *long*, forming out of it a term for the time when the
days grow longer (Old-High-German *langiz*, *lenzo*, *lenzin*; Middle-High-
German *lenze*; Dutch *lente*; Anglo-Saxon *lengten*, *lencten*; English *lent*),
which, however, cannot be traced beyond the Western Germanic, not to
mention the common Germanic.[5]   This makes it rather likely that it was
not the name of an old three-score-day tide, but was formed new.   The
term adopted to correspond to *autumnus* is also confined to Western Germanic, although its root is common Aryan property.   It is Old-High-

---

[1] Grotefend, *Die Zeitrechnung des deutschen Mittelalters*, 1891, I., 79.

[2] Grotefend, *Zeitrechnung*, I., 87.

[3] *Die deutschen Monatnamen*, Halle, 1869, pp. 1, 2.

[4] If Neocorus, II., 315, explains *in howman edder in der howarne* (Weinhold, *Ibid.*,
p. 13), it follows that he regarded the term *howarne* as still more popular than the newly
formed word *howman*.

[5] Since the fifteenth century it has been in German supplanted by the term *Frühling*
(from *früh*, Gothic *frô*,* early; Greek πρωΐ), and in English by *spring* (cp. 1 *Sam.* ix. 26,
"about the spring of the day"; Shakespeare, 2 *Henry IV.* iv. 4. 35, "since the middle
summer's spring").

German *herbist*, Middle-High-German *herbest*, Dutch *herfst*, Anglo-Saxon *hærfest*, English *harvest*, and belongs to Latin *carpere*, to pluck, and Greek καρπός, fruit.[1]

Yet more important than these rather vague terms are several others which can be proved to have exactly covered a Germanic tide of three-score days. They are the more striking since, in two cases, it is simply Roman month-names which are used for denoting a tide of two months, so that two subsequent Roman months among the Germanics are frequently called by the same name, the first being called the former, and the second the latter month of that designation; whilst some Germanic names of the same kind are of very great age.

The Scandinavian summer of six months is divided into three tides called *Vaarmoaner*, *Sumarmoaner*, and *Haustmoaner*;[2] *herbst* as denoting the two months September and October is very common in the Middle Ages, so that the former month is called *der erste herbst*, and the latter *der andere herbst*.[3]

In a Gothic *calendarium* of the sixth century[4] November, or *Naubaimbair*,

---

[1] Scandinavian *haust* or *höst* is probably to be derived from *August*, which in the Middle Ages appeared as *aust*. In English the Germanic word *harvest* in the later sense of a season was completely superseded by Romance *autumn*.

[2] Weinhold, *Altnordisches Leben*, Berlin, 1856, pp. 371-383.

[3] Grotefend, *Zeitrechnung des deutschen Mittelalters*, I., 84; Weinhold, *Deutsche Monatnamen*, pp. 15, 42. There appears even a *dritt herbst* for November. The naming of three subsequent months as first, second, and third *augst* or *herbst* admits of several explanations. The Roman quarter of a year having taken the place of the old third, it was but natural that all the three months forming it should have received a common name; there is no doubt that in this way *herbst*, which simply meant *harvest*, advanced to the meaning of the season of autumn. This is the more likely, since the tripling of the month-name is found just in that season, which, according to Tacitus, among the Germanics had no name. Beda also has such a tripling in the case of the Lida month, though for another purpose, viz., for forming an intercalary month for the leap year. His June, July, and third Lida covering to a large extent the same ground as the July, August, and September, called the three *herbste* or *augste*, it may seem probable that the leap year had also to do with the origination of the series of three months bearing the same name. That it was August which was doubled may be inferred from Northic *tvîmânadhr*, double-month, which is the name for August, and has not been understood by Professor Weinhold.

[4] Moritz Heyne, *Ulfilas*, Paderborn und Münster, 1885, p. 226.

is called *fruma Iiuleis*, which presupposes that December was called **aftuma Iiuleis*; in Beda's list of Germanic month-names[1] it is stated that the Anglo-Saxons called December and January together *Giuli*, for which, later, the terms *ærra Geola* and *æftera Geola* were used; in the same place Beda states that the Anglo-Saxons called June and July *ærra Lida* and *æftera Lida* respectively; in Middle Germany up to this day January is called *der grosse Horn*, February *der kleine Horn*. Both names together occur in Christian Wolf's *Mathematical Dictionary*, Leipzig, 1742, which borrowed all kinds of things from the dialects spoken in Saxony; but *Hornung* (*i.e.*, small Horn or son of Horn) is found among the list of German month-names composed by Charlemagne, and brought down to us by his biographer Eginhart.[2] It being the only name in the list which is not a compound of *mânôth*, it is bound to be of ancient German origin. The forms occurring elsewhere are *Hornung*, *Horning*, *horner* and *horn*.[3]

As a rule, *der erst herbst* is September,[4] and *der ander herbst* October.[5] But November also appears as *der ander herbst*,[6] though more frequently as *der drit herbst*,[7] September also being called *Überherbst*.[8] It shows a state of things a little further advanced when, as is frequently the case, *der erste* and *der andere herbst* are replaced by *der erste* and *der andere herbstmonat*;[9] likewise there are numerous examples for November

---

[1] *De Temporum Ratione*, chap. xv.　　[2] *Vita Caroli Magni*, chap. xxix.

[3] Grotefend, *Zeitrechnung des deutschen Mittelalters und der Neuzeit*, 1891, I., 86. I should be inclined to see in *Horn* the name of an old German three-score-day tide, just as in Yule and Lida. Compare on *Horn*, however, Weinhold, *Deutsche Monatnamen*, p. 45.

[4] Diefenbach, *Novum Glossarium*, 32; *Codex Germanicus Monacensis*, 93, 398, 700, 730; *Gräzer Kalender*; "der erst heribst," *Codex Germanicus Monacensis*, 349.

[5] *Klingenberger Kronik*, 343; Diefenbach, *Novum Glossarium*, 32; *Codex Germ. Monac.*, 93, 398, 480, 700, 730, 771; *Gräzer Kalender*; Huber, "der ander herbst," *Giess. MS.*, 978; Weinhold, *Die deutschen Monatnamen*, pp. 41, 42.

[6] *Codex Germ. Monac.*, 32.

[7] Diefenbach, *Novum Glossarium*, 32; *Codex Germ. Monac.*, 349, 730.

[8] *Tegernseer Kalender*; Weinhold, *Ibid.*, p. 42.

[9] Grimm, *Geschichte der deutschen Sprache*, I., p. 85; *Zellweger*, No. 191, a. 1407; Weinhold, *Deutsche Monatnamen*, p. 15, note, and pp. 42, 43, where a long list of cases is given. November is sometimes called *der dritt herbistmanot* (*Ibid.*, p. 43), and December *der vierd herbistmonad* or *letst herbistmoneth* (Grotefend, *Zeitrechnung*, I., 84), a fact which leads us beyond Roman quarters of years into Germanic thirds of years. *Unser frauen*

being called *der erst winter*, and December being called *der ander winter* (and even January being named *manot des hindrosten winters*) ;[1] so November is also called *der erst wintermaneid*,[2] and December *der ander wintermaneid*,[3] or *der lest wintermond*.[4] On Bavarian ground, a Tegernsee calendar[5] calls March and April *das erst ackermonat* and *das ander ackermonat* ;[6] to these cases two others are to be added, in which Roman month-names are used for the same purposes. There is quite an abundance of instances in which May is called *der erst may*, and June *der ander may* ;[7] the same holds good for *der erst augst*, meaning August, and *der ander augst*, meaning September, so that even the term occurs : *in den tzweyen augsten*.[8] In the Diocese

---

dulttag in dem ersten herbstmanode, Sept. 8, A.D. 1290, Pilgram ; Grotefend, *Zeitrechnung*, I., 68.

[1] See Weinhold, *Deutsche Monatnamen*, p. 61.   [2] *Ibid.*, p. 62.   [3] *Ibid.*, p. 62.

[4] Grotefend, *Zeitrechnung*, I., 208, where also an instance is given of February being called *der letzte wintermonat*, A.D. 1536, Ulm, which again points to four winter months or Germanic thirds of years.

[5] Pfeiffer, *Germania*, IX., 192 f. ; Weinhold, *Deutsche Monatnamen*, 14.

[6] Grotefend, *Zeitrechnung*, I., 1.

[7] Weinhold, *Deutsche Monatnamen*, pp. 13, 50, where a whole group of old Bavarian almanacs is mentioned which has this peculiarity ; Grimm, *Geschichte der deutschen Sprache*, 1848, I., 84, according to a Cassel manuscript of A.D. 1445. About some Alemannic and Swabian almanacs, comp. Weinhold, *Ibid.*, p. 15.

[8] *Muglen bei Kovachich*, p. 4 ; Grimm, *Geschichte der deutschen Sprache*, 1848, I., p. 85. In some Bavarian almanacs August and September are called *der erste* and *der andere augst* (Diefenbach, *Novum Glossarium Latino-germanicum*, Francofurti, 1857, 34, and *Tegernseer Fischbüchlein*) ; so it is on Alemannic and Swabian ground (Weinhold, *Deutsche Monatnamen*, p. 15 ; *Codex Germanicus Monacensis*, 32 ; Diefenbach, *Novum Glossarium*, 34 ; Mone, *Anzeiger*, VIII., 496) ; *der ander ougst* is September (Grimm, *Geschichte der deutschen Sprache*, p. 85). Among the German communities of Valsugan and on the hills between Brenta and Drau, August is called *erster Aux*, and September *änderts Aux*, a form in which it also appears in some Roman documents of Rhaetia (Hormayr, *Geschichte der gefürsteten Grafschaft Tirol*, Tübingen, 1806, Part I., Section 1, p. 141). *Der erste augst* means August in *Tegernseer Fischbuch* ; *der erst awgst*, *Giessen MS.*, 978 ; *der erst awst*, *Codex Germanicus Monacensis*, 32 ; whilst *der ander augst* may be August (*Codex Germanicus Monacensis*, 93, 398, 700, 848, 3384 ; *Giessen MS.* 978 ; Gmund's *Kalender* ; *Gräzer Kalender* ; Huber's *Kalender* ; *der andere auste*, Diefenbach, *Novum Glossarium*, 4), or September (Megenberg, Diefenbach, *Novum Glossarium*, 34 ; *Tegernseer Fischbuch* (*der ander augst*)). In the xiii. comuni there are even three *Agester*, meaning August, September, October (*Cimbr. Wörterbuch*, 107 ; Weinhold, *Die deutschen Monatnamen*, p. 32).

of Constanz August is called *ougst*, and September *Haberougst*,[1] or August is called *erster aux*, and September *ander aux*,[2] or August is called *augest*, and September *Augstin, oegsten, auwestin*, *i.e.*, the small *augest*.[3] Sometimes July is called *der erste augst*, and August *der ander augst*.[4] Though *Augstine* and *Aygsten* appear a few times as meaning August,[5] on the whole *Ougstine*, *i.e.*, small August, means September ;[6] nay, there even appears for September the compound *Herbistouwistinne*[7] and the word *Haberougst*.[8] So Konrad von Dankrotsheim in his *Namenbuch*[9] names August and September *ougst* and *oegstin*. On the other hand, *augstmänd, auistmaent, austmaent, owest-man* mean August exclusively.[10]

There is nothing whatever in the Roman calendar which can be said to have been suggestive of that strange custom, so that we have good reason for claiming it as a relic of a pre-Roman Germanic usage. If it was able to influence the Roman calendar so far as to force upon it the three-score-day tide, it must needs have been most deeply rooted and firmly established among the Germanic tribes in East and West, North and South. Not only is the six-fold division of the Germanic year a most important fact in itself, but it also furnishes us with the means of reconciling the seeming contradiction, according to which the Germanics at the same time had a dual division and a tri-partition of the year. The units of which

---

[1] *Ehinger Spitalbuch*, Germanic Museum, Nürnberg, No. 7008.

[2] *Sette communi* ; Schmeller-Frommann, *Bayrisches Wörterbuch*, 54 ; Grotefend, *Zeitrechnung*, I., 14.

[3] Schmeller-Frommann, *Bayrisches Wörterbuch*, 54 (1453, Baselland) ; Grotefend, *Zeitrechnung*, I., 14. Grimm explained the term wrongly as the wife of August.

[4] Grotefend, *Zeitrechnung*, I., 14. [5] *Codex Germanicus Monacensis*, 771.

[6] *Codex Germanicus Monacensis*, 558 (Schmeller, I², 54), *Ougstin*, Dankrotsheim ; *Augstin*, Dasypodius 488d (1537) ; *Ougsten*, Diefenbach, *Novum Glossarium*, 40 ; *Oegstin*, Dankrotsheim ; *Ouwestin*, Köditz, *Leben des heiligen Ludwig*, Leipzig, 1851, 40, 61 ; *Owestin*, Hermann von Fritslar (*Myst.* I., 195) ; Weinhold, *Deutsche Monatnamen*, p. 32 ; Grotefend, *Zeitrechnung*, I., 14.

[7] Köditz, *Leben des heiligen Ludwig*, Leipzig, 1871, 66.

[8] *Ehinger Spitalbuch* ; Weinhold, *Deutsche Monatnamen*, p. 39.

[9] Weinhold, *Ibid.*, p. 16 ; Strobel, *Beiträge zur deutschen Literatur und Literatur-geschichte*, Paris, Strassburg, 1827, p. 109 ss.

[10] Grotefend, *Zeitrechnung des Mittelalters*, Hannover, 1891, I., 14.

their year consisted were sixths, and it is apparent that of these tides either two could each time be grouped together to form thirds, or three could be grouped together each time to form halves. At the same time the simple fact of sixths being the units constituent of the Germanic year excludes any quartering of the year, since a quarter would consist of one-sixth and a half, and would thus most seriously interfere with the unity of the three-score-day tide. If Professor Weinhold [1] says the dual division of the Germanic year was dislodged by a tri-partition, he is entirely in error; for so little can be said of a dislodgment of one mode by the other that for a long prehistoric period both existed peacefully alongside each other, and appear thus at the dawn of history. The Oriental tri-partition of the year would probably not have so deeply rooted itself in the Germanic mind had it not been supported by the economic and climatic conditions of the country they emigrated to. There the most decided season, the winter, fills, on an average, a period of exactly four months, which naturally leads to a division of the rest of the year into two equal parts of four months each. And the economic year was no less naturally divided into three parts—the rest of the plough, the cultivation and reaping of the grass, and the harvest.[2] There is no reason to take refuge in speculations about symbols and the religious opinions of the early Germanics to explain their division of the year. Economic conditions have at all times weighed much heavier than fancies. The centre of animal activity, as well as of the strivings, hopes, and dreams of men, was in pre-Roman Germanic times, as it is now, to win food and to get on in life—in early times by hunting and keeping cattle, later on by cultivation of meadows, and finally by agriculture in addition. Then as now the endless generation of human beings and the endless competition for the means of subsistence among them, which two factors have at all times determined the fates of families, tribes, nations, and races, pressed upon individuals, and compelled them to work by leaving them, if unwilling to do so, the alternative of perishing.

---

[1] *Deutsche Jahrteilung*, 1862, p. 7.
[2] Weinhold, *Deutsche Jahrteilung*, 1862, p. 7.

CHAPTER II.

THE BEGINNING OF THE ANGLO-GERMAN YEAR.

BOTH Caesar and Tacitus tell us that the Germans did not count by days as the Romans did, but by nights, reckoning the *vigilia* or eve as part of the following day.[1]   This habit lived on unbroken through the Middle Ages, and is still living among us, so that we count by fortnights instead of by fourteen days, and speak of the Twelve-nights of Christmas-time.   It was taken over by the early Church, as we know by so good an authority as the Venerable Beda, as regards festivals at least.[2]   In the same way the Germanics reckoned by winters instead of by summers, counting the winter and the summer which followed it as one year, a custom which, however, is not exclusively Germanic.[3]   The *Saxon Chronicle*

---

[1] Caesar, *Bellum Gallicum*, Book VI., chap. xviii. : "Spatia omnis temporis non numero dierum, sed noctium finiunt ; dies natales et mensium et annorum initia observant, ut noctem dies subsequatur."   Tacitus, *Germania*, chap. xi. : "Coeunt nisi quid fortuitum et subitum incidit, certis diebus, cum aut inchoatur luna aut impletur ; nam agendis rebus hoc auspicatissimum initium credunt.   Nec dierum numerum, ut nos, sed noctium computant ; sic constituunt, sic condicunt ; nox ducere diem videtur."   Later instances are given from law literature by Weinhold, *Deutsche Jahrteilung*, notes 2, 3, 11, 12, and 13 ; from documents by Grotefend, *Zeitrechnung des deutschen Mittelalters*, Hannover, 1891, I., p. 131, and 1898, II., 202, under *Nacht*.

[2] *De Temporum Ratione*, chap. v. : "Merito autem quaeritur, quare populus Israel, qui diei ordinem iuxta Moysi traditionem a mane semper usque ad mane servabat, festa tamen omnia sua, sicut et nos hodie facimus, vespere incipiens, vespere consummarit dicente legislatore : A vespera usque ad vesperam celebrabitis sabbata vestra."

[3] Manilius, *Astronomicon*, "per quinquaginta brumas" ; and Martialis, "ante brumas triginta."   On the parallels between night and winter and between day and summer, see O. Schrader, *Die aelteste Zeitteilung des indogermanischen Volkes*, Berlin, Habel, 1878, pp. 12, 44 ss.

B

abounds with examples of that usage.[1] Though it is generally the term *winter* which is used thus, it is by no means exclusively so, other terms, like *louprise* in the Alemannic dialects, being employed in the same sense.[2] Thus there can be no doubt that the Germanic year began with the beginning of winter, and not in the middle of it, as did the Roman year with its dogmatic and unpractical way of dividing time. But when exactly was the Germanic New Year? On an average, in Germany actual winter sets in about the middle of November, when it ceases to be possible to leave cattle, swine, sheep, and horses on the pasture grounds to seek their own food; when it begins to freeze; and when snowfalls become very frequent. There is no doubt that for purely nomadic cattle-keeping tribes, such as at the dawn of history the Germanics certainly were, this is the term which compels them to change all their summer habits, and therefore marks the beginning of a new season in the most incisive way. It may, therefore, be regarded as certain that the Germanic winter did not begin later than at mid-November. But in order to determine whether it did not, perhaps, begin earlier, we need other means than mere economic speculation. We saw above that the Germanics in prehistoric times took over the Oriental year, which was divided into six three-score-day tides. Now the oldest such tide we know of among Germanics was the *Iuleis* tide among the Goths of the sixth century.[3] It exactly covered the Roman months, November and December, November being called *fruma Iuleis*. It is more than unlikely that the beginning of the year should have interfered with any

---

[1] The Parker MS. of the *Saxon Chronicle* (ed. by Earle in " *Two of the Saxon Chronicles Parallel*," Oxford, 1865, p. 2) begins : "thy geare the wæs agan fram Cristes acennesse cccc. wintra and xciiii. uuintra," and in the second paragraph *gear* and *winter* are used as synonyms ("and he hæfde thæt rice xvi. gear . . . and heold xvii. winter . . . heold vii. gear . . . ricsode xvii. gear . . . riscode xxxi. wintra . . . heold xxxi. wintra," *Ibid.*, p. 2). The oldest part of the version belongs to the second half of the ninth century (R. Wülker, *Grundriss zur Geschichte der angelsächsischen Literatur*, Leipzig, 1885, § 509).

[2] Weinhold, *Deutsche Jahrteilung*, pp. 12 and 19 ; just as the Bavarians counted after autumns (*Lex Baiuvariorum*, VIII., 19, 4 ; Weinhold, *Ibid.*).

[3] The periods of three scores of days I call *tides*, the unities of two tides I call Germanic *seasons*, and the unities of three tides I call *half-years*.

such three-score-day tide ; therefore the conclusion will be allowed that it
rather began with the beginning of one. Thus we should have to assume
either November 1 or September 1 to have been the beginning of the
Germanic year. But September bearing in Germany entirely the character
of a summer month,—nay, towards the end of August, the heat frequently
being the greatest in the whole course of the year,—the beginning of
the Germanic year at the beginning of September is practically out of
the question, so that only November 1 remains as a possible beginning.
Among the Goths of the sixth century *fruma Iiuleis* and November were
apparently absolutely identical, as appears from St. Andrew's day—which
is marked down in that calendar as *Fruma Iiuleis* 31—and from some
other saints' days. All we are allowed to conclude from the fact, however, is that the Goths of the sixth century had taken over the Roman
calendar, naming the Roman months by the home-made names of those
Germanic tides which approximately covered them. It by no means follows
from this fact that each of the Germanic pre-Roman three-score-day tides
exactly covered two Roman months. It would be an astounding incident
indeed if that had been the case, and only an extremely rare chance could
account for it. Knowing that the Indian months began shortly after the
middle of the Roman months,[1] we have every reason to assume something
similar for the Germanic three-score-day tides. This assumption is supported by a great number of singular facts. Had each of the six ancient
Germanic tides not exactly, but fairly covered two subsequent Roman
months, we should have to expect that the same would be the case with
the German month-names which sprung up for the denomination of the
Roman months. But the contrary is the case. To quote a witness beyond suspicion, I cite Professor Weinhold,[2] who says : "We find a wavering
of the names between several months : *ackermonat* wavers between March
and April ; *hartmonat* between November, December, and January ; *lasemânt*
means December and January ; *hornung* means January and February ;
hundemân is found to be applied to June, July, and August ; *rosenmânt* to

---

[1] Grimm, *Geschichte der deutschen Sprache*, 1848, I., p. 75.
[2] *Die deutschen Monatnamen*, Halle, 1869, p. 2.

June and July; *sâtmânt* to September and October; *slachtmân* to October,
November, and December; and *sommermonat* to June and July : the names
containing the constituent *vol* (ful) occur for September, November, December, January, and February, and *wolfmonat* appears denoting November,
December, and January "—a list which could easily be increased.   It is now
generally admitted that the Germanic month-names are a very late product, and
that they were merely formed for the purpose of replacing the Latin names.
If, then, the ancient Germanic three-score-day tides extended from about the
middle of one Roman month to the middle of the second next, it was
bound to happen that, at the time when the Roman month-names were
taken over, they were applied to the interval between the middles of two
consecutive Roman months, which means neither more nor less than that
each month-name could be used for two months ; so during the period
of transition it could scarcely be avoided that *e.g.* the term November was
at some places used for the time from October 15 to November 15; whilst on
others it was, with equal right, made to cover the time from November 15 to
December 15.   When, later, the Latin name was replaced by a German word,
the characteristic held good.   In consequence it could not fail to happen,
even in neighbouring places, that, of two consecutive Roman months, sometimes the first and sometimes the second was called by the one Latin name.
Finding, as we do, that the Goths called *Iuleis* the time from November 1 to
December 31, and the Anglo-Saxons called *Geola* the time from December 1
to January 31, we can scarcely help assuming that *Iuleis* originally covered a
period from about November 15 to January 15, and that, at the taking over
of the Roman calendar, among the Goths that name was shifted a fortnight
back, and among the Anglo-Saxons a fortnight forward, so as to create an
incongruence of a whole Roman month.   This argument must needs lead us
to the conclusion that the Germanic *Iuleis* tide extended originally from
about mid-November to mid-January ; for had it extended from mid-October
to mid-December, we should have to expect a wavering of the Yule tide
between October-November and November-December, and not between
November-December and December-January.   All this points to the conclusion that a Germanic three-score-day tide began originally about the
middle of November, and that the beginning of it was at the same time

the beginning of the Germanic year. This result is supported by the Rhenish Urbary of the fourteenth century from the Monastery of St. Victor, Xanten,[1] in which the terms of the six three-score-day tides are July 12, Sept. 17, Nov. 11, Jan. 13, March 17, and May 12, Martinmas being marked out as a term as close to the middle of November as possibly can be expected.

The idea of the Germanic year beginning about Martinmas is not new. Fin Magnusen[2] remarked, about a century ago, that the Germanics began their year about the Advent tide, which for a long time began with the Sunday after Martinmas. Even Weinhold admits that Martinmas coincides with the actual beginning of winter,[3] in which character it is clearly marked by the popular rimes:

<blockquote>
"Sanct Martin
Feuer im Kamin"[4]
</blockquote>

and

<blockquote>
"Sanct Märten Miss
Is der Winter wiss";[5]
</blockquote>

whilst, on the other hand, he maintains that the Germans began their year about the same time as the Romans began a new quarter of the year, i.e., on September 29, St. Michael's Day. It is true he does not even attempt to prove that assertion historically, but with a few vague remarks, which can scarcely be taken seriously, jumps over the whole point which ought to have been the centre of his investigation. It never occurs to him that the Goths regarded November and December as their *Iuleis* tide, and that, if their year was not begun at the 1st of November, it was bound to commence on the beginning of September, when another three-score-day tide took its inception. Only a man who has never in his life left his study for fresh air can maintain that winter began at the close of

---

[1] Staatsarchiv, Düsseldorf, under "Stift Xanten," R, No. 8ª, leaf 8ª.

[2] *Specimen Calendarii gentilis*, p. 1018, according to Pfannenschmid, *Germanische Erntefeste*, p. 512: "Suspicor vulgarem inter veteres Germanos anni adventum posterius inter christianos certo modo mutatum fuisse in adventum domini sive initium anni ecclesiastici."

[3] *Über die deutsche Jahrteilung*, Kiel, 1862, p. 5.

[4] Graesse, *Des deutschen Landmanns Practica*, Dresden, 1858, p. 178.

[5] *Ibid.*, p. 178.

September!¹ Did Professor Weinhold realize that spring began then at
the end of January, when Germany as a rule is ice-bound for another
month and a half—two to three months before cattle are able to pasture
on the meadows? He had not even the courage to follow out the consequences; but makes spring begin "in March," and summer at the summer
solstice! To do him no injustice in any respect, I shall assume that the
phrase "in March" (which implies thirty-one days to select from) is meant
to mean the middle of March. Then we have a winter extending from the
end of September to the middle of March; a spring extending from the
middle of March to June 24; and a summer extending from June 24 to
the end of September (which seems to mean September 29), i.e., a winter
of more than five months and a half! a spring of three months and nine
days! and a summer of three months and five days!—a calculation which
certainly does all honour to the arithmetical attainments of our Germanic
ancestors and their distinct sense of the equality of three thirds! Would
one take the phrase "in March" as "in the end of March," the time
when storks and swallows return in flocks and the grass begins to grow
green again, we should have a winter of full six months, a spring of not
quite three months, and a summer of a little more than three months.

But perhaps one must not draw the consequences from these ill-considered
assumptions. The truth is, that a beginning of the Germanic winter about
the end of September is absolutely untenable, that it really took place
about the middle of November, while the end of September did not
become of importance as a dividing-point of the year until the introduction of the Roman quartering of the year, under the reign of which a new
quarter began on October 1, and was fixed by the Church on September 29,
i.e., on Michaelmas.

Having, at last, arrived at the starting-point, it will be necessary to
cast a glance over the whole of the Germanic year, and to draw once and
for all the theoretical conclusions from that result. Counting by original
Germanic half-years, *summers* and *winters*, we have to fix the other
junction-point of the two at mid-May, a term dear to all who have the

---

¹ Graesse, *Des deutschen Landmanns Practica*, Dresden, 1858, p. 718.

happiness of receiving house rents in Scotland.   Counting with Oriental-made thirds of years, or Germanic seasons, we have to close the winter and begin the early summer at mid-March, and to close the early summer and begin the late summer at mid-July.   If this really be the old Germanic division of the year, it is bound to be preserved in all kinds of recollections and institutions: above all, in legal institutions, in popular tradition, in folk-belief and rustic custom, in festivals and bonfires, and, last but not least, in ecclesiastical habits which, as far as they were created after the fifth century of our era, reflect an enormous amount of Germanic tradition and thought.

CHAPTER III.

THE FEAST OF MARTINMAS.

THE term at which Roman legions in Gaul and Germany withdrew into winter quarters varied a little, although not considerably. As a rule it seems to have been before the middle of October, when the rainy season begins in those countries. It was the frequent rain which prevented any continuation of warfare, not the cold. No Roman general seems to have been bold enough to try to extend warlike operations till frost set in. When Caesar, for once, tried to keep his legions engaged in war beyond the usual term, he was compelled to retreat, as his soldiers could no longer sleep in the open field because of the rain.[1] On the other hand, he did not like to retire into winter quarters too early; and when he had to do so, because no more work was to be done, he expressly mentioned it.[2] Now, A.D. 14, Germanicus was fighting some German tribes. The autumn came, and he withdrew into winter quarters. The winter was imminent, but had not yet set in.[3] The fifth and twenty-first legions were in winter quarters at the sixtieth stone, which place was called Castra

---

[1] Caesar, *Bellum Gallicum*, Lib. III., chap. xxix.: "Incredibili celeritate magno spatio paucis diebus confecto, cum iam pecus atque extrema impedimenta ab nostris tenerentur, ipsi densiores silvas peterent, eiusmodi sunt tempestates consecutae, uti opus necessario intermitteretur et continuatione imbrium diutius sub pellibus milites contineri non possent."

[2] *Bellum Gallicum*, Lib. I., chap. liv.: "Caesar, una aestate duobus maximis bellis confectis, maturius paullo, quam tempus anni postulabat, in hiberna in Sequanos exercitum deduxit."

[3] Tacitus, *Annales*, Lib. I., chap. xliv.: "Ob imminentem . . . hiemem."

Vetera,[1] when they mutinied. In order to turn their minds to something else, Germanicus undertook—autumn being far advanced, but apparently no snow having fallen yet and there being no frost—another small military expedition. He crossed the frontier, and invaded the enemy's territory. There were two ways to take. He chose the longer one, and hurried on; for scouts had informed him that a certain night was a festival night for the Germans, and gave occasion for gay banqueting. In a beautiful clear night he reached the village of the *Marsi*, and surprised them completely during their feasting.[2] This can only refer to a festival held at the beginning of winter, before snow and frost had set in, which, in the German climate, can hardly have been at any other time than in the first half of November. In the second half Germanicus would have had to encounter the most serious difficulties as to the weather, whilst to assume that the festival had been in October would not leave sufficient time for the withdrawing of the legions into winter quarters, the mutiny, and the warlike expedition after it. So we have a right to say that a German festival was held in the first half of November as far back as A.D. 14, while the date of the report of it is certainly to be set down before A.D. 117, in which year Tacitus died. It is the oldest Germanic festival on historical record; and although half a millenium elapsed before it was mentioned again, we have no reason to doubt its existence. And it is mentioned again before the Christian Church had got proper hold of all the Western Germanic tribes, towards the end of the sixth century, when St. Martin had become a great saint of the Church, and November 11, the date of his death, had been made his day of commemoration.

---

[1] Tacitus, *Annales*, Lib. I., chap. xlv.: "Quintae et unaetvicesimae legionum sexagesimum apud lapidem (loco Vetera nomen est) hibernantium."

[2] *Ibid.*, chap. l. : "Delecta longiore via cetera accelerantur: etenim attulerant exploratores festam eam Germanis noctem ac solemnibus epulis ludicram. Caecina cum expeditis cohortibus praeire et obstantia silvarum amoliri iubetur: legiones modico intervallo sequuntur. Iuvit nox sideribus illustris, ventumque ad vicos Marsorum, et circumdatae stationes, stratis etiam tum per cubilia propterque mensas, nullo metu, non antepositis vigiliis. Adeo cuncta incuria disiecta erant, neque belli timor; ac ne pax quidem nisi languida et soluta inter temulentos," etc.

St. Martin was born in A.D. 336, and died in 401. About the middle of the sixth century there was definitely given as his own day November 11, which had before been celebrated in Gaul in his commemoration. Whilst France knows nothing of a popular celebration of it, Martinmas[2] in early times was held as the highest festival of the year wherever Western Germanics lived, the banqueting lasting, in the sixth century, all night long till morning broke. We know this from the terms in which the Synod of Auxerre in 578 forbade its celebration.[3] Beda, in *De Temporum Ratione*, testifies to a Germanic festival in November, saying that in that month, which they called *Blot-monath* or Offering-month, the heathen Germanics devoted to their gods their cattle, which they intended to kill.[4] Martinmas, probably, was in chief view when in 589 the Council of Toledo interdicted the same nightly feasting for all saints' days,[5] and the *Concilium Cabilonense* of 650 A.D. repeated the prohibition.[6]

---

[1] A very brilliant sketch of his life and activity is given by Heino Pfannenschmid, *Germanische Erntefeste*, Hannover, 1878, pp. 193 ss., with numerous notes, pp. 464 ss.

[2] Pfannenschmid, *Ibid.*, p. 466, note 10.

[3] "Omnino et inter supradictas conditiones, pervigilias, quas in honore domni Martini observant, omnimodo prohibete," *Acta Conciliorum*, Parisiis, 1714, Vol. III., col. 444, *Synodus Autissiodorensis*, A.D. 578, v. The *supradictae conditiones* can only be the contents of Canons iii. and iv., which run as follows: "iii. Non licet compensos in domibus propriis, nec pervigilias in festivitatibus sanctorum facere; nec inter sentes, aut ad arbores sacrivos, vel ad fontes vota exsolvere: sed quicumque votum habuerit, in ecclesia vigilet, et matriculae ipsum votum, aut pauperibus reddat: nec sculptilia aut pede, aut homine lineo fieri penitus praesumat. iv. Non licet ad sortilegos, vel ad auguria respicere, non ad caragios, nec ad sortes, quas sanctorum vocant, vel quas de ligno, aut de pane faciunt, aspicere: sed quaecumque homo facere vult; omnia in nomine Domini faciat." It is important to notice that the only two feasts which are mentioned by their name by that Synod of Auxerre are the Calends of January and Martinmas, and from that the conclusion may be drawn that the heathen customs were more prominent at these two tides than at any other.

[4] *De Temporum Ratione*, chap. xv., *De Mensibus Anglorum*: "*Blotmanoth*, mensis immolationum, quia in ea pecora quae occisuri erant, Diis suis vovebant."

[5] *Acta Conciliorum*, Parisiis, 1714, Vol. III., col. 483, *Concilium Toletanum*, III., A.D. 589, xxiii.: "Exterminanda omnino est irreligiosa consuetudo, quam vulgus per sanctorum solemnitates agere consuevit; ut populi, qui debent officia divina attendere, saltationibus et turpibus invigilent canticis."

[6] *Acta Conciliorum*, Parisiis, 1714, Vol. III., col. 950, *Concilium Cabilonense*, A.D. 650, xix.: "Multa quidem eveniunt, quae dum levia minime corriguntur, saepius majora consurgunt."

The veneration of St. Martin spread very rapidly in the old Church. After God, the holy cross, and the Virgin Mary, the blessed confessors Hilarius and Martinus were held in the highest reputation in the Gaul of the sixth century,[1] and in Great Britain things were not much different,[2]

Valde enim omnibus noscitur esse indecorum, quod per dedicationes basilicarum, aut festivitates martyrum, ad ipsa solemnia confluentes chorus femineus turpia quidem et obscena cantica decantare videntur, dum aut orare debent, aut clericos psallentes audire. Unde convenit, ut sacerdotes loci talia a septis basilicarum, vel porticibus ipsarum, ac etiam ab ipsius atriis vetare debeant et arcere. Et si voluntarie noluerint emendare, aut excommunicari debeant, aut disciplinae aculeum sustinere." It was then the habit to sing in these days worldly love songs in the church, to dance in accompaniment of them, and to banquet in the same sacred place. "Non licet in ecclesia choros secularium, vel puellarum cantica exercere, nec convivia in ecclesia praeparare : quia scriptum est : *Domus mea, domus orationis vocabitur,*" *Acta Conciliorum,* Parisiis, 1714, Vol. III., col. 445, *Synodus Autissiodorensis,* A.D. 578, ix. *Acta Conciliorum,* Parisiis, 1714, Vol. III., col. 1920-1, *Concilium Germanicum,* A.D. 742, v. : "Decrevimus quoque, ut secundum canones unusquisque episcopus in sua parochia solicitudinem gerat, adjuvante gravione, qui defensor ecclesiae ejus est, ut populus Dei paganias non faciat, sed omnes spurcitias abjiciat et respuat ; sive profana sacrificia mortuorum, sive sortilegos, vel divinos, sive phylacteria et auguria, sive incantationes, sive hostias immolatitias, quas stulti homines juxta ecclesias ritu pagano faciunt, sub nomine sanctorum martyrum vel confessorum, Deum et sanctos suos ad iracundiam provocantes : sive illos sacrilegos ignes, quos Niedfyr vocant ; sive omnes, quaecumque sunt, paganorum observationes diligenter prohibeant."

[1] *Acta Conciliorum,* Parisiis, 1714, Vol. III., *Epistola Sanctae Radegundis ad Episcopos,* A.D. 567, col. 370 : "Dei et sanctae crucis, et beatae Mariae incurrat judicium : et beatos confessores Hilarium et Martinum, quibus post Deum sorores meas tradidi defendendas, ipsos habeat contradictores et persecutores." The *Concilium Turonense, Ibid.,* col. 371-72, replied to this letter mentioning Martin in almost equal terms, saying of God : "Beatum Martinum peregrina de stirpe ad inluminationem patriae dignatus est dirigere misericordia consulente. Qui licet apostolorum tempore non fuerit, tamen apostolicam gratiam non effugit. Nam quod defuit in ordine, suppletum est in mercede," etc.

[2] When the Roman missionaries under Augustine, sent by Pope Gregory to Great Britain, settled down in Canterbury, they found there a St. Martin's Church, as Bede states, of Roman origin—a church which, after some medieval reconstructions, still exists, and is not the least interesting of the antiquities of Canterbury. Beda, *Historia Ecclesiastica gentis Anglorum,* I., chap. xxvi., ed. Plummer, Oxford 1896, p. 47 : "Erat autem prope ipsam civitatem ad orientem ecclesia in honorem sancti Martini antiquitus facta, dum adhuc Romani Brittanniam incolerent, in qua regina, quam Christianam fuisse praediximus, orare consuerat." (Her name was Bercta, and she was a Frankish princess.) St. Martin, besides, had at Canterbury a porticus, in which King Aedilberct was buried (Beda, *Hist. Eccl.* II., chap. v. : "Defunctus vero est rex Aedilberct die XXIIII. mensis

whilst in Germany the cult of the same saint spread simultaneously with Christianity.[1] The popularity of St. Martin was bound to increase from the fact that his day was placed at the greatest ancient Germanic festive tide; and however scarce is our information about medieval popular festivals, we know of no other so much as we do about Martinmas as a time of feasting and banqueting. If Martin is called the drunken saint, there is no doubt about the significance of that expression, nor is there any about the so-called Martin-geese. The oldest St. Martin's goose of which we know is a silver one, and belongs to the year 1171, although the testimony by which it is warranted is not contemporaneous. A monk of Corvei,

Februarii post xx. et unum annos acceptae fidei, atque in porticu sancti Martini intro ecclesiam beatorum apostolorum Petri et Pauli sepultus ubi et Bercta(e) regina condita est.") St. Ninian had a bishop seat, which was later on celebrated through the name and the church of St. Martin (Beda, *Hist. Eccl.*, III., chap. iv.: "Cuius sedem episcopatus, sancti Martini episcopi nomine et ecclesia insignem . . . iam nunc Anglorum gens obtinet"). Ninian probably died earlier than St. Martin (*Lives of St. Ninian and St. Kentigern*, ed. Forbes, 1874, xxvii., xxxviii., 256, 266, 271-273). There was also a monastery called after that saint (Beda, *Hist. Eccl.*, IV., xvi.: "Et abbas monasterii beati Martini, . . ." and "corpusque eius ab amicis propter amorem St. Martini, cuius monasterio praeerat, Turonis delatum atque honorifice sepultum est"; and Beda, *Historia Abbatum*, § 6, ed. Plummer, p. 369 : "Ab Agathone papa archicantore ecclesiae beati apostoli Petri et abbate monasterii beati Martini Johanne . . ." and *Historia Abbatum auctore Anonymo*, ed. Plummer, in *Venerabilis Baedae Opera Historica*, Oxford 1296, Vol. I., p. 391, § 10: "Abbatemque monasterii beati Martyni"). Mr. Plummer, in his edition of Bede's *His-torical Writings* (Vol. II., p. 43) says: "To the popularity of the cultus of St. Martin (who died between 397 and 401) in Britain, Venantius Fortunatus (born about 530 at Ceneta and having died as bishop of Poitiers after 600) bears striking testimony, saying of him : "Quem Hispanus, Maurus, Persa, Britannus amat." Cf. Haddan and Stubbs, *Councils and Ecclesiastical Documents relating to Great Britain and Ireland*, I., 13, where see note for references illustrating the connection of St. Martin with the British Isles ; Venantius Fortunatus, *Vita S. Martini*, Lib. IV., vv. 621 ss. (*Monumenta Historica Germaniae*, 4to series).

[1] Boniface also speaks of "fundamenta cuiusdam destructae a paganis ecclesiolae, quam Willibrordus . . . in castello Traiecto repperit, et eam proprio labore a funda-mento construxit et in honore S. Martini consecravit (*Monumenta Moguntina*, pp. 259-260, ed. Jaffé). Ducange, *Glossarium*, under *Festum S. Martini*: "Recensetur inter festa quae celebrari debent, in Lib. VI. *Capitul.*, c. 189; in *Capitulari Aquisgran.*, A.D. 817, c. 46; in *Capitulis Walterii Aureliani*, c. 18; in *Concilio Lugdunensi sub Inn. III.*, etc.; in *Capitulari Ahytonis Episcopi*, Basiliensis, c. viii. ; Beletus, c. 163."

who, in the middle of the fifteenth century, compiled the Annals of that monastery,[1] tells that in 1171 Othelricus of Svalenburg, on the feast of St. Martin, because he was a member of the fraternity of Corvei, gave the monks as a present a silver goose. This gift was probably in compensation for a payment of some annual duty on Martinmas.[2]

In the thirteenth century there was a song on St. Martin known through large parts of Gaul and Germany, which, like almost all songs in use at Germanic offering tides, was repudiated by the clergy as indecent. It was then ascribed to some evil spirit, and a story was popular according to which, in 1216, a demon had boasted that he and a friend of his composed that song, and promulgated it over a large territory.[3] Public bonfires on Martinmas can be proved to have existed as early as 1448, when Martinmas for that reason was called *Funkentag*;[4] and are again mentioned about the end of the sixteenth century in Fischart's (+1590) *Gargantua*, where baskets are stated to have been burnt in the St. Martin's fire. Perhaps it has also to do with St. Martin's fires that, when in 1557, at Augsburg, a house was burnt

---

[1] Leibnitz, *Scriptores*, II., 308 ; Pfannenschmid, *Germanische Erntefeste*, p. 229.

[2] *Annales Corbejenses* in Leibnitz's *Scriptores*, II., 308 : "Othelricus de Svalenberg argenteum anserem in festo S. Martini pro fraternitate (obtulit)." Pfannenschmid, *Germanische Erntefeste*, 1878, p. 505. Old Leibnitz, *Scriptores*, II., *Introductio*, p. 28 : "Anserem assatum in festo S. Martini per omnes fere domos, mensis inferunt Germani. . . . Invitat anni tempus : tum enim anseres pingues habentur." Pfannenschmid, *Ibid.*, p. 505, beats all speculators about the connection between St. Martin and geese, by the simple declaration that St. Martin's day is just the time of the year when geese are fat. This was of even greater moment in former centuries, when the accumulation of food was attended with considerable difficulties, and domestic animals were difficult to feed during winter time. Compare also D. Georg Joachim Marks, *Geschichte vom Martini-Abend und Martins-Mann*, Hamburg und Güstrow, 1772, p. 20.

[3] The story is told by Thomas Cantipratensis, who in 1263 wrote his book on the bee state. It is contained in his treatise *Bonum universale de apibus*: "Quod autem obscoena carmina finguntur a daemonibus et perditorum mentibus immittuntur, quidam daemon nequissimus, qui in Nivella urbe Brabantiae puellam nobilem anno domini 1216 prosequebatur, manifeste populis audientibus dixit : cantum hunc celebrem de Martino ego cum collega meo composui et per diversas terras Galliae et Theutoniae promulgavi. Erat autem cantus ille turpissimus et plenus luxuriosis plausibus."

[4] In a document of Count Friedrich zu Moers (A. J. Wallraf, *Altdeutsches Wörterbuch*, Köln, p. 23). Comp. Grotefend, *Zeitrechnung*, I., p. 71.

down, a report expressly remarks that the young fellows when feasting and holding Martinmas had neglected it.[1]

According to a seventeenth century source,[2] in Holland the boys, on the eve of Martinmas, lit fires, singing:

> " *Stoockt vyer, mackt vyer* :
> *Sinte Marten komt hier*
> *Met syne bloote armen* ;
> *Hy sonde hem geerne warmen.*"

About 1230 an Austrian poet represents peasants drinking to the praise and memory of St. Martin.[3] A joke connected with the Martinmas of the thirteenth century is preserved to us in the poem *St. Martinsnacht*.[4] A rich farmer and his people have got drunk in honour of St. Martin. A thief breaks into the farmer's stable, and, when surprised by the owner, shakes off his clothes, pretending to be St. Martin. The farmer, believing him, goes on with his banquet, with the result that in the morning he finds his stable empty. That the festivity was equally familiar to monasteries is apparent from some documents. The monastery of Eilenrostorf received every year, from 1353, a quantity of wine—half for the mass and half for the convent who were to drink it *in vigilia sancti Martini*.[5] What it received before that date is not known.

A.D. 1369 we have a description of a celebration of Martinmas. A knight, von Schwichelt, possessor of Liebenburg, asked Duke Otto of Göttingen to spend Martinmas with him. Duke Otto had gone to Harzburg, which he had taken from the Count of Wernigerode, at the same time compelling, by surprise of the town of Alfeld, the Bishop of Hildesheim

---

[1] Birlinger, *Aus Schwaben*, II., p. 132. This happened on October 10. Nevertheless that feasting was called *Martinsnacht*, apparently because in olden times it had been held on November 11.

[2] Gisbertus Voëtius, *Selectae Disputationes Theologicae*, Utrecht, 1659, p. 448.

[3] Der Stricker, *Kleine Gedichte*, V., 167, Grimm's *Wörterbuch*, IV. 1, 1263: "Dem guoten sant Martine ze lobe und zu minnen."

[4] Hagen, *Gesammtabenteuer*, Stuttgart und Tübingen, 1850, No. 50.

[5] Reimann, *Deutsche Volksfeste*, 284; Pfannenschmid, *Germanische Erntefeste*, p. 222; Marks, *Geschichte vom Martini-Abend und Martinsmann*, Hamburg, 1772, p. 20.

to provide the castle of Harzburg with food. On Martinmas eve he arrived
with his army before Liebenburg, and was invited for St. Martin's banquet.
He accepted the invitation, and on the following day presented his host
with the castle of Harzburg.[1] Oswald von Wolkenstein (1367-1445) sings:
Trinckh martein wein, und genss iss Ott,[2] and bones of Martin's geese
were used for prophecy about the middle of the fifteenth century.[3] Sebastian
Franck (1500-1545) says in his *Weltbuch* of the Francs: "Firstly they praise
St. Martin with good wine and geese, until they are drunk. Unblessed is
the house which has not a goose to eat that night; then they also tap
their new wines which they have kept so far," to which he adds a description
of a St. Martin's game: "In Franconia at that day people enclosed in a
circuit or circle two boars, which tore each other to pieces. The meat was
divided among the people, the best bits being given to the authorities."[4]

---

[1] *Bodonis Chronicon pict.* in Leibnitz's *Scriptores Br.*, III., 385, H. Pfannenschmid,
Germanische Erntefeste, p. 500; and *Uralte Sachsen Chronic* by Caspar Abel, written
about 1455 (ad annum 1375). Pfannenschmid, *Ibid.*: "Hertog Otto de bose to Gotting
halde eyn grot hop des Quecks uth Holt-Lande van der Wulfesborch, unde wolde darmidde
driven in dat Lant to Gotting, so legerde he sick under der Levenborch, unde was St.
Martens-Avend, dar spysen se öne myt alle sinen Volke, unde dem Quecke, des Morgens
wolde he de Koste betalen, des wolden de van Schwichgelde nyn Gelt vore hebben, unde
ėreden sine Gnaden darmidde, do dreyff he sin Roffqueck in dat Lant to Götting, unde
spisede dar sine Borghe midde, unde gaff do denen Schwichgelde vor de Woldad de
Hartesborch to erve unde to egen, de worden so derna der Borch Goddes Frünt, unde
aller werlde vyent."

[2] *Odo* = November 13.

[3] Dr. Hartlieb, physician-in-ordinary to Duke Albrecht ot Bavaria, in his *Buch aller
verboten kunst, ungelaubens und der zauberei* (1455) says: "Als man zu sant Martinstag
oder nacht die gans geessen hat, so behalten die eltesten und die weisen das prustpain, und
lassen das trucken werden bis morgens fru und schawen dan das nach allen umbstenden,
vorn hinden und in der mitt. Darnach so urtailen si dan den winter wie er sol werden kalt
warm trucken oder nass, und sind so vest des gelauben, das si darauf verwetten ir gut und
hab." A hundred and fifty years later that habit was still in use, as we know from J.
Colerus, *Calendarium Oeconomicum* (1591), and from Olorinus Variscus and his writing
on St. Martin's geese.

[4] "Nach dem kompt S. Martin, da jsset ein jeder Haussvater mit seinem Haussgesinde
eine Ganss, vermag ers, kaufft er jnen Wein vnd Medt, vnd loben S. Martin mit voll seyn,
essen, trincken, singen"; Heinrich Panthaleon, of Bâle (1522-1595), writes in *Der deutschen
Nation Heldenbuch*: "Die Leute pflegen zum Gedächtniss S. Martini in Deutschland mit

A writer of the same century says; "We Germans think Shrove Tuesday, St. Burkhard, and St. Martin, Pentecost, and Pasch, the times when people should be gay and banquet more than at other seasons of the year: on St. Burkhard's eve for the sake of the new must; on Martinmas perhaps for the sake of the new wine; then people roast fat geese, all the world rejoicing."[1]

Sermons of the seventeenth century, even when coming from Protestant pulpits, have many things to tell about Martinmas and its geese.[2] The popular rime says:

> "Auff Martini schlacht man feiste Schwein,
> Und wird allda der Most zu Wein."[3]

On the eve of Martinmas the devil had free play. On that night, in the

---

fröhlichem Gemüth St. Martensnacht zu begehen, die Martensganss zu essen, und mit den Nachbaren und dem Hausgesinde fröhlich zu sein, gleich als wenn aller Dinge Ueberfluss mit Sanct Martino der Armen Patron vorhanden sey;" Jod. Lorichius, *Aberglauben*, 1593, p. 52. Simrock, *Martinslieder*, xiv.; Pfannenschmid, *Germanische Erntefeste*, pp. 500-1, where other proofs for similar festivities are given from Thomas Naogeorgus (Thomas Kirchmaier of Straubingen, 1511-1563), *Regnum Papisticum*, Lib. IV.; Joannes Boemus Aubanus, *De Omnium Gentium Ritibus*, 1520, fol. lx.; G. Forster, *Frische Liedlein*, II Parts, Nürnberg, 1540, No. 5, and many items of later dates.

[1] Scheible, *Schaltjahr*, II., 95, from Agricola.

[2] Scheible, *Schaltjahr*, I., 187, *Aus einer protestantischen Martinspredigt des 17. Jahrhunderts*: "Und weil heute der Tag Martini gefället, daran es die Gänse leider übel haben, als will ich zu einer Martinsgans bitten, und dieselbe anatomieren und zutheilen. Nicht aber wie die Abergläubischen, nach jetzt erzähltem heidnischem Gebrauch, von künftiger Winterwitterung aus dem Brustbein weissagen, sondern was wir bei einer Gans christlich zu lernen haben, anzeigen. Richtet ihr hierauf eure beharrliche Andacht. —Es isset Mancher eine Gans nach der andern, und ist und bleibet selbst eine Gans, versteht und weiss nicht, was Gott und die Natur uns an derselben zu studiren gegeben." *Ibid.*, I., p. 194: "Gänse geben Speis, sonderlich um diese Martinszeit. Drum ihnen auch der Martinstag sehr gefährlich ist. . . . Verständige Köche wissen sie mit gutem Beifusz, Aepfeln und Kastanien zu füllen und zu einem lieblichen Schmack zu geben." On Martinmas gaieties a mass of material is contained in Mussard, *Ceremoniae Ecclesiasticae*, p. 117; Blumberg, *Delineatio fraternitatum Calendarum*, p. 155; Calvör, *Ritual Eccl.*, P. II., p. 362; Keisler, *Antiquitates Septentrionales*; Pirnische *Chronick* in *Mencken*, II., p. 1554; Marks, *Geschichte vom Martini-Abend und Martinsmann*, Hamburg, 1772.

[3] Grässe, *Des deutschen Landmanns Practica*, Dresden, 1858, p. 27.

shape of a man dressed in a long wolf-skin coat, he appeared in 1594 at Spandau, Brandenburg, to a young fellow, and raged about in an indescribable fashion, so that all the persons possessed had to be brought to the high altar of the church for protection.[1]

In the seventeenth century the police began to become an important factor in the development, or rather suppression, of popular usages. So on February 4, 1605, and June 22, 1649, in old Frankfurt-on-the-Main, it was forbidden to bake *Mertins hörnichen* for sale. The same happened to the other Martin's festivities at many places.[2] Yet some lived on for a considerable time as *quasi* legal institutions, *e.g.*, in the Rhine country, where such festivities existed till after 1750,[3] being given as a gift in return for the duties paid at that term.

---

[1] Scheible, *Schaltjahr*, IV., 462, *Schreckliche Zeitung.*

[2] "Die übel practicirten Martins- oder Herbsttrünke" ("Würzburger Herbstinstruction" in *Werndii Tractatus vom Zehntrechte*, p. 324 (ed. de anno 1708); Pfannenschmid, *Germanische Erntefeste*, p. 224; comp. also Schilter's *Glossar.*, p. 123.

[3] At Oberaussem, in 1750, at the banqueting (*Hofessen*) on Sunday after Martinmas, the persons who took part were sixty-one. They dined at two tables, at a *tisch auffm söller* and a *specktisch im haus* (Armin Tille, *Archivübersicht*, p. 102).

CHAPTER IV.

MARTINMAS, AND THE TRI-PARTITION OF THE YEAR.

MARTINMAS is the earliest term occurring in the Anglo-Saxon Laws. Church-scot had to be paid then, so early as the seventh century,[1] though the church to which it was to be paid was that of the place at which a man stayed in the beginning of the calendar year.[2] He who failed to do so was to forfeit sixty shillings, and render the church-scot twelve-fold.[3]

---

[1] Haddan and Stubbs, *Councils and Ecclesiastical Documents*, Oxford, 1871, III., 215, *Laws of King Ine of Wessex*, about A.D. 690 (688-693): " Be Ciric-sceattum. Ciric-sceattas sin agifene be Sancte Martines mæssan."

[2] *Ibid.*, III., 217, lxi. : " Be ciric-sceatte. Ciric-sceat mon sceal agifan to tham healme and to tham heordhe the semon on bidh to middum wintra."

[3] In Thorpe's *Ancient Laws and Institutes of England* (London), 1840, II., 460. In the canons enacted under King Edgar (ca. A.D. 967) it was enjoined that plough-alms were to be given XV. days after Easter; and a tithe of young by Pentecost; and of earth-fruits by All Saints; and Rome-"feoh" by St. Peter's mass; and church-scot by Martinmass ("ærest sulh-celmessan XV. niht onufan Estron. and geôgudhe teodhunge be Pentecosten. and eordh-westma be Omnium Sanctorum. and Rom-feôh be Petres-mæssan. and ciric-sceat be Martinus-mæssan "). This is the reading of MS. D, a small folio of the middle of the eleventh century, *Corpus Christi*, 201 (v. 18); X, a large octavo MS. of the tenth century, *Bodleana, Junius*, 121, has *Ealra Hâlgena mæssan* instead of *Omnium Sanctorum*, and has the following sentence immediately preceding to the quoted Anglo-Saxon text: " and riht is that man thisses mynegige to Eastrum. odhre sidhe to gang-dagum. thriddan sidhe to middan-sumera. thonne bidh mæst folces gegaderod ; " whilst it adds after the above sentence from D the following : "and leoht-gesceotu thriwa on geare. ærest on Easter-æfen. and odhre sidhe on candel-mæsse æfen. thriddan sidhe on Ealra Hâlgena mæsse æfen." *Acta Conciliorum*, Parisiis, 1714, Vol. VI., 1, col. 657-8, *Leges Ecclesiasticae Regis Edgari*, ca. A.D. 967, iii. : "Quisque fetuum decimas omnes ante

This term lived on a considerable time. It was, at any rate, preserved as late as the reign of Henry the First (1100-1135), but probably a good deal longer.[1] It is like many other Germanic institutes also found in

---

Pentecosten persolvito : terrae quidem fructuum decimas ante aequinoctium pendito : ipsas autem seminum primitias sub festum divi Martini reddito." *Ibid.*, col. 659, iii. : "Et omnis decimatio juventutis reddita sit ad Pentecosten, et terrae frugum ad aequinoctium, et omne ciricsceattum ad festum sancti Martini, per plenam forisfacturam quam judicialis liber dicit." *Ibid.*, col. 776 (*Concilium Aenhamense*, A.D. 1009) x. : "Jura Deo debita unusquisque annuatim recte pendito : aratri scilicet eleemosynam decimaquinta nocte a Paschate : fetuum seu novellorum gregum decimas, ad Pentecosten ; et terrae fructuum, ad festum omnium Sanctorum. xi. Census Romae debitus [quem denarium sancti Petri vocant] and festum sancti Petri ad vincula (alias Missam Petri) persolvatur : et ecclesiae census, qui cyrick sceat appellatur, ad Missam sancti Martini. xii. et. xiii. Luminarium census ter quotannis penditor ". A mention of this institute occurs in Cnut's letter from Rome (Thorpe, *Ancient Laws and Institutes of England* (London) 1840, I., p. 104 : "Et in festivitate Sancti Martini primitiae seminarum ad ecclesiam sub cujus parochia quisque degit, quæ Anglice 'ciric-sceatt' nominatur") (*Ibid.* in the notes). Also Heming, 21 : "De cirisceato de Perscora dicit vicecomitatus, quod illa ecclesia de Perscora debet habere ipsum cirisceattum de omnibus cc. hidis, scilicet de unaquaque hida ubi francus homo manet unam summam annonæ, et, si plures habet hidas, sint liberæ, et si dies fractus fuerit, in festivitate Sancti Martini ipse, qui retinuerit det ipsam summam, et undecies persolvat abbati de Perscora, et reddat forisfacturam abbati de Westminstre quia sua terra est" (*Ibid.*). Cnut's letter is also printed in the *Acta Conciliorum*, Parisiis, 1714, Vol. VI., I. col. 846, *Epistola Canuti Regis ad Anglorum proceres*, A.D. 1031 : "Omnium debita, quae secundum legem antiquam debemus, sint persoluta : scilicet eleemosyna pro aratris, et decimae animalium ipso anno procreatorum, et denarii, quos Romam ad sanctum Petrum debetis, sive ex urbibus, sive ex villis, et mediante Augusto decimae frugum, et in festivitate sancti Martini primitiae seminum, ad ecclesiam sub cujus parochia quisque degit, quae Anglice Cureset nominatur." Bye and bye Easter creaps into the number of these terms (*Acta Conciliorum*, Parisiis, 1714, VI., 1, col. 899, *Leges Ecclesiasticae Canuti Regis*, A.D. 1032), where the terms enumerated are : "a fortnight after Easter ;" "Pentecost ;" "All Saints," whilst, besides, Peter's penny is to be paid at Peter and Paul, and the firstlings of the seeds at Martinmas ; also three times a year the candle money has to be paid (*Ibid.*, col. 899, xii.): "at Pasch," "at All Saints," and "at Mary's Purification" ; *Ibid.*, col. 908, xvi. ; col. 909, xvii., xix ; Thorpe's *Ancient Laws*, II., 524.

[1] Thorpe, *Ancient Laws*, I., 520 (*Leges Regis Henrici Primi*, xi., § 4) : "Qui cyric-sceattum tenebit ultra festum Sancti Martini, reddat eum episcopo, et undecies persolvat, et regi l. solidos." This institute is commented upon by Lingard, *Altertümer der angelsächsischen Kirche*, ed. by von Ritter, Breslau, 1847, p. 56. Compare David Wilkins, *Concilia Magnae Britanniae et Hiberniae*, London, 1734, I., pp. 59, 302 ; and Pfannenschmid, *Germanische Erntefeste*, p. 204.

Spain, whither the Goths apparently had carried it,[1] and in Germany, where it obtained all through the Middle Ages. There the church tax falling due at Martinmas was even called St. Martin's penny,[2] when the payment of it had been shifted to Christmas, a change which seems to have taken place in the thirteenth or in the beginning of the fourteenth century. A similar shifting of terms is to be observed in England in the eleventh century.[3] Church-scot was not the only payment to be made at the beginning of winter. Then was also paid an instalment of the wages of female servants, which were due three times a year, viz., at the beginning of winter, at mid-Lent, and at the beginning of later summer.[4]

In Germany Martinmas was legally recognised as a general term for paying

---

[1] *Vita Sancti Isidori Agricolae, Madriti in Castelia* (+1130), *auctore Iohanne Diacono* (1275, comp. Potthast., Wegweiser, 766), No. 15 (Ducange-Henschel, *Glossary*, 1845, IV., 304): "Accidit, quendam virum ex eius curia ad colligendam exactionem regiam, quae vulgariter dicitur Martiniega, in tempore hiemis sub mense Decembri Majorinum certissime advenisse." H. Pfannenschmid, *Germanische Erntefeste*, 1878, p. 466.

[2] Norrenberg, *Geschichte der Pfarreien des Dekanates München Gladbach*, Cöln, 1889, p. 276, No. 23. A.D. 1324, Dec. 24: Among the revenues of the church at Giesenkirchen is named: "denarium, qui dicitur Mertyns pennynge."

[3] John Earle, *A Hand-Book to the Land-Charters and other Saxonic Documents*, Oxford, 1888, pp. 344-345. Eadward (1042-1066), his Writ of Privileges to the Abbey of Ramsey, co. Huntingdon (Manuscript of century XII., *Cottoniana*, Otho, B, xiv., f. 257): "and ealle dha gyltes dha belimpedh tô mîne kinehelme inne Iol and inne Eâsterne and inne dha hâli wuca æt Gangdagas on ealle thingan al swâ ic heô meseolf âhe, and tolfreo ofer ealle Engleland, widhinne burhc and widhûtan, æt gâres cepinge and on æfrice styde, be wætere and be lande; habeant et omnes forisfacturas quae pertinent ad regiam coronam meam in natali dominico, in pascha, et in sancta ebdomada rogationum, in omnibus rebus sicut ipse habeo, et per totam Angliam infra ciuitatem et extra, in omni foro et annuis nundinis et in omnibus omnino locis per aquam et terram, ab omni telonii exactione liberi sint."

[4] Thorpe, *Ancient Laws*, I., 436-7, "Rectitudo Ancillae: ad hiemale companagium; ad quadragesimalem convictum; and in aestate, *i.e.* to winter-sufle, to længten-sufle, and on sumera." A similar state of things survived up to the present time. *Notes and Queries*, Ninth Series, February 4, 1899, p. 85, in a note on *Pack Rag Feast* by R. Hedger Wallace: "The agricultural labourers in some of the North Derbyshire villages, among other old customs, retain that of having a social gathering on Old Martinmas Day (23 November), which is, not over politely, designated the Pack Rag Dinner. The name refers to the fact that the indoor menservants about the farms, who are changing masters at Martinmas, gather together their belongings for removal from one house to another."

duties about the time of Charlemagne, and in the ninth century it was in general use.[1] In thirteenth century ordinances about leases, geese or fowls are mentioned which are delivered at Martinmas.[2] We know of such gifts to the clergy on saints' days from about the middle of the sixth century.[3]

---

[1] Anton, *Geschichte der Landwirtschaft*, I., p. 341, and Pfannenschmid, *Germanische Erntefeste*, p. 204, confuse the legal recognition of an existing status with the introduction of it.

[2] *Pfründenordnung of the Monastery of Geisenfeld*, ed. by Wittmann, München, 1856; Lexer, *Mittelhochdeutsches Ergänzungswörterbuch*, I., p. 736; Pfannenschmid, *Germanische Erntefeste*, p. 205 : "Ieclichen hof und vourt unde sunderlich hus verzendet man mit eyme hune ze sente Mertinstage," *Sachsenspiegel*, ed. by Weiske, Landrecht, Book II., Art. 48, § 5; or, as another version has it : "Jeglichen hoff, odder wüste hofstadt vnd sonderlich heuser, verzehent man mit einem hune, am S. Martinstag." "An St. Martinstag sind allerhand pfleg und zins verdient," *Ibid.* II., 58, from the thirteenth century, Middle Germany.

[3] *Acta Conciliorum*, Parisiis, 1714, Vol. III., col. 352; *Concilium Bracarense*, I., xxi. : "Item placuit, ut si quid ex collatione fidelium, aut per festivitates martyrum, aut per commemorationem defunctorum offertur, apud unum clericorum fideliter colligatur; et constituto tempore, aut semel, aut bis in anno, inter omnes clericos dividatur : nam non modica ex ipsa inaequalitate discordia generatur, si unusquisque in sua septimana quod oblatum fuerit, sibi defendat." Ample evidence on Martinmas as a term I have given in my *Geschichte der deutschen Weihnacht*, Leipzig, 1893, pp. 23-28, and pp. 291-296. Mark's *Geschichte vom Martini-Abend und Martins-Mann*, Hamburg, 1772, contains on pp. 26, 27 a chapter (13), *Von der Zahlungsfrist auf Martini*, and mentions there documents of A.D. 1294, 1318, 1460, to which are to be added those mentioned in E. J. Westphalen's *Monumenta Inedita*, Part IV., Preface, p. 95. Nicolaus von Werle, A.D. 1297, gave the town of Waren *exemtionem ab angariis et petitionibus omnibus* under the condition that the citizens every year at Martinmas would send him on a cart *quantitatem seminum*; Georg Joachim Mark's *Geschichte vom Martini-Abend und Martins-Mann*, Hamburg, 1772, p. 49. *Ibid.*, p. 81, mentioned that two generations earlier Graf Heinrich of Schwerin concluded a bargain with Archbishop Engelbrecht of Köln to the effect that the archbishop had to send him annually at Martinmas fifteen *harradas* or barrels of wine. That book is devoted to the question of the origin of the custom of the so-called *Martinsmann* at Lübeck, which, however, it fails to answer. The origin of the habit is unknown, but it is certain that in 1567 it was called an old habit, that on Martinmas the Town Council of the Imperial city of Lübeck sent a barrel of old *Rheinweinmost* to the Court of Schwerin. The story is frequently related in modern times, *e.g.*, by Mark; by Reimann, *Deutsche Volksfeste*, p. 288; by Pfannenschmid, *Germanische Erntefeste*, pp. 222, 223. As a gift in return for the duties paid—a kind of Germanic New Year's gift—the Town Council of Lübeck received some deer. The same was the case in Würtemberg monasteries. There the prelate was under obligation

That Martinmas was not merely a term like other terms, but the
beginning of the economic year, is evident from the fact that, in the
Middle Ages, accounts run from Martinmas to Martinmas, and appointments
were made for the same period, which is also understood to cover a year
of taxation.

As long as the duties were paid in natural products, the terms were
the last days within which the duties had to be paid; but when the taxes
were paid in money, they became the days on which the payment had to
be made.[1] As early as A.D. 1253 money payments for the whole of the
year of taxation were made at Martinmas.[2] In medieval Frankfurt a. M. the
year for which officials were appointed ran from Martinmas to Martinmas,
or the Sunday previous.[3] So did the period of imperial taxation,[4] and so

---

to give the Martin's wine to all people of his place.   In the provostship of Hellingen
each holder of a tenure received a pint, each old man and each woman half a pint, and
male and female servants, and even the baby in the cradle, a quarter (Nork, *Festkalender*,
p. 684 ; Reinsberg-Düringsfeld, *Das festliche Jahr*, p. 340).   Wine was also given at
Martinmas at the court of the Archbishop of Mayence, at Erfurt, about 1494 (Michelsen,
Der Mainzer Hof zu Erfurt am Ausgange des Mittelalters (1494), Jena, 1853, p. 26, Regulations for the Küchenmeister (the highest economic official) : " Uff sanct Martins abent sal
er wein, uff weihenachten opffergelt und uff das neue jhor zum neuen jhor geben, wie
das rothbüchlein und die rechnung in helt, und auch christsemeln wie sich gehurth
geben,") and about 1520 at Würzburg, as Martin Boëmus tells us.

[1] Arnold, *Zur Geschichte des Eigentums in den deutschen Städten*, Basel, 1862, p. 68.

[2] Grimm, *Deutsche Rechtsaltertümer*, III., 607, Oeringen, A.D. 1253 : "Swer dirre
stete reht hat, der sol geben ze sante Mertins naht achte heller, und sol daz jar alles fri
sin zolles halp."

[3] *Frankfurt a. M. Rechenbuch*, 1358-59, fol. 16ᵇ : "Hartmude an fizscher porten synen
jarlon 3 lb. 3 ss. und geng sin jar an des suntags vor sant Mertinsdag."   *Ibid.*, 1374, fol.
93ᵃ : "Sabbato ipso die divisionis apostolorum Gultsmede dem wechter uff dem thorne
zu Bonemesse 1 lb. sines penning lones unde 2 lb. fur 3 achtel kornes unde ist da midde
sines halben jarlons bezalet unde ged sin jar uz unde an uff sand Mertinsdaig unde pliget
man yme eyn jar zuo gebin 6 lb. 6 achteil kornes unde 1 rog ;" *Ibid.*, 1474, fol. 22ᵇ, under
"Einzelinge Innemen:" "Item 295 lb. 14 ss. 4½ h. han wir enphangen von Johan Heller,
schriber im spitale zum heiligen geiste als der uns rechnunge getan hat von dem jare das
Martini anno 74 ussgangen ist."   Actum sabbato post dominicam Esto mihi anno 1475.

[4] *Frankfurt Rechenbuch*, 1435, fol. 39ᵃ, under "Einzelinge ussgeben:" "1100 lb.,
14 lb. mynner 3½ ss. han wir ussgeben und bezalt unserm gnedigen herren dem keiser
keiser Sigmund die gewonliche des rijchs sture von sant Mertinstag izunt vergangen die im

it came that the tax had to be paid for all people who lived to see St. Martin's day, but not for those who died before it, because their lives did not cover the whole of the taxation year.[1] On the other hand, the amount of corn and wine requisite for maintaining the owner and his servants from the date of paying the taxes till Martinmas was free from duty,[2] Martinmas being the last term for paying the duties.[3] In the medieval Frankfurt a. M., all through the fourteenth century, the taxes were raised in November or December,[4] as they are now in Scotland, the taxation year beginning with Martinmas.[5] In the thirteenth century the winter, during which all agricultural work was interrupted, was counted from Martinmas till *St. Petri ad cathedram* (Feb. 22), for during that time, in 1297, the *Pfahlbürger* of Frankfurt a. M. were required to have a household within the ramparts of the city.[6] That on the banks of the Rhine Martinmas in the twelfth century also was considered as the beginning of the economic year is evident from a document of A.D. 1149, of Hirzenach, near Boppard, according to which once a year judgment was held, and the day of it proclaimed the day after Martinmas,[7] *i.e.*, at the beginning of that year economic.

In medieval Tirol Martinmas began the business year for which all officials

---

Walther Swarzenberg, Heinrich vom Rijne und andere des rades frunde umb siner sunderlichen begerunge willen zu Pressburg zuvor bezalten und ussrichten uff sine quertancil."

[1] *Bedebuch of Frankfurt a. M. of* A.D. 1476, *Ob.* 19ᵇ: "6 ss. von siner swieger seligen wegen, die nach sant Mertins dage von dodes wegen abegegangen ist."

[2] Karl Bücher, *Die Bevölkerung von Frankfurt a. M.*, I., p. 263.

[3] *Ibid.*, I., p. 354, from the *Citizenbook* of 1378. He who does not pay his citizen money, "sal geben zuschen hie vnd sant Mertins dag neist kommet 10 lb. und 4 ss. hell ; wo he det nit entede, so mochte man sie uff in zun juden uff sinen schaden nemen ;" *Ibid.*, I., p. 485, A.D. 1372, the inhabitants of the villages which are under the protectorate of the city have to give "eyme schultheizsen eynen schilling phennige vnd ein hun uff sant Martins dag"; *Ibid.*, I., p. 486, A.D. 1383, "Und sal . . . dem schultheiszen sin recht uff sant Mertins dag."

[4] Karl Bücher, *Zwei mittelalterliche Steuerordnungen* in *Kleinere Beiträge zur Geschichte von Dozenten der Leipziger Hochschule*, Leipzig, 1894, p. 139.

[5] *Ibid.*, p. 150: The duties are to be raised (A.D. 1474) "eyn iglich der nehst komenden dry jare zu heben und zu sant Mertins dag schirst kommend anetzufahen."

[6] Bücher, *Bevölkerung von Frankfurt a. M.*, I., p. 370.

[7] *Annalen für Rheinische Geschichtskunde*, Vol. LXII., p. 39.

were elected,[1] and for which duties and interests were paid.[2] If anybody's
property was burnt before St. Martin's day, he needed to pay no duties that
year.[3] Besides, Martinmas began the rustic winter in Tirol so late as the
fifteenth and seventeenth centuries.[4] When drawing conclusions from his
discussion of popular Martinmas, Heino Pfannenschmid, who firmly believes
that the Germanic year began with the winter solstice, arrives at the result[5]
"that Martinmas forms the conclusion of the peasant agricultural year. This
is also shown by the fact that most leases end about Martinmas, when the
rent has to be paid, which might have been hard for many a one, though
the harvest had been reaped and turned into money. To this refer the
sayings, 'Martin is a severe man,' and 'Martin is a bad man.'[6] So other
payments are made, and accounts handed in, at Martinmas;[7] all sorts of
duties in kind and money are paid to monasteries, churches, parishes; church
accounts are made up and paid. The conclusion of the old agricultural
and crop year on Martinmas is finally marked by the changing of servants.
With this end of the old agricultural and crop year a new one began. Then
the new lease year begins both in Germany and England; new servants are
hired. . . . In France Martinmas was considered the beginning of winter

---

[1] Zingerle, *Tiroler Weistümer*, II., p. 173, A.D. 1580, of Nassereit and Torminz, Upper
Engadine: "Sollen drei erbare verstendige mannspersonen . . . järlich an sanct Martins
des heiligen bischofs tag . . . zu gwalthabern und dreierern . . . furgenomen, erwölt und
erkiest werden;" *Ibid.*, III., p. 258, A.D. 1607, of Latsch, Vintschgau: "Ein feldsaltner
soll, wo es kann, auch am kassuntag, wo nit doch neyst darnach angenomen und seinen
dienst, als hernach folgt unzt auf Martini zu verrichten schuldig sein;" *Ibid.*, III., p. 193,
A.D. 1614, of Kortsch, Vintschgau: "Der messner allhier hat auch järlich am st Martinstag
urlaub, und soll auch jährlich vor der ganzen gemeinde stehen und um solches amt bitten;"
Ibid., II., p. 168, A.D. 1674; I., p. 79, A.D. 1727.

[2] *Ibid.*, II., p. 310, A.D. 1303; II., p. 104, A.D. 1416; III., p. 351, A.D. 1427.

[3] *Ibid.*, III., p. 7, A.D. 1440, of Glurns, Vintschgau: "Und ob dann ainer verprent wurd
oder verprunne vor sand Martins tag, derselb sol umb dieselben zins desselben jars ledig und
los sein." A long list of other cases is given in the apparatus to my *Geschichte der deutschen
Weihnacht*, p. 293.

[4] Zingerle, *Tiroler Weistümer*, IV., p. 33, A.D. 1431, of Partschins; *Ibid.*, III., p. 65,
A.D. 1630, of Burgeis.

[5] *Germanische Erntefeste*, Hannover, 1878, p. 237.

[6] Nork, *Festkalender*, p. 683, and Simrock, *Martins Lieder*, xv.

[7] Leoprechting, *Aus dem Lechrain*, p. 200; Birlinger, *Aus Schwaben*, II., 132.

and of the *new year*, the legend of St. Martin explaining the latter fact as a proof of the high esteem and reverence in which that Saint was held. But in Germany also the time about Martinmas must have been considered as, in a certain respect, the beginning of the year. As the day began with the eve, so for the ancient Germans the new year could begin with the beginning of winter at Martinmas. After the time of Gregory of Tours, even a new era was computed from St. Martin's death, just as an era was computed from Christ's death."[1] Montanus[2] noted that formerly everywhere, and in his time still on the left bank of the Rhine, the lease year and agricultural year closed with Martinmas, to which Pfannenschmid[3] added that that was also the case in Lower Saxony and in other provinces of Germany. The Church Ordinance of Hoya of 1573[4] fixed Martinmas as the date for the elders of the church to lay the accounts before the officials in presence of the minister. Pfannenschmid gives a long list of facts in support of Martinmas being an old term. Male and female farm servants changed their places at Martinmas.[5] About Martinmas, at Seelze near Hannover, male farm servants changed.[6] Elsewhere female farm servants changed,[7] and in other regions all servants did.[8] In the Havel country it was so till a short time ago. Now they change at Christmas.[9] Also the lease year began at Martinmas in Germany and England.[10] Even Grotefend (who has been completely led astray by Weinhold's theories, according to which the Germanic year was divided by solstices and equinoxes) has to confess[11] that among the country folk in various districts Martinmas means the beginning of winter, where a dual division of the year prevails.

---

[1] Pfannenschmid, *Germanische Erntefeste*, p. 511.
[2] *Volksfeste*, I., 55.   [3] *Germanische Erntefeste*, p. 511.
[4] Richter, II., 359; Pfannenschmid, *Germanische Erntefeste*, p. 511.
[5] Schambach, *Wörterbuch*, 131.   [6] Waldmann, *Eichsfelder Gebräuche*, 15.
[7] Danneil, *Altmärkisches Wörterbuch*, 132.
[8] Kuhn und Schwartz, *Norddeutsche Sagen*, II., 401; Birlinger, *Aus Schwaben*, II., 132.
[9] *Ibid.*
[10] Nork, *Festkalender*, p. 683; Simrock, *Mythologie*, 574; Mülhause, *Urreligion*, p. 308; Rochholz, *Wandelkirchen*, p. 14.
[11] "Martinstag ist bei der Zweiteilung des Jahres provinciell als Anfang des Winters gebräuchlich" (*Zeitrechnung*, I., 119).

In German folk-belief there is still a faint recollection of Martinmas being the old Germanic New Year. It is in some phrases still used as identical with year, or with winter, as the phrase went previously. Instead of: "a man has lived through many years," the folk say: The man has helped to eat many a St. Martin's goose.[1] The old hexameter,

"Iss Gänss Martini, trink Wein ad circulum anni,"

also alludes to Martinmas as the beginning of the year, when people drank good luck to a new annual course.

Beside the legal institution of termly duties stands that of regular assemblies, the so-called not-ordered law courts. It was shown before that there existed among the Germanics sometimes three (originally held at mid-November, mid-March, and mid-July),[2] sometimes two (originally held at mid-November and mid-May), according to a dual division or a tri-partition of the year. It is a fact of great weight that they adhere to these terms, even when one or two of them disappear.

The only foreign impost imposed by the Church upon her believers was the Peter's penny. It was by a perfectly voluntary act that the payment of it was fixed at St. Peter's mass. Thus it has nothing to do with ancient Germanic institutions. Its name *Rome-feoh* on British ground showed the foreign origin and purpose of it only too clearly. Keeping this in mind, we cannot fail to see that the ordinary taxes as well as duties like *light-scot*

---

[1] Grimm's *Wörterbuch*, IV., 1, 1262. The explanation of that phrase, given there by Rudolf Hildebrand, is wrong. The time from one St. Martin's goose to the next is properly regarded as a complete year.

[2] A curious interpretation of the word *Trithinga*, which shows that its meaning had been forgotten entirely, is given by *Fleta seu Commentarius Juris Anglicani sic nuncupatus, sub Edwardo Rege primo seu circa annos abhinc* CCCXL. *ab Anonymo conscriptus, atque e Codice veteri, autore ipso aliquantulum recentiori, nunc primum typis editus*, Londini, 1647, p. 134, Lib. II., chap. lxi., § 23: "De tritingis, sciendum quod aliae potestates erant super wapentakia quae tritinga dicebantur, eo quod erat tertia pars provinciae; quia vero super eos dominabantur, trithingreves vocabantur, quibus differebantur causae quae non in wapentakiis poterint diffiniri in Schiram, sicque quod Anglici vocant hundredos, jam, per variationem locorum et idiomatis, wapentakia appellantur, et tria, vel quatuor, vel plura hundredi solebant Trithinga vocari; et quod in Trithingis non potuit diffiniri, in Schiram id est, in comitatum differebatur terminandum: modernis autem temporibus pro uno eodemque habentur apud homines hundredi, wakentakia, et Trithinga."

had to be paid three times a year, though their exact terms vary a little in the several districts.   Under King Ethelred (991-1016) plough-alms were to be paid xv. days after Easter, and a tithe of young by Pentecost, and of earth fruits by All-hallows' mass (and *Rome-feoh* by St. Peter's mass), and *light-scot* thrice in the year,[1] one of the days of payment for them being Candlemas.[2]

In the *Rectitudo Ancillae*[3] mid-Lent is named as the second of the three terms of the year, the term used being *to lœngten-sufte* and *ad quadragesi-*

---

[1] Thorpe's *Ancient Laws*, I., p. 306: "xi. And gelæste man Godes gerihta georne ræghwylce geare. that is. sulh-ælmessan xv. niht on ufan Eastran. and geôgodhe teodhunge be Pentecosten. and eordh-wæstma be Ealra Hâlgena mæssan. and Rom-feoh be Petres mæssan. and leôht-gescot thriwâ on geare"; and *Ibid.*, I., p. 318, in the resolutions passed at the Council of Enham: "xvi. And gelæste man Godes gerihta. æghwilce geare rihtlice georne. that is. sulh-ælmessan huru xx. niht ofer Eastron: xvii. And geôgodhe teodhunge be Pentecosten. and eordh-wæstma be Ealra Hâlgena mæssan: xviii. And Rom-feôh be Petres mæssan. and ciric-sceat tô Martinus mæssan: xix. And leôht-gescot thrîwa on geare"; *Ibid.*, I., 338, under King Ethelred: "iv. Et præcipimus, ut omnis homo, super dilectionem Dei et omnium sanctorum, det cyricsceattum et rectam decimam suam, sicut in diebus antecessorum nostrorum stetit, quando melius stetit; hoc est, sicut aratrum peragrabit decimam acram."

[2] *Ibid.*, I., p. 342 (also under King Ethelred): "ix. And sî ælc geogudhe teodhung gelæst be Pentecosten be wîte. and eordh-wæstma be emnihte. oththe huru be Ealra Hâlgena mæssan." (Here the equinox was probably substituted for the older All-Hallows term.) "x. And Rom-feôh gelæste man æghwilce geare be Petres mæssan. and sethe that nelle gelæstan sylle thar-tô-eâcan. xxx. peninga. and gilde tham cyninge cxx. scillingas. xi. And ciric-sceat gelæste man be Martinus-mæssan. and sethe that ne gelæste for gilde hine mid twelffealdan. and tham cyninge cxx. scillingas. xii. Sulh-ælmessan gebyredh that man gelæste be wîte æghwilce geare. thonne xv. niht beodh âgân ofer Easter-tîd. and leoht-gescot gelæste man tô Candel-mæssan. dô oftor sethe wille." The same is ordained in the *Laws of King Cnut*, 1017-1042 (*Ibid.* I., 366: "viii. And gelæst man Godes gerihta æghwylce geare rihtlice georne. that is. sulh-ælmesse huru fiftene niht ofer Eastran. and geogudhe teodhunge be l'éntecosten. and eordh-wæstma be Ealra Hâlgena mæssan. ix. De Nummo Romano. And Rom-feôh be Petres mæssan. x. De Primitiis Seminum. And cyric-sceat to Martines mæssan. xii. De Pecunia Pro Lucernis. And leôht-gesceot. thrîwâ on geare. ærest on Easter-æfen healf-penig-wurdh wexes æt ælcere hîde. and eft on Ealra Hâlgena mæssan eall swa mycel. and eft to thæm Sanctan Mariam clænsunge eal swa" (Feb. 2); *Ibid.*, I., 434-35: "Et det suum cyric-sceatum in festo Sancti Martini (and sylle his cyric-sceat to Martinus mæssan "), (*Rectitudines Singularum Personarum*).

[3] Thorpe's *Ancient Laws*, I., 436-7.

malem convictum. The fourteenth century Rhenish Urbary of St. Victor, Xanten,[1] gives St. Gertrudis Day (March 17) as the spring term, whilst Tirol documents of the fifteenth century call it simply *mitte merzen;*[2] whilst, two centuries later,[3] summer was reckoned to begin on April 23,[4] the beginning of winter being in both cases Martinmas. In Flanders St. Gertrudis Day (March 17) is called *Sommer tag.*[5] Just as the mid-May term, which halved the year beginning at Martinmas, was easily replaced by the Rogation Days, and afterwards by Pentecost, so the nearness of the Christian festival of Easter could scarcely fail to become detrimental to a mid-Lent term, or rather to a mid-March term. The earliest date on which Easter could fall was March 22, a date only a week distant from March 15. Grimm has shown[6] that the three old Germanic offering-tides coincided with the Thing tides, nay, represented one side of them. There is no doubt that the autumn Thing and the spring Thing were the most important, while the summer Thing could not be so significant, for the very simple reason that, in time of war, almost all men able to bear arms were away. A festival about the middle of July I should be the last to deny to Germanics, Slavs, and Celts, but that it had any early relation to a summer solstice which fell about three weeks earlier must be most emphatically gainsaid. It is true the festivals which appear in medieval poetry are almost all celebrated either at Pentecost or *ze einer sunnenwenden* (about June 24). But to that date the festival of the beginning of late summer at mid-July had been shifted in the tenth or eleventh century, whilst the legal term in many places remained where it had been. As the expression *ze einer sunnenwenden* is foreign, so the date itself is foreign. Were it otherwise, and had June 24 been an old Germanic date (so that the other two had originally fallen on October 24 and February 24), it would be quite inexplicable how the term could have moved away from it to mid-July, which was equally out of keeping with October 1, with Christmas, and with

---

[1] State-Archive, Düsseldorf, under " Stift Xanten," R. No. 8ᵃ, leaf 8ᵃ.
[2] Zingerle, *Tiroler Weistümer,* IV., p. 33, A.D. 1431, at Partschins.
[3] A.D. 1630, at Burgeis.   [4] Zingerle, *Tiroler Weistümer,* III., p. 65.
[5] Grotefend, *Zeitrechnung des deutschen Mittelalters,* I., 178.
[6] *Deutsche Rechtsaltertümer,* 821 ss. 245, 745.

Easter. Besides, there is no trace of sun-worship whatever in Germanic religion,[1] and in the Scandinavian North the existence of a midsummer Thing is as well vouched as any fact of Old Norse history, without it showing the slightest trace of a relation to a sun-cult. Quite in accordance with the fact that the Scandinavian year began between October 9 and 14, and had a *Góiblót* between February 9 and 14, the summer Thing was held between June 9 and 14. In Germany, where the terms of both the beginning of winter and of the beginning of early summer fell one month later, the festival at the beginning of later summer must have been held about July 15. In the Rhenish Urbary of St. Victor, Xanten,[2] July 12 (St. Margaret's day) was marked, not only as the beginning of a new season, but even as the beginning of a new year. At other places July 17 appears as the joyous day. So in Swabia children and gilds received gifts—the latter of wine.[3] It is also the day of old bonfires in Villingen, Swabia.[4]

In the Netherlands the old season of four months, from March 15 to July 15, was till very late called May,[5] just as in Germany a Roman quarter of a year was taken as identical with spring, and counted from February 22 to May 25.[6] That that popular summer festival had originally nothing to do with a solstice appears from the fact that even July 25 was called *te midzomer* (1419) or *na midden-somere* (1351).[7] In 1461 it was still taken as corresponding to Christmas, and was the occasion of a local fair like that festival.[8] It was still regarded also as one summer term in the Tirol of the sixteenth century. It divided the time of pasture into two halves, and he who, at Laatsch, Tirol, in 1546, bought oxen after that term, and put them

---

[1] Holtzmann, *Germanische Altertümer*, Leipzig, 1873, pp. 127 and 173; Grimm, *Deutsche Mythologie*, 591.

[2] State-Archive, Düsseldorf, under "Stift Xanten," R. No. 8ᵃ, leaf 8ᵃ.

[3] Birlinger, *Aus Schwaben*, II., p. 118.

[4] *Ibid.*; and Mone, *Quellensammlung*, II., 88ᵃ.

[5] *Tijdschrift v. nederl. Taalk*, IX., 134; Grotefend, *Zeitrechnung*, I., 116.

[6] *Baltische Studien*, XIX., 49: "de Mey beginnet in sunte Peters daghe, de summer in sunte Urbans daghe" (Grotefend, *Zeitrechnung*, I., 116).

[7] Grotefend, *Zeitrechnung*, I., 87.

[8] *Annalen des historischen Vereins für den Niederrhein*, Vol. LXV., p. 42 (Town-Archive of Kempen, Docs. Nos. 367 and 387). It there appears as St. Jacob's day.

on the common pasture ground of the community, had to pay to the community four Bernese pounds for each pair,[1] whilst, a century later (in 1647), the term had been shifted to St. Vitus Day, June 15.[2] In the Anglo-Saxon *Rectitudo Ancillae*[3] this term is called *on sumera* or *in aestate* (an expression corresponding to Old Icelandic *at sumri*, *i.e.*, June 9 to 14), meaning a day about mid-July. When it had been shifted to June 24, it was called *midsummer*. *Midsummer* was a later Anglo-Saxon term recognized by law : " A sheep shall go with its fleece until Midsummer, or let the fleece be paid for with two pence," is a doom in King Ine's Laws.[4] But occasionally the regular law courts and assemblies were held still later. More than once the day of the beheading of St. John the Baptist (August 29) is fixed as the term at which the bishops and reeves are to adjudge the king's commands to all whom it behoveth.[5]

The tri-partition of the year—Martinmas, mid-March, mid-July—was, till late in the Middle Ages, more than an artificial division of the year carried on by tradition without apparent reason. It was deeply rooted in economic life, and in conditions affecting pasture and agriculture. In connection with the keeping of domestic animals, as well as with the ploughing of the fields, traces of an old tri-partition have come down to us. The anonymous Anglo-French Seneschaucie of the thirteenth century[6] ordains : " The bailiff ought, after St. John's Day, to cause all the old and feeble oxen with bad teeth to be drafted out, and all the old cows, and the weak and the barren, and the young avers that will not grow to good, and put them in good pasture to fatten, so the worst shall then be worth a better. And he ought, three times a year, to cause all the sheep in his charge to be inspected by men who know their business—that is, to wit, after Easter, because of the disease of May, and later, for then sheep die and perish by the disease; and all

[1] Zingerle, *Tiroler Weistümer*, Vol. III., p. 103.

[2] In the neighbouring community of Schleiss (Zingerle, *Tiroler Weistümer*, Vol. III., p. 89).

[3] Thorpe's *Ancient Laws*, I., 436-7.

[4] Thorpe, *Ancient Laws*, I., p. 146 : "odh midne sumor."

[5] *Laws of King Athelstan*, I., Thorpe's *Ancient Laws*, I., p. 194 : "ond thæs sie to thæm dæg thær beheafdunges Seint Iohannes thæs fulhteres."

[6] Ed. by Elizabeth Lamond in Walter of Henley's *Husbandry*, London, 1890, p. 97.

that are found so, by the sure proof of killing two or three of the best, and as many of the middling, and as many of the worst, or by proof of the eye or of the wool, which separates from the skin, let them be sold with all the wool. And again, let all the old and weak be drafted out before Lammas, and let them be put in good pasture to fatten, and when the best have presently mended and are fat, let them be sold to the butchers; so can one do well, for mutton flesh is more sought after and sold then than after August; and let all the rest of the draft beasts which cannot be sold then be sold before Martinmas. And the third time, at Michaelmas, let all the sheep be drafted out."[1] In the same century elsewhere the day of testing the health of wethers was October 28. Walter of Henley, in his *Husbandry*, laid it down that two of the best wethers, two of the middling, and two of the worst should be killed on that day. If they were found not to be sound, a part was to be sold by true men for good security, until Hockday (Thursday after Easter), and then replaced.[2] Almost the same way of denoting a third of a year is found in connection with sheep-keeping; from Martinmas to Pasch sheep were to spend their nights under shelter.[3]

In agricultural life in the middle of the thirteenth century the three terms were known in low Latinity as *Hibernagium*, *Tratmesium*, and *Warectum*. They then continued to determine the ploughing times, which seem to have occupied the latter half of each of the old three seasons.[4]

---

[1] "E tote le remeignant de creim ke ne put estre uendu adonkes seit vendu deuant la seint martin."

[2] Walter of Henley's *Husbandry*, ed. by Elizabeth Lamond, London, 1890, p. 33 : "A la seynt symon e seyn Iude facet tuer deus de meylurs e deus de myuueyns e deus de pyres e si vos trouet ke eus ne seyent mye seyens fetes vendre vne partye a lele genz par bone surte iekes a la hokeday e donc fetes releuer autres."

[3] *Fleta seu Commentarius Juris Anglicani*, London, 1647, p. 167, Lib. II., chap. lxxix., § 7 : "Inter festa autem sancti Martini et Paschae, infra domum oves expedit noctanter custodire, nisi terra sicca fuerit, ovileque bene reparatum, tempusque serenum."

[4] *Registrum sive Liber Irrotularius et Consuetudinarius Prioratus Beatae Mariae Wigorniensis*: with an Introduction, Notes, and Illustrations by William Hale Hale, Londini, Sumptibus Societatis Camdensis, 1865 ; Redditus Prioratus Wigorniae Anno Incarnationis Domini MCCXL., p. 14[b]: "Praeterea arabit ad yvernagium, tramesium, et ad warrectum, per unum diem, excepto opere, et vocatur 'benherthe.'" *Ibid.*, p. 14[b]: "Praeterea arabit et herciabit 1. die ad yvernagium ; et Prior inveniet semen, et si necesse

fuerit quaelibet herciabit pro opere, donec perventum fuerit ad carucas, praeterea arabit uno die ad tramesium, et uno die warectabit," etc., *ut supra*. *Ibid.*, p. 18^b: "Nova assisa de vilenagio de Mora. In hoc manerio sunt XXVII. dimidiae virgatae Quarum quaelibet ad firmam posita reddit ad quemlibet terminum II^{os} solidos et in Purificatione I quarter. avenae. Quaelibet etiam debet X^{cem} summagia apud Wygorniam et terram arare sicut sibi arat; scilicet semel ad yvernagium et ad tratmesium et ad warectum et debent sarclare et metere et intassare una cum cottariorum operibus et aliorum in autumpno totum bladum de dominico, et debent Thac et Thol et pannagium et gersummationem prolis et hujusmodi." *Ibid.*, p. 19^b: "Et dat auxilium, scilicet XVIII. denarios Et in Purificatione dimidiam quarterium avenae et facit IIIes aruras scilicet ad yvernagium ad tratmesium et ad Warectum et IIIes Benrip."

CHAPTER V.

MARTINMAS, AND THE DUAL DIVISION OF THE YEAR.

IN Germany mid-May and Martinmas appear as the two half-yearly terms as late as 1525. In that year the peasants of his district reproached the Count of Fürstenberg for having increased the taxes, the same being then raised twice a year as May tax and autumn tax. In reality these taxes had, as is shown by the Fürstenberg *Urbaria*, been raised almost regularly through the whole of the fifteenth century. The holders petitioned the Count to reduce these two taxes to one, which should be paid at Martinmas.[1] In the *Exchequer Rolls of Scotland*[2] almost all accounts of provosts of burghs are dated Whitsunday and Martinmas, while the dates of the custumars' accounts vary considerably. Even accounts "for four years ending Martinmas, 1331" occur. Martinmas appears considerably oftener than Whitsunday, thus being shown to have been the more important term, at which not only half a year but a whole year ended. In the second volume, which covers the years 1359 to 1379, Whitsunday and Martinmas are also the two main terms occurring in accounts.[3]

---

[1] The application of the small-holders is printed by Baumann, *Akten zur Geschichte des deutschen Bauernkrieges aus Oberschwaben*, Freiburg i. B., 1877, and is commented upon by Hössler, *Zur Entstehungsgeschichte des Bauernkrieges in Südwestdeutschland*, Leipzig Dissertation, 1895, p. 49.

[2] *Rotuli Scaccarii Regum Scotorum*, edited by John Stuart and George Burnett, Vol. I., 1264-1359, Edinburgh, 1878.

[3] On pages viii., x., xi., xii., xv., xvii. to xx., xxiii. to xxv., long lists of accounts, beginning and ending at those days, are enumerated, just as in the contents of Vol. III.,

D

In England this state of things was codified by Edward the Confessor (1042-1066), perhaps with a slight alteration of the existing usage. Whilst mid-May or Rogation Days as a rule appear as the old legal term, Edward ordained that the great assembly of his people was to take place on May 1.[1] As regards the Franks[2] it has been finally proved that their great annual assembly took place in the middle of May. Can the name of this assembly *Campus Martius* (to be translated May-field) suggest that previously, when the tri-partition prevailed and there were three such meetings, the most important of them was held in the middle of March, and thus has nothing to do with *Mars = Ziu*? This institution extended all over German soil as far as to the Italian frontier. As late as 1281 the community of Fleims, in the secular territory of Trient, reserved to itself the right of keeping two *placita*— the one in May and the other in November.[3] It took a very long time to uproot this institution, and replace it by meetings held according to Roman quarters of years and Christian high festivals.

Legal institutions were not the only form in which the Germanic terms survived. Very early the Christian Church in Gaul was compelled to make considerable concessions to the Germanic mode of dividing the year, which,

---

which covers the time from 1379-1406. The most frequent phrases of Vol. II. are: "de termino beati Martini ultimo preterito" (p. 475); "de termino Sancti Martini" (p. 621 twice; p. 281); "de duobus terminis huius compoti, videlicet Pentecostes et Sancti Martini" (pp. 72, 73); "de termino Pentecostes ultimo preterito" (pp. 72, 73); "de terminis Pentecostes et Sancti Martini" (pp. 72, 73 twice); "de eodem termino Pentecostes" (pp. 72, 73 twice).

[1] *In capite Calendarum Maji*, Hampson, II., 94, Grotefend, *Zeitrechnung*, I., 20ᵃ. The spring term appearing probably with most frequency in other connections is the Rogation Days. "And we ordain that every 'burh' be repaired XIV. days over Rogation Days." *Laws of King Athelstan*, Thorpe's *Ancient Laws*, I., p. 206, No. 13: "XIIII. niht ofer Gang-dagas." "And every man that will may make 'bôt' for every theft with the accuser, without any kind of 'wite,' until Rogation days; and be it after that as it was before." *Ibid.*, p. 222, *Laws of King Athelstan*, iii.: "odh Gong-dagas."

[2] H. L. Ahrens, *Über Namen und Zeit des campus Martius der alten Franken*, Hannover, 1872.

[3] *Fontes Rerum Austriacarum*, Second Division, *Diplomata*, Vol. V., No. 212, p. 417: "Allegando, quod ipsi homines et communitas de Flemmis sicut de jure et ex antiquo est observatum, nisi bis in anno quolibet non debeant conveniri in foro temporali et juri parere in civilibus et sub judicio esse, videlicet ad placitum in festo s. Martini et in placito in Majo. . . ."

about the year 500 A.D., found expression in processions and litanies at the two terms of mid-May and mid-November. Two closely corresponding Church celebrations were held at these tides, so that their relationship cannot fail to appear. In 511 A.D. the Council of Orleans instituted the so-called Rogations before the Ascension day,[1] and decreed a three days' liberation from all work for servants of both sexes. Because of a suspicion that the clergy might try to ignore this new institution, as too great a concession to the Germanic field processions about mid-May, a special canon was added, threatening them with punishment in case of non-compliance with the command of the Church. Bye and bye some change took place in the date of the praying processions round the fields, further concessions being made to the Germanic celebration, or *uoba*, in the corresponding tide of the year in November. The Synod of Gerunda of June 8, 517, at which six bishops and one archbishop were present, ordained in its second and third canons that litanies and fasts should be held in the weeks subsequent to Pentecost and to the Calends of November respectively,[2] so that the latter were held between November 1 and November 9. That this was a permanent institution appears from Canon VI. of the second Synod of Lyon in 567,[3] from which we also learn that, between 517 and

---

[1] *Acta Conciliorum*, Parisiis, 1714, Vol. II., col. 1011-12; *Concilium Aurelianense*, I., A.D. 511, Canon xxvii. : "Rogationes, id est, litanias ante Ascensionem Domini ab omnibus ecclesiis placuit celebrari; ita ut praemissum triduanum jejunium in Dominicae Ascensionis festivitate solvatur: per quod triduum servi et ancillae ab omni opere relaxentur, quo magis plebs universa conveniat: quo triduo omnes abstineant, et quadragesimalibus cibis utantur." Canon xxviii. : "Clerici vero qui ad hoc opus sanctum adesse contempserint, secundum arbitrium episcopi ecclesiae suscipiant disciplinam."

[2] *Acta Conciliorum*, Parisiis, 1714, Vol. II., col. 1043; *Concilium Gerundense*, A.D. 517, ii. : "De litania, ut expleta solemnitate Pentecostes, sequens septimana, a quinta feria usque in sabbatum, per hoc triduum abstinentia celebretur. iii. Item secundae litaniae faciendae sunt Kalendis Novembris, ea tamen conditione servata, ut si iisdem diebus Dominica intercesserit, in alia hebdomada, secundum prioris abstinentiae observantiam, a quinta feria incipiantur, et in sabbato vespere missi facta finiantur. Quibus tamen diebus a carnibus et a vino abstinendum decrevimus."

[3] *Acta Conciliorum*, Vol. III., col. 355; *Concilium Lugdunense*, II., A.D. 567, vi.: "Placuit enim universis fratribus, ut in prima hebdomada noni mensis, hoc est, ante diem Dominicam, quae prima in ipso mense illuxerit, litaniae, sicut ante Ascensionem Domini sancti patres fieri decreverunt, deinceps ab omnibus ecclesiis, seu parochiis celebrentur."

567 A.D., the Church had returned to the older date of the spring litany, to the days preceding Ascension day, which apparently almost coincided with the ancient Germanic May term. The autumn litany was then ordained to be held before November 7—which implied almost no alteration.[1] In 517 there existed neither a forty days' fasting-tide from Martinmas to Christmas nor even Martinmas itself. Martin of Tours had died in 401, but he was not made St. Martin till long after. His feast appears first in a *Sacramentarium* by Pope Gelasius I. (492-496), and in the *Liber Sacramentorum* of Gregory the Great (590-604);[2] but it was only Pope Martin I. (649-654) who made it a great Church festival.[3] So the excuse is not possible that the praying procession was instituted as a preparation for St. Martinmas, or the fasting-tide beginning with it, as has been suggested by a man so ingenious as Heino Pfannenschmid.[4] For, according to his own words, the first certain traces of an Advent-tide are found in some homilies,[5] probably written by Caesarius of Arles, who died in 542. Yet even there it is only the question of a general preparation for Christmas, and by no means of a prevailing custom or an ecclesiastical statute.[6] According to Gregory of Tours,[7] who died in 595, it was Bishop Perpetuus of Tours (who died as Bishop of Toulouse in 506) who ordained for his diocese a fast of three days a week, from St. Martin's burial day till Christmas.[8] From the bishopric of Tours the habit of keeping an Advent-tide seems then to have spread over the whole territory of the Church.

First the new fast-tide referred to monks only. In the second Synod of Tours in 567 (where nine bishops were gathered, and among them those of Tours, Rouen, and Paris), with the consent of King Charibert, a daily

---

[1] About *nonus mens* = November, comp. Eccard, *Commentarius de Rebus Franciae*, I., 131.

[2] Pfannenschmid, *Germanische Erntefeste*, p. 464.

[3] Wandalbert, *Martyrologium* in *d'Archery, Specilegium veterum Scriptorum*, T. II.; Pfannenschmid, *Ibid.*, p. 465.

[4] *Germanische Erntefeste*, p. 515.

[5] In *Appendix Augustianus*, Tom. V. *Operum St. Augustini, nova edit.*, No. 115 et 116.

[6] Binterim, *Denkwürdigkeiten*, V., i., 164.   [7] Lib. X., *Hist.*, chap. xxxi.

[8] "A depositione domini Martini usque ad Natale domini."

fast was decreed for monks during December up till Christmas day, a period bye and bye extended to forty days, and made applicable to laymen also. The first testimony as to a general celebration of an Advent-tide is an ordinance on fasting for laymen given by the first Synod of Macon, which was called in 581 by the Frankish king, Guntram, and was attended by twenty-one bishops from various provinces of the Church, among others by the bishops of Lyon, Vienne, Sens, and Bourges. Its Canon IX. runs as follows : " From St. Martin's day till Christmas every Monday, Wednesday, and Friday is to be a day of fast." [1] At the end of the sixth century Rome took over that forty-day fast-tide preceding Christmas, and in the seventh century it was kept all over Italy, Spain, and England. In Germany it was ordained by the Synods of Aix-la-Chapelle in 836, and at Erfurt in 932. The period of fast as well as its strictness varied, however, considerably. Finally, the whole fortnight preceding Christmas was declared a continuous fast-tide, and the week preceding Christmas a time void of any legal process. In 1022 it was even decreed that from the beginning of Advent till Epiphany nobody was to marry. [2]

In the beginning of the seventh century the Calends of November received a new ecclesiastical significance. About the year 608 the Pantheon of Rome, which until then had been devoted to the service of all Roman gods, was by Boniface IV. dedicated in honour of "the holy Mother of God, and of all Saints;" and it was ordained that a commemoration of them should be observed during the Kalends of November. [3] This feast was received through all Gaul by the authority of the Emperor, Louis the Pious (A.D. 835). [4] In 694 the seventeenth Council of Toledo extended the litanies, which so far had been held twice a year—in May

---

[1] " Ut a feria sancti Martini usque ad Natale Domini, secunda, quarta, et sexta sabbati jejunetur, et sacrificia quadragesimali debeant ordine celebrari " (*Acta Conciliorum*, Parisiis, 1714, Vol. III., col. 451).

[2] Pfannenschmid, *Germanische Erntefeste*, p. 514, Hefele, IV., 565, 564, 640.

[3] Alcuin, *De Divino Officio.*

[4] Sigeberti Gemblacensis, *Chronicon ab anno* 381 *ad* 1113, under A.D. 835 : "Monente Gregorio papa et omnibus episcopis assentientibus Ludouicus imperator statuit ut in Gallia et Germania festiuitas omnium sanctorum in Calen. Nouemb. celebraretur, quam Romani ex instituto Bonifacij papae celebrant."

and in November—over the whole twelve months of the year, at the same time specifying the reasons for the change.[1]

If proof were requisite that the Rogation Days took the place of a most important Germanic festival, it would be supplied by the description of their celebration given by the Council of Cloveshou, II., A.D. 747, in the canons of which games, horse-races, and extensive dinners were named as the characteristics of that tide.[2] In the ninth and tenth centuries these regulations were more than once repeated by Councils and Synods.[3]

---

[1] *Acta Conciliorum*, Parisiis, 1714, Vol. III., col. 1815, *Concilium Toletanum*, XVII., vi. : "Quamquam priscorum patrum institutio, per totum annum, per singulorum mensium cursum, litaniarum vota decreverit persolvendum, nec tamen specialiter sanxerit pro quibus causis idipsum sit peragendum : tamen, quia cooperante humani generis adversario, multa inolevit oberrandi consuetudo, et jurisjurandi transgressio ; ideo secundum evangelistam, qui ait : *Vigilate et orate, ne intretis in tentationem* ; in commune statuentes decernimus, ut deinceps per totum annum, in cunctis duodecim mensibus, per universas Hispaniae et Galliarum provincias, pro statu ecclesiae Dei, pro incolumitate principis nostri, atque salvatione populi, et indulgentia totius peccati, et a cunctorum fidelium cordibus expulsione diaboli, exhomologeses votis gliscentibus celebrentur : quatenus dum generalem omnipotens Dominus afflictionem perspexerit, et delictis omnibus miseratus indulgeat, et saevientis diaboli incitamenta ab animis omnium procul efficiat."

[2] *Acta Conciliorum*, Parisiis, 1714, Vol. III., col. 1956, *Concilium Cloveshoviae*, II., A.D. 747, xvi. : "Sextodecimo condixerunt capitulo, ut litaniae, id est, rogationes, a clero omnique populo his diebus cum magna reverentia agantur : id est, die septimo Kalendarum Maiarum [this date must mean May 7], juxta ritum Romanae ecclesiae : quae et litania maior apud eam vocatur. Et item quoque, secundum morem priorum nostrorum, dies ante ascensionem Domini in coelos cum jejunio usque ad horam nonam, et missarum celebratione venerentur ; non admixtis vanitatibus, uti mos est plurimis, vel negligentibus, vel imperitis : id est, in ludis, et equorum cursibus, et epulis majoribus : sed magis cum timore et tremore, signo passionis Christi, nostraeque aeternae redemptionis, et reliquiis sanctorum ejus coram portatis, omnis populus genu flectendo divinam pro delictis humiliter exorat indulgentiam."

[3] *Acta Conciliorum*, Parisiis, 1714, Vol. IV., col. 1014-5, *Concilium Moguntiacum*, A.D. 813, xxxiii. : "Placuit nobis, ut litania maior observanda sit a cunctis Christianis diebus tribus, sicut legendo reperimus, et sicut sancti patres nostri instituerunt, non equitando, nec pretiosis vestibus induti, sed discalceati, cinere et cilicio induti, nisi infirmitas impedierit." *Ibid.*, Vol. IV., col. 1395, *Concilium Aquisgranense*, II., A.D. 836, x. : "De Litania quoque maiore atque de Rogationibus ventilatum est : sed communi consensu ab omnibus electum atque decretum, juxta morem Romanum, VII. Kalendas Maii illam celebrationem, secundum consuetudinem nostrae ecclesiae non omittendam." *Ibid.*, Vol. V., col. 456, *Herardi Turonensis Capitula*, A.D. 858, xciv. : "De Letania Romana VII. Kalendis Maii, ut rememoretur." xcv. : "De diebus Rogationum, ut reverenter ac studiose absque turpibus

Just as the Church sanctified the older Germanic celebration of mid-May and mid-November by special litanies, so it took over the meetings wont to be held at those terms.   In 578, at the Synod of Auxerre,[1] it was decreed that every year priests should meet at mid-May and abbots at November 1. When (in 589, at the Council of Toledo) it was resolved that the Synods, instead of meeting twice a year (on mid-May and November 1), were to meet only once, November 1 was fixed for that meeting [2]—a date observed for more than a century.[3]

Not before A.D. 755 were these terms superseded by March 1 and October 1,[4] but even after the middle of the ninth century the annual meetings of the priests of the Church were held in the beginning of November.[5] In Great Britain the Rogation Days were, under the name of

---

jocis et verbis celebrentur.   Ut nullus in eis prandia, comessationes diversasque potiones per diversa loca facere praesumat."   *Ibid.*, Vol. VI., I., col. 606, *Concilium Engilenheimense*, A.D. 948, vii. : "Ut litania majore jejunium, sicut in Rogationibus ante Ascensionem Domini exerceatur."

[1] *Acta Conciliorum*, Parisiis, 1714, Vol. III., col. 444, *Synodus Autissiodorensis*, Canon vii. : "Ut medio Maio omnes presbyteri ad synodum in civitatem veniant, et Kalendis Novembris omnes abbates ad concilium conveniant."

[2] *Acta Conciliorum*, Parisiis, 1714, Vol. III., col. 482, *Concilium Toletanum*, III., A.D. 589, xviii. : "Praecipit haec sancta et veneranda synodus, ut stante priorum auctoritate canonum, quae bis in anno praecipit congregari concilia, consulta itineris longitudine, et paupertate ecclesiarum Hispaniae, semel in anno in locum quem metropolitanus elegerit episcopi congregentur : judices vero locorum, vel actores fiscalium patrimoniorum, ex decreto gloriosissimi domini nostri simul cum sacerdotali concilio, autumnali tempore, die Kalendarum Novembrium in unum conveniant."

[3] The decree was repeated at another Council of Toledo in 681.   *Acta Conciliorum*, Parisiis, 1714, Vol. III., col. 1725, *Concilium Toletanum*, XII., A.D. 681, xii. : "Placuit huic venerando concilio, ut juxta priorum canonum instituta, episcopi singularum provinciarum annis singulis in unaquaque provincia Kalendis Novembribus concilium celebraturi conveniant.   Quisquis autem in praedictis Kalendis Novembribus pro celebratione synodi venire distulerit, excommunicationi debitae subjacebit."

[4] *Acta Conciliorum*, Parisiis, 1714, Vol. III., col. 1995, *Concilium Veronense*, A.D. 755, iv. : "Ut bis in anno synodus fiat.   Prima synodus mense primo, quod est Martiis Kalendis, ubicumque domnus rex jusserit, in ejus praesentia.   Secunda synodus Kalendis Octobris, aut ad Suessiones, aut alibi, uti in Martiis Kalendis inter ipsos episcopos convenit."

[5] *Acta Conciliorum*, Parisiis, 1714, Vol. V., col. 391, *Hincmari Archiepiscopi Remensis Capitula*, A.D. 852, i. : "Anno DCCCLII. Kalendis Novembris, conventu habito presbytorum in metropoli civitate Remorum," etc.

Gangdagas, as popular as on the continent, they being one of the great tides of the year by which people computed time.

In the Parker MS. (A) of the *Saxon Chronicle*, in the same year in which Martinmas appears for the first time (A.D. 913), there are also found the Rogation Days: *betweox gangdagum and middum sumera*. They are held to be fixed on Monday, Tuesday, and Wednesday of the Ascension week, and appear once more in 921 *to gangdagum*, and in 922 *betweox gangdagum and middan sumera*.[1] In the other group of chronicles represented by the Laud MS. (E), the entry of 913 A.D. is the same, whilst the next two are lacking. Then the Rogation Days appear in 1016.[2]

The term denoting at once the beginning of the Germanic year, and of the winter season, varies from the Calends of November to mid-November, thus keeping clearly within the time which had to be assumed as the beginning of the old Germanic *Iuleis* tide.[3]

---

[1] The only similar term other than Martinmas and *gangdagas* appearing is *hlafmæssa*, the later *Lammas*; it is the first of August, *Sti Petri ad vincula (Augusti)*, frequently abbreviated as *Gula Augusti*, which, of course, has nothing to do with *gula* (the throat or palate), but is merely a mutilation of *vincula*. C and *g* are frequently interchanged; comp. *Gumplete* for *Completa*; Grotefend, *Zeitrechnung des deutschen Mittelalters*, I., p. 78, where the current mistaken explanation of *Gula Augusti* is also found. *Lammas* appears in 921 (*betwix hlafmæssan and middum sumera*); whilst in the little interpolation of later date in B and C, which is styled by Earle *The Annals of Æthelflæd*, it occurs as early as 913 and 917 (*thæs foran to hlafmæssan* and *foran to hlæfmæssan* respectively). It seems to have been the term dividing the economic summer-tide, instead of July 15.

[2] *Hlafmæssa* appears in 917, in 1085, in 1100, in 1101, and 1135, whilst *ane dæge ær sanctes Petres mæssan æfene* and *on sanctes Petres mæssa dæg* are mentioned in 1048, 1131, 1132.

[3] It is a mere exception when the term is shifted back as far as October 18. In the thirteenth century it was in the south of England usual and right that plough beasts should be in the stall between the feast of St. Luke (October 18) and the feast of the Holy Cross (on May 3), five-and-twenty weeks (Walter of Henley's *Husbandry*, ed. by Elizabeth Lamond, London, 1890, p. 13: "Custume est edreyt ke bestes des charues seyent a la creche entre la feste de seynt luc e la feste de la seyt croys en may par vint e cynk semeynes"). At the same time sheep were kept in houses between Martinmas and Easter (*Ibid.*, p. 31: "Veet ke vos berbyz seyent en mesun entre la seynt martyn e pasche"). Even in these five-and-twenty weeks the wintry half of the year is clearly recognisable.

CHAPTER VI.

MARTINMAS AND MICHAELMAS.

IN Professor Weinhold's opinion Michaelmas is an older term and festival than Martinmas—a view not tenable for a moment, as he easily might have seen himself. For, in the text of his book on the division of the German year,[1] he says that the four not-ordered law courts, mentioned in some legal documents, are Michaelmas or Martinmas, Epiphany, Easter, John Baptist's Day; and when, in the apparatus,[2] he has to give the proof, he instances seven cases, in five of which Martinmas appears, whilst no other occurs so often, and Michaelmas and John Baptist's Day only in two. If any generalisation is to be gathered from these facts, it is that, even when the Roman quartering had superseded the Germanic tri-partition of the year, for a long time Martinmas by far prevailed over Michaelmas. He further talks[3] of all kinds of usages and customs having been transferred from Michaelmas to Martinmas, without giving a single historical instance of such a transference; nay, even without attempting any proof of the assertion that they were found earlier at Michaelmas than at Martinmas. The fact is that, after eighteen hundred years of effort to force upon the Germanics the quartering of the year and a beginning of the winter on September 29, the attempt has succeeded so little, that up to this day Martinmas has in many places, preserved its character as the popular beginning of the winter. Grotefend[4] shares the view of a shifting of the beginning of winter from

---

[1] *Über die deutsche Jahrteilung*, Kiel, 1862, p. 10.   [2] *Ibid.*, p. 19.   [3] *Ibid.*, p. 5.
[4] *Zeitrechnung des deutschen Mittelalters*, 1891, I., 89, *Jahreszeiten*.

September 29 to November 11, and adds to it an imaginary shifting of the beginning of summer from April or Easter to the middle of May, whilst in reality the middle of November and the middle of May are the most ancient Germanic terms, and in Scandinavia (as Weinhold and Grotefend know very well) a shifting by one full month has taken place, so that October 14 and April 14 divide the year.

In the *Saxon Chronicle* Martinmas appears first in 913, Michaelmas first in 1014; but after 1066 the mentions of the latter quickly outnumber those of the former. From the Parker MS. of the *Saxon Chronicle* Martinmas appears to have existed long before Michaelmas. We have in 913 *ymb Martines maessan*, in 918 and 919 *foran to Martines mæssan*, in 921 *thæs ilcan geres foran to Martines mæssan*, whilst Michaelmas does not occur a single time; in the Laud MS.[1] things are a little different. Its oldest part was written in the tenth century, so that it is quite irrelevant that under A.D. 759 appears a solitary *to sancte Michaeles tyde*. This can only be a dating after a later fashion. Then Martinmas is mentioned under 913, 915, 971 (B), 1009, 1021, 1089, 1097, 1099, 1100, 1114, whilst Michaelmas appears again as late as 1014 (also in MS. C); but its occurrences become very frequent after 1066.[2]

Nobody will deny that Dr. Heino Pfannenschmid, author of *Germanische Erntefeste*,[3] is the first authority on everything connected with the festivities held in autumn on Germanic ground. His book, though written more than twenty years ago, is still the best on the subject, and unparalleled by another book on cognate matter. By the most thorough investigation he was led to the conclusion that only very slight traces of a thanksgiving for the corn harvest can be discovered in the later Michaelmas, and that it almost exclusively, in Christian times, bears the character of a celebration for the sake of the dead and of a festival in honour of angels,[4] whilst "an abundance

---

[1] *Two of the Saxon Chronicles parallel*, ed. by John Earle, Oxford, 1865.

[2] They are 1066, 1086, 1089, 1091, 1095, 1097 (twice), 1098, 1099, 1100, 1101, 1102, 1103, 1106, 1119, 1125, 1126 (twice), 1129 (twice). Asserius, *De Rebus Gestis Ælfredi, Monumenta Historica Britannica*, I., p. 492, has *in venerabilis Martini festivitate* as early as between 886 and 893.

[3] Hannover, 1878.　　　　　　　[4] *Ibid.*, p. 193.

of customs, which point to the ancient heathen autumn-festival celebrated in November, have clung round the festival held in honour of St. Martin." The expression *Herbstfeier* (autumn-festival) is perhaps the only thing in this statement which might be improved upon; it should be: Festival of winter's beginning and summer's close.[1]

Whilst Martinmas can be proved to have been a popular festival in 578, when the banqueting at Martinmas eve was forbidden by the Synod of Auxerre, it was not before the ninth century that the Church made an attempt to give to the end of the third quarter of the Roman year a special importance by a festival—that of St. Michael and of the angels and guardian angels in general—called in Germany *Engelweihe* or *Fest der Engel*.[2] It was the Council of Mayence of 813 which added that angel-festival to two others (on March 15 and on May 2).[3] Round this festival there gathered from that time a number of habits and customs, all of them inaugurated by certain Church practices, but becoming a little more popular with every century, although their popularity cannot, even so late as the seventeenth century, compete with that of Martinmas. Had there been any Germanic festival about that time which the Church thought it worth while to absorb and use for its own purposes, it would long before the ninth century have instituted some saint's day of special prominence in that part of the year. The payment of a tax or duty at Michaelmas cannot be proved before the tenth century, when the Anglo-Saxons paid the fruit-

---

[1] When, in 1893, dealing with this matter in my book, *Die Geschichte der deutschen Weihnacht*, I did not suppose that any folklorist could be unfamiliar with the results of Dr. Pfannenschmid's book, and, consequently, endeavoured solely to supplement his arguments, instead of restating them and summing them up. But Professor Weinhold seems really to have overlooked them. Otherwise he could no longer be in favour of Michaelmas as the ancient Germanic festival of winter's beginning.

[2] II. Pfannenschmid, *Germanische Erntefeste*, p. 169; Ducange, *Glossarium* under *Festum S. Michaelis*: "Est illa dies, inquit Honorius Augustod., Lib. III., cap. 167, qua populus Christianus cum paganis pugnavit, et victoriam per S. Michaelem Archangelum obtinuit; *Cathwlphi Epistula ad Carolum Magnum*, Vol. II.; *Historia Franconum*, p. 667; Beletus, c. cxxix., cliii.; Durandus, Lib. VII., c. xii."

[3] *Acta Conciliorum*, Parisiis, 1714, Vol. IV., col. 1015; Pfannenschmid, *Ibid.*, p. 175.

tithe to the Church on St. Michael's day,[1] and lease-rents seem not to have
been paid in England at Michaelmas prior to the fifteenth century. The
rent day is marked in the fifteenth and sixteenth centuries by the fact
that the landlords used to invite their tenants for Michaelmas, a roast
goose being the festive dish.[2] Under King Edward IV. (1461-1483), John
de la Hay paid to William Barneby of Lastres, in the county of Hereford,
among other things as rent for part of his land, a goose for Michaelmas.[3]
We still are able to trace the way in which the quarterly division of the
Roman year was made popular by the Church. In England the four
quatembers or ember days were introduced by Gregory the Great (+604),
in the Frankish empire in the *Statuta Bonifacii*,[4] and emphasised by Charlemagne's *Capitulare* of 769, chapter xi., and the Synod of Mayence of 813,[5]
whilst it is not earlier than about the year 1000 that a fast-tide is brought
into connection with Michaelmas.[6]

---

[1] Lingard, *Altertümer der angelsächsischen Kirche, Aus dem Englischen übersetzt von Ritter*, p. 55.

[2] N. Drake, *Shakespeare and his Times*, p. 165.

[3] *Fragmenta Antiquitatis; Antient Tenures of Land, and Jocular Customs of some Mannors*, by T[homas] B[lount], London, 1679, p. 8: "Johannes de la Hay cepit de Will. Barneby Domino de Lastres in Com. Heref. unam parcellam terrae de terris Dominicalibus. Reddend. inde per annum xx. d. et unam Aucam habilem, pro prandio Domini in Festo S. Michaelis Archangeli, Sectam Curiae et alia Servitia inde debita, etc. i. Paying a Goose fit for the Lord's dinner on Michaelmas day."

[4] "Doceant presbyteri populum quatuor legitima temporum jejunia observare, hoc est in mense Martio, Junio, Septembri et Decembri."

[5] *Acta Conciliorum*, Parisiis, 1714, Vol. IV., col. 1015; Pfannenschmid, *Germanische Erntefeste*, 425.

[6] *Acta Conciliorum*, Parisiis, 1714, Vol. VI., i., col. 794; *Leges Ecclesiasticae Aethelredi regis circa annum* 1012 *apud Habam conditae*, chap. ii.: "De jejunio et feriatione trium dierum ante festum Michaelis," etc. "Et instituimus, ut omnis christianus, qui aetatem habet, jejunet tribus diebus, jejunet in pane, et aqua, et herbis crudis, ante festum Sancti Michaelis. Et omnis homo ad confessionem vadat, et nudis pedibus ad ecclesiam; et peccatis omnibus abrenunciet emendando et cessando. Et eat omnis presbyter cum populo suo ad processionem tribus diebus nudis pedibus, et super hoc cantet omnis presbyter triginta Missas, et omnis diaconus et clericus triginta psalmos: et apparetur tribus diebus corrodium unuscujusque sine carne in cibo et potu, sicut idem comedere deberet, et dividatur hoc totum pauperibus. Et sit omnis servus liber ab opere illis tribus, quo melius jejunare possit: operetur sibimet quod vult. Hi sunt illi tres dies; dies Lunae, dies

The first time that Michaelmas appears alongside Martinmas is in 813, in the decrees of the Council of Mayence,[1] where also the birthday of John Baptist (June 24) and the day of Peter and Paul (June 29) appear to mark the ultimate quartering of the year according to solstices and equinoxes. In 858 the list considerably differs from that prevalent before,[2] but even then sometimes Michaelmas is not in the list, whilst the Rogation Days are.[3]

In England St. Michael's day seems not to have taken root much before the end of the tenth century, King Ethelred's Laws being the first collection of institutes to contain an ordinance for keeping it, while so far only the Apostle's days, the Mary's days, and Martinmas had been kept, besides the three great Church festivals of Christmas, Easter, and Pentecost.[4] Sometimes both terms appear together.[5] The mentions of Michaelmas became

---

Martis et dies Mercurii proximi ante festum sancti Michaelis." This ordinance bears the complete stamp of being a mere church invention.

[1] *Acta Conciliorum*, Parisiis, 1714, Vol. IV., col. 1015, *Concilium Moguntiacum*, A. D. 813, xxxvi.: "Festos dies in anno celebrare sancimus. Hoc est, diem Dominicum Paschae, cum omni honore et sobrietate venerari: simili modo totam hebdomadam illam observari decrevimus. Diem Ascensionis Domini pleniter celebrare. Item Pentecosten similiter ut in Pascha. In natali apostolorum Petri et Pauli diem unum, Nativitatem sancti Ioannis Baptistae. Assumptionem sanctae Mariae, dedicationem sancti Michaelis, natalem sancti Remigii, sancti Martini, sancti Andreae. In Natali Domini dies quatuor, octavas Domini, Epiphaniam Domini, Purificationem sanctae Mariae. Et illas festivitates martyrum, vel confessorum observare decrevimus, quorum in unaquaque parochia sancta corpora requiescunt. Similiter etiam Dedicationem templi."

[2] *Acta Conciliorum*, Parisiis, 1714, Vol. V., col. 454, *Herardi Turonensis Capitula*, A. D. 858, lxi.: "De festivitatibus anni, quae feriari debeant, id est, Natali Domini, sancti Stephani, sancti Ioannis, et Innocentium, octavas Domini, Epiphania, Purificatione sanctae Mariae, et Assumptione, Ascensione Domini et Pentecoste. Missa sancti Ioannis Baptistae, Apostolorum Petri et Pauli, sancti Michaelis, atque omnium sanctorum, sancti Martini, et sancti Andreae, et eorum, quorum corpora ac debitae venerationes in locis singulis peraguntur."

[3] *Ibid.*, V., col. 462, *Walterii Aurelianensis Capitula*, xviii., about A.D. 850.

[4] *King Ethelred's Laws* (991-1016) in Thorpe's *Ancient Laws*, I., viii., p. 337, ii. (*Acta Conciliorum*, Parisiis, 1714, Vol. VI., I., col. 793-4, *Leges Ecclesiasticae Aethelredi Regis*, ca. A.D. 1012, ii.); and in the concluding passage vii. in p. 339: "Et reddatur pecunia eleemosinae hinc ad festum Sancti Michaelis, si alicubi retro sit, per plenam witam," etc.

[5] Thorpe, *Ancient Laws*, I., 479, XXVIII. of the *Laws of William the Conqueror*: "De qualibet hida in hundredo IIII. homines ad stretwarde invenientur a festo Sancti Michaelis, usque ad festum Sancti Martini."

more frequent after the middle of the eleventh century, the time when the quartering of the year according to Roman custom had been effected all over the realm governed by the Church. From A.D. 877 the term *intra tres menses* appears in the Councils of the Church,[1] which shows that quarters of years had become the unities to be reckoned with.

Probably the institution of a quartering term at the division between September and October would not have been so easy had it not had a certain economic basis in an important change which took place contemporaneously. Up to the third and fourth centuries of our era the Germanics had, for their livelihood, almost entirely depended upon pasture. It was only in the Carolingian age that the cultivation of meadows began to develop; and in consequence of the vast increase in produce of cattle, the continental Germanic tribes grew quickly in numbers. But for several centuries the improved cultivation of meadows for the purposes of pasture continued to surpass agriculture in importance, and it seems to have been not much before A.D. 1000 that agriculture took equal rank with pasture as a means of livelihood. The pasture time did not end before the beginning of actual winter. After Martinmas it was no longer considered possible to pasture foals, so that before A.D. 800 it was not customary to let them be out at pasture after that term.[2] For the same length of time swine were kept in the oak forest in the Westphalia and Tirol of the fifteenth century.[3] The time in which no pasture was possible extends there down to the sixteenth century *von St. Martanstag bis auf mitten meien.*[4]

---

[1] *Acta Conciliorum*, Parisiis, 1714, VI., 1, col. 185, *Synodus Ravennae habita*, A.D. 877, i., ii.

[2] *Capitulare de Villis*, by Charlemagne: " Ut poledros nostros missa sancti Martini hiemale ad palatium omnimodis habeant."

[3] "Op S. Remigy dach (Oct. 1) in tho driven in den wolde twelff schwine vnd een beer vnd die Martin wieder vuith tho driven ; weer saecke die beer daer nicht mede en ist, mach men die schwine uthschütten" (A.D. 1465, *Speller Waldweistum*, Westphalia), Freiherr von Löw, *Über die Markgenossenschaften*, Heidelberg, 1829, p. 99; Piper, *Beschreibung des Markenrechts in Westphalen*, Halle, 1763, pp. 158, 159.

[4] Zingerle, *Tiroler Weistümer*, III., pp. 72, 73, A.D. 1542 ; on the meadows which were the common property of the communities of Mals and Burgeis. A long list of cases from Tirol legal documents, which shows that Martinmas was throughout the beginning of

At least as regards the beginning of winter, similar conditions ruled the economic year of the Anglo-Saxons of the eleventh century. Just as Tirol documents of the fifteenth century considered the season of the year to be summer from *mitte merzen* to Martinmas,[1] the *Rectitudo Geburi* treated the season of winter as from Martinmas till Easter, Martinmas being given as the date at which the ploughing of the fields came to an end, and the time between February 2 and Easter being denoted as no less busy than the harvest-tide.[2] It is in this latter state, however, that a change is contained. Whilst the real pasture time does not begin much before mid-May, the field work sets in about two months earlier, though in Germany nowhere at the beginning of February.

But soon enough in autumn also a change was wrought by the spreading of agriculture. All grain and aftermath are stored in the barns towards

---

winter, is given in the apparatus to my *Geschichte der deutschen Weihnacht*, Leipzig, 1893, pp. 291-3. As late as the fifteenth century the *libe Herr sant Martein* is addressed as the keeper and patron of cattle (Grimm, *Deutsche Mythologie*, 1189).

> " Ich treip heut aus
> in unser lieben frauen haus,
> in Abrahames garten
> der lieber herr sant Martein
> der sol heut meines vihes warten."

Karl Gödeke, *Deutsche Dichtung im Mittelalter*, Dresden, 1871, p. 243-5. Hirtensegen from a fifteenth century MS.

[1] Zingerle, *Tiroler Weistümer*, IV., p. 33, A.D. 1431, of Partschins, whilst the seventeenth century began it on April 23, and ended it on Martinmas. Zingerle, *Ibid.*, III., p. 65, A.D. 1630, of Burgeis.

[2] Thorpe's *Ancient Laws*, I., 434-435, : " Rectitudines Singularum Personarum : Geburi consuetudines inveniuntur multimodae, et ubi sunt onerosae et ubi sunt leviores aut mediae. In quibusdam terris operatur opus septimanae, II. dies, sic opus sicut ei dicetur per anni spatium, omni septimana ; et in Augusto III. dies pro septimanali operatione, et a festo Candelarum ad usque Pascha III. Si averiat, non cogitur operari quamdiu equus eius foris moratur. Dare debet in festo Sancti Michaelis x. denarios de gablo, et Sancti Martini die XXIII., et sestarium ordei, et II. gallinas. Ad Pascha I. ovem juvenem, vel II. denarios. Et jacebit a festo Sancti Martini usque ad Pascha ad faldam domini sui, quotiens ei pertinebit. Et a termino quo primitus arabitur usque ad festum Sancti Martini arabit unaquaque septimana I. acram, et ipse parabit semen domini sui in horreo. Ad haec III. acras precum, et duas de herbagio. Si plus indigeat herbagio, arabit proinde sicut ei permittatur." Here August is in the Anglo-Saxon text corresponded by *herfest*.

the end of September. In Anglo-Saxon time August was the month of harvest.[1] Except Professor Weinhold, nobody doubts any longer the late origin of the harvest festivals. Professor Mogk agrees with Heino Pfannenschmid, author of *Germanische Erntefeste*, who maintains that Michaelmas is rooted in economic conditions, the existence of which the Germanics owe to the Romans.[2] In the same degree as, in the centuries which followed, agriculture excelled pasture as a means of producing food, Martinmas was bound to decay in favour of Michaelmas, which was bound to receive ever new stress. But another economic force also set in, with a tendency destructive of a Martinmas celebration, though without anything in it to raise the significance of Michaelmas. In olden times it had been the most economical course to leave cattle, swine, sheep, and horses on the pasture grounds till the actual winter came, and then at once to kill all such of those animals as could not be kept over the winter. Thus, in the first half of November, a great killing time for the domestic animals had begun, which was apparently distinguished by the festival at the beginning of winter. With the improvement which took place in the cultivation of meadows in the Carolingian age, the quantity of hay produced annually

---

[1] This appears plainly from Thorpe's *Ancient Laws*, I., 432-33: "Rectitudines Singularum Personarum : Cot-setle rectum est juxta quod in terra constitutum est. Apud quosdam debet omni die Lunae, per anni spatium, operari domino suo, et tribus diebus unaquaque septimana in Augusto. Apud quosdam, operatur per totum Augustum, omni die, et unam acram avenae metit pro diurnale opere." The word corresponding to August in the Anglo-Saxon text of this *Rectitudo* is again *hærfest* : " Kote-setlan riht. be dham dhe on lande stent. On sumon he sceal ælce Mon-dæge ofer geares fyrst his laforde wyrcan. odhdh III. dagar ælcre wucan on hærfest ne dhearf he land-gafol syllan." When Jacob Grimm explains *evenmant* (September) as meaning oats-month (from Latin *havena*, *Geschichte der deutschen Sprache*, 1848, I., p. 87), he is probably wrong, for oats were reaped before September. The term, which is of very late origin, is rather to be put beside *even-naht* (equinox), and means the month of equinox on Frisian ground. So is Grotefend wrong (*Zeitrechnung*, I., p. 54). From the quotations given there it is apparent that the term *Evenmaend* is confined to the Nether-Rhine up to Cologne.

[2] "Auch auf deutschem Boden scheinen wir noch Überreste dieser alten Sommer- und Herbstopfer zu haben : jener in der Hagelfeier, dem Johannisopfer, an dem es besonders galt, Menschen, Vieh und Erzeugnisse des Bodens vor bösen Geistern zu schützen, dieser in den Erntefesten oder den Martinsschmäusen, doch sind die Nachrichten auf diesem Gebiete mit Vorsicht für altgermanischen Kult zu verwerten, da sie in Kulturverhältnissen

was increased, and consequently it was no longer necessary to slaughter at once all the domestic animals designed for food. They could now in part be kept for some time in the stable, and fattened whilst they did not move about very much. Thus the great killing time slowly advanced further into winter—to St. Andrew's day (November 30)[1] or St. Nicolas day (December 5).[2]

So late as the time of King David I. of Scotland (1124-1153) the usual time of slaughter for cattle, swine, and sheep was from Martinmas till Christmas, and these forty-four days were in legal language called "tyme of slauchter."[3] Almost contemporaneously a pig appeared as a duty

ihre Wurzel haben, die wir hauptsächlich den Römern verdanken" (*Mythologie*, 1127, in Paul's *Grundriss der germanischen Philologie*, Strassburg, 1891, Vol. I.). This argument does not, however, hold good for the *Martinsschmäuse*; for the impossibility to pasture cattle, sheep, and horses beyond Martinmas is much older than the Roman influence upon the Germanics is.

[1] A St. Andrew's feast is mentioned *e.g.* by Melchior Goldast of Haiminsfeld, *Rerum Alamannicarum Scriptores Aliquot Vetusti*, Francofurti, 1661, I., p. 97, in *Ephemerides Monasterii S. Galli*: "Andreae Apostoli. Eodem festo dat Hospitarius x. fercula, scilicet bis carnes, bis pisces, bis caseos, bis ova, duos ciatos, et unum stuopum, maximum leibonem, et minorem leibunculum, et in vespera stuopum, lunulas et oblatas de Linkinwiller."

[2] Thorpe, *Ancient Laws*, I., 461, *Leges Regis Edwardi Confessoris* (1042-1066): "De Occisionibus Animalium contra natale. xxxix. Cum autem dictum est, quod non emerent animalia praeter plegios, clamaverunt macecrarii, quos Angli vocant fleismangeres, de civitatibus et burgis, quod quaque die oportebat eos emere animalia, occidere et vendere [L. add: nam in occisione animalium erat vita eorum]. Clamabant etiam cives et burgenses pro consuetudinibus suis, quod circa festum Sancti Martini emebant animalia [L. instead: consueverant animalia in foro mercari] sine plegiis, ad faciendas suas occisiones contra Natale Domini, quas consuetudines justas et sapienter ductas non auferimus eis, tamen in mercatis emptis cum testibus et cognitione venditorum." As to the masting of swine and the varying thickness of their fat, compare the *Laws of King Ine* in Thorpe's *Ancient Laws and Institutes of England*, I., p. 133 (xlix.), where different fines are prescribed for taking forbidden mast, according to the thickness of the fat of the swine. There were rules laid down for the swine-herd, how many swine of each class had to be slaughtered every year (Thorpe, *Ancient Laws*, I., pp. 436 437: "Gafolswane, id est, ad censum porcario, pertinet, ut suam occisionem det secundum quod in patria statutum est. In multis locis stat, ut det singulis annis xv. porcos ad occisionem, x. veteres et v. juvenes; ipse autem habeat super-augmentum"), though the exact time of killing the swine is not stated in any *Rectitudo* of the Anglo-Saxon period.

[3] *Leges Burgorum Scocie*, or *Leges et Consuetudines Quatuor Burgorum Berewic Rokisburg Edinburg et Strivelin, constitute edite ac confirmate per Regem David, titulo*

to be paid at Christmas in Germany,[1] which, of course, meant that it was to be killed at once.

In Scotland Martinmas was, so late as 1800, "the term at which beeves are usually killed for winter." This was "commonly called Martlemas in England, whence the phrase mentioned by Serenius,[2] 'Martlemas beef.' "[3] Brand's *Popular Antiquities*[4] tell of a little later time: "Two or more of the poorer sort of rustic families still join in purchasing a cow, etc., for slaughter at the time (called in Northumberland a Mart), the entrails of which, after having been filled with a kind of pudding meat consisting of blood, suet, groats, etc., are formed into little sausage links, boiled, and sent about as presents, etc. From their appearance they are called Black Puddings." Jamieson[5] mentions that the Black Puddings were, at the beginning of our

---

LXIV. *De Officio Carnificum* (in *The Acts of the Parliaments of Scotland*, Vol. I., A.D. 1124 to 1423; 1844, p. 346):

LXIV. "DE OFFICIO CARNIFICUM

"Quicunque carnes vendere voluerit vendat bonas carnes scilicet bovinas ovinas et porcinas et vendat secundum consideracionem proborum hominum ville et ponat eas in fenestra sua ut sint communes omnibus emere volentibus   Carnifices vero servient burgensibus tempore occisionis scilicet a festo sancti Martini usque ad natale Domini de carnibus suis preparandis et conficiendis in lardariis   Si vero carnes male preparentur carnifex restituet ei dampnum suum cuius erant animalia   Carnifices dum serviunt burgensibus comedent ad mensam illorum scilicet cum servientibus eorum   Et habebunt pro uno marto obolum pro quinque ovibus obulum pro uno porco obulum"

"OF FLESCHEWARIS IN THE BURGH

"Quha that wyl sell flesche he sal sell gude flesche beyff muttone and pork eſtir the ordinans of gud men of the toune and he sal sett his flesche opynly in his wyndow that it be sene communly till al men that will tharof   And fleschewaris forsuth sal serve the burges in tyme of slauchter that is to say fra the feſt of saynct Martyne quhil yhule of the flesche in thar lardyner to be graythit and dycht   And gif the fleschewar graythis ivil flesche he sal restor hym the scathis that aw the bestys   And the fleschewaris quhilis thai serve thaim thai sal ete at thair burde wyth thair servandis   And thai sal hafe for a cow or ane ox a halpeny and for v shepe a halpeny and for a swyne a halpeny"

[1] Grimm, *Deutsche Rechtsaltertümer*, V., 537, Baubach, Lower Alsace, A.D. 1143, § 5: "Ipse villicus mansum cum omnibus iustitiis habebit, porro in natale domini curiam visitabit, 12 panes, 4 sextaria vini et unum porcum, quem pascalem vocant, apportabit."

[2] *English and Swedish Dictionary*, Nykoping, 1757.

[3] Jamieson, *Etymological Dictionary of the Scottish Language*, under "Mart."

[4] P. 355.   [5] *Ibid.*

century, as they still are, an appendage of the Mart in Scotland. They were made of blood, suet, onions, pepper, and a little oatmeal.[1] A cow or ox which was fattened, killed, and salted for winter provision was at least from the fifteenth to the nineteenth century in Scotland called a *Mart* (Gaelic = cow), *Marte*, or *Mairt*.[2]

The sculptured capitals of the choir-pillars of Carlisle Cathedral present a probably unrivalled fourteenth century series of figures, depicting the occupations of the seasons.[3] While June is there described as the month of hunting with a hawk, and July as the time of mowing with a scythe, the representative of August, holding in one hand a crutch and in the other a weed-hook, is cutting off with the latter the thick succulent stalk of a thistle-leaf which borders the opening; and it is September which is denoted as the month of grain-harvest, its symbol being a man in a field of wheat, holding a handful in his right hand, and cutting it with a sickle in his left. October is the tide of grape-harvest, the bunch of grapes in the left hand,

---

[1] The eighteenth century song says:

> "It fell about the Martinmas time,
> And a gay time it was than,
> When our gudewife got puddings to mak',
> And she boil'd them in the pan."

(*The Songs of Scotland chronologically arranged*, London, 2nd ed., p. 158; "Get up and bar the door," from Herd's Collection).

[2] Jamieson, *Etymological Dictionary of the Scottish Language*, under "Mart." He gives the following instances: "Of fleshers being burgesses, and slaying mairts with their awin hands" (*Chalmerlan Air*, c. 39, s. 68). "That all—martis, muttoun, pultrie,—that war in the handis of his Progenitouris and Father—cum to our Souerane Lord, to the honorabill sustentation of his hous and nobill estate" (Acts of James IV., 1489, c. 24, edit. 1566; Skene, *Laws and Acts of Parliament*, Fol., Edin., 1597, c. 10). "In 1565, the rents were £263 19s. 2d. sterling,—60 marts or fat beeves, 162 sheep," etc. (*Statistical Account*, V., 4). The same word is also used metaphorically to denote those who are pampered with ease and prosperity: "As for the fed Marts of this warlde, the Lord in his righteous judgement, hes appoynted them for slaughter" (Bruce's *Eleven Sermons*, 1591, A. 4 a., Jamieson, *Ibid.*). There can be no doubt that this Celtic word *Mart* = cow was very early brought into connection with Martinmas.

[3] Described by James Fowler in the *Transactions of the Cumberland and Westmorland Antiquarian and Archaeological Society*, IV., p. 280, which description is extracted in R. S. Ferguson's *Guide to Carlisle*, Carlisle, 1890, pp. 45-46.

the hooked knife in the right hand of the vine-dresser, and the basket upon the ground by his side denoting it as such. It is November and December which bring in the domestic animals. The emblem of November is a man in boots, sowing corn broadcast with his right hand out of a wicker basket hanging at his left side, suspended by a strap from his right shoulder. Oak-leaves and acorns are on the bell of the western member of this capital; on the eastern member of the next capital is seen a swine-herd in the midst of oak-leaves and acorns tending a herd of swine feeding, one of the swine having its head raised as if to catch a falling acorn. December is a man with an axe grasped by the handle in both hands, raised, and with the back of it about to fall on the forehead of an ox, which is held fast by its horns by a man, in similar costume to the first, standing behind it. January is the time of gay drinking, its representative having three smooth unbearded faces under one skull cap, drinking by the right and left mouths out of shallow cups held respectively in the right hand and in the left, and with the central face looking impassively forward. A jug wherewith to replenish his cups stands on the ground at his left side. February is nothing but the month of cold and wet weather; March digs up the ground round still leafless trees; April, with a crooked knife, cuts dry branches down from them; and May is the gay month of young foliage and flowers, its symbol being a woman holding in each hand a *fleur-de-lys*-shaped bunch of sprouting foliage, and presenting them to a young man, who, by his right hand, takes from her the bunch in her hand.

On the Nether Rhine, about A.D. 1400, the killing time of swine was about Christmas,[1] just as in England, a little later, December was the principal month of slaughter.[2] In the Germany of the sixteenth century, under the

---

[1] *Annalen des Historischen Vereins für den Niederrhein*, Instalment LIV., 1892, p. 12; *Book of Expenditure of Herr von Drachenfels*, 1395, p. 21, Jan. 4, 1396, No. 56: "1 alb um spiskraut, 1 alb um eier up dat huis, doe man die verken affdeide;" p. 37, Nov. 29, 1396: "Ich haen Heynen Volrait gegen 55 m van den verken die zuo jair up vur kirsnacht wurden gegulden."

[2] Bartholomaeus Anglicus, IX., chap. xix. (ed. 1488): "De Decembre. In hoc mense propter asperitatem frigoris sunt altilia et animalia domestica multae quietis et parvi motus, et ideo plurimum impinguantur. Unde tunc temporis interficiuntur potissime et mactantur;

influence of agricultural progress, the killing time of pigs extended to Epiphany,[1] and shortly afterwards to St. Anthony's Day (January 17),[2] thus reaching the second half of January.[3] To February it was shifted not earlier than the seventeenth century, when the cultivation of potatoes had become popular and productive enough to keep especially swine through the greater part

---

propter quod depingitur tanquam carnifex qui cum securi percutit et mactat porcum suum.' That the slaughter began in November is shown by the following passage : " Of our tame boars we make brawn, which is a kind of meat not usually known to strangers. . . . With us it is accounted a great piece of service at the table from November until February be ended, but chiefly in the Christmas time. With the same also we begin our dinners each day after other ; and, because it is somewhat hard of digestion, a draught of malvesey, bastard, or muscadel is usually drank after it." . . . (*Elizabethan England :* from "A Description of England," by William Harrison (in *Hollinshed's Chronicles*), edited by Lothorp Withington, with Introduction by F. J. Furnivall, London, The Scott Library, p. 658).

[1] Lauterbach Document of 1589, Grimm, *Deutsche Rechtsaltertümer*, III., 369: a young pig which had not reached maturity was led round through the benches (and, probably, killed afterwards).

[2] Montanus, p. 17 ; Sebastian Franck, *Weltbuch*, I., p. 131 ; Ulrich Jahn, *Deutsche Opfergebräuche*, p. 266.

[3] At the end of the sixteenth century the occupations of the time of October to January are described in the following way :

OCTOBER.

" Frigoribus coelum magis intractabile reddit,
October, stabula hinc cogit adire pecus.
Arboribus fructus adimit, spoliatque decore,
Atque etiam cupide turbida musta bibit.

Aliter.

October mustum calcatis exprimit uvis
Et serit hoc anno quae redeunte metat.

NOVEMBER.

Ligna vehit mactatque boves, et laetus ad ignem
Ebria Martini festa November agit.
Ad pastum in silvam porcos compellit, et ipse
Pinguibus interea vescitur anseribus.

Aliter.

Autumnus quaecunque dedit, consumo November,
Et pinguem hyberna glande trucido suem.

of the winter. This movement was, on legal ground, accompanied by a shifting of a great number of duties and taxes to the beginning of the new year, reckoned either as at Christmas or on January 1, so that Michaelmas, Christmas, Easter, and St. John's Day came to be the four great terms all over Europe, wherever the Roman Calendar and the Roman Church succeeded in uprooting the ancient Germanic tri-partition of the year.[1] The economic evolution, more especially the prevalence of agriculture over cattle-keeping, thus tended to destroy the ancient Germanic mid-November celebration, whilst favouring both a harvest festival held earlier in the year and the development of a festival about the middle of the German winter.

DECEMBER.

In nive persequitur vestigia pressa ferarum,
Abluit et calida membra December aqua.
Affert Solstitium, celebrat cunabula Christi,
Et iugulat porcos, tribula dura ferit.

Aliter.

Haud avis, haud fera venanti deest ulla Decembri,
Quamvis ningat atrox et gelet usque vadum.

JANUARIUS.

Ianus vina bibit, crepitantique assidet igni.
Et pingues carnes torret, editque suem.
Annum praeteritum claudit, reseratque futurum,
Sed venam ferro tangere, iure vetat"

(*Ranzovii Exempla, Quibus Aetrologicae Scientiae Certitudo Comprobatur*, Coloniae, 1585, pp. 304, 306, 307, which latter two are there wrongly numbered 400 and 303). Another piece from the same time says of December :

"Prassen will ich und leben wol,
Eine Sau ich itzunder stechen sol."

(Grässe, *Des deutschen Landmanns Practica*, Dresden, 1858, p. 28).

[1] Michaelmas appears as a term for paying duties very frequently from the sixteenth century. *Landesordnung des Herzogtums Preussen von* 1525, Pfannenschmid, *Germanische Erntefeste*, p. 118; Richter, *Kirchenordnungen*, I., 32; *Ibid.*, II., 355; *Hoyaische Kirchenordnung von* 1573, where Michaelmas is called the *vierte Hochfesttag,* and put into parallel with Christmas, Pasch, and Whitsunday, thus clearly standing in relation to the Roman quartering of the year.

CHAPTER VII.

SOLSTICES AND EQUINOXES.

JACOB GRIMM, as has been shown already, had a perfect grasp of the six-fold division of the year found among the Germanics at the dawn of history. And though he did not know that it had been borrowed from the Orient, and probably ultimately from Egypt, and that it was by no means genuine and common Aryan property, yet he did not fail to see how deep-rooted it was in the legal, cultural, and economic conditions of our ancestors. It is a very strange fact that he should have thought a knowledge of two solstices and two equinoxes, together with a quartering of the year, reconcilable with the conclusions as to the Aryan year in general, which of necessity must be drawn from a six-fold division. Had he been aware that these two ways of looking at the course of the year were mutually exclusive, he would have been led to a further examination of each, and then would have found that a cognizance of solstices and equinoxes must be denied to the early Aryans, as well as to the Germanics before their acquaintance with the Roman calendar; that the quartering of the year is of purely Roman origin, and is not found elsewhere; that there is no historical evidence whatever for a celebration of solstices and equinoxes among the Germanics in their pre-Roman time; that philology and folklore, the history of the Christian Church, and the history of agriculture all point to a three-fold partition of the year with the beginning about the middle of November. It was Jacob Grimm's way to regard our ancient ancestors as speculative philosophers who stood aloof from the struggle for existence, and who shaped their yearly course according to their own fancies and their belief in gods; and he failed to see that it is the economic conditions which, in primeval times, as they do in our own, fixed all the more important features of daily and yearly life, leaving only a very limited realm to a manifestation of personal likes and dislikes; nay, that that realm gets smaller and smaller every step we go further back into the past.

Jacob Grimm was a king in his kingdom of Germanic philology, and even where he stumbled on his royal road, he could not help indicating the way to walk safely.   But what about those who followed his route? Was it not strange that they should think his stumbles worthy, above all, of imitation, that they should altogether neglect his useful hints and the material gathered by him which pointed in the right direction?   It looks like a joke in the history of Germanic antiquarian studies, that the man who after Grimm made this subject his special study, and devoted years to it, should have wasted all his energy in the attempt to prove that the Germanics in pre-Roman times had exactly the same year as the Romans; that they, therefore, had nothing to get from them, and rejoiced in quartering their year and celebrating imaginary solstices and equinoxes.[1]

The observation of the change of cold in winter and heat in summer is one thing, that of the movement of the rising-point of the sun on the horizon is another.   If some peoples of antiquity sought to find a causal connection between the two things, that connection was hopelessly wrong, the proper relation of the two lines of observation having been known only since Copernicus, *i.e.*, since the sixteenth century.   That primitive people were bound to connect them is by no means true, and it is more than doubtful whether the next thing would be to observe so-called solstices and equinoxes.   The fixing of the date at which day and night are exactly equal lacks entirely in economic interest and significance, and certainly never affected the minds of primitive peoples.   The observation of so-called

---

[1] So even Heino Pfannenschmid seems to think when he explains his theory of the Germanic year in his otherwise excellent book on *Germanische Erntefeste im heidnischen und christlichen Cultus* (Hannover, 1878, pp. 16 ss. and 326 ss).

solstices, on the other hand, is extremely difficult. Whilst in autumn and spring the rising-point of the sun visibly shifts from day to day, it scarcely shifts at all from the beginning of December to the middle of January, and from the beginning of June to the middle of July. Even the astronomers whom Caesar had at his disposal were not able to fix the solstices and equinoxes actually; and although he ordered the winter solstice to take place December 25, and the summer solstice on June 24, they persistently and obstinately disobeyed—the winter solstice making a point of taking place on December 23, A.D. 1; on December 22, A.D. 101; on December 21, A.D. 201; on December 20, A.D. 301; on December 19, A.D. 401; on December 18, A.D. 601; on December 17, A.D. 801; and so on; so that in 1501 it was wicked enough to take place on December 12. The spring equinox and autumnal equinox apparently shared the delight in moving backward by eighteen hours a century, and shifted in the same degree away from March 21 and September 22.

It was not earlier than at their close contact with the Romans that the Germanics became acquainted (as with other Roman institutions) with solstices and equinoxes,[1] although not with their true astronomical dates, but with the pseudo-equinoxes and solstices of the Julian calendar, to which their wise men faithfully stuck for a millenium, whilst popular tradition knew nothing of these foreign-made goods. Nevertheless these innovations brought the ancient Germanics face to face with a task which may be called philological. They were compelled to create new words for the new conceptions with which they were made familiar, and they chose the simplest way that offered, by merely translating the Latin terms. But not all tribes fulfilling that task in the same way, there arose considerable divergence in the expressions used, from which divergence even now we can see that the Germanics had no ancient common word for them, such as they had for *winter* and *summer*. Nay, they even took over the particular limitations with which the Latin expression *solsticium* was used. *Solsticium* is in Latin, with a few late exceptions, exclusively used for the

---

[1] Kuhn's article in Zacher's *Zeitschrift für deutsche Philologie*, 1868, I., 118, is not to be taken seriously, at least so far as the Germanics are concerned. He fails to give any proof for their knowledge of a solar year with solstices and equinoxes.

summer solstice. How well aware the Roman mind was of that appears from the fact that the adjective *solsticialis* refers, even in late Latin, exclusively to summer and the middle of it, and is used as the contrary of *brumalis*. The name for the shortest day of the year was simply *bruma* (supposed to be a contraction of *brevissima* [*dies*]), which also meant the whole of winter. Germany herself has evolved four words for solstice, all four of which apply to the summer solstice alone: *sunwende, sungiht, sunstede,* and *sommertag.* Grotefend,[1] who maintains that by *solsticium* without an additional qualification the summer solstice is, in most cases, meant, is unable to give even a single instance from a medieval document in which a winter solstice occurs, and (although he heads his paragraph *Solsticium estivale, brumale*) gives examples solely of *solsticium estivale.* In another paragraph, however,[2] he quite properly remarks that the whole of the following expressions: *sonnwenden, sonnabenden, sonnenbenttag, sunnbenden, sunnewenttag, sunibentag, sunwende, sunnstede, sungichten, sungicht, suniich,* apply to the summer solstice alone. This amounts to the fact, that no medieval instance is known of December 25, or any of the days about it, having ever been called solstice in the German language: nay, that there is no medieval word *wintersonnwende* or the like, the corresponding term in New-High-German being of quite modern growth. Wherever the word *sunnewende* occurs in the Middle-High-German poetry of the twelfth and thirteenth centuries there is no doubt that it can apply to the summer solstice solely. No poet or writer of prose thinks of adding any adjective to make that clear.[3] *Sonnenwende* is turning of the sun; *sungicht* is walk of the sun; and *sunstede* is standing of the sun—three quite different things. These terms do not occur all over Germany, but are restricted to several dialects. So *sunstede* is exclusively Frisian, at least

---

[1] *Zeitrechnung des deutschen Mittelalters*, 1891, I., p. 178.
[2] *Zeitrechnung des deutschen Mittelalters*, I., p. 181.
[3] "Hiute ist der ahte · tac nâch sunewenden," Iwein, 114; "ze einen sunewenden," *Nibelungenlied*, 32, 4, and Lachmann's *Nibelungen Not*, 2023, 1; "vor disen sunwenden," *Ibid.*, 678, 3; 694, 3; "zen næhsten sunwenden," *Ibid.*, 1352, 4; 1424, 4; *Wigalois*, 1717; "an sunwenden âbend," *Nibelungen Not*, 1754, 3; "ze sunewenden," *Tristan*, 5987; "Sant Johans sunewenden tac," Ls., 2, 708.

as far as the continent is concerned, for it also occurs in Anglo-Saxon, thus appearing to be an Anglo-Frisian term.[1] From this we may conclude that the Germanics became acquainted with the Roman summer solstice at a time when the Western Germanics had already separated into Germans and Anglo-Frisians, but before the community of speech between Angles and Frisians was broken up. This is the more likely, as Frisian and English have in common another word for the same notion: Frisian *sumerdey*, English *summer night*, whilst *sommertag* for solstice is sporadic in German. This being the state of matters among the Western Germanics, nobody will wonder that the several Northern Germanic tribes evolved almost each a name of their own. How could it have been otherwise, since they were not acquainted with the summer solstice until after they had settled in the several parts of the north! Thus Danish has *Solhverv*, or throwing of the sun, from which in modern times is derived *Vintersolhvers-festen*. Norwegian, likewise, has *Solkverv* and *Solhverv* with the modern derivatives *Sommersolhverviet* and *Vintersolhverv*. But Swedish has *Solstaud* with the modern derivative *Vintersolstand*, and Icelandic has *Sólstödur* with the modern derivative *Vetrarsólstödur*.

In German the word *sonnwende* (solstice), though never used for winter solstice, is sometimes used for *equinox*, so that Germany can boast of having three solstices, which she certainly deserves on account of her ancient three seasons.[3] In Flanders the equinoxes are called *summer day* (March 17) and *winter day* (September 21),[4] whilst in Frisian and English

---

[1] It is found, *e.g.*, in an Anglo-Saxon treatise on astronomy based entirely on Beda's work, *De Ratione Temporum*: Thomas Wright, *Popular Treatises on Science* written during the Middle Ages in Anglo-Saxon, Anglo-Norman, and English, London, MDCCCXLI., Historical Society of Science Publication, pp. 8, 9: "Aestas is sumor, se hæfdh sunn-stede; hiems is winter, se hæfdh otherne sunn-stede."

[2] Grotefend, *Zeitrechnung des deutschen Mittelalters*, 1891, I., p. 178.

[3] "Sonnwende der ander in der vasten," Grotefend, *Zeitrechnung*, 1891, I., 181. Grotefend maintains the same usage to have existed among the Frisians, *Ibid.*, I., 189: "A sunna ewenda bifara sente Liudgeris dei" (Richthofen, *Friesische Rechtsquellen*, 169); but I should be rather inclined to think that we have there to do with Saturday instead of equinox.

[4] Grotefend, *Zeitrechnung*, 1891, I., p. 178.

summer day means summer solstice. In Middle-High-German the literal
translation of *equinox* (*ebennaht*) is very rare and very late, so that it
almost seems to have been borrowed from Frisian.[1] At any rate it never
was a popular date or an early term. It is not before the fifteenth
century that the equinox is used for dating documents, and even then it
is supplemented by other things.[2] The complicated expression *Tag und
Nachtgleiche*, which bears the stamp of artificial manufacture, is of quite
modern origin. Frisian and English evolve a little earlier than German
their common term for equinox, A.S. *evenniht* or *emnihte*,[3] Frisian *evennaht*.[4]
Among the Northern Germanics the term is exceedingly rare and very
late. Modern Icelandic has *jafn-dægur* and *jafn-dægri*, equal days; Modern
Danish has *iævndogn*; Modern Norwegian has *jafndægri*, *jevndogn*, and
jafnnætti.

If we knew nothing about the actual division of the Germanic year, it
would, on the authority of these philological facts, be safe to assume that
the ancient Germanics did not base their seasons and tides on solstices
and equinoxes. There was once a theory current according to which
everything—myth, cult, custom—was traced back to an alleged sun worship
or observations of the events visible in the sky, such as the rising of the
sun, the hiding of the sun behind clouds, and the shifting of the rising-
point of the sun on the horizon. But, as regards Germanic tribes, that
theory is so little applicable as to make it quite certain that among our

---

[1] " Der onager, in dem merzen an dem funf und zweinzigsten tage sô luot er zwelfstunt
unde sam ofte in der naht, davon bekennet man sint, daz ebennaht belouhtet ir sunne unde
wæt ir wint," Karajan, 82, 26; Müller und Zarncke, *Mittelhochdeutsches Wörterbuch*,
Leipzig, 1863, I., 301. *Ibid.*, "Ebennahtec, equinoxialis obent-nehtig," Diefenbach,
Glossen., 109; " Equinoxium, ebennachtig," *Ibid.*; "aequinoctium ewennachtig," Mone,
VIII., 249.

[2] " 1402 als equenoxium was umme sunte Gregorius dge uten" (*Magdeburger Schöppen-
chronik*, 304), Grotefend, *Zeitrechnung*, 1898, II., 2, 194.

[3] Thomas Wright, *Popular Treatises on Science*, London, 1841, pp. 8, 9, " Ver is
lencten-tid, seo hæfdh emnihte; autumnus is hærfest, the hæfdh odhre emnihte," *Saxon
Chronicle*, Laud MS., E, 1048; "to hærfestes emnihte," John Earle, *Two of the Saxon
Chronicles Parallel*, Oxford, 1865, pp. 179, 180.

[4] Richthofen, *Friesische Rechtsquellen*, 390-392. "Letera evennaht." is the September
equinox, Grotefend, *Zeitrechnung*, I., 54.

ancestors the sun was no deity. We have not only absolutely no traces of sun worship among the Germanic nations, but even in historical times the sun has been of different gender in different Germanic languages. Nay, different Germanic tribes even had different words for *sun*, which, though coming from the same root, were formed with different suffixes (Gothic *sunnô*, fem., and *sunna*, masc.; German *Sonne*, fem.; English *sun*, masc.; Gothic *sauil*, neut.; Anglo-Saxon *sôl*; Old Scandinavian *sôl*). As to deities, the Germanics seem to have originally had one god only, his name being *Tiwaz* (Greek Ζεύς, Latin *Dies-piter*), to whom in common Germanic times another was added, named *Thonaraz*, whilst North Germany still later produced a third, *Wodanaz*, who in the Middle Ages immigrated to Scandinavia, but never won the adoration of the High-German tribes. Besides, there was one goddess, called *Frija*. At any rate we may affirm that at the time when, probably in the first century of our era, the Germans took over from the Romans the Phœnician week of seven days, and replaced their names by German terms which corresponded exactly to the Roman terms, there was not even a god to take the place of *Saturnus*.

Whilst the summer solstice was probably taken over directly from popular Roman tradition, the equinoxes seem to have become familiar to the clerical Germanic mind through the bearing the spring equinox had on the fixing of Easter, the more so because violent discussions about the proper time for holding Easter were going on for several centuries, and most seriously affected the Anglican Church. It is in connection with this controversy that we get our first information about our ancestors' ability to find the term of the spring equinox. Ceolfrid's Letter on Easter and the Tonsure, written circa A.D. 710,[1] shows that about that time the capacity to

---

[1] Haddan and Stubbs, *Councils and Ecclesiastical Documents*, Oxford, 1871, III., 289 : "Aequinoctium autem, juxta sententiam omnium Orientalium, et maxime Aegyptiorum, qui prae ceteris doctoribus calculandi palmam tenent, duodecimo kalendarium Aprilium die provenire consuevit, ut etiam ipsi horologica inspectione probamus." What stress was laid by the Middle Ages on the coincidence of Christmas and the winter solstice is evident from the fact that the keeping up of that coincidence is given as the reason for the institution of the leap year. Bracton's *Note Book*, ed. by F. W. Maitland, Vol. III., London, 1887, p. 301 (fol. 196): "Sed hoc fit propter quandam necessitatem ad evitandam illud inconveniens, quod esset intemperies hiemalis in signis aestivalibus, et quia si possit

fix the date of the equinoxes by observation had been attained in Great Britain, though several centuries elapsed after their first acquaintance with them before equinoxes and solstices were accepted as terms quartering a solar year of 365 days and a quarter. It was probably not before the eleventh century that this took place. The Anglo-Saxon treatise of astronomy, which is entirely based on Beda's *De Temporum Ratione*[1] and on Roman views, calls the four Roman quarters of the year, which are halved by solstices and equinoxes, *lencten-tid*, *sumor*, *hærfest*, and *winter*, of which *lencten-tid*, by its very name a compound with *tide*, is shown to be not an old term.

Notwithstanding all these facts, Professor Weinhold goes on talking about Germanic solstices and equinoxes as if nothing in the world were a fact better established. After having wrongly fixed the terms of the dual division of the year at the end of September and of March, and two of the terms of the three-fold partition on almost the same days, he proceeds[2] to declare that the Germanics halved their two seasons, summer and winter, and thus arrived, absolutely like the Romans, at four seasons (which, however, were no longer seasons, but broke entirely through the system of actual seasons). In his fanciful way he sets down the following bold guesses:[3] "Midwinter and midsummer, Christmas and the feast of John Baptist, according to ecclesiastical denomination, stand out in the German year as very ancient high tides. Through the standing still of the sun, which, according to the opinion of that time, stopped in turning round to a new

---

contingere quod Natale Domini celebraretur in aestate et Nativitas B. Johannis Bapt. in hieme." This passage was in all probability written before A.D. 1256; Henrici de Bracton, *De Legibus et Consuetudinibus Angliae*, Londini, 1640, Lib. V., 2, *De Essoniis*, fol. 359b: "Ille vero dies excrescens qui non est computabilis, ea ratione propter necessitatem ad vitandum illud inconveniens ne festum Natalis Domini celebretur in aestate et Nativitas Sancti Johannis Baptistae in hieme, quod contingere posset infra quingentos vel sexcentos annos, et etiam ita contingeret intemperies hiemalis in signis aestivalibus."

[1] Historical Society of Science, *Popular Treatises on Science* written during the Middle Ages, ed. by Thomas Wright, London, 1841, pp. 8, 9: "Feower tida synd ge-tealde on anum geare, that synd, ver, æstas, autumnus, hiems. Ver is lencten-tid, seo hæfdh emnihte; æstas is sumor, se hæfdh sunn-stede; autumnus is hærfest, the hæfdh odhre emnihte; hiems is winter, se hæfdh otherne sunnstede."

[2] *Deutsche Jahrteilung*, p. 9.　　　　　　　　[3] *Ibid.*, p. 9.

journey, the people felt themselves driven to solemn rest and the service of the deity of the sky which led the sun. Divination and prophecy prevailed during those tides, and with their mysterious thrill interrupted the noisy joy which wreathed round heathen sacrifices." Yet there is not a shadow of historical evidence for these fancies. The Germanics neither had a festival about Christmas nor about the day of John Baptist. The Twelve-nights, of which he talks a little further on, are simply the *Dodekahemeron* of the old Church, which existed there for centuries before they appeared among any Germanic tribe.[1] Nay, all through the Middle Ages the term *Sonnenwende*, or solstice, has not a single time been shown to have been applied to December 25: its use is absolutely restricted to June 24, just as the word *solsticium* was among the Romans. If Weinhold[2] places the Anglo-Saxon word *lîdha* for June and July alongside the Dutch *lauwe, louwmænt* for January, explains them as *lind* and *lau*, transforms these meanings to "resting," and refers that adjective to the "rest of the sun," which, according to popular belief, *i.e.*, according to his belief, took place about midwinter and midsummer, one may well be doubtful whether that serves to strengthen the position of his own hypothesis. The goddesses *Ostara* and *Hrêda*, on whom he[3] lays much stress, he has later given up himself. But he still deduces from the facts that the Scandinavians divided their year by October 9 to 14 and April 9 to 14 (*vetrnâtt* and *sumarnâtt*), and that the Germans are shown to have had the Roman seasons, one of which began about October 1, the conclusion that equinoxes, of which the Germanics knew absolutely nothing, "divided the most ancient German year."[4]

In his *Weihnacht-Spiele und Lieder aus Süddeutschland und Schlesien*[5] there is even a chapter headed in the index as "The Germanico-heathen celebration of the winter solstice," in which he gives a still more enrapturing delineation of that alleged Germanic festival, without being in the least disturbed by the fact that such a thing never existed. There even the

---

[1] Compare my own book *Geschichte der deutschen Weihnacht*, Leipzig, 1893, p. 282.
[2] *Deutsche Jahrteilung*, p. 14.
[3] Weinhold, *Deutsche Jahrteilung*, 1862, p. 15.   [4] *Ibid.*, p. 6.
[5] Wien, 1875, pp. 4, ss.

error occurs, that the solstice had been called *Jul*, accompanied by another, that the winter solstice was the beginning of the Germanic year. We learn that that time was devoted to Wodan, and Fricke, or Holda, or Berchta or Hera, or Gode; that the boar (*bär*) led about through the village was not a boar at all, but a bear; that it was not the central figure of the procession, but probably merely accidental: and we have a hundred other products of unscientific imagination. The description given of the holy Twelve-nights of the Germanics [1] is almost touching. That the Christmas fires have a close relation to the sun; that *yule* has etymologically to do with *wheel*; that the Christmas tree is to be derived from Wodan; that a great number of the customs in use from Martinmas to Easter should properly be held on Christmas eve, or, at least, on the Twelve-nights; these and an extensive list of other most surprising fancies can be learned from that book. So the whole of the thirty-six pages which Professor Weinhold's disciple, Dr. Ulrich Jahn, in his book *Die deutschen Opfergebräuche bei Ackerbau und Viehzucht*,[2] devotes to the offerings about the time of the winter solstice, contain, in so far as they are meant to apply to pre-Christian times, nothing but unhistorical speculations, and would have been better omitted from that book, which, in various respects, may be called useful, and certainly represents a much more critical attitude on the part of its author than any of the attempts of Professor Weinhold to deal with the problems of German popular tradition.

---

[1] Given Wien, 1875, p. 11.   [2] Breslau, 1884, pp. 253-289.

CHAPTER VIII.

THE CALENDS OF JANUARY.

IN the first century before Christ a number of Germanic tribes, through
commerce and war, came into close contact with the Romans, taking over
from them in rapid succession the Roman capital alphabet of Egyptian
origin to turn it into their runes, the Phœnicio-Roman week, the pre-Julian
calendar with its beginning of the year on March 1, some astronomical
wisdom, and a variety of other things. They took over the institution of
the ancient Roman leap year with its intercalary month,[1] although they
did not add this *mensis Mercidonius* every second year between February 23
and 24, but about the middle of summer and at intervals which we do not
know. This intercalary period of apparently about thirty days was the
first thing to interfere with the congruity of the German year, which, so
far, had known only tides of sixty days, but had not taken account of
lunar periods for the purpose of dividing time, however conscientiously
they might observe them as bringing good or bad luck to the affairs of
daily life. Tacitus[2] keeps that usage quite distinct from the Germanic
division of the year. So it continued for at least three-quarters of a

---

[1] We know this from Beda, *De Temporum Ratione*, chap. xv., who expressly testifies
to the existence of an intercalary month among the ancient Angles.

[2] *Germania*, chap. xi.: "Coeunt nisi quid fortuitum et subitum incidit, certis diebus, cum
aut inchoatur luna aut impletur; nam agendis rebus hoc auspicatissimum initium credunt."

F

millennium.[1] The introduction of Roman months instead of tides of about sixty days necessarily led to a breaking-up of the latter into two parts of equal length, for which new names were required. The fact that the six Germanic tides, which formed the course of a year, began about the middle of the Roman months made things a little difficult. Yet the Roman month-names were taken over and bye and bye replaced by new German terms, which were formed by means of a word probably identical with Germanic *moon*, *mânôdh* (Gothic *mênôths*, Old Saxon *mônadh*). It is, however, doubtful whether Latin *mensis* is exactly of the same derivation. Similarly, the relation of the root of *moon* to Sanskrit *mâ*, to measure (Greek μέτρον), is disputed with good reason. The moon was, among the Aryans and among the Germanics in particular, anything but the medium for dividing the course of the year, for which they received, at a very early date, a ready-made theory of probably Egyptian origin. The word *mânôdh* was added to each of the sections in order to mark them clearly out from the old three-score-day tides, the names of which were used for forming the new compounds. So the old *Iuleis* tide of sixty days at the beginning of winter was divided into a first *Iuleis* month and a second *Iuleis* month, the *Lida* tide in summer into a first *Lida* month and a second *Lida* month, to which, in intercalary years, a third *Lida* month was appended, whilst the words *Iuleis*, *Lida*, etc., without any addition, continued to mean a tide of about sixty days, two of which formed a Germanic season of a long hundred of days. Only gradually self-dependent names were developed for these half-tides which were denoted months, most of these names being taken from economic life, which naturally varied considerably between the coasts of the Baltic and the south of France, and from the British Isles down to the coasts of the Adriatic,[2] and remained an ever new source of name-giving, especially during the time of transition from prevalent pasture to

---

[1] *Acta Conciliorum*, Parisiis, 1714, Vol. III., col. 1686, *Concilium Quinisextum sive in Trullo*, A.D. 706, lxv.: " Qui in noviluniis a quibusdam ante suas officinas et domos accenduntur rogos, supra quos etiam antiqua quadam consuetudine salire inepte ac delire solent, iubemus deinceps cessare. Quisquis ergo tale quid fecerit, si sit quidem clericus, deponatur: sin autem laicus, segregetur."

[2] Weinhold, *Die deutschen Monatnamen*, Halle, 1869, pp. 24-28.

prevalent agriculture. The inexhaustible variety of circumstances which led to names for these new half-tides made impossible the development of one and the same series of home-made month-names for all Germanic tribes, or even for each of the principal groups of them; nay, for individual tribes. The several hundreds of Germanic month-names found on Germanic territory from the sixth century down to the present time, with their innumerable variations of meaning, make impossible of attainment a system which would embrace them all.

In the year of Rome 707, *i.e.*, forty-five years before the date from which later the Christian era was counted, the Julian calendar began to reign in Italy and Gaul, and on the coasts of the Mediterranean in general. Within the hundred and fifty years which followed, Roman legions and Roman administration carried it over the Rhine into Germany, and beyond the channel into the British Isles. As long as Gaul remained a Roman province entirely Romanized; as long as down the banks of the Rhine there flourished large Roman towns; as long as hundreds of thousands of Germans served in Roman armies, visiting Italy, Greece, Asia Minor, Egypt, fighting all over the world then known, and more than once disposing of the Roman imperial throne; as long as invading Goths went down to Italy and Vandilian invaders to the north of Africa without losing contact with those Germanic tribes which remained northward of the Alps—there was practically no limit to the entry of Roman knowledge into Germanic territory; and in the suite of every-day experience there came Roman learning with its poets, historians, philosophers, rhetoricians, scientists, and physicians. All along the Rhine there flourished Roman rhetoric schools in considerable number, in which the noble science of grammar and the *trivium* as well as the *quadrivium* were taught thoroughly. Among the Germanics there was no self-dependent scholarship that could successfully compete with those finest products of a higher civilization, and so it became, for about a thousand years, the task of the Germanics to receive and ever receive mental gifts from the civilization of the empire they destroyed.

In the suite of the new calendar which, after Julius Caesar, began the year with the Calends of January (at which date, subsequently to 153 B.C., the Roman consuls had entered their offices), the whole annual course of Roman festivals passed by degrees to Gaul, Germany, and the south of Great Britain; above all, the *Saturnalia*, *Brumalia*, and *Kalendae Januariae*, which, during the first three centuries of our era, were with great regularity observed in all the great towns along the Rhine, and thence spread to the inner parts of Germany, as far as Bohemia; nay, even to the Slave tribes east of the Germans, and to the Lithuanians north of them.[1]

Since even Professor Weinhold admits that the Roman calendar was one of the three forces which shaped the medieval German calendar,[2] it will be worth while to see of what kind the Roman customs were which could be transferred to Germany along with the institution of the Calends of January and the neighbouring festivals. There was first of all the custom of New-Year's gifts or *Strenae*.[3] In imperial Rome the people and the Senate were expected to present New-Year's gifts to the emperors,[4] it being related that Augustus had had a nocturnal vision requiring that people should annually, on a certain day, present money to him, which he received with a hollow hand.[5] During his reign they were given on the Capitol; but Caligula was so lost to a sense of shame,

---

[1] The Lithuanians, according to the old significance of their winter festival, called many centuries later their Christmas *Kalledos*, a name which has wrongly been brought into connection with Lithuanian *Kalada*, log (Grimm, *Deutsche Mythologie*, 4th ed., p. 522), but is certain to have sprung from *Calendae*, since the Czechic word for Christmas is up till to-day *Koleda* (Polish *Kolenda*, Russian *Koljada*); a fifteenth century source calling Bohemian Christmas processions *calendisationes* (Usener, *Christlicher Festbrauch*, Bonn, 1889; Johannes von Holleschau's *Treatise on Christmas*), and a verb *colendisare* appearing in old sources of Bohemian law (Rössler, *Prager Recht*, p. 95, No. 140). Compare my own *Geschichte der deutschen Weihnacht*, Leipzig, 1893, p. 287, note to p. 14,[3] where the quotations from Holleschau's treatise are given.

[2] *Über deutsche Jahrteilung*, Kiel, 1862, p. 3.

[3] The habit of New-Year's presents *boni ominis causa* is first mentioned by Plautus (+ 184 B.C.) in his *Stichus*, iii. 2, 6; v. 2, 24. Their purpose is explained by Ovid, *Fasti*, i. 187. Cakes and fruits were the principal gifts (Martialis, viii. 33; xiii. 37; Seneca, *Epistulae*, lxxxvii.). It seems to have been under Augustus that money took the place of these eatables. The custom still prevailed about A.D. 400 under the Emperors Arcadius and Honorius.

[4] Suetonius, in *Augustus*, chap. lvii.; in *Tiberius*, chap. xxxiv.; in *Caligula*, chap. xlii. Compare Preller, *Römische Mythologie*, p. 161.

[5] "Cavam manum asses porrigentibus praebens," *Ibid.*, in *Augustus*, chap. xci.

as to publish an edict expressly requiring such gifts, and to stand in the porch of the palace, on the Calends of January, in order to receive those which people of all descriptions brought to him.[1] It was reckoned a handsome enough way of receiving gifts, when the bosom-fold of the cloak was expanded; but when they were received with both hands hollow,[2] or in "goupins," to use the Scotch word, it was accounted objectionable. Hence rapine was proverbially expressed in that manner.[3]

But the celebration of the Calends of January was by no means the only festivity of that time of the year in ancient Rome; there was a whole series of festivals, so that Seneca (+A.D. 39) could write to his friend Lucilius: "It is now the month of December, when the greatest part of the city is in a bustle. Loose reins are given to public dissipation; everywhere may you hear the sound of great preparations, as if there were some real difference between the days dedicated to Saturn and those for transacting business. Thus, I am disposed to think, that he was not far from the truth who said that anciently it was the month of December, but now the year. Were you here, I would willingly confer with you as to the plan of our conduct; whether we should live in our usual way, or, to avoid singularity, both take a better supper and throw off the toga. For what was not wont to be done, except in a tumult or during some public calamity to the city, is now done for the sake of pleasure, and from regard to the festival. Men change their dress. It were certainly far better to be thrifty and sober amidst a drunken crowd, disgorging what they had recently swallowed."[4]

These festivals were the *Saturnalia*, with their equality between rich and poor, freemen and slaves, and their presents of all descriptions,[5] lasting from December 17 to December 19; or seven days, from December 17 to

---

[1] Suetonius, in *Caligula*, chap. xlii.

[2] "Utraque manu cavata."

[3] Ammianus Marcellinus, Lib. XVI.; Rosin, *Antiquitates*, p. 29.

[4] Seneca, *Epistulae*, xviii.; Jamieson, *Etym. Dict. of Scot. Lang.*, "Yule," IV.

[5] "Cereos Saturnalibus muneri dabant humiliores potentioribus, quia candelis pauperes, locupletes cereis utebantur," Festus Pompeius, Lib. III. The new year's gift was called *Kalendaticum*. Ducange, *Glossarium*, explains "Kalendaticum praestatio quae Januarii

December 23. All labour rested, and, under the call *Io Saturnalia!* *Io Saturnalia!* people gave themselves to a wild joy. Then followed the *Brumalia*, fixed by Caesar erroneously on December 25, the alleged shortest day of the year, called since that time occasionally *Dies Invicti Solis*, day of the unconquered sun. The character of *Saturnalia*, *Brumalia*, and *Kalendae Januariae* was very wild and lascivious, so wild that, together with the *Matronalia* of the first of March (and sometimes with the *Septimontium*, the feast of incorporation of the seven hills with the city of Rome, also celebrated in December), they were, by the fathers of the Christian Church, regarded as a perfect essence of heathendom, which was by no means meant to be a compliment. So Tertullian (+A.D. 220) could say: "By us who are strangers to sabbaths and new moons, once acceptable to God, the *Saturnalia*, and the feasts of January, and *Brumalia*, and *Matronalia*, are frequented; gifts are sent hither and thither; there is the noise of the *Strenae*, and of games and feasting. O! better faith of the nations in their own religions, which adopts no solemnity of the Christians."[1]

Kalendis fiebat." *Charta Rogerii Siciliae Regis an.* 1137, *apud Falconem Beneventanum,* p. 315: "Angarias, terraticum, herbaticum, carnaticum, kalendaticum, vinum, olivas, relevum, etc. Καλανδικὸν in Justiniani edicto XIII." In England, as late as the thirteenth century, the custom of benevolences exacted by kings was connected with the Roman Calends custom: "Rex autem Regalis magnificentiae terminos impudenter transgrediens, a civibus Londinensibus, quos novit ditiores, die Circumcisionis Dominicae, a quolibet exegit singulatim primitiva, quae vulgares nova dona novi anni superstitiose solent appellare." The king is Henry III., A.D. 1249 (Matthaei Paris, Monachi Albanensis Angli, *Historia Major*, London, 1640, p. 757, under the year 1249). Matthew Paris goes on to say: "Veruntamen festo beati Aeduwardi, quod est in vigilia Epiphaniae, appropinquante, vocavit dominus Rex per literas suas copiosam Magnatum multitudinem: ut simul cum eo, qui in vigilia sancti, videlicet die Lunae in pane et aqua et in vestibus laneis jejunaverant, prout de more solet, ipsum festum magnifice celebrarent in ecclesia S. Petri apud West-monasterium."

[1] Tertullian, *De Idolatria*, chap. xiv. These sweetmeats, called by the name of *Strenae*, were therefore prohibited by the early church (V. Rosin, *Antiquitates*, p. 29). The *Strenae* are traced as far back as to King Tatius, who at this season used to receive branches of a happy or fortunate tree from the grove of *Streniae* as favourable omens with respect to the new year. In another passage (*De Idolatria*, chap. x.) Tertullian says: "Saturnalia, strenae captandae, et septimontium, et brumae, et carae cognationis honoraria exigenda omnia." Compare also Tertullian's *De Fuga in Persecutione*, chap. xiii.

With the introduction of the Julian calendar all kinds of southern Calends rights found entrance to the Germanics: the making of processions through the streets and singing of songs, the lighting of candles and lamps, the adorning of their houses with laurel and green trees, the giving of presents, men dressing up in women's garments, masquerades in the hides of animals, and the erection of a table of fortune for the good luck of the new year.[1]

Half a century before the beginning of our era the first Roman legion had entered Great Britain, and not much later British soil was in constant occupation by Roman legions. The great mass of Roman inscriptions found in Britain gives ample evidence as to their sojourn there. It is not astonishing that among these we find one devoted to the "God The Unconquered Sun" (*Deus Invictus Sol*),[2] which further supports the general assumption that these legions did not only celebrate the Calends of January, but the *Brumalia* as well, and *a fortiori* the *Saturnalia*. The exact date when the Roman legions were withdrawn from Great Britain is not known, but there is no doubt that Roman civilization and Roman religious tradition survived them there, so that when Augustine and his Roman fellow-missionaries of Christianity landed in Britain (A.D. 592) they found there December 25 as a day marked in the festive calendar, at least

---

[1] *Acta Conciliorum*, Parisiis, 1714, Vol. III., col. 365, *Concilium Turonense*, II., A.D. 567, xxii.: "Enim vero quoniam cognovimus nonnullos inveniri sequipedas erroris antiqui, qui Kalendas Ianuarii colunt cum Ianus homo gentilis fuerit: rex quidem, sed Deus esse non potuit." And eight years later: "Non liceat iniquas observationes agere Kalendarum, et otiis vacare gentilibus, neque lauro aut viriditate arborum cingere domos. Omnis haec obsevatior paganismi est." (Caput lxxiii. of the *Capitula Martini Episcopi Bracensis*, circa A.D. 575.) *Ibid.*, Vol. III., col. 399.

[2] *Monumenta Historica Britannica* in the chapter, "Ex Inscriptionibus Excerpta de Britannia," p. 116, No. 103: "Deo Invicto Soli Soc Sacrum Pro Salute Et Incolumitate Imp. Caes. M. Aureli Antonini Pii Felic. Aug. L. Caecilius Optatus Trib. Coh. I. Vardul Cum Con* braneis Votum. Deo * * A Solo Extruct * * * *" (Riechester or Rochester, Northumberland). The Inscriptions, No. 102, "Deo Invicto Herculi Sacr. L. Aemil. Salvianus Trib. Coh. I. Vangi V.S. P.M." (Risingham, Northumberland), and No. 75, "Silvano Invicto Sacrum C. Tertius Veturius Micianus," etc., show, however, that *Invictus* was a rather general divine predicate, which excludes the possibility of interpreting Inscription No. 103 as dedicated to the sole unconquered God, taking *soli* as the dative singular of *solus*.

of the south of England, which naturally paved the way for a celebration of Christ's Nativity on the same day.

As regards the continental Germanics, as late as the middle of the eighth century there existed a perfect unity of popular sacramental usage as to the Calends of January between them and the Romans, the German Calends rites not only resembling the Roman ones absolutely, but even being felt to be identical with them by the people celebrating them. We know this from an incident of A.D. 742. In that year, Winfrid (Bonifacius), the "apostle of the Germans," in a letter written to Pope Zacharias, complained of a strange fact which hindered his getting on better in sowing the gospel in the souls of the *Alamanni, Boioarii*, and *Franci*. For when he interdicted them from certain heathen customs, they justified themselves by the excuse that they had seen similar things at Rome, close to St. Peter's Church, where these things were regarded as perfectly permissible. And they told Boniface they had seen that every year on the eve of the Calends of January, after heathen custom, processions went through the streets singing unchristian songs and using heathen exclamations, that people erected tables of fortune and kept a Calends fire from which they would not give anything away, just as they refused to lend anything else to their neighbours during that time, and that women went publicly about wearing amulets round arms and legs, and offered them to others for sale. The Pope could not deny that such things actually happened in Rome; but, of course, declared in his answer to Boniface that he detested them, as all Christians should do.[1] In the next year he brought the matter

---

[1] *Acta Conciliorum*, Parisiis, 1714, Vol. III., col. 1880, *Epistola Bonifacii Episcopi ad Zachariam Papam* (741-752): V. "Quia carnales homines idiotae, Alamanni, vel Bajuarii, vel Franci, si juxta Romanam urbem aliquid fieri viderint ex his peccatis quae nos prohibemus, licitum et concessum a sacerdotibus esse putant: et dum nobis improperium deputant, sibi scandalum vitae accipiunt. VI. Sicut affirmant se vidisse annis singulis in Romana urbe, et juxta ecclesiam sancti Petri, in die vel nocte quando Kalendae Ianuarii intrant, paganorum consuetudine choros ducere per plateas, et acclamationes ritu gentilium, et cantationes sacrilegas celebrare, et mensas illa die vel nocte dapibus onerare, et nullum de domo sua vel ignem, vel ferramentum, vel aliquid commodi vicino suo praestare velle. Dicunt quoque se ibi vidisse mulieres pagano ritu phylacteria et ligaturas in brachiis et in cruribus ligatas habere, et publice ad vendendum venales ad comparandum

before the Synod of Rome, which promptly interdicted all usages of that kind at the Calends of January and *Brumalia*.[1] An interdiction which was for several centuries repeated and repeated again, was in the form of a question taken over into all more important Penitentials of the Church, and there probably lived longer than the usages of which it was meant to be destructive. The question was: "Didst thou observe the Calends of January after heathen custom, so as to lead singers and choirs through the streets and open places?"[2]

From the letter by Bonifacius to Pope Zacharius (741-752) it appears that, according to Roman custom, the fire at the Calends of January was regarded as holy, and custom did not permit anything to be taken away from it.[3] The Calends fire was an entirely private affair, not kept in public; a fire on the hearth of the home, not a bonfire; whilst all Germanic festive fires are bonfires in the open air.

---

alis offerre. Quae omnia eo quod ibi a carnalibus et insipientibus videntur, nobis hic improperium et impedimentum praedicationis et doctrinae faciunt." To this the Pope replied (*Ibid.*, III., col. 1883, vi.): "De Kalendis vero Januariis, vel ceteris auguriis, vel phylacteriis, et incantationibus, vel aliis diversis observationibus, quae gentili more observari dixisti apud beatum Petrum apostolum, vel in urbe Roma; hoc et nobis, et omnibus Christianis detestabile et perniciosum esse judicamus," etc. The Letters are reprinted in *Epistolae Merowingici et Karolini aevi*, I., Berlin, 1892, p. 301, and commented upon by Rudolf Koegel, *Geschichte der deutschen Literatur bis zum Ausgang des Mittelalters*, Strassburg, 1894, p. 29, though Koegel fails to recognize their proper bearings.

[1] *Acta Conciliorum*, Parisiis, 1714, Vol. III., col. 1929, *Concilium Romanum*, I., A.D. 743, ix.: "Ut nullus Kalendas Januarias et broma colere praesumpserit, aut mensas cum dapibus in domibus praeparare, aut per vicos et plateas cantationes et choros ducere, quod maxima iniquitas est coram Deo: anathema sit." Compare R. Koegel, *Geschichte der deutschen Literatur*, I. 28.

[2] "Observasti Calendas Ianuarias ritu paganorum . . . ita ut per vicos et per plateas cantores et choros duceres," Penitentiary of Burchard von Worms (Friedberg, *Aus deutschen Bussbüchern*, p. 84; Rud. Koegel, *Geschichte der deutschen Literatur*, 1894, I., p. 29).

[3] *Acta Conciliorum*, Parisiis, 1714, Vol. III., col. 1880, *Epistola Bonifacii Episcopi ad Zachariam Papam*, vi., where it is said of the Calends of January: "Et nullum de domo suo vel ignem, vel ferramentum, vel aliquid commodi vicino suo praestare velle." At the *Saturnalia* candles were given as presents, nay, even torches of wax. "Cereos Saturnalibus muneri dabant humiliores potentioribus, quia candelis pauperes, locupletes cereis utebantur," Festus Pompeius, Lib. III. The same custom is witnessed by Martialis and Macrobius.

There is not a single case on record of a New Year's or Christmas fire held in the open air in ancient times; when such fires are recorded, towards the end of the twelfth century, they are of a perfectly private character.[1] It can scarcely astonish anybody that, in the coldest time of the year, good care was taken to have a good warm fire, and that for that

---

[1] The oldest cases of *quasi* public Christmas fires are found in 1577 and 1591. They are, however, kindled in the private houses of the sexton or provost. Wahlscheid, Sieg District, Archive of the Protestant Parish, Document of April 23, 1577, on the Münchhof of Wahlscheid, property of the Monastery of Maer near Neuss, paragraph 5: "Zum funfften soll der opferman haben von dem vorschrieben munchhoff heixholtz, notturfftigen brandt sonder schaden, undt zu christmissen einen stock, des soll der halffman schuldig sein zu leiden, dasz die nachparn, wem solches gefellig, muegen gehen zu desz opffermans hausz, umb sich bei dem christock zu wermen"; Schröteler, *Herrlichkeit und Stadt Viersen*, Köln, 1861, pp. 349, 350, Article 32 of the *Viersener Landrecht* of 1591. "Item wan ein donner wetter ist soll der scholtis den küster die klocken helffen trecken oder sein diener, desgleichen in der *Christnacht* so lang helffen trecken, dass ein man auss Theys hoff an die kirch gahn magh und in der selbe fruhe morgen stondt sall der scholtiss einen stock oder hartholtz ein grot feur in brandt halten bist der Gottesdienst auss ist, das die jenighe, so zur metten und zur kirchen kommen, sich etwas wermen mogen." The old new year's fire seems, under the influence of the special conditions of early morning service, to have become an institute and servitude. But it is not sure that there is any special connection between this fire for warming the church-goers and the fire of the Calends of January. How great is the danger of regarding as sacramental customs which merely spring from the requirements of the season, can be seen from the following case: *The Boke of Curtasye* from the Sloane MS., 1986, in the British Museum, A.D. 1430-40, ed. by Furnivall for the Early English Text Society, London, 1868, in *The Baabees Book*, etc., p. 311 says of the Marshall:

> " 383 Gomon-vsshere, and grome also,
>   Vndur hym ar thes two :
>   Tho grome for fuelle that schalle brenne
>   In halle, chambur, to kechyn, as I the kenne,
>   He shalle delyuer hit ilke a dele,
>   In halle make fyre at yche mele ;
>   Borde, trestuls, and formes also,
>   The cupborde in his warde schalle go,
>   The dosurs cortines to henge in halle,
>   Thes offices nede do he schalle ;
> 393 Bryng in fyre on alhalawgh day,
>   To condulmas euen, I dar welle say
> Per quantum tempus armigeri habebunt liberatam et ignis ardebit in aula.
>   So longe squiers lyuerés schalle hafe,

purpose large pieces of wood were put on, but a thorough proof would be requisite before such fires could be regarded as of Germanic origin. Besides, they are by no means confined to Christmas, but appear on Epiphany as well. An old Bavarian manuscript contains the item: "*Ignes qui fieri solent in vigilia Epiphaniae.*"[1]

We know from a *Weistum* that (A.D. 1184) one of the privileges of the manse of Ahlen, Westphalia, was the right of delivery to it of a whole tree for the festive fire at Christmas eve. But that fire is at the same time denoted as the clergyman's private festive Christmas fire;[2] and in another

---

Of grome of halle, or ellis his knafe ;
But fyre shalle brenne in halle at mete
To Cena domini that men hase ete ;
Ther browgt schalle be a holyn kene,
That sett shalle be in erber grene,
And that schalle be to alhalawgh day,
And of be skyfted, as y the say ;"

and p. 327 :

" 833 In chambur no lygt there shalle be brent,
Bot of wax ther-to, yf ge take tent ;
In halfe at soper schalle caldels brenne
Of parys, ther-in that alle men kenne ;
Iche messe a candelle fro alhalawghe day
To candelmesse, as I gou say ;
Of candel liueray squiyers schalle haue,
So long, if hit is mon wille kraue."

This fifteenth century book states that fires are to burn in the hall from November 1 to February 2, whilst squires shall have a fire during their dinner from November 1 to Maunday Thursday (*Cena Domini*). A daily candle they receive from November 1 to February 2. Had mention of these customs been made about Christmas-tide, they might easily have been supposed to be popular Christmas customs. In churches, no doubt, the number of candles used at Christmas was very great, as can still be seen from church accounts, *e.g.*, at the manse of Engelskirchen, District of Wipperfürth, Rhine-country, of A.D. 1596-7: "In Anno 96 auff christmess funff und ein firdel pont wachfs zu kertzen gemacht vur jeder pont gegeben 22 alb. facit 4 guld. 19 alb. 6 heller, und in der christnacht ein halff pont kleiner kertzen, costen 4 alb."

[1] Ulrich Jahn, *Deutsche Opfergebräuche*, 1884, p. 255.

[2] When stating the privileges of his parsonage the clergyman: "Et arborem in nativitate domini ad festivum ignem suum adducendum esse dicebat." Kindlinger, *Münstersche Beiträge*, II., document 34 ; Grimm, *Deutsche Mythologie*, 2nd ed., p. 594.

Weistum, of Riol and Velle on the Mosella, the *Scheffe* is said to be entitled to a *Winnachtploech*;[1] whilst a third *Weistum*, of Tavern on the Mosella, remarks: "*Item ein bochg zu hawen vff Christabend vor den Christbraten*;"[2] so that we have no more to do with a festive fire, but merely with a fire for roasting meat in the kitchen, if there was one, and if the roasting was not rather done over the fire of the common room. There occur also public payments for a common *Christbraden* of burghers.[3]

That the festive fire at Christmas was a private affair, and that poor people were not always able to have one of their own, appears from a little medieval story, either from the thirteenth or fourteenth century, which contains an allusion to the Yule-log, although it seems to point to the fact that it was by no means common, so that a blacksmith could rejoice to get a Yule-log contrary to expectation, by a mere play of seeming chance.[4]

---

[1] Grimm, *Deutsche Rechtsaltertümer*, II., 302.   [2] *Ibid.*, II., 264.

[3] Town-Archive of Bingen on the Rhine, No. 90, Town accounts of A.D. 1501, "Item 14 s. 6 hllr. hain wir geben zum Christbraden uff die christnacht den burgern und nachbern."

[4] "Quidam in partibus de Winchelse sibi aggregavit pecuniam in cista, de qua nec sibi nec aliis voluit subvenire. Veniens igitur una die ut eam videret, vidit super eam quendam diabolum sedere nigerrimum, dicentem sibi, 'Recedere, nec est pecunia tua, sed Godewini fabri.' Quod ille audiens, et nolens eam in alicujus commodum pervenire, cavavit magnum truncum, ipsamque imposuit, reclusit, et in mare projecit. Quem quidem truncum marinae undae ante ostium dicti Godewini, viri justi et innocentis, manentis in proxima villa, super litus in siccum projecerunt, circa vigilium Dominici Natalis. Exiens itaque idem Godwinus mane, invenit truncum projectum, multumque gavisus pro habendo foco in tanto festo, eum in domum suam traxit, et ad locum foci gaudens apposuit. Intrante itaque festi praedicti vigilia, ignis trunco supponitur, metallum intro latens liquescit, et exterius defunditur. Quod videns uxor dicti Godwini, ignem subtrahit, truncum movet et abscondit. Sicque ut dominus praedictae pecuniae victum quaereret hostiatim, dictusque faber de paupere fieret inopinate dives, devulgatur quia in vicinio quod miser ille pecuniam suam demersisset, cogitavit ergo uxor dicti Godwini quod eidem misero in aliquo cautius subveniret, cogitans dictam pecuniam fuisse suam, fecit uno die panem unum, et in eo XL. solidos abscondens dedit ei. Quem infortunatus ille accipiens piscatoribus super litus obviavit, panem eis pro uno denario vendidit, et recessit. Venientes itaque piscatores ad domum dicti Godwini, prout fuerunt assueti, dictum panem extrahunt et suis equis elargiri proponunt. Quem agnoscens domina domus, avenam pro eis dedit et eum recepit. Idemque miser finetenus pauper undique remansit," Thomas Wright, *A Selection of Latin Stories* (from Manuscripts of the thirteenth and fourteenth centuries: a Contribution to the History of Fiction during the Middle Ages. London, printed for the Percy Society, 1842), pp. 220, 221, from *Altdeutsche Blätter*, Vol. I., p. 75

On British soil an early instance of a Yule-clog or Yule-log has yet to be given.   Ulrich Jahn's generalizations,[1] according to which a pre-Christian winter-solstice fire would have to be supposed as a general custom, are void of any historical foundation, and merely represent fantastic speculations. Nay, the very fact that the British version of the above story[2] makes the blacksmith use the tree trunk as an anvil seems to indicate that the Yule-log is only a more modern intrusion into that story.   For the fact that the figure of the blacksmith is kept in the German story shows that the anvil has been replaced by the Yule-log, and not *vice versa*.[3]

The privilege of cutting wood in the forest about Christmas appears also in Switzerland, where it is connected with a local legend.   On December 27, 1375, the women of the Berne village Hetteswil are said to have surprised and slain the knightly army of the Count of Coucy.   As a reward they received, from the Prior of the monastery, the privilege to go, on St. John's day at Christmas, with a hatchet into the forest of the monastery and cut as much wood for boiling their Christmas soup as they needed.   But when it was found that the forest suffered too great damage, because the women used to boil too tough Christmas fowl, the privilege was changed to the effect that instead of the firewood they received a meadow, which, in 1826, was still in the possession of the women of Hetteswil, and the yearly yield of which was spent for a meal called the fowl-soup.[4]   That we have here to do with an old term servitude is evident from the fact that in some cases the servitude of driving a cart-load, or several cart-loads, of wood to a castle or landlord's dwelling, known to medieval Latinity as *truncagium*, and in early English as *wodlade*,[5] appears not at Christmas

---

[1] *Die deutschen Opfergebräuche bei Ackerbau und Viehzucht*, Breslau, 1884, p. 258.

[2] Thomas Wright, *A Selection of Latin Stories*, p. 27, No. 25.

[3] The passage of the English story runs : "Dixit quidam puer ad magistrum navis, 'Da mihi truncum istum, quia faber istius villae amicus meus est, et volo ei dare truncum ut faciat sibe exinde incudem.' Et magister concessit. Cum autem faber quadam die operaretur super truncum illum et feriret, exilierunt denarii de trunco per quoddam foramen, et obstupuit faber, sed omnes collegit, et consilio uxoris suae illos abscondit."

[4] *Berner Neujahrsblatt*, 1826, 28 ; Rochholz, *Deutscher Glaube und Branch*, Berlin, 1867, II., p. 317.

[5] *Notes and Queries*, 7th series, x., 472, 1890, Geo. Neilson: *Truncagium*.

alone, but at Christmas and May, whilst the old terms were Martinmas and mid-May (or Rogation Days or Pentecost), of which the former had been shifted to Christmas.[1]

So late as about 1712 the wood for the Christmas fire is mentioned, it being a servitude of the holders to drive it into the castle.[2]

When the tenant of a small. holding paid his duties at the old terms, he was, as a rule, entertained to dinner by his landlord. The meal he got was not a free gift of the landlord, but something to which the tenant had a claim, and which had to be of a certain substantiality and duration. Its duration was, in the fifteenth century, fixed by the time requisite for burning away a wet wheel on the open fire in the hall in which the meal took place. We know that custom to have been observed at various terms, in autumn as in winter.[3] As long as the only instance known fell on

[1] Bürgermeisteramt Osterath, district Crefeld, *Schatzregister des Kirspels Osteraht*, made in 1683, after models of 1603 and 1640, contains the regulation that the community has the duty to drive to the castle of Linn twelve cart-loads of wood every eight weeks: "Item noch jahrligs drey Christ- und drey Meyfuhren beyfahren." In the sixteenth century Christmas and Pentecost (instead of Martinmas and Pentecost) appear together in the same way (Klotz, *Beschreibung der Herrschaft und Stadt Gera*, 1816, p. 237; the first article of the *Reussische Kirchenvisitation* of 1533 is: "Zu gedenken das Opfer-Geld zu Besserung des Pfarrers jährlich auf zwo Tagzeit, als nämlich zu Weyhnachten und Pfingsten ordentlich einzubringen und zusammlen").

The Archive of the Protestant parish of Leuscheid, Rhine country, contains, under IV. *b¹*, a complaint about the withdrawal of the Christmas allowance of wood of November 17, 1696. According to it, it was customary, "dass ein jedweder kirspels eingesessener, der welcher ein gefähr unter henden hat, auff *christmess* umbtrent ein karrich hotz, dass Christ-holtz, zu unterhaltung der hauss-steur an dass widem hauss unentgeltlich zu liefferen schuldig."

[2] Bürgermeisteramt Liedberg, district München Gladbach, *Acts*, No. 16, 4, Manuscript of about 1712, fragment of a Weistum on the services to be rendered to the family of Liedberg, paragraph 10, "Item ist auch das gantze amt nach advenant schuldig auf Christ-messen die corstbrende dem haus Liedberg aufzufahren" (*advenant* is the document which regulates the distribution among the several communities of the servitudes to be borne by the whole district).

[3] In an unprinted document on the privileges of the family of Lüftelberg in the Sürst, a district between Bonn and Euskirchen, Rhine country, of 1579, which is copied from the same original as is an eighteenth century manuscript in the Archive of the family of Lüftelberg, it is decreed that the holders have to deliver their duties to the landlord on St. Kunibert's day (October 10): "Wann · solches geschehen, so soll der grundherr

December 26, there was at least some possibility of connecting this habit with the Calends-log and later Christmas-log, but now this no longer holds good. Speculative mythologists found in that wheel an image of the sun, and regarded its burning as a solstice-celebration. In all probability the holders had to deliver the wheels—of course simple tree sections[1]— and the time requisite for burning them was made the duration of their meal, in order that they might not make them too thin.

The custom of Christmas fire no doubt has its root in the Roman Calends of January rite of the same description. But that fact did not hinder it from receiving an intrinsically Christian interpretation. It was an old institute for the landlord to give his tenant a cart-load or wheelbarrow-load of wood at the birth of a child. Christ being regarded, in the fourteenth and fifteenth centuries, as a kind of little universal brother to mankind, the occasion of his birth was taken as an opportunity for gifts similar to those which children received at the birth of a baby brother or sister. ·In the beginning of the sixteenth century such gifts to children were called in North Germany *kindsvôt*, or child's-foot,[2] the same name

darentgegen schuldig sein den geschwornen ein frei kost zugeben, drei gericht von einem schwein, erbsen und pfeffer, weck und brod, wein und bier, wie von alters gebrauchlich. Wann die geschwornen ihre zeit sitzen, so soll man ein rad an das feur legen, welches 3 tag und 6 wochen im wasser gelegen hat, so lang den geschwornen essen und trinken geben, bis ein auswendiger mann komt und nicht erkennen mag, was das gewesen sei" (communicated to me by Dr. Armin Tille of Bonn). It was the custom that the peculiarities of such dinners as were legal institutions should be prescribed exactly. Compare Lamprecht, *Deutsches Wirtschaftsleben im Mittelalter*, III., p. 32, Urbary of the Stift St. Trond of A.D. 1274 (Bridal on the Mosella): "Item autumpno facto debent praedicti feodales habere servitium sive prandium de tribus ferculis ab ecclesia sancti Trudonis, olera cum carnibus bovinis, carnes porcinas cum pipere et porcinas carnes assas." Another example of this custom was published by Grimm, *Deutsche Rechtsaltertümer*, II., p. 615, 616, 693: "Uff sant stephans tage solle der lehenmann liefern vnd bezalen pfenningzins vnd weissbroit, dan soll man dem lehenman guitlich thuin auff dem hofe, zweyerley wein zweyerley fleischs, zweyerley brot vnd alles desjeniges, wass vom tage zeitig iss. abe der lehenher bedoecht, dass der lehenman zu lange seess, so solle der lehenher ein naeff sechs wochen vnd drey tag in ein mistphole legen laissen, dieselb nit rödeln noch stochen, vnd wannehe die verbrandt, dass der dauon keyner mehr erkandt möcht werden, soll der lehenman vffstehen."

[1] A broad cross section of a tree still often forms the Scottish peat barrow wheel.
[2] Franz Wessel's description of the Roman Catholic service at Stralsund, A.D. 1523,

being given to the present of straw which the cattle, swine, geese, and ducks received that day, in order that they might take part in the rejoicing over Christ's birth. Similarly it was a custom that, at Hippetsweiler, the *Kelner* gave to the small holders at Christmas three cart-loads of wood, and one cart-load on the birth of a child.[1] The *Gotteshausleute* of the monastery of Petershausen, Schlatt, in the first half of the fifteenth century, received at Christmas a wheelbarrow-load of wood—on the birth of a boy a cart-load, and on the birth of a girl a wheelbarrow-load of wood.[2]

There is another Italian custom connected with the Calends of January which found its way through Gaul to Great Britain and Germany, though comparatively late. It is the habit of walking about in the hides of calves and deer and doing all kinds of indecency under the protection of these masks. Even Rudolph Koegel, who has a great inclination for finding something Germanic everywhere, admits this custom to be of Italian origin.[3] That this habit was unknown in inner Germany comparatively late can be shown by a misunderstanding made by a glossator when translating a passage relating to it.[4] There was a German custom to sit down on a cow's hide, or deer's hide, at a cross road, or on the roof of the house, on certain nights and wait for oracles. This was called *liodorsâza*. When the glossator found the phrase *in cervulo* mentioned, he thought it referred to that custom, and translated: *in cervulo, in liodersâza*, whilst *in vetula* he interpreted *in deru varentun truchti*, i.e., in the procession.[5] About these masquerades,

---

Höfer in Bartsch's *Germania*, xviii., 1 : "sô drôgen sê garuen in de koppele efte sus in de lucht, dadt se de windt snê rîp efte sus de lucht beschînen konde, dadt hêtede men des morgens kindesvôdt, dadt deelde men des morgen allem ûtth, schlôch eine garue 2 efte 3 ûth undt gaf den swînen koyen enten gensen dad se alle des kindesvôthes genêten scholdenn."

[1] Weistum of A.D. 1400, from Hippetsweiler, Upper Rhine, *Fürstenbergisches Urkunden-buch*, Tübingen, 1877, Vol. VI., No. 132, p. 216.

[2] A.D. 1444, *Ibid.*, Vol. VI., No. 240, Hössler, *Zur Entstehungsgeschichte des Bauernkrieges in Südwestdeutschland*, Leipzig Dissertation, 1895, pp. 25, 26.

[3] *Geschichte der deutschen Literatur*, Strassburg, 1894, I., p. 30.

[4] *Althochdeutsche Glossen.*, II., 365, 17.

[5] Koegel, *Geschichte der deutschen Literatur*, I., 30, note, explains *in deru varentun truchti* quite rightly as procession, while Müllenhoff, *Zeitschrift für deutsches Altertum*, XII., 351, thought it to refer to the Wild Huntsman, who, however, is in no way connected with the Twelve-nights, as Koegel assumes, these Twelve-nights themselves being of Christian origin, the *Dodekahemeron* of the old Church.

which are till very late associated with the Calends, and have for a long
time no relation to the Church festival of Christ's Nativity, we have various
reports, the most important being the homily *De Sacrilegiis*, written in Gaul
in the seventh or eighth century, but commonly ascribed to Augustine.[1]
"Reversing the order of things, the heathens in those days dress themselves up into indecent monsters. These miserable men and, still worse,
some baptized Christians take on false likenesses and monstrous faces, of
which people should rather be ashamed and sad. For what reasonable
man would believe that men in the possession of their senses should, by
playing a stag, turn themselves into the nature of animals? Others dress
themselves up in the hides of their cattle; others put on the heads of
animals, rejoicing and exulting that they are turned into the shape of
beast to such an extent that they no more appear to be human beings.
How horrible is it, further, that those who have been born men take on
women's dresses, and effeminate their manhood by girls' dresses in an
abominable masquerade! They who do not blush to put their warlike
arms into women's dresses! Bearded faces are displayed by them, and yet
they wish to be taken for women!" "What is so insane as, by a disgraceful
dress, to give the male sex the appearance of the female? What so insane
as to spoil one's face and put on masks by which even demons might be
terrified? What so insane as with indecent gestures and improper songs
to sing the praise of vices in shameless delight? To turn one's self into a
wild beast, to resemble the goat or the stag, in order that man, created

---

[1] Ed. by Caspari, Christiania, 1886, who gives a large number of parallels to the
customs related and expressions used. Compare Friedrich Panzer, *Bayerische Sagen und
Bräuche*, München, 1855, Vol. II., pp. 466-468: "Cervulum seu vitulam facere."
Caspari's text says about the Calends of January, § 24: "In istis diebus miseri homines
cervolo facientes vestiuntur pellibus pecodum. Alii sumunt capita bestiarum, gaudentes et
exultantes ut homines non essent. Et illud quid turpe est! Viri tunicis mulierum
induentes se feminas videri volunt." The usual phrases are: "cervulum et vetulam
facere; in cervulo aut vetula vadere; cervulos aut vetulas ducere." Koegel, *Geschichte der
deutschen Literatur*, I., 30, note. The Council of Auxerre, 573-603 (in *Concilia aevi
Merovingici*, ed. by Frid. Maassen, Hannover, 1893, p. 179), forbade: "Non licet
Kalendis Januarii vetolo aut cervolo facere vel streneas diabolicas observare, sed in ipsa
die sic omnia beneficia tribuantur sicut et reliquis diebus" (*Acta Conciliorum*, Parisiis,
1714, Vol. III., col. 444).

G

to be the likeness and image of God, may become the sacrifice of demons!"
"Therefore he who gives to anyone of those miserable men any human
requirement in the Calends of January, when in the sacrilegious rite
they rather rage than play, shall know that he does not give it to men
but to demons. Therefore, if you do not want to participate in their sins,
do not permit that the stag or the cow or any such portent come before
your house."[1] It almost looks as if the *Matronalia* of March 1, the
lascivious festival of the ladies of ancient Rome, had, with the beginning
of the year through the Julian calendar, been shifted to January 1, and
there revived in ever-new glory and licentiousness! In less eloquent
speech the same habit was repeatedly forbidden by Councils and mentioned
in Penitentials, especially during the eighth century.[2]

---

[1] A list of other allusions to this custom is given in my *Geschichte der deutschen Weihnacht*, pp. 15 and 288.

[2] " Kalendas quae dicuntur, et vota, et brumalia quae vocantur; et qui in primo Martii mensis die fit conventum, ex fidelium universitate omnino tolli volumus: sed et publicas mulierum saltationes multam noxam exitiumque afferentes: quin etiam eas, quae nomine eorum, qui falso apud Gentiles dii nominati sunt; vel nomine virorum ac mulierum fiunt, saltationes ac mysteria, more antiquo et a vita Christianorum alieno, amandamus et expellimus; statuentes, ut nullus vir deinceps muliebri veste induatur, vel mulier veste viro conveniente. Sed neque comicas, vel satyricas, vel tragicas personas induat; neque execrandi Bacchi nomen, uvam in torcularibus exprimentes, invocent; neque vinum in dolis effundentes, risum moveant; ignorantia vel vanitate, ea quae ab insaniae impostura procedunt, exercentes" (*Acta Conciliorum*, Parisiis, 1714, Vol. III., col. 1683, *Concilium Quinisextum sivi in Trullo*, A.D. 706, lxii.). The same appears in England: Thorpe, *Ancient Laws*, II., 34 (xxvii. "De Idolatria et Sacrilegio, et qui . . . in Kalendas Januarii in cervulo et in vitula vadit," etc.). § 19. "Si quis in Kalendas Ianuarii in cervulo aut vetula vadit, id est, in ferarum habitus se communicant, et vestiuntur pellibus pecudum, et assumunt capita bestiarum; qui vero taliter in ferinas species se transformant, III. annos poeniteant; quia hoc daemoniacum est" (seventh century). . . . § 24. "Qui observat divinos, vel praecantatores, philacteria etiam diabolica, et somnia, vel herbas; aut v. feriam, honore Iovis, vel kalendas Ianuarii, more paganorum, honorat; si clericus est, v. annos poeniteat; laicus III. annos poeniteat." Haddan and Stubbs, *Councils and Ecclesiastical Documents*, Oxford, 1871, Vol. III., p. 424; Egbert's Penitential, A.D. 732-766, viii. 4: "Caraios et divinos praecantatores, filecteria etiam diabolica vel herbas vel facino suis vel sibi impendere vel quinta feria in honore Jovis vel Kalendas Januarias secundum paganam causam honorare, si non, quinque annos peniteat clericus, si laicus, tres annos peniteat." Ducange, *Glossarium*, under *Cervula*, adds a long list of instances: "*Concilium Toletanum*, iv., Can. x.; S. Isidorus, Lib. I., *De Officio Ecclesiae*, cap. xl.; *Concilium*

When, through the Julian calendar, the Calends of January became a
festive tide among the Germanics, they were at first probably a festive tide
like others, without any special reference to the new year.   But in the course

---

Turonense, ii., Can. xvii. ; St. Augustinus, *Sermo de Tempore*, 215: 'Si adhuc agnoscatis
aliquos illam sordidissimam turpitudinem de hinnula, vel cervula exercere, ita durissime
castigate, ut eos poeniteat rem sacrilegam commisisse'; *Vita S. Eligii*, Lib. II., cap. xv. :
'Nullus in Kalendis Januarii nefanda et ridiculosa, vetulas, aut cervulos, aut jotticos faciat;'
Halitgarius Cambrensis in *Libro Poenitentiali*, cap. vi. : 'Si quis in Kalendis Ianuarii, quod
multi faciunt, et in cervulo ducit, aut in vetula vadit, tres annos poeniteat;' *Burchardus
Wormaciensis*, Lib. XIX., cap. v.: 'Fecisti aliquid tale, quod pagani fecerunt, et adhuc
faciunt in Kalendis Ianuarii in cervolo et vetula : si fecisti, triginta dies in pane et aqua
poeniteas;' St. Pacianus in *Paraenesi ad Poenitentiam* ; S. Ambrosius in *Psalmo* xli. : 'Sed
iam satis in exordio tractatus, sicut in principio anni, more vulgi cervus allusit ;' Faustinus
Episcopus in *Sermone in Kalendas Ianuarias*: 'Quis enim sapiens credere poterit inveniri
aliquos sanae mentis, qui cervulum facientes, inferarum se velint habitus commutari? Alii
vestiuntur pellibus pecudum, alii assumunt capita bestiarum, gaudentes et exultantes, si taliter
se in ferinas species transformaverint, ut homines non esse videantur ;' Aldhelmus, Abbas
Malmesburiensis initio *Epistolae ad Eahfridum* ; *Epistolae Petri Damiani*, p. 384, editionis
A.D. 1610; Durandus, Lib. VI., *De Ratione* ; cap. xv." Ducange, *Glossarium*, under
Kalendae, quotes a large number of other prohibitions of the Calends of January celebrations:
"*Concilium Romanum sub Zacharia*, Can. viii.; *Concilium Turonense*, ii., Cann. xvii.-xxii.;
Capitulare Gregorii, ii., P.P. pro Bavaris, cap. viii.; *Attonis Episcopi Basilensis Capitula*, cap.
lxxix.; *Epistula ipsius Zachariae ad Bonifacium Moguntinum* ; *St. Ambrosii Sermo* ii.; S. Maximi
Taurinensis, *Petri Chrysologi Sermo*, cxv. ; Faustini Episcopi apud Bolandum, I Januariis :
Joannis Chrysostomi ; S. Asterii ; Tertullianus *De Idolatria*, c. xiv.; Isidorus, Lib. I., *De
Ecclesiae Officio*, cap. xl.; Alcuinus, *Lib. de Divino Officio*, c. iv.; Cyprianus in *Vita S.
Caesarii Arelatensis*, sub. fine. ; Anonymus in *Vita S. Sansonis Episcopi Dolensis*, Lib. II.,
c. xiii. ; *Vita S. Hugonis Abbatis S. Martini Eduensis*, n. xv." Direct continuations of these
turbae impudicae are the Calends guilds or Calends brethren.   Ducange, *Glossarium*, under
Kalendae: "Sodalitates ad pias causas, inquit Sambucus.   Fratres Calendarum, qui vulgo
Confratres, forte quod singulorum mensium Kalendis invicem convenirent, occurrunt in
Lib. I., *Decret. S. Ladislai Regis Hungariae*, c. xiv., 39, et in *Capitulis Laurentii Archiep.
Strigon.*, c. xlvi." Under the influence of a Greek rite these wild enjoyments in the course
of centuries became even an unholy ecclesiastical institution.   Ducange, *Glossarium*, under
Kalendae: *Octava Synodus*, Can. xvi., *ex versione Anastasii* (Canon xvi. is wanting in the
Greek version), says: "Fuisse quosdam Laicos qui secundum diversam Imperatoriam
dignitatem videbantur capillorum comam circumplexam involvere atque reponere" (ita
namque, ait hoc loco Anastasius, a cervice usque ad capita contorquebant, ut clericali more
in rotundam tonsi viderentur) "et gradum quasi sacerdotalem per quaedam indusia et
vestimenta sacerdotalia sumere, et ut putabatur, Episcopos constituere, superhumeralibus,
id est, palliis, circumamictos, et omnem aliam Pontificalem indutos stolam, qui etiam
proprium Patriarcham adscribentes, eum qui in adinventionibus risum moventibus Praelatus

of time that side was bound to come into the foreground, to rival and, later on, to replace the old Germanic New Year towards the middle of November. So it could not fail that Germanic usages having special

et Princeps erat, et insultabant, et illudebant, quibusque divinis, modo quidem electiones, promotiones, et consecrationes, modo autem acute calumnias, et depositiones Episcoporum quasi ab invicem et per invicem miserabiliter et praevaricatorie agentes et patientes; tales autem actio nec apud gentes a saeculo unquam audita est," etc. The later medieval ecclesiastical *Festum Fatuorum* or *Hypodiaconorum* is the outcome of the marriage between the Calends of January and that Greek habit. In the shape of an *Abbot of Unreason*, a *Lord of Misrule*, or *Boy-bishop*, and similar types, it lived on for centuries, and is, in Great Britain, even to-day not quite extinct. Ducange, *Glossarium*, under *Kalendae*: "Beletus (vivebat in Ecclesia Ambianensi, A.D. 1182), chap. cxx. : 'Sunt nonnullae Ecclesiae, in quibus usitatum est, ut vel etiam Episcopi et Archiepiscopi in Coenobiis cum suis ludant subditis, ita ut etiam sese ad ludum pilae demittant. Atque haec quidem libertas ideo dicta est Decembrica, quod olim apud ethnicos moris fuerit, ut hoc mense servi et ancillae, et Pastores velut quadam libertate donarentur, fierentque cum dominis suis pari conditione, communia festa agentes post collectionem messium: quanquam vero magnae Ecclesiae, ut est Remensis, hanc ludendi consuetudinem observent, videtur tamen laudabilius esse non ludere.' *Ibid.* in *Libro de Divinis Officiis*, chap. lxxii: 'Festum Hypodiaconorum, quod vocamus Stultorum, a quibusdam perficitur in Circumcisione, a quibusdam vero in Epiphania, vel in eius octavis. Fiunt autem quatuor tripudia post Nativitatem Domini in Ecclesia, Levitarum scilicet, Sacerdotum, Puerorum, id est, minorum aetate et ordine, et Hypodiaconorum, qui ordo incertus est. Unde fit ut ille quandoque annumeretur inter sacros Ordines, quandoque non,'" etc. Ducange, *Glossarium*, under *Kalendae*, also mentions: "Litterae Petri Capuani Cardinalis Legati in Francia, A.D. 1198, quibus praecipit Odoni Episcopo Parisiensi et aliquot Canonicis eiusdem Ecclesiae, ut hocce 'festum' quod 'Fatuorum' appellabatur, et in Ecclesia Parisiensi, ut in caeteris, invaluerat, penitus abolerent: quod dictus Episcopus aliique ad id nominati Commissarii executi sunt, facta ordinatione in Ecclesia deinceps observanda, quae habetur apud Gusanvillam post Notas ad Petrum Blesensem. Illud etiam interdixit *Concilium Parisiense*, A.D. 1212, Part IV., Can. xvi.: 'A festis vero follorum, ubi baculus accipitur, omnino abstineatur.' Id est, baculus Episcopalis." About the end of these festivities the following remark is made by Ducange, *Glossarium*, under *Kalendae*: "At in Gallia videtur desiisse, ex quo serio manum admovit Facultas Theologiae Parisiensis ann. 1444, 12 Martii, missa ad id Epistola encyclica ad Galliae Praesules, damnatoque, pleno Theologorum consessu, hocce festo, in quo Sacerdotes ipsi ac Clerici Archiepiscopum, aut Episcopum, aut 'Papam' creabant, eumque 'Fatuorum' appellabant: 'Divini ipsius Officii tempore larvati, monstruosi vultibus, aut in vestibus mulierum, aut leonum, vel histrionum, choreas ducebant, in Choro cantilenas inhonestas cantabant, offas pingues supra cornu altaris juxta celebrantem Missam comedebant, ludum taxillorum ibidem exarabant, thurificabant de fumo foetido, ex corio veterum sotularium, et per totam Ecclesiam currebant, saltabant,' etc. Verba sunt citatae Epistolae, quam edidit Savaro, et ex eo Gussanvilla." The boy bishop is a comparatively late development

reference to the beginning of the year should bye and bye be transferred to the Calends of January, where we find them in the eighth and in the eleventh centuries.[1] The passage evincing this Koegel for the first time satisfactorily explained in his *Geschichte der deutschen Literatur*.[2] At New Year's eve people girt with their swords sat down on the roofs of their houses to find out what good and bad things would be brought by the new year. Others sat down at a cross road on a cow-hide. As was mentioned before, this was called *liodorsâza* or sitting down for the purpose of receiving an oracle, whilst the person who did so was called *hleotharsâzzo* (Keronic Glossary) or *hleodarsizzeo* (Hrabanic Glossary), which was thought to correspond to Latin *negromanticus*.[3] But this habit was not confined to the Calends of January, probably appearing at all holy tides, and certainly at the time of the waning of the moon, nor were oracles the only purpose of it, as it was resorted to for the cure of fever and probably of other illnesses. So say the sentences of Pope Gregory III. (731-741),[4] in which, among others, Janus is referred to as the god in whose honour the *liodorsâza* is done.

---

from this group of customs. Early documental evidence for it seems to be lacking entirely. Ducange, *Glossarium*, under *Kalendae*, mentions an "Inventarium ornamentorum Ecclesiae Eboracensis, ann. 1530," in *Monast. Anglic.*, Vol. III., p. 169, where we find: "Item una mitra parva cum petris pro Episcopo puerorum," and "Item unus annulus pro Episcopo puerorum, et duo archys, unus in medio ad modum Crucis cum lapidibus in circumferentiis," etc.

[1] To a custom like that refers the following (*Acta Conciliorum*, Parisiis, 1714, Vol. III., col. 1863, *Gregorii Papae II. Capitulare* (circa A.D. 720), ix.): "Ut incantationes, et fastidiationes, sive diversae observationes dierum Kalendarum, quas error tradidit paganorum, prohibeantur, sicut maleficia, et magorum praestigia, seu etiam sortilegium, ac divinantium observatio execranda." Burchard von Worms in Friedberg, *Aus deutschen Bussbüchern*, p. 84: "Vel in bivio sedisti supra taurinam cutem, ut et ibi futura tibi intelligeres?"

[2] Vol. I., p. 29.

[3] *Althochdeutsche Glossen.*, I., 215, 33; II., 763, 9; II., 365, 35.

[4] *Acta Conciliorum*, Parisiis, 1714, Vol. III., col. 1875, *Gregorii Papae III. Judicia*, xxiii.: "Si quis maleficus aut malefica filium suum aut filiam supra tectum aut in fornace pro sanitate febrium posuerit, vel quando luna obscuratur; vel clamoribus suis, vel maleficiis sacrilego usu se defensare posse confidunt, vel ut frater in honore Jovis vel Beli aut Iani, secundum paganam consuetudinem, honorare praesumpserit, placuit secundum antiquam constitutionem sex annos poeniteat. Humanius tres annos judicaverunt."

Other kinds of prophecy were by the observation of the moon,[1] of the months, and of the effective potency of the several hours. Even the Church could not, in the long run, keep apart from the celebration of Calends. An ecclesiastical observance at the Calends existed at least in the middle of the ninth century.[2] At the Councils of Oxford, A.D. 1222, and of Lyon, 1244, the Calends of January were, as *Circumcisio Domini*, proclaimed a general festive day to be strictly kept by the Church. Johannes von Holleschau[3] speaks in 1426 of *calendisationes* in a little treatise on Christmas called *Largum Sero* or *Liberal Evening*, which is a slight modification of a booklet written by a priest, Alsso, about A.D. 1400. Alsso even tells us more.[4] At the beginning of every month the Bohemians carried about the image of their god Bel, singing a Czechic song. They rejoiced in the god thus visiting their houses, hoping faithfully that, in consequence, the whole month long he would send them good luck, and lead all their fortune and life. Therefore people brought gifts to the image of Bel, as it were a tribute, regarding themselves as his true worshippers in order that he might bring them luck. But St. Adalbert, because it was too circumstantial to do so at the beginning of every month, and in order that the Christians might not also celebrate the beginning of the months according to heathen custom, changed this celebration of the beginnings of months into a celebration of Christ's Nativity and of the week following it, thinking that it would be better to exercise

---

[1] *Acta Conciliorum*, Parisiis, 1714, Vol. VI., I., col. 207, *Synodus Generalis Rodomi* (circa A.D. 878), xiii. : "Si quis in Kalendis Ianuariis aliquid fecerit, quod a Paganis inventum est, et dies observat, et lunam, et menses ; et horarum effectiva potentia aliquid sperat in melius aut in deterius verti, anathema sit."

[2] *Acta Conciliorum*, Parisiis, 1714, Vol. V., col. 394, *Hincmari Remensis Capitula*, A.D. 852, xv. : "Ut quando presbyteri per Kalendas simul convenerint, post peractum divinum mysterium, et necessariam collationem, non quasi ad prandium ibi ad tabulam resideant, et per tales in convenientes pastellos se invicem gravent, quia inhonestum est, et onerosum. Saepe enim tarde ad ecclesias suas redeuntes majus damnum de reprehensione conquirunt, et de gravedine mutua contrahunt, quam lucrum ibi faciunt." A large number of quotations as to the monthly meetings of the clergy on the Calends are given by Ducange, *Glossarium*, under *Kalendae*.

[3] Usener, *Christlicher Festbrauch*, Bonn, 1889, p. 72.

[4] Usener, *Ibid.*, p. 63.

that habit in the time in which Christ was born, than at the beginning of months, at which honour had once been bestowed upon Bel. He also is said to have altered the name and the sense of that celebration, making of *kalendisare colendisare* (from *colere*, to revere), because through that usage Christ was revered at his birthday, and not in the Calends. If this report does not imply that medieval Christmas in South Germany took the place of an older Calends celebration according to Roman usage, I do not know what it implies. The confusion in which the minds of both authors are is best shown by the fact that they not only regard the Calends rites as an imitation and distortion of Christmas rites caused by the devil, but at the same time inform us that up to St. Adalbert's time the Calends alone prevailed, and that it was this Saint who transferred to Christmas the *Calendisationes* or Calends processions,—two statements which are mutually exclusive.[1]

When the Chapters of Bishop Martin of Bracae, A.D. 575,[2] forbade the faithful to observe dangerous Calends customs, to keep the heathen times of leisure, and to adorn their houses round about with laurel and green trees,[3] he rendered a very great service indeed to folklore, for this seems to be the only prohibition of that Calends custom which has come down to us, and it is not until eight hundred years later that we can show houses to have been adorned with green and trees at New Year and Christmas. It is told, however, of the Sabinian king Tatius, to whom by the legend a date is given about the middle of the eighth century B.C., that in winter he received branches of a happy or fortunate tree from the grove of Streniae as favourable omens with respect to the new year. It is true that story is told by a Roman writer of about 400 A.D., Q. Aurelius Sym-

---

[1] Usener, *Christlicher Festbrauch*, Bonn, 1889, p. 63.

[2] *Acta Conciliorum*, Parisiis, 1714, Vol. III., col. 399, *Capitula Martini Episcopi Bracensis* (circa A.D. 575), chap. lxxiii. : "Non liceat iniquas observationes agere Kalendarum, et otiis vacare gentilibus, neque lauro aut viriditate arborum cingere domos. Omnis haec observatio paganismi est."

[3] *Viriditate arborum* can only mean the same as *viridibus arboribus*, and not "with green branches of trees"; *viriditas* never meaning leaves or branches, but referring simply to the colour.

machus, and it cannot therefore be regarded as affording any evidence on a state of things twelve hundred years before that time. But the one thing certain from it is that, in the time of the Roman empire, there existed the habit of presenting to people, on the Calends of January, branches of trees for the sake of good luck in the new year.[1] It is again solely from this custom that we learn the meaning of the adornment of houses with

---

[1] Rosinus, *Antiquitatum Romanarum Corpus Absolutissimum*, (ed. Dempster, Genevae, 1620), Lib. IV., chap. v., remarks: "Kalendas Ianuarii laetis precationibus faustum sibi invicem ominabantur teste, praeter Plinium et alios, Ovidio:

> 'At cur laeta tuis dicuntur verba Kalendis,
> Et damus alternis, accipimusque preces.'

Item munera sibi invicem mittebant boni ominis causa, videlicet caricas, coriotides, et mella, ut dulces dies anni a dulcibus rebus auspicarentur: et stipem, id est, nummum signatum: quae omnia simul strenas appellarunt: cuius rei origo ad ipsum T. Tatium regem a Symmacho refertur, quod is verbenas e luco Streniae Deae acceperit, significans strenuis viris istas deberi. Strenam, inquit Festus, vocamus, quae datur die religioso, ominis boni gratia, a numero, quo significatur alterum, tertiumque venturum similis commodi, veluti trenam, praeposita S. litera, ut in loco, et lite solebant antiqui. Constituta autem per C. Octavium Augustum Monarchia, hic mos inolevit, ut equites ac reliquus populus ipsis etiam Imperatoribus strenam Kalendis Ianuarii conferrent: qua de re saepe loquitur Suetonius." The mention of Quintus Aurelius Symmachus refers to his *Epistolae*, Lib. X., Ep. xxviii.: "Ab exortu paene urbis Martiae strenarum usus adolevit, auctoritate Tatii Regis, qui verbenas felicis arboris ex luco Strenuae anni novi auspices primus accepit, D.D. Imperatores. Nomen indicio est viris strenuis haec convenire ob virtutem: atque ideo vobis huiusmodi insigne deberi; quorum divinus animus magis testimonium vigilantiae quam omen expectat." The *verbenae felicis arboris* mentioned here played an important part in Roman ceremonies. Compare Ammianus Marcellinus, Lib. XXIX.: "Verbenas felicis arboris gestans." According to Servius, the term included branches of laurel, olive, and myrtles. A great number of instances are enumerated in the Lib. X. of the *Miscellanies* which accompany the *Epistles of Symmachus*, under Ep. xxviii., in the Paris edition of 1604, by A. Fr. The Christian poet Metellus, in his *Quirinales*, has put into eloquent verse the passage quoted above from Symmachus:

> "Strenae praeterea nitent—Plures aureolae, munere regio,
> Olim Principibus probis—Iani principiis auspicio datae,
> Fausto temporis omine—Ut ferret Ducibus strenua strenuis
> Annus gesta recentior.—Illas nobilitas Caesaribus piis,
> Rex dignis Procerum dabat.—Urbi quas latiae tum iuveni dedit
> Rex Titus Tatius prior,—Festas accipiens paupere munere
> Verbenas studio Patrum.—Solleres posteritas quas creat aureas.
> Servant dona tamen notam—A luco veteri nomine Strenuae."

laurel and green trees in the sixth century. These things were put up as
good omens for the luck of the year. Even later evidence of this custom
is very scarce. That in Italy it lived on we know at the end of the
fifteenth century, through Polydore Vergil, who says: "Trimmyng of the
Temples with hangynges, floures, boughes, and garlandes, was taken of the
Heathen people, whiche decked their Idoles and houses with suche arraye."[1]
In Germany the two fifteenth century witnesses for that usage come both
from the Rhine country, from Strassburg, and both mention that at New
Year's day the houses were adorned with green fir branches.[2]

In Strassburg it is also that, a hundred years later, the first Christmas
tree appears, a usage which seems to have sprung out of the union of the
habit of adorning houses with green branches and trees according to
Roman Calends custom, and of a Christian tenth century legend, according
to which, in the night when the Saviour was born, all trees bloom and
bring forth fruits in the forest. This legend can be proved to have been
very popular in the Germany of the fifteenth and sixteenth centuries.

In England the same custom must have been popular, at least in the
fifteenth century, even in the form of trees or artificial trees. "Against
the Feast of Christmas, euery mans house, as also their parish Churches,
were decked with Holm, Iuy, Bayes, and whatsoeuer the season of the yeere
aforded to be greene. The Conduits and Standards in the streetes were,
likewise, garnished. Amongst the which, I read, that in the yeere 1444,

---

[1] *An abridgegment of the notable worke of Polidore Vergile*, by Thomas Langley, London, 1551, Book V., chap. i., fol. 98ᵃ. This remark refers to festivals in general.

[2] Sebastian Brant, *Narrenschiff*, 1494, 65, 37 ss. in Zarncke's edition, Leipzig, 1854,
p. 64:

> " Vnd wer nit ettwas nuwes hat
> Vnd vmb das nuw jor syngen gat,
> Vnd gryen tann riss steckt in syn huss
> Der meynt er leb das jor nit uss
> Als die Egyptier hieltten vor,
> Des glichen zuo dem nuwen jor
> Wem man nit ettwas schencken duot
> Der meynt das gantz jar werd nit guot."

And Geiler von Kaisersberg, *Die Emeis Dis ist das Buch von der Omeissen*, Strassburg,
Grieninger, 1516.

by tempest of thunder and lightning, on the first of February at night, Pauls steeple was fiered, but with great labour quenched, and toward the morning of Candlemas day, at the Leaden Hall in Cornhill, a Standard of tree being set up in the midst of the pauement, fast in the ground, nayled full of Holme and Iuy, for disport of Christmas to the people, was torne up and cast downe by the malignant Spirit (as was thought), and the stones of the pauement all about were cast in the streets, and into divers houses, so that the people were sore aghast at the great Tempests."[1] Gay, in his *Trivia*, sings :

> " When *Rosemary* and *Bays*, the poet's crown,
>   Are bawl'd in frequent cries through all the town ;
>   Then judge the festival of Christmas near,
>   Christmas, the joyous period of the year !
>   Now with bright *Holly* all the temples strow
>   With *Laurel* green, and sacred *Mistletoe*."

And from that time on there is a complete continuity of tradition as regards the adornment of houses and churches by holly and ivy, evergreen and mistletoe, box and bay.   There are the well-known fifteenth century carols about the contest between Holly and Ivy :

> " Holly and Ivy, Box and Bay,
>   Put in the Church on Christmas day."

---

[1] John Stow, *The Survay of London* (written A.D. 1598), London, 1618, pp. 149, 150. On p. 667, Stow, speaking of a long pole preserved in Gisors or Gerrards Hall in the city, says : "The Pole in the Hall might be vsed of old time (as then the custome was in euery Parish) to be set up in the Summer a May-Pole, before the principall house in the Parish or Street, and to stand in the Hall before the Scrine, decked with Holme and Iuy at the Feast of Christmas.   The Ladder serued for the decking of the May-Pole, and roofe of the Hall."   To this he adds the marginal note : "Euery mans house of old time was decked with Holly and Iuy in the winter, especially at Christmas."   In the edition of 1598 the passage is found on p. 284.   Compare Ritson's *Ancient Songs and Ballads*, 3rd ed., by Carew Haslitt, London, 1877, p. 113.   This undeniable correspondence between Christmas customs and May customs in later times, which is also found in the servitude of *woodlade* or *truncagium*, is one of the conclusive proofs that Christmas has taken the place which had been held before by Martinmas.

CHAPTER IX.

TABULA FORTUNAE.

AMONG the Roman Calends-of-January customs which were taken over by Germanic tribes there is one deserving special attention, because it gave rise to the belief, among modern mythologists, that the Germanics celebrated a festival of the dead about the darkest time of the year. In fact, this view in a certain sense replaced the alleged Germanic celebration of a winter solstice, in which Professor Weinhold and a few others still believe. When this view seemed to be no longer tenable, Professor Eugen Mogk yet thought it too daring to deny that the Germanics had had any festival about the middle of the winter, and assumed that there had been about that time some celebration in honour of the dead or ancestors. He took as the basis a rite which, at first sight no doubt, has the appearance of an offering to the dead, but in reality is of Mediterranean origin, having been known in the early centuries of our era from Egypt to Rome.

Isaiah lxv. 11 says: "But ye are they that forsake the Lord, that forget my holy mountain, that prepare a table for that troop, and that furnish the drink offering unto that number."[1] Jerome (+A.D. 420), in

---

[1] The meaning of the Hebrew version is: "Et vos qui dereliquistis dominum, et obliti estis montem sanctum meum. Qui ponitis fortunae mensam et libatis super eam"; which, however, the Septuagint translated as meaning: "Vos autem qui dereliquistis me et obliti estis montis sancti mei, et paratis fortunae mensam: et impletis daemoni potionem." The English revised version of 1885 has: "But ye that forsake the Lord, that forget my holy mountain, that prepare a table for Fortune, and that fill up mingled wine unto Destiny."

his *Commentary* to Isaiah, remarks:[1] "But there is in all towns, and most of all in Egypt and Alexandria, the old custom of idolatry that, on the last day of the year and of the last month, people erect a table full of eatables of various kind, and a cup mixed with mead, in order to try to find out the fertility either of the year past or the year to come. This also was done by the Israelites, who, adoring the portents of all ghosts, did not offer slain animals at the altar, but brought their offerings to a table of this kind."[2] In the *Sermo de Sacrilegiis*, ascribed to St. Augustine (+A.D. 430), a penalty is threatened to anyone who, for the Calends of January, adorns the tables with loaves and other dishes.[3] The wandering to the north of that Table of Fortune can be traced through the mentions of it by St. Eligius (588-659);[4] by Boniface in his letter to Pope Zacharias, of A.D. 742,[5] in which he testifies to that usage still existing both in Rome and among the Germans, with the consequence that it was interdicted at the Council of Rome A.D. 743;[6] and by Burchard von Worms (+A.D. 1024).[7] In his first reference the latter simply mentions the custom, but

---

[1] *Operum D. Hieronymi*, Quintus Tomus, *Commentarios in Prophetas Quos Maiores Vocant Continet*, Basileae, 1537 (ed. Reuchlin), p. 240.

[2] "Est autem in cunctis urbibus, et maxime in Aegypto, et in Alexandria idololatriae vetus consuetudo: ut ultimo die anni et mensis eius qui extremus est, ponant mensam refertam varii generis epulis, et poculum mulso mixtum: vel praeteriti anni vel futuri fertilitatem auspicantes. Hoc autem faciebant Israelitae, omnium simulacrorum portenta venerantes: et nequaquam altari victimas, sed huiusce modi mensae liba fundebant."

[3] § 17: "Quicunque in calendas ianuarias mensas panibus et aliis cybis ornat."

[4] "Nullus in cal. Ian. nefanda aut ridiculosa, vetulas, aut cervulos, aut jotticos faciat, neque mensas super noctem componat, neque strenas aut bibitiones superfluas exerceat." Grimm, *Deutsche Mythologie, Aberglaube* A.

[5] *Acta Conciliorum*, Parisiis, 1714, Vol. III., col. 1880: "Mensas illa die vel nocte dapibus onerare."

[6] *Acta Conciliorum*, Parisiis, 1714, Vol. III., col. 1929, *Concilium Romanum*, I., A.D. 743, ix.: "Ut nullus Kalendas Januarias et broma colere praesumpserit, aut mensas cum dapibus in domibus praeparare."

[7] *Decreta*, Coloniae, 1548, 193[c]: "Observasti calendas januarias ritu Paganorum, ut vel aliquid plus faceres propter novum annum, quam antea vel post soleres facere, ita dico, ut aut mensam tuam cum dapibus vel epulis in domo tua praeparares eo tempore, aut per vicos et plateas cantores et choros duceres"; and p. 198[d]: "Fecisti ut quaedam mulieres in quibusdam temporibus anni facere solent, ut in domo tua mensam praeparares et tuos cibos et potum cum tribus cultellis supra mensam poneres,

in the second he adds an explanation, which shows a further evolution of the Table of Fortune into an offering to the goddesses of fate. The further we advance, the more distinct that belief grows, and is shifted to Epiphany and then to Christmas. About the middle of the thirteenth century, Martin von Amberg, in his *Gewissensspiegel*, tells that people on the eve of Epiphany put food and drink on the table for Percht with the iron nose;[1] and the poem "Von Berhten mit der langen nase"[2] seems to allude to a very similar custom.

In the fifteenth century, in the *Thesaurus Pauperum*,[3] the old Egyptian and Italian custom from the eve of the Calends of January has, like the sacredness of that day, become part and parcel of German folk-belief. Some of the ancient goddesses of the people have become connected with the new holy tide, extending from December 25 to January 6, and are supposed to be honoured by that alleged sacrifice. So it is in other parts of the country, for example in Bohemia, where the custom was transferred to Christmas eve, as the report shows which is given in Presbyter Alsso's *Largum Sero* of 1426.[4] Money and trinkets were built up on a table, people believing that thus they would increase. Below the dishes coins were laid for the same purpose. He tells: "The fourth custom is, that on Christmas eve people eat a large and lengthy roll. . . . We use for it leaven to make

---

ut si venissent tres illae sorores, quas antiqua posteritas et antiqua stultitia Parcas nominavit, ibi reficerentur. Et tulisti divinae pietati potestatem suam, et nomen suum, et diabolo tradidisti, ita dico, ut crederes illas quas tu dicis esse sorores tibi posse aut hic aut in futuro prodesse."

[1] Grimm, *Deutsche Mythologie*, 2nd ed., p. 256: "*Percht mit der eisnen nasen an der Perchtnacht.*"

[2] My *Geschichte der deutschen Weihnacht*, 1893, pp. 48 and 307.

[3] *Codex Tegernseeensis*, 434, Ulrich Jahn, *Deutsche Opfergebräuche*, Breslau, 1884, p. 282: "Multi credunt sacris noctibus inter natalem diem Christi et noctem Epiphaniae evenire ad domos suas quasdam mulieres, quibus praeest domina Perchta. . . . Multi in domibus in noctibus praedictis post coenam dimittunt panem et caseum, lac, carnes, ova, vinum et aquam et huiusmodi super mensas et coclearea, discos, ciphos, cultellos et similia propter visitationem Perhtae cum cohorte sua, ut eos complaceant . . . ut inde sint eis propitii ad prosperitatem domus et negotiorum rerum temporalium." On similar statements about such seeming offerings, compare Schmeller, *Bayrisches Wörterbuch*, 2nd ed., I., p. 270.

[4] Edited by H. Usener, *Christlicher Festbrauch*, Bonn, 1889.

it tastier.   Old and honourable people of orthodox belief and fair mind
on that night put those large rolls on the tables, and dishes and knives
beside them, permitting their family, if they choose, to eat it or to leave it
to the poor.—I am sorry to say that in that custom, as in the rest, the
devil has invented a great illusion in his own favour; for, as I was told,
in some regions the Christians put the rolls and knives on the tables and
dishes, not for the praise of the childhood of Christ, but in order that in
the night the gods might come and eat them.   But that is a gross delusion
of the heathens who have many gods; faithful Christians, however, have one
only.   And it is rather a gross conception that those spirits, which are
demons, should eat bodily food—being spirits."[1]

Not much later, about the middle of the fifteenth century, a very similar
custom was observed in the Monastery of Scheyern near Pfaffenhofen.   There
at Christmas a plough was put under the table, and a *Frau Perthatisch* was
prepared.[2]   This custom lived on German soil till close to the present
time.   In Kärnthen, on the eve of Epiphany, bread and a pie were put
outside for *Berchtl.*   If she comes and eats of it, there will be a good year.
At Vordernberg, Ober-Steiermark, milk and bread, after people have eaten
some of it, are placed in the porch for *Berschte*, whilst all the inner doors are
locked.   In the morning milk and bread have disappeared.   In other parts
of the same region food is left on the table for the *Persteln*, in order that
they may not hurt people.[3]   That the *Perchten* represent a plurality is evident
from the form *Geperchten*, in which *ge* is the collective prefix.[4]

---

[1] Usener, *Christlicher Festbrauch*, Bonn, 1889, pp. 51-58.

[2] *Merkzettel für die Beichte aus Kloster Scheyern*, written 1468 and 1469, ed. by Usener in
his *Christlicher Festbrauch*, Bonn, 1889, p. 83, ss.

[3] M. Lexer in Wolf's *Zeitschrift*, IV., p. 300; Karl Weinhold, *Weihnachtspiele*, p. 25;
Schmeller, *Bayrisches Wörterbuch*, 2nd ed., I., p. 271.   The items were collected by Ulrich
Jahn, *Deutsche Opfergebräuche bei Ackerbau und Viehzucht*, Breslau, 1884, p. 283, where
more modern cases of the same custom are mentioned.

[4] *An dem geperchtentag den man haizet der zwelfte*, 1334, *Innicher Stiftsarchiv*,
Grotefend, *Zeitrechnung*, I., 73.   The *Bächeltag, bachtag*, however, or day preceding
Christmas, which Schmeller-Fromman, *Bayrisches Wörterbuch*, 271, 194, and Grotefend,
Zeitrechnung, I., 14, derive from *Berchta*, is *dies baculi episcopalis* (compare the note
on p. 100), the day on which children are "driven out of school," because the Christmas
vacation begins.   The same is the case with *Bächlboschen*.   Bavarian *Berchta* seems to

There are sundry other fifteenth century cases on record.[1] A sixteenth
century report shows the purely Christian evolution of this custom. On
the distribution of the Epiphany cake, besides all the members of the household,
Christ, the Virgin, and the holy three kings also get their piece,[2] while here
and there the Table of Fortune has been preserved rather more purely,
the three kings merely taking the place of *Berchta*. In Rothenkirchen,
Frankenwald, the peasant, before going to bed on the eve of Epiphany,
puts even now on his table a loaf and a jug of water, inviting the three
kings to be his guests. In the Saxony of the seventeenth century, bread
and knives were laid on the table.[3] In other regions the same custom has
been shifted to St. Andrew's night, and appears together with a prophecy
about a girl's future husband or a man's future wife,[4] or has been preserved at
Christmas eve as a completely set dinner table.[5]

About the beginning of our century it was "customary, among the
peasants in the north of Europe, at Christmas-time, to make bread in the
form of a boar-pig. This they placed upon the table, with bacon and

---

be simply another name for Saxonio-Thuringian *Holda*; the former being now derived from
Gothic *balrgan*, German *verbergen*, to hide; the latter from Old-High-German *helan*, New-
High-German *verhehlen*, to hide; and both names appearing also as names of a whole
host of inferior female deities, the latter frequently in *die Holden*, *Hulden*, or *Hollen*,
beside *Frau Holle*, the former at least in the word *Geperchtentag* mentioned above.

[1] "Also versünden sich ouch, die an der Perchtnacht der Percht speiss opfernt und dem
schtetlein, von der Hagen's *Germania*, I., 349, 356; II., 64; Die am ersten jar monden
des abentz ein tisch mit guter speiss seczen die nacht den schretelen," *Codex Germanicus
Monacensis*, 234, f. 152b, of 1458; Panzer, *Beiträge zur deutschen Mythologie*, II., p. 262, 2,
from "Buch der zehen gebot, sprüche der lehrer, tafel der christlichen weisheit," of 1458; and
"Die am jahrsstag dez abentz einen tisch mit guter speyss setzen die nacht der schretlein,"
Codex Germanicus Monacensis, 523, fol. 233; Panzer, *Beiträge zur deutschen Mythologie*,
II., p. 263, 3, from "Epitome brevis ex sacris libris mosaicis de creatione coeli et terrae."
In modern times the table remained set at Christmas eve in Silesia, in order that the poor
souls, or the angels, might come and eat of the food; Peter, *Volkstümliches*, II., p. 274;
Weinhold, *Weihnachtspiele*, p. 25; Ulrich Jahn, *Deutsche Opfergebräuche*, p. 286.

[2] Sebastian Franck, *Weltbuch*, 1567, Part I., fol. 50.

[3] Praetorius, *Saturnalia*, 1663.

[4] Englien und Lahn, *Der Volksmund in der Mark Brandenburg*, Berlin, 1868, p. 237.

[5] Schulenburg, *Wendische Volkssagen und Gebräuche aus dem Spreewald*, Leipzig, 1880,
p. 248. This table is by mythologists of the older generation taken as devoted to the
ancestors (Wolff-Mannhardt, *Zeitschrift für Mythologie*, III., 123).

other dishes : and, as a good omen, they exposed it as long as the feast continued. To leave it uncovered was reckoned a bad omen, and totally incongruous to the manners of their ancestors. They called this kind of bread *Julagalt.*"[1]

At the time when the Table of Fortune began to be regarded as an offering to certain spirits, the prophecy which had been connected with it was disconnected from it and evolved into a self-dependent custom. The same *Strenae* or sweet cakes, which we know from Tertullian (+ A.D. 220),[2] as found on the *Saturnalia, Brumalia*, and Calends of January, and the rising of which was regarded as a favourable omen for the new year, appear again in the sixth century in Gaul. There, as in the south three hundred years before, the baking of them was observed for the sake of fortune-telling, wherefore the Church called them devilish.[3]

About A.D. 700 these *Strenae* had been transferred to Christmas, and were eaten in honour of the Virgin Mary, or rather in commemoration of her afterbirth, a view to which the Council of Trullus of A.D. 706 took serious objection, punishing the rite with death in the case of its being practised by a priest, and with excommunication in the case of the heretic and blasphemer being a layman. It declared in its Canon lxxix. : "Confessing that He who came into existence without seed of man, was born from the Virgin without afterbirth, and announcing this to the entire flock, we subject to correction those who from ignorance do anything which is not decent. For because some are shown to bake a cake after the day of the holy birth of Christ our God and to divide the same amongst one another, that is, under the pretext of honour to the afterbirth of the immaculate Virgin mother, we decree that henceforth nothing of the kind be done by the faithful. For this is no honour to the Virgin—who, beyond understanding and speech, gave birth in the flesh to the Word that cannot be

---

[1] Jamieson, *Etymological Dictionary of the Scottish Language*, Paisley, 1882, Vol. IV., p. 865ᵇ, after *Verel. Not. ad Hervarar Saga*, p. 139.

[2] *De Idolatria*, chap. xiv.

[3] " Non licet Kalendis Ianuarii vetula, aut cervolo facere, vel strenas diabolicas observare : sed in ipsa die sic omnia benéficia tribuantur, sicut et reliquis diebus." *Acta Conciliorum*, Parisiis, 1714, Vol. III., col. 444, *Synodus Autissiodorensis*, A.D. 578, 1.

understood—to define, measure, and describe her unutterable birthgiving according to common births and what happens in ourselves. If therefore anybody will attempt to do so again, he shall die, if he be cleric; and he shall be excommunicated, if he be a layman."[1] At the time of the Council of Trullus that question had occupied the most serious attention of the Church for several centuries. In the Decrees of Pope Hormisdas (514-523) those problems are treated most thoroughly.[2] Another instance occurs in passage III. of the Lateran Council of A.D. 649, under Pope Martin I.,[3]

---

[1] *Acta Conciliorum*, Parisiis, 1714, Vol. III., col. 1690, *Concilium Quinisextum sive in Trullo*, A.D. 706, Canon lxxix.: "οθ'. Ἀλόχευτον τὸν ἐκ τῆς παρθένου θεῖον τόκον ὁμολογοῦντες ὡς καὶ ἀσπόρως συστάντα, καὶ παντὶ τῷ ποιμνίῳ κηρύττοντες, τοὺς ἐξ ἀγνοίας πράττοντάς τι τῶν οὐ δεόντων διορθώσει καθυποβάλλομεν. ὅθεν ἐπειδή τινες μετὰ τὴν ἡμέραν τῆς ἁγίας τοῦ Θεοῦ ἡμῶν γεννήσεως δείκνυνται σεμίδαλιν ἕψοντες, καὶ ταύτην ἀλλήλοις μεταδιδόντες προφάσει τιμῆς δῆθεν λοχείων τῆς ἀχράντου παρθενομήτορος, ὁρίζομεν μηδὲν τοιοῦτον ὑπὸ τῶν πιστῶν τελεῖσθαι. οὐ γὰρ τιμή γε τοῦτο τῇ παρθένῳ, τῇ ὑπὲρ νοῦν καὶ λόγον τὸ ἀχώρητον τεκούσῃ λόγον σαρκί, ἐκ τῶν κοινῶν τε καὶ καθ' ἡμᾶς τὰ κατὰ τὸν ἄφραστον αὐτῆς τόκον ὁρίζειν καὶ ὑπογράφειν. εἴ τις οὖν ἀπὸ τοῦ νῦν πράττων τοιοῦτόν τι φωραθείη, εἰ μὲν κληρικὸς εἴη, καθαιρείσθω. εἰ δὲ λαϊκὸς, ἀφοριζέσθω." lxxix.: "Absque ullis secundis ex Virgine partum esse confitentes ut qui sine semine constitutus sit, idque toti gregi annuntiantes, eos, qui propter ignorantiam aliquid faciunt quod non decet, correctioni subiicimus. Quare quoniam aliqui post sanctae Christi Dei nostri nativitatis diem similam coquere ostenduntur, et eam sibi invicem impertiri, honoris scilicet praetextu secundinarum impollutae Virginis matris, statuimus, ut deinceps nihil tale fiat a fidelibus. Neque enim hoc honor est Virginis, quae supra mentem et sermonem, quod comprehendi non potest Verbum peperit carne, ex communibus et iis quae in nobis fiunt, inenarrabilem ejus partum definire, metiri, ac describere. Si quis ergo deinceps hoc facere agressus fuerit, si sit quidem clericus, deponatur: si vero laïcus, segregatur."

[2] *Acta Conciliorum*, Parisiis, 1714, Vol. II., col. 1014, iii.: "Proprium quoque Filii Dei, ut juxta id quod scriptum est, in novissimis temporibus *Verbum caro fieret, et habitaret in nobis*: intra viscera sanctae Mariae Virginis genitricis Dei unitis utrisque sine aliqua confusione naturis: ut qui ante tempora erat Filius Dei, fieret filius hominis; et nasceretur ex tempore hominis more, matris vulvam natus non aperiens, et virginitatem matris deitatis virtute non solvens. Dignum plane Deo nascente mysterium, ut servaret partum sine corruptione, qui conceptum fecit esse sine semine: servans quod ex Patre erat, et repraesentans quod ex matre suscepit."

[3] Haddan and Stubbs, *Councils and Ecclesiastical Documents Relating to Great Britain and Ireland*, Oxford, 1871, Vol. III., p. 146: "De Beata Virgine. Si quis secundum sanctos patres non confitetur proprie et secundum veritatem Dei genitricem sanctam semperque virginem et immaculatam Mariam, utpote ipsum Deum Verbum specialiter et veraciter, qui a Deo Patre ante omnia saecula natus est, in ultimis saeculorum absque semine concepisse ex Spiritu Sancto, et incorruptibiliter eam genuisse, indissolubili permanente et post partum ejusdem virginitate, condemnatus sit."

H

the canons of which were brought from Rome to Great Britain by John the Precentor, and adopted by the Council of Hatfield, A.D. 680.

About the year 1000, in Germany, loaves were baked in the name of special persons. When they rose very high, it was considered a sign of prosperity in the new year; and when they did not rise, it was deemed prophetic of bad luck.[1] In the course of time these customs developed and took a great variety of forms. When the Church transferred the beginning of the year from the Calends of January to Christmas, these usages were also transferred thither, where we find them in the fourteenth and fifteenth centuries.[2] Another usage was to measure water into a pot on the eve of December 25, and again next morning. If its quantity had increased, it was supposed to be an indication of a plentiful year; if it was just the same, an average harvest was expected; and if less than before, it was the announcement of a poor year.

About 1800, in Scotland, on Christmas morning, one of the family used to rise before the rest and prepare food for them, which had to be eaten in bed. This frequently consisted of cakes baked with eggs, called care-cakes. A bannock or cake was baked for every person in the house. If any one of these broke in the toasting, the person for whom it was baked would not, it was supposed, see another Yule.[3]

It is no wonder that mythologists who did not know the passage from Jerome should have taken this custom for an offering to the dead or the chthonic deities of the Germanic tribes. But it is not true that the

---

[1] In the *Decreta* of Burchard von Worms (+1024), Coloniae, 1548, p. 193⁴, Ulrich Jahn, *Deutsche Opfergebräuche*, Breslau, 1884, p. 280, the question is put about New Year's eve: "Vel si panes praedicta nocte coquere fecisti tuo nomine: ut si bene elevarentur, et spissi et alti fierent, inde prosperitatem tuae vitae eo anno praevideres."

[2] Grimm, *Deutsche Mythologie, Aberglaube* F, No. 43, from an Austrian MS. of the Monastery of St. Florian: "Item an dem weihnachtabend noch an dem rauchen so messent die lewt 9 leffl wasser in ain hefen, vnd lassent es sten vncz an den tag vnd messent herwider auf. Ist sein mynner das dy mass nicht ganz ist, so chumpt es des jars in armüt. Ist sy gancz so pestet es. Ist sein aber mer, so wirt es vberflussikleich reich." In the sixteenth century J. Colerus, *Calendarium Oeconomicum et Perpetuum*, Wittenberg, 1591; and in the seventeenth century Praetorius, *Saturnalia*, Leipzig, 1663, p. 407, bear testimony of the same custom. Ulrich Jahn, *Deutsche Opfergebräuche*, p. 284.

[3] Jamieson, *Etymological Dictionary of the Scottish Language*, under "Yule," vii.

chthonic and wind-deities, Wôdan, Holda, Perchta, did by preference hover about Christmas, as Professor Mogk thinks.[1] Plain statistics show that they appear with about equal frequency at all seasons of the year. Nor can the later popular belief of Germany be adduced in favour of a Germanic festival of the dead about the beginning of January, because apparitions of spirits do not occur in any larger percentage about the time of Christmas than at any other time of the year, and more especially the Christmas rides of the wild huntsman and his host cannot be proved to be older than the sixteenth century. The mummings and masquerading of men in guise of animals, by covering themselves with hides—although Professor Mogk takes them for a kind of artificial appearance of souls of the dead in beast shape—are, as far as they appear in old Gaul and the farthest west of old Germany, in the form of a general masquerade, of Roman origin, as has been shown above.

The dressing up of artificial animals, however, which is found all over German soil, from Martinmas till mid-Lent—confined in olden days to the time about Martinmas, extended from the sixteenth century to about Christmas, and since then prolonged till mid-Lent—is a slaughtering custom, probably of purely Germanic growth. Originally the real animals destined to be killed were dressed up, whilst bye and bye, in part at least, artificial animals were placed in their stead. The domestic male animals which had been kept for stud purposes to the close of the season were killed at the beginning of December—December 5 being, in ancient Tirol, the day for killing the boar. The slaughtering of these animals was a kind of public affair, since, wherever the *Markgenossenschaft* existed, only one bull, one stallion, and one boar were kept for the whole community, so that those who, not being members of the community, wished to use the animal for their own herds had to pay extra for it.[2]

---

[1] Hans Meyer's *Deutsches Volkstum*, Leipzig, 1898, p. 292.

[2] This state of things survived in Tyrol down to 1800: "Hat der Stammser zehend und der Mathias Walch . . . ieder einen brauchbaren herdstier alter observanz nach, und ein ieweilliger herr pfarrer den s. v. schwilch zu stöllen, deren der eine von Martini, bis mann mit dem rever küevich am längets auffahrt, und der andere von Martini an bis st. Peters tag dienen muss, hingegen aber sind diese 2 stier in denen

That *Nicolaus*—familiar to English children as Santa Claus—is not a ghost of a dead person, as Dr. Mogk thinks, need scarcely be proved; and that *Knecht Ruprecht* (German Father Christmas), who has so long been thought a descendant of *Wuotan Hruodperaht* (Wodan shining in glory) merely represents a type of a man servant, and had originally nothing whatever to do with Christmas, was proved by myself in 1894.[1] In 1832 H. Hoffmann published, in the *Anzeiger für die Kunde der deutschen Vorzeit*, a conversation between master and servant, in which the servant has the name *Ruprecht*, being called "*Knecht Ruprecht*." The conversation, which belongs to the sixteenth century, stands in no connection with Christmas customs. In 1847 J. Scheible, in the third volume of his *Schaltjahr*, reprinted a fly-leaflet in quarto of the time about 1530, which is called: "*Ein Gespräch von den gemeinen Schwabacher Kasten, als durch Bruder Heinrich, Knecht Ruprecht, Kämmerin, Spuler, und ihrem Meister, des Handwerks der wollen Tuchmacher.*" Here also are master and servant contrasted. Here also every connection with Christmas is lacking. Here also *Knecht Ruprecht* is simply a *Knecht*, a servant, who might as well be named *Knecht* alone. From these two cases his popular significance appears very clearly: he is the popular type of a servant, and has exactly as much individuality of social rank and as little personal individuality as the *Junker Hanns* and the *Bauer Michel*, the characters representative of country nobility and peasantry respectively. The probable cause of the combination is the rime of *Knecht* and *Ruprecht*. For a whole century after his first appearance this *Knecht Ruprecht* has no relationship to any Christmas customs. The first instance in which, so far as I know, he appears in a Christmas play is a printed Nürnberg Christmas procession play, the only copy of which known to me is preserved at the Royal Library of Berlin. It is printed in 1668, and in it he appears as the servant of

---

gemeinds-alpen, wo sie wollen, frei zu sommern, 1801. Fliess-Oberinnthal," Zingerle and Inama-Sternegg, *Die Tirolischen Weistümer*, II., 234. About the payment of non-members of the community, compare Vol. III., p. 182. A more extensive explanation of these economic matters is contained in my *Geschichte der deutschen Weihnacht*, Leipzig, 1893, pp. 27-30 and 297.

[1] *Die Zukunft*, Berlin, 1894, Heft 12, *Wintersonnenwende*, p. 551.

Holy Christ. The list of characters calls him *Kindleinfresser*, and Christ addresses him as Acesto. But the stage directions call him *Ruprecht*, and he himself says to Holy Christ about the children: " *Christe, Du thust recht daran,—Dass Du keine Bitt nimmst an.—Ich Dein Knecht—Der Ruprecht,—Will sie striegeln—Und zerprügeln.*" Through these little printed plays, *Knecht Ruprecht* as a character of Christmas procession plays became popular so quickly, that as early as 1680 his appearance could be interdicted by law, and the term *Rupert* became identical with spirit from below, so that a minister could say about these popular Christmas processions, that in the suite of Christ there went about, " *etliche Rupert oder verdammte Geister.*" [1]

Hitherto no proof has been given that the drinking in honour of the dead, the so-called drinking of *Minne* [2] was confined to, or even prevalently occurring on, a hypothetical Germanic mid-winter festival. As far as I know, *alfablót* and *disablót*, offerings for elves and *geniae* never occur in the description of any early Scandinavian Yule festival, so that an argument as to the Scandinavian Yule festival being a dead-festival cannot be based upon that fact. These offerings took place late in winter, or towards the end of winter, but not at midwinter, which, in the later terminology, would be identical with "at Yule-tide." [3] And if in late sources even giants are said to have taken part in Yule feasting, it is difficult to see how this can support the supposition that the Yule feast was a festival for the dead. [4] If Professor Mogk explained the Voigtlandic

---

[1] (*Drechsuler*) *Curiöser Bericht wegen der schändlichen Weynacht Larven, so man insgemein Heiligen Christ nennet, herausgegeben Von MM.*, Dressden und Leipzig, 1702. There seems to be an older Latin edition of this pamphlet: *Christianorum Larvas natalitias Sancti Christi nomine commendatas post evolutam originem confodit stylo theologico conscientiosus Christi cultor Chresulder* (ed. auctior cum apologia, Lipsiae anno 1677, 12°), which I, however, have never seen.

[2] *Minnetrinken*; *minne* has the same stem with Latin *memini* and Greek μιμνήσκω.

[3] According to the *Olafssaga ins Helga*, 80, Sighvatr the Scald came late in winter to a farm in which *alfablót* was celebrated (Mogk, *Mythologie* in Paul's *Grundriss der germanischen Philologie*, I., 1126).

[4] *Ibid.*, according to Maurer, *Bekehrung des norwegischen Stammes zum Christentum*, München, 1855-56, II., 235.

name *Unternächte* as being the nights of the subterranean beings, of the
" *Unterirdischen*," I as early as 1893[1] proved that to be erroneous; and
it makes evident Professor Weinhold's carelessness that he, in his review
of my book,[2] accuses me of following Mogk in his erroneous explanation.[3]

Whether there was a Germanic commemoration tide for the dead is
very uncertain. Shrovetide has been supposed to be the period, and
that festive time a relic of it. It is true, besides the Scandinavian
customs just mentioned, we have express testimony from the sixth century
that it was at February 22, when the Germanics made offerings to their
dead.[4] But therein they followed again the course of the Romans, whose
festival of the dead, the *Ferialia*, was held on February 21.

---

[1] *Geschichte der deutschen Weihnacht*, p. 282: "Der Voigtländische Name 'Unternächte,' den Mogk, *Mythologie*, 1126 (Paul's *Grundriss der germanischen Philologie*, 1891,
I.), als Nächte der Toten deutet, bedeutet nur 'Nächte vor dem Feste' (vor Epiphanias
[das oberster Tag heisst: Oberster tag, obrister tag, obroster tag, oberstag, uberster tag,
zu oberstn, am hailigen oberstn, Grotefend, *Zeitrechnung des Mittelalters und der Neuzeit*,
1891, I., p. 137]) wie 'unter Mittag' eigentlich die Zeit unmittelbar vor Mittag, 'über
Mittag' die Zeit unmittelbar nach Mittag bedeuten, bis dann beide 'um Mittag' heissen. So
heisst Weihnachten lateinisch sub calendas januarias (Beatus Rhenanus, *Rer. Germ.*, Lib. III.)."

[2] *Zeitschrift des Vereins für Volkskunde*, 1874, Heft I., p. 100.

[3] "Nur wolle man das nicht, wie E. Mogk, und ihm nach A. Tille thun, durch den
vogtländischen Namen der Zwölften *Unternächte* beweisen, der nichts als *Zwischen*nächte
bedeutet: die Nächte zwischen Weihnacht und Epiphanias." After the examples of *oberster
tag* I gave above, I need scarcely state that Weinhold's explanation as "*Zwischennächte*"
is probably wrong also. In Hans Meyer's *Deutsches Volkstum*, Leipzig, 1898, p. 292,
Professor Mogk repeated the error that the ancient Germanics celebrated a dead festival
in the darkest time of the year, but gave up his former explanation of *Unternächte*,
adopting instead the explanation suggested by Professor Weinhold.

[4] *Acta Conciliorum*, Parisiis, 1714, Vol. III., col. 365, *Concilium Turonense II.*,
A.D. 567, xxii.: "Sunt etiam qui in festivitate cathedrae domni Petri apostoli cibos mortuis
offerunt, et post missas redeuntes ad domos proprias, ad gentilium revertuntur errores, et
post corpus Domini, sacratas daemoni escas accipiunt. Contestamur illam solicitudinem
tam pastoies quam presbyteros gerere, ut quemcumque in hac fatuitate persistere viderint
vel ad nescio quas petras, aut arbores, aut ad fontes, designata loca gentilium, perpetrare
quae ad ecclesiae rationem non pertinent; eos ab ecclesia sancta auctoritate repellant, nec
participare sancto altario permittant, qui gentilium observationes custodiunt." The same
habit seems referred to in caput lxix. of the *Capitula Martini Episcopi Bracarensis*, *Ibid.*,
Vol. III., col. 398: "Non liceat Christianis prandia ad defunctorum sepulchra deferre, et
sacrificare de re mortuorum" (about A.D. 575).

CHAPTER X.

THE NATIVITY OF CHRIST.

For centuries after Julius Caesar had ordered the winter solstice to take place on December 25, the *Brumalia*, celebrated at that date, could not compete in splendour with the Calends of January. Their later fame and significance they owe not to ancient Rome, but to the new religion which, since the first century of our era, was spreading in all directions from Palestine. They owe it to Christianity. The year in which the two, *Brumalia* and Christianity, were brought into contact by an energetic Roman bishop was A.D. 354.

The historical date of Christ's birth is unknown; and though some early fathers of the Church tried to find out by speculation at what date He ought to have been born, the matter apparently lacked interest for the Church. November 17 and March 28 were contended for, but without any success, as the date of the miraculous birth in the stable at Bethlehem. Clemens of Alexandria was as little able to gain authority for the former date as a writing on Easter ascribed to Cyprian was to gain it for the latter.

The early Church did not regard Christ as a God from birth, but merely as having become one when He was thirty years old, and when the Holy Ghost descended upon Him at the baptism in Jordan. Distinct traces of that dogma are even preserved in the common text of the New Testament,[1]

---

[1] *Gospel according to St. Matthew*, i. 16, where, for the purpose of proving that Christ was a descendant of David, it is shown that His father Joseph was such: "And Jacob begat Joseph the husband of Mary, of whom was born Jesus, who is called Christ." The medieval Church noticed this incongruity, and got over it by decreeing that Mary had been a cousin of Joseph's, and consequently of the same stock as he was.

the Gospels of St. Mark and St. John beginning with that story, as being the first important event in Christ's career. The festival in commemoration of the deification of Christ was Epiphany—the festival of Christ's appearance in the glory of God, as it was called later. Along with Easter and Pentecost it is, in the early Church, named as one of the three greatest Church festivals.

About the beginning of the third century there arose in the Western countries a new opinion on the person of the Saviour. He was now held to have been a God from birth, His Father having been God Himself. It was the Church of Rome which made itself the advocate of this doctrine, and evolved the necessary basis for it in her own Gospel, which is called "according to St. Luke." Within little more than a century that new dogma conquered the countries round the Mediterranean, though it seems never to have reached the far East. In the face of that view it could scarcely any longer appear proper to celebrate the memory of the deification of Christ in the festival of Epiphany on January 6. It was the Roman Bishop Liberius (A.D. 352-366) who had the courage to draw the consequence from the new belief. On January 6, 354, he celebrated, as before, the appearance of Christ in God-like glory, but in the same year he celebrated a second birthday of the God in Christ on December 25, and used henceforth all his authority to lead this new festival to victory throughout the whole Church. The mere choice of the day shows that the step which was taken had been considered well beforehand.[1]

The assumed days of solstices and equinoxes were days with regard to which the Julian calendar had not been consistent. Whilst attaching all possible importance to them and making them the measure of the duration of the year, it did not make them the beginnings of months, nor the winter solstice the beginning of the year. Its year rather began seven days (or, as it was counted then, eight days) after the winter solstice. When Bishop Liberius made his choice of a new birthday for the Redeemer, he was no doubt conscious of the fact that thereby he would get into his hands a

---

[1] Christ's birthday on December 25 is first mentioned in the chronology of Furius Dionysius Filocalus (Usener, *Das Weihnachtsfest*, Bonn, 1889, p. 267), where the year begins with December 25, and the entry: "viii. Kl. ianu. natus Christus in Betleem Judeae."

means of beating, in the long run, the entire Roman calendar—an idea for which the Church fought for a whole millennium, though without ever winning a complete victory; so that the doctrinaire and unpractical Roman beginning of the year, though a little reformed by a Pope himself, now rules the time wherever Christian civilisation has come. But the new festival at least conquered, or did even more. Whilst Easter, having a basis beyond the world of the Roman calendar, and therefore being something strange to the Western world, gave rise to endless discussions about the proper date of its celebration and to two different traditions,[1] Christmas from its very first origins bore the mark of being a Roman creation, stood firmly on the basis of the Roman[2] system of the year, and in the course of time even managed to shake that very system, by making itself the beginning of the year instead of the Roman Calends of January. Up to the time of the Reformation its sanctity was never disputed, neither was its historical foundation attacked, so that, if not outshining in splendour Easter and Whitsunday, it soon gained a position certainly equal to theirs.

With the triumph won by the belief of Athanasius and the heirs of St. Peter at Rome, the new custom of the Roman Church came to the East. In Constantinople the first festival of Christ's birth on December 25 was celebrated in 379, in Nyssa of Cappadocia in 382, in Antioch in 388. It took about a century and a half to win for it legal authority among the Eastern Germanics. By the commentary to the Law Book of Alarich, which originated with it in 506, Christ's birthday became a day on which no law courts were allowed to be held. In Eastern Rome it gained the same position not much later, the *Codex Justinianus* of 543 ordaining it to be a *dies nefastus*. On the other hand, the Church tried to make it a real day of worldly joy, excluding from it all fasting as early as A.D. 561.[4]

---

[1] Beda, *Historia Ecclesiastica*, III., 3, 25, 26.

[2] Beda knew the bearing of that difference between the two festivals quite well. Comparing Easter and Christmas, he says (*De Temporibus*, chap. xv.): "Ideo autem pascha non ad eundem redit anni diem, sicut tempus Dominicae nativitatis, quod ibi nativitatis ipsius memoria tantum solemnis habeatur: hic vero vitae venturae et mysteria celebrentur, et munera capiantur."

[3] Usener, *Das Weihnachtsfest*, pp. 262, 247, 238.

[4] The *Concilium Bracarense* of 561 ordains: "Siquis Natalem Christi secundum carnem

The new day of Christ's deification could only be successful in outshining the old one if it was celebrated earlier than the old one and at the same time with higher splendour. Although everything was done in that direction, attempts were not lacking to build a bridge from the new day to the old one, by proclaiming holy the twelve days between them. This was done as early as the fourth century by Ephraim the Syrian, and became bye and bye an ecclesiastical institution; so that the Synod of Tours of 567 declared it to be a festive tide of the Church under the name Δωδεκαήμερον or Twelve-days tide—called on Germanic soil, several centuries later, the *Twelve nights*—and in the course of time becoming so popular that a thousand years later so great a mythologist as Professor Weinhold could mistake them for a relic of ancient Germanic worship.

After having gained a new centre at Rome, Christianity went out to convert the nations—following in the footsteps of old Roman civilisation. It spread over Gaul and came to the Rhine, in the sixth century passed the Rhine, and in the course of two other centuries won over almost all the Western Germanics. Wherever it came it fought against heathen custom, whether Roman, Celtic, or Germanic; and in pressing Christ's birthday, Pasch and Pentecost, as the main festivals of the new faith, had to fight a hard struggle with hard-headed Germanics. The Edicts of the Councils of the Church, especially of those held in Gaul, are eloquent documents on the various ways in which the Germanics and their evil demons attempted to put Christ's Church to shame, and on the energetic ways in which the representatives of the right belief frustrated that audacious undertaking.

To Great Britain Christianity had come about A.D. 200 from Asia Minor, and spread somewhat in the course of the third century, so that the persecution of the Christians by Diocletian (284-305)[1] threw its shadows over this country as over others. When some time later three heathen Germanic tribes crossed the Channel—the Angles, the Saxons, and the Jutes—Christian tradition on British soil was not entirely interrupted, although it

---

non bene honorat, sed honorare se simulat, jejunans in eodem die, et in Dominico: quia Christum in vera hominis natura natum esse non credit, sicut Cerdon, Marcion, Manichaeus, et Priscillianus anathema sit." *Acta Conciliorum*, Parisiis, 1714, III., col. 348.

[1] Beda, *Historia Ecclesiastica Gentis Anglorum*, chap. vi.

seems not to have specially flourished. It was in 592 that Pope Gregory the Great sent the first Roman missionaries to Britain, led by Augustine, who was to be their bishop if they should succeed. They were kindly received by King Ethelbert of Kent, and settled in Canterbury. The ancient British Christian Church, having sprung up in the second century from Asia Minor, cannot have had any celebration of Christ's nativity on December 25. So the first celebration of that festival, it must be assumed, was held in Britain in 592 by Augustine and his fellow-missionaries, though we have no knowledge of that fact. If there was such a celebration, it consisted, in all probability, in a specially splendid mass, and was supported by worldly dining and drinking.[1]

From the famous letter of Pope Gregory the Great to the Abbot Mellitus in Britain we know that, so late as the end of the sixth century, the Pope attached the principal weight to the celebration of the proper sacred *days*, however heathenish the customs might be of which that celebration consisted, provided only that what so far had been done in honour of the heathen demons was now done in honour of the one God of the heavens, and if it took the shape of offering and feasting.[2]

---

[1] Adamnan's *Life of St. Columba* (A.D. 521-597) (*Adamnani Vita S. Columbae*, edited from Dr. Reeves's Text, with an Introduction on early Irish Church History, Notes, and a Glossary by J. T. Fowler, Oxford, Clarendon Press, 1894), which belongs to the first half of the eighth century and to Ireland and Iona, knows of Christmas as being one of the two great festivals of the Church, the other being the *Paschales dies* (*Ibid.*, p. 46). It names it *Natalitium Domini*. It tells of a manuscript by Columba which remained in the water uninjured from Christmas to Easter: "Qui videlicet libellus, a Natalitio Domini usque ad Paschalium consummationem dierum in aquis permanens . . . postea repertus" (*Ibid.*, p. 79, Book II., chap. ix.); whilst elsewhere the *dies natalis* of a saint is the day on which he died, *i.e.*, was born into heaven, the word usually applied to the birthday of a saint being *nativitas*. Compare Fowler's book, p. 124, note: "Quia ut saeculo et mundo moriuntur, ita tunc caelo nascuntur" (Beleth, *Div. Off.*, 4). Of course, in this case the evidence is lacking that the story was told the same way during Columba's life-time.

[2] *Venerabilis Baedae Historiam Ecclesiasticam Gentis Anglorum, Historiam Abbatum, Epistolam ad Ecgberctum una cum Historia Abbatum, Auctore Anonymo ad fidem codicum manuscriptorum denuo recognovit commentario tam critico quam historico instruxit Carolus Plummer*, Tomus Prior, Oxonii, 1896, p. 65 (chap. xxx.): "Cum ergo Deus omnipotens vos ad reverentissimum virum fratrem nostrum Augustinum episcopum perduxerit, dicite ei, quid diu mecum de causa Anglorum cogitans tractavi; videlicet, quia fana idolorum

So Germanic and Roman customs were drawn to those festivals by the
Christian missionaries, just for the purpose that those festive days might
at least be celebrated, and new Church customs, partly of Oriental heathen
origin, were introduced in order to compete with the native customs
originally belonging to other days of the year. A second stage in that
evolution of Christian festivals on Germanic ground is that the Church
began to combat the very same native customs which it first had drawn
to its new festivals, and to interdict them wherever they might occur. Of
that stage also the Edicts of the Church Councils afford abundant proof.
Whilst up to about A.D. 550 they fight against the participation of Christians
in heathen festivals, after that date they start a struggle against heathen
and heterodox usages practised on the festivals of the Church. This
second attempt, however, seems to have been less successful, or, at least,
to have succeeded much more slowly. It was, apparently, easier to induce
those Germanic tribes to alter the days of their celebrations than to
practise new usages altogether.[1] Just as, according to the letter of Pope

destrui in eadem gente minime debeant ; sed ipsa, quae in eis sunt, idola
destruantur ; aqua benedicta fiat, in eisdem fanis aspergatur, altaria construantur, reliquiae
ponantur. Quia, si fana eadem bene constructa sunt, necesse est, ut a cultu daemonum
in obsequio veri Dei debeant commutari ; ut dum gens ipsa eadem fana sua non videt
destrui, de corde errorem deponat, et Deum verum cognoscens ac adorans, ad loca, quae
consuevit, familiarius concurrat. Et quia boves solent in sacrificio daemonum multos
occidere, debet eis etiam hac de re aliqua sollemnitas immutari ; ut die dedicationis, vel
natalitii sanctorum martyrum, quorum illic reliquiae ponuntur, tabernacula sibi circa easdem
ecclesias, quae ex fanis commutatae sunt, de ramis arborum faciant, et religiosis conviviis
sollemnitatem celebrent ; nec diabolo iam animalia immolent, et ad laudem Dei in esu
suo animalia occidant, et donatori omnium de satietate sua gratias referant ; ut dum
eis aliqua exterius gaudia reservantur, ad interiora gaudia consentire facilius valeant.
Nam duris mentibus simul omnia abscidere impossibile esse non dubium est, quia et is,
qui summum locum ascendere nititur, gradibus vel passibus, non autem saltibus elevatur.
Sic Israelitico populo in Aegypto Dominus se quidem innotuit ; sed tamen eis sacrificiorum
usus, quae diabolo solebat exhibere, in cultu proprio reservavit, ut eis in suo sacrificio
animalia immolare praeciperet ; quatinus cor mutantes, aliud de sacrificio amitterent,
aliud retinerent ; ut etsi ipsa essent animalia, quae offerre consueverant, vero tamen
Deo haec et non idolis immolantes, iam sacrificia ipsa non essent."

[1] *Acta Conciliorum*, Parisiis, 1714, Vol. III., col. 334, *Childeberti Regis Constitutio
sive Constitutionis quae supersunt Capita duo* (511-558); Boretius, *Capitularia Regum
Francorum*, I., 2 : "Ad nos querimonia processit, multa sacrilegia in populo fieri, unde

Gregory to Mellitus, it was the policy of the Church to change the places of heathen cult into places of worship of the God of the Christians, the new Christian churches are expressly and more than once reported to have been used for celebrations after the old Celtic and Germanic manners,[1] and so late as the beginning of the ninth century the repetition of an interdict of that habit was thought expedient.[2] Nay, the very festivals of the new religious community were constantly used for celebrations according to ancient heathen Germanic customs.[3] Certainly Professor Koegel

---

Deus laedatur, et populus per peccatum declinet ad mortem. Noctes pervigiles cum ebrietate, scurrilitate, vel canticis, etiam in ipis sacris diebus Pascha, Natale Domini, et reliquis festivitatibus, vel adveniente die Dominico, dansatrices per villas ambulare. Haec omnia, unde Deus agnoscitur laedi, nullatenus fieri permittimus. Quicunque post commonitionem sacerdotum, vel nostrum praeceptum, sacrilegia ista perpetrare praesumpserit, si servilis persona est, centum ictus flagellorum ut suscipiat iubemus: si vero ingenuus aut honoratior fortasse persona est, districta inclusione digna. Sunt hi autem in poenitentiam redigendi: ut qui salubria et a mortis periculo revocantia audire verba contemnunt, cruciatus saltem corporis eos ad desiderandam mentis valeat reducere sanitatem."

[1] *Council of Autun* (573-603), chap. ix., in *Concilia ævi Merowingici*, ed. Frid. Maassen, Hannover, 1893, p. 180: "Non licet in ecclesia choros saecularium vel puellarum cantica exercere nec convivia in ecclesia praeparare, quia scriptum est: domus mea domus orationis vocabitur."

[2] *Statuta Bonifacii*, chap. xxi.: "Non licet in ecclesia choros secularium vel puellarum cantica exercere nec convivia in ecclesia praeparare."

[3] *Acta Conciliorum*, Parisiis, 1714, Vol. III., col. 445, *Concilium Autissiodorense*, A.D. 578, Canon xi.: "Non licet in vigilia paschae ante horam secundam noctis vigilias perexplere, quia in illa nocte non licet post mediam noctem bibere [nec manducare], nec in Natali Domini, nec in reliquis solemnitatibus." *Ibid.*, Vol. III., col. 444, Canons iii. and v.: "Canon iii. Non licet compensos in domibus propriis, nec pervigilias in festivitatibus sanctorum facere; nec inter sentes, aut ad arbores sacrivos, vel ad fontes vota exsolvere: sed quicumque votum habuerit, in ecclesia vigilet, et matriculae ipsum votum, aut pauperibus reddat: nec sculptilia [sub tilia] aut pede, aut homine lineo fieri penitus praesumat. Canon v. Omnino et inter supradictas conditiones, pervigilias, quas in honore domni Martini observant, omnimodis prohibet." *Council of Chalons-sur-Saône* (639-654), chap. xix., in *Concilia ævi Merowingici*, ed. Frid. Maassen, Hannover, 1893, p. 212: "Valde omnibus nuscetur esse decretum, ne per dedicationes basilicarum aut festivitates martyrum ad ipsa solemnia confluentes obscina et turpea cantica, dum orare debent aut clericos psallentes audire cum choris foemineis, turpia quidem, decantare videantur."

is wrong when [1] he expresses the opinion that these days of saints were
just the ancient Germanic festive days on which people continued their
old practice of worship.[2] / Among these Church festivals used for popular
rejoicing were, of course, the Sundays and the two greatest festivals of the
sixth century Church—Christmas and Easter [3]—at which processions after the
ancient Celtic and Germanic fashion apparently were very frequent in
the Gaul of the early sixth century.[4] It is to be admitted that, in fixing
the saints' days, the Church had a certain liberty, although very many of
them had definitely been marked down before any Germanic tribe got
anything like a decisive influence over Church affairs; but the three festivals,
Epiphany, Easter, and Pentecost—or, as they run in the Western countries
from the middle of the fourth century, Christmas, Easter, and Pentecost—
were absolutely fixed previous to a contact of the supreme authority in the

---

[1] *Geschichte der deutschen Literatur bis zum Ausgange des Mittelalters*, Strassburg,
1894, p. 25.

[2] Professor Koegel, *Ibid.*, has put together a number of further evidences of heathen practices
at Christian festive days: "Caspari, *Kirchenhistorische Anecdota*, Christiania, 1883, pp. 176,
188; *Benedictus Levita*, VI., 96, in *Monumenta Germaniae, Scriptores*, IV., 2; Wasserschleben, *Bussordnungen der abendländischen Kirche*, p. 607 (Preuso-Theodorean Penitential);
Indiculus Superstitionum: *De Sacrilegiis per ecclesias* (among the Saxons newly converted);
Regino von Prüm, ed. by Wasserschleben, p. 179 (Council of Mayence, 813); Boretius,
Capitularia Regum Francorum, I., p. 376: 'Sunt quidam, et maxime mulieres, qui festis
ac sacris diebus atque sanctorum nataliciis non pro eorum quibus debent delectantur
desideriis advenire, sed balando et verba turpia decantando, choros tenendo ac ducendo,
similitudinem paganorum peragendo, advenire procurant.'"

[3] Beda's Letter to Egbert, Bishop of York, on the state of the Northumbrian
Church, which was written A.D. 734 (Haddan and Stubbs, *Councils and Ecclesiastical
Documents*, Oxford, 1871, III., p. 323: "Quod videlicet genus religionis, ac Deo
devotae sanctificationis tam longe a cunctis pene nostrae provinciae laicis per incuriam
docentium quasi prope peregrinum abest, ut hi qui inter religiosiores esse videntur, non
nisi in Natali Domini et Epiphania et Pascha sacrosanctis mysteriis communicare
praesumant"), mentions even, as the three festivals of the Church most popular in his
time, Christmas, Epiphany, and Easter.

[4] Rudolph Koegel as late as 1894 maintained that Christmas and Easter were
originally Germanic festivals (*Geschichte der deutschen Literatur bis zum Ausgang des
Mittelalters*, Strassburg, 1894, I., p. 28); but that part of his book was printed before he
had come to know my own *Geschichte der deutschen Weihnacht*, which had appeared
in Leipzig, 1893.

Christian Church with the Germanics. It does not seem to have occurred to anybody what a number of singular and unexplainable coincidences would have to be assumed, if each of these festivals had fallen on a day sancrosanct to the Germanics before their contact with the Romano-Christian world!

Professor Weinhold somewhat underrates the power and influence of Christianity on the Germanic nations. What a poor religion would it require to have been had it influenced them no more than he supposes it to have done! He overlooks the world of tradition, of tales, of customs, of beliefs, it called into existence, and has some feeling that he does a patriotic work when he ascribes to our heathen ancestors all those creations of fancy, and the experience of life and the human heart, which the religion of the cross gave them as an entirely unearned present. To ascribe to Germanic heathendom whatever is popular among the Germanic nations in modern times means nothing but to assume that the Germanics were touched by Christianity only in the most superficial way, and that all efforts which the Church made in order to bring home to the Germanic mind its institutions were of no consequence.

The establishment of the *Dodekahemeron*, or the twelve holy days from Christmas to Epiphany which was mentioned above, was one of the means to make Christmas an important feast. Another was the institution of a preparatory tide of forty days which immediately preceded it, and which gained ground after the middle of the sixth century, spreading from Gaul over almost the whole Christian world.

The Advent-tide, with its beginning at Martinmas, is of Gallic growth, that date having been decidedly fixed under Germanic influence. It is important, for the purpose of understanding the relation between Martinmas and the autumnal equinox, to notice that there was in the early Church another and later Advent-tide, which competed with that of Gaul. It was of southern growth, and began on the autumnal equinox. According to a letter which pretends to be written by St. Augustine of Hipporegius, Numidia, to Biblianus, Bishop of Santonae, Gaul, living about 450,[1] the Advent-tide was to begin on

---

[1] " Episcopus Sanctonensis," now Saintes in the Département Charente-Inférieur. Compare Potthast, *Wegweiser*, 634; Pfannenschmid, *Germanische Erntefeste*, p. 514.

September 24, that being the day of the autumnal equinox, because that
was the day of the conception of John Baptist. It being preserved only
in a manuscript of the eighth century, and stating expressly that the
beginning of the holy tide with the equinox was more fitting than its
beginning with Martin's burial-day, it cannot have been written before the
middle of the sixth century, before which date an Advent-tide, beginning
with Martinmas, cannot be proved to have existed. It is clearly a falsifi-
cation intended to supersede the Germanic term Martinmas by the Italian
term of the autumnal equinox, of which the Germanics knew nothing. The
Advent-tide, beginning with Martinmas, became an ecclesiastical institution
in the latter half of the sixth century.[1] It was the policy of the Church
to impress on people's minds its three great festivals by making each of
them a gay time of worldly joy, and by rendering their gaiety the more
attractive by letting them be preceded by periods of strict fasting, which were
extended to forty days each, a space of time which, however, seems seldom
to have been exceeded. To be sure it was long enough—the three fasting-
tides together comprising, as they did, an entire third of a year. Nor
were the saints' days times of penitence or fasting, but the very contrary.
The Judæo-Christian and also Roman conception of sanctifying festive days
by dropping every kind of work was understood to refer to the toil of
every-day life—to business and law proceedings only—whilst every allowance
was made for enjoyment of various kinds, and, above all, for eating and
drinking. In truth, it was not before the time immediately following the
Reformation that another view was taken which turned, though only within the
small area of Puritanism, the festive days of the Church into true *dies nefasti*
of Roman strictness, making it a sin to enjoy one's self in any way on a
Sunday, and dropping the old festivals of the Catholic Church almost
completely. In the seventh century, even the worst sinners who had to
do penitence for fifteen years were allowed to break their fasting on Sundays.[2]

---

[1] " Ut a feria sancti Martini usque ad Natale domini, secunda, quarta, et sexta sabbati
jejunetur, et sacrificia quadragesimali debeant ordine celebrari." *Acta Conciliorum*, Parisiis,
1714, Vol. III., col. 452, *Concilium Matisconense*, I., A.D. 581, ix.

[2] Haddan and Stubbs, *Councils and Ecclesiastical Documents*, Oxford, 1871, III., 179,
Theodore's Penitential, ii., 16: "Si cum matre quis fornicaverit, xv. annos peniteat, et
nunquam mutet nisi Dominicis diebus."

As far as I am aware, the three *Quadragesimae* occur in Britain for the first time shortly before A.D. 570.[1] The mention of them without any specifying remark presupposes a general establishment of the three great Church festivals, as to which it is, however, uncertain whether the third was Epiphany or Christmas.[2] Whitsunday and Easter are for the first time mentioned between A.D. 616 and 627.[3] A.D. 704 the Strathclyde Britains adopted the Roman Easter.[4] In Armorica the first Easter is mentioned as early as A.D. 541,[5] the first mentioning of Christmas taking place in 598.[6] Between A.D. 597 and A.D. 604 Gregory is said to have given the English a rule on the Ember Feasts, or feasts of the four Roman seasons of the year.[7]

---

[1] Haddan and Stubbs, *Councils and Ecclesiastical Documents Relating to Great Britain and Ireland*, Oxford, 1869, Vol. I., p. 113, in *Praefatio Gildae de Penitentia*, where to the penitent sinner it is permitted: "Per tres quadragesimas superaddat aliquid, prout virtus admiserit."

[2] The mention occurs again and again. *Ibid.*, I., p. 114, xi.: "Tres quadragesimas;" xvii.: "Quadragesimam; duas quadragesimas;" *Ibid.*, I., p. 117 (A.D. 569), *Sinodus Aquilonalis Britanniae*, ii.: "Tribus quadragesimis;" iv.: "Tres quadragesimas;" *Ibid.*, I., p. 118 (A.D. 569), *Excerpta quaedam de Libro Davidis*, ii.: "Quadragesimam; tribus quadragesimis."

[3] *Ibid.*, I., 124, Nennius, Appendix: "Eanfled filia illius duodecimo die post Pentecosten baptismum accepit cum universis hominibus suis de viris et mulieribus cum ea. Eadguin vero in sequenti Pascha baptismum suscepit, et duodecim millia hominum baptizati sunt cum eo;" *Ibid.*, I., 124 (A.D. 731), *Baedae Historica Ecclesiastica*, III., 28: "Dominicum paschae diem."

[4] *Ibid.*, II., ii., 6, and II., ii., 110, *Baedae Hist. Ecclesiastica*, V., 15: "Quo tempore plurima pars Scotorum in Hibernia, et nonnulla etiam de Brittonibus in Brittannia, rationabile et ecclesiasticum Paschalis observantiae tempus Domino donante suscepit."

[5] Haddan and Stubbs, *Councils and Ecclesiastical Documents*, II., Oxford, 1873, p. 75, *Concil. Aurelian.*, IV., Can. i.: "Placuit itaque, Deo propitio, ut sanctum Pascha secundum laterculum Victorii ab omnibus sacerdotibus uno tempore celebretur" (in Armorica); *Ibid.*, II., 77 (A.D. 577, 590); *Greg. Tur.*, V., 17 (A.D. 577): "Eo anno dubietas Paschae fuit," etc. About the Easter dispute, compare Beda, *Hist. Eccl.*, III., 3 and 25, 26.

[6] *Ibid.*, Vol. III., Oxford, 1871, p. 12, Letter by Gregorius to Eulogius, Bishop of Alexandria: "In solemnitate autem Dominicae Nativitatis quae hac prima indictione transacta est plus quam decem milia Angli ab eodem [Augustino] nuntiati sunt fratre et coepiscopo nostro baptizati."

[7] Haddan and Stubbs, *Councils and Ecclesiastical Documents Relating to Great Britain and Ireland*, Vol. III., Oxford, 1871, p. 52 (after Mansi, X., 446, *ex Additamentis ad Codicem Burchardi*, who, however, is inclined to regard it as spurious, following therein Muratorius, II., p. 262, in his *Dissertatio de Jejuniis Quatuor Temporum*, chap. vii.,

I

That Gregory gave that rule was at least believed in the English Church of the eighth century.

Prescriptions about the three fasting tides are very frequent.[1] Of these periods the forty days preceding Pasch were reckoned the holiest,[2] at least as regards chastity. As regards abstinence from work Sunday stood first.[3]

---

p. 449) : "Haec sunt jejunia, quae S. Gregorius genti Anglorum praedicari praecepit— Sunt quatuor jejunia quatuor temporum anni ; id est, veris, aestatis, autumni et hiemis. Jejunium primum in prima hebdomada Quadragesimae ; jejunium secundum in hebdomada post Pentecosten ; jejunium tertium in plena hebdomada ante autumnale aequinoctium ; jejunium quartum in plena hebdomada ante natale Domini. Jejunium in feria sexta per totum annum nisi a Pascha usque ad Pentecosten, aut si major festivitas fuerit."

[1] Haddan and Stubbs, *Councils and Ecclesiastical Documents*, Oxford, 1871, III., p. 182, Theodore's Penitential (668-690), VI. 1, 2 : "Quis perjurium facit in ecclesia undecim annos peniteat. (2) Qui vero necessitate coactus sit tres quadragesimas." *Ibid.*, III., p. 184, viii., 11 ; *Ibid.*, III., 186, xi. : "De his qui damnant Dominicam et indicta jejunia ecclesiae Dei. (1) Qui operantur die Dominico, eos Graeci prima vice arguunt, secunda tollunt aliquid ab eis, tertia vice partem tertiam de rebus eorum, aut vapulent, vel VII. diebus peniteant. (2) Si quis autem in Dominica die pro negligentia jejunaverit, ebdomadam totam debet abstinere ; si secundo, XX. dies peniteat ; si postea, XL. dies. (3) Si pro damnatione diei jejunaverit, sicut Judaeus abominetur ab omnibus ecclesiis catholicis. (4) Si autem contempserit indictum jejunium in ecclesia et contra decreta seniorum fecerit sine XLma, XL. dies peniteat. Si autem in XLma, annum peniteat ; si quis autem contempserit XLmam ; XL. dies peniteat. (5) Si frequenter fecerit, et in consuetudine erit ei, exterminetur ab ecclesia, Domino dicente, 'Qui scandalizaverit unum de pusillis istis' et reliqua." *Ibid.*, III., 196, viii. : "De moribus Graecorum et Romanorum. (1) In Dominico Graeci et Romani navigant et equitant, panem non faciunt, neque in curru pergunt nisi ad ecclesiam tantum, nec balneant se. (2) Graeci in Dominica non scribunt publice ; tunc pro necessitate seorsum in domu scribunt. (3) Graeci et Romani dant servis suis vestimenta et laborant sine Dominico die. . . . (5) In illa die ante Natale Domini hora nona, expleta missa, id est, vigilia Domini, manducant Romani, Graeci vero dicta vespera et missa coenant. . . . (8) Lavacrum capitis potest in Dominica esse, et in lexiva pedes lavare licet, sed consuetudo Romanorum non est haec lavatio pedum."

[2] *Ibid.*, III., 199, xii. : "(2) Vir abstineat se ab uxore XL. dies ante Pascha usque octavas Paschae," which prescription is enlarged in another version by the addition : "post Pentecosten una ebdomada" (*Ibid.*, III., published in *Cap. Theodor.*, ed. Wasserschleben, No. 56).

[3] *Ibid.*, III., 215, *King Ine's Laws*, touching the Church (688-693 ; probably A.D. 693) : iii. "Gif theowmon wyrce on Sunnan-dæg be his hlafordes hæse, sie he frioh ; and se hlaford geselle xxx. scillingas to wite. Gif thonne se theowa butan his gewitnesse wyrce, tholie his hyde [oththe hyd-gyldes]. Gif thonne se frigea thy dæge wyrce butan his hlafordes hæse tholie his freotes [oththe sixtig scillingas ; and preost si twy-scildig]" ; the same, *Ibid.*, III., 235, *Laws of Wihtred* (693-731), 9·11.

Nevertheless, the Church had considerable difficulty in making the new Christians see a difference between their old Germanic and the new Christian festivals. The Anglo-Saxons came to church dancing, and there sang their love-songs, as they had done at their traditional festivals, so that this kind of thing had to be forbidden in England as it had to be on the Continent.[1] Otherwise, especially as regards feasting at the proper times, the Church was very liberal. Theodore's Penitential (A.D. 668-690) regarded it as an excuse if a man ate too freely at Christmas, so long as he did not pass the limits allowed by the Church.[2]

The state of the ecclesiastical observance of Christmas among the people about Beda's time can be seen from several Penitentials contemporaneous or almost contemporaneous.[3]

---

[1] Haddan and Stubbs, *Councils and Ecclesiastical Documents*, Oxford, 1871, III., 227, in the *Judicium Clementis*, probably written by Willibrord (690-693), 20: "Si quis in quacunque festivitate ad ecclesiam veniens pallat foris, aut saltat, aut cantat. orationes amatorias, ab Episcopo aut presbytero aut clerico excommunicetur et, dum paenitentiam non agit, excommunicetur." The same in Kunstmann, *Die Lateinischen Pönitentialbücher der Angelsachsen*, p. 177, and Wasserschleben, *Die Bussordnungen der Abendländischen Kirche*, p. 433.

[2] Haddan and Stubbs, *Councils and Ecclesiastical Documents*, Oxford, 1871, III., p. 177: Liber Primus I., De Crapula et Ebrietate. "(4) Si vero pro infirmitate aut quia longo tempore se abstinuerit, et in consuetudine non erit ei multum bibere vel manducare, aut pro gaudio in Natale Domini aut in Pascha aut pro alicujus Sanctorum commemoratione faciebat, et tunc plus non accipit quam decretum est a senioribus, nihil nocet. Si Episcopus juberit, non nocet illi, nisi ipse similiter faciat." It was mentioned above that the *Concilium Bracarense*, I., A.D. 561, ordained a celebration of Christmas, expressly forbidding any fasting on that day (*Acta Conciliorum*, Parisiis, 1714, Vol. III., col. 348, iii.: "Si quis Natalem Christi secundum carnem non bene honorat, sed honorare se simulat, jejunans in eodem die, et in Dominico . . . anathema sit"). The same prohibition occurs as late as about A.D. 725 (*Acta Conciliorum*, Parisiis, 1714, Vol. III., col. 1863, *Gregorii Papae II.* (A.D. 715-731) *Capitulae*, x.: "Ut dominicis diebus doceantur non licere omnino jejunare, propter resurrectionis dominicae sacramentum, neque in festivitatibus Dominicis Nativitatis, aut Apparitionis, sive Ascensionis").

[3] Thorpe, *Ancient Laws*, II., 95-96; Haddan and Stubbs, *Councils and Ecclesiastical Documents*, Oxford, 1871, Vol. III., 412, Dialogue of Egbert between A.D. 732 and 766: "De Quarto Jejunio: Quartum jejunium mense Novembrio a veteribus colebatur, juxta praeceptum Domini ad Jeremiam dicentis: 'Tolle volumen libri, et scribe in eo omnia verba, quae locutus sum adversus Israel et Judam. Et factum est in mense nono, praedicaverunt jejunium in conspectu Domini omni populo in Jerusalem.' Hac ergo

Unwise regulations do not always attain the purpose for which they are made. Just as the forty days' fast preceding the Nativity was bound to lead to

---

auctoritate Divinarum Scripturarum ecclesia catholica morem obtinet, et jejunium atque observationem in mense celebrat decimo, sabbato quarto, propter advenientem venerabilem solemnitatem Domini nostri Jesu Christi; ubi ante plures dies et continentia carnis et jejunia exhibenda sunt, ut unusquisque fidelis praeparet se ad communionem corporis et sanguinis Christi cum devotione sumendam.   Quod et gens Anglorum semper in plena ebdomada ante Natale Domini consuevit, non solum quarta et sexta feria, et sabbato, sed et juges XII. dies in jejuniis, et vigiliis, et orationibus, et elemosinarum largitionibus, et in monasteriis, et in plebibus, ante Natale, quasi legitimum jejunium exercuisse perhibetur.   Nam haec, Deo gratias, a temporibus Vitaliani papae, et Theodori Dorobernensis Archiepiscopi inolevit in ecclesia Anglorum consuetudo, et quasi legitima tenebatur, ut non solum clerici in monasteriis, sed etiam laici cum conjugibus et familiis suis ad confessores suos pervenirent, et se fletibus et carnalis concupiscentiae consortio his duodecim diebus cum elemosinarum largitione mundarent, quatenus puriores Dominicae communionis perceptionem in Natale Domini perciperent.   Praeter haec namque constituta jejunia quarta et sexta feria, propter passionem Christi, et sabbato, propter quod ipso die jacuit in sepulcro, plerique jejunaverunt." Thorpe's *Ancient Laws*, II., 65, *Capitula et Fragmenta Theodori Operum*: "Jejunia legitima tria sunt in anno * * * * praeterea quadraginta ante Natale Domini, et post Pentecosten quadraginta dies." *Ibid.*, II., 66: "Poenitentia illius anni unius, qui in pane et aqua jejunandus est, isto ordine observari debet. Poenitentia illius anni unius, qui in pane et aqua jejunandus est, talis esse debet in unaquaque hebdomada. Tres dies, id est feriam quintam et sabbatum, a vino, medone, mellita et cervisia, a carne et sagimine, a caseo et ovis, et ab omni pingui pisce se abstineat.   Manducet autem minutos pisciculos, si habere potest.   Si habere non potest, tantum unius generis piscem, et legumina, et olera, et poma, si vult, comedat, et cervisiam bibat; et in diebus Dominicis, et in Natali Domini illos quatuor dies; et in Epiphania unum diem; et in Pascha, usque ad octavum diem; et in Ascensione Domini, et Pentecostes quatuor dies; et in festo Sancti Johannis Baptistae, et Sanctae Mariae, et sanctorum duodecim Apostolorum, et Sancti Michaelis, et Sancti Remigii, et Omnium Sanctorum, et Sancti Martini, et in illius Sancti festivitate, qui in illo episcopatu celebris habetur.   In his supradictis diebus faciat charitatem cum ceteris Christianis, id est, utatur eodem cibo et potu quo illi, sed tamen ebrietatem, et ventris ingluviem semper in omnibus caveat." In the second year the sinner of the same kind has to do the following: "Poenitentia istius anni talis esse debet, ut duos dies, id est secundam feriam et quartam in unaquaque hebdomada, jejunet ad vesperam, et tunc reficiatur sicco cibo, id est, de pane et leguminibus siccis sed coctis, aut pomis, aut oleribus crudis; unum eligat ex his tribus, et utatur, et cervisiam bibat sed sobrie.   Et tertium diem, id est, sextam feriam, in pane et aqua observet, et tres quadragesimas jejunet ante Natale Domini unam, secundam ante Pascha, tertiam ante missam Sancti Joannis.   Et in his tribus quadragesimis jejunet duos dies ad nonam in hebdomada, et de sicco cibo comedat, ut supra notatum est.   Et sextam feriam jejunet in pane et aqua,

gluttony at the festival, so the injunctions about the sexual relations for the same forty days were bound to have reactionary consequences in the holy tide.[1]

---

et in Dominicis diebus, et in Natali Domini, et in Pentecoste quatuor illos dies; et in Epiphania unum diem, et in Pascha usque ad septimum diem, et in Ascensione Domini, et in missa Sancti Ioannis Baptistae, et reliqua ut supra." *Ibid.*, II., 68: "De illis qui jejunare non possunt, et nesciunt quomodo poenitentiam unius anni, quem jejunare debent in pane et aqua, redimere possint. Qui vero psalmos non novit, et jejunare non potest, pro uno anno, quem in pane et aqua jejunare debet, det pauperibus in eleemosynam viginti duos solidos, et omnes sextas ferias jejunet in pane et aqua, et tres quadragesimas, id est, quadraginta dies ante Pascha, quadraginta dies ante festivitatem Sancti Johannis Baptistae (et si ante festivitatem aliquid remanserit, postea adimpleat, ét quadraginta dies ante Natale Domini. In istis tribus quadragesimis, quidquid ori suo praeparatur in cibo, vel in potu, vel cujuscumque generis sit, illud aestimet quanti pretii sit, vel esse possit; et medietatem illius pretii distribuat in eleemosynam pauperibus, et assidue oret, et roget Dominum, ut oratio ejus, et eleemosynae ejus, apud Deum acceptabiles sint." The penitence for incest is a little more restricted; *Ibid.*, II., 83, *Capitula et Fragmenta Theodori*: "Ut septem annos agant poenitentiam, tres primos annos tres dies in hebdomada, id est, feria secunda, et quarta, et sexta; quadraginta dies ante Pascha; viginti ante missam Sancti Iohannis, viginti ante Natale Domini: quatuor vero reliquos annos, feria quarta et sexta, et quatuordecim noctes ante missam Sancti Johannis, et alias ante Natale Domini."

[1] Thorpe, *Ancient Laws*, II., 12, *Liber Poenitentialis*, xvii.: "De Observatione Conjugatorum. § 1. Qui in matrimonio sunt, abstinent se in III. Quadragesimas, et in Dominica nocte, et in Sabbato, et feria IIII. et VI. quae legitimae sunt, et III. noctes abstineant se antequam communicent, et I. postquam communicent, et in Pascha usque ad octabas. . . . § 3. Qui autem in Quadragesima ante Pascha cognoscit mulierem suam, et non vult abstinere, I. annum poeniteat, vel suum pretium reddat ad ecclesias, vel pauperibus dividat, vel XXVI. solidos reddat. Si per ebrietatem vel aliqua causa acciderit, sine consuetudine, XL. dies poeniteat. § 4. Qui vero in Quadragesima post Pentecosten, aut ante Natale Domini, non vult a sua conjuge abstinere, XL. dies poeniteat." *Ibid.*, II., 81, *Ex Fragmentis Theodori*: "De temporibus quibus se continere debent conjugati ab uxoribus. Uxoratus contineat se quadraginta dies ante Pascha et Pentecosten, seu ante Natale Domini, et omnem Dominicam noctem, et quartam et sextam feriam." "Uxoratus contineat se quadraginta dies ante natale Domini vel Pascha et omni dominica" (Haddan and Stubbs, *Councils and Ecclesiastical Documents*, Oxford, 1871, III., 329, Beda's Penitential, 731-34). Thorpe's *Ancient Laws*, II., 149, *Ecgberti Confessionale*, xxi.: "Vir cum uxore ne coeat XL. dies ante Pascha, nec VII. dies ante Pentecosten, nec XL. dies ante Natalem Domini. Wer ne hæme mid his wife XL. nihta ær Eastron. ne VII. nihtum ær Pentecosten. ne XL. nihtum ær middan-wintra." Thorpe's *Ancient Laws*, II., 103, *Ecgberti, Arch. Ebor., Excerptiones* xxxviii., *Sinodus Agatensis*: "Seculares qui in Natale Domini, et Pascha, et Pentecosten, non communicaverint, catholici esse non credantur." Christmas

In the first half of the sixth century Christmas received a new significance for the Church by the foundation of a new era through Dionysius
Exiguus. It began on the first day of January in the 753rd year of the
building of Rome, in which Christ was supposed to be born, although it is
now generally admitted that that date is wrong either by three or by five
years. That new era was introduced into Italy in the sixth century, and
into France and England in the seventh, the first instance occurring in
England belonging to the year 680.[1] The Venerable Beda uses throughout
this year—the year "of Grace," "of the Incarnation," "of our Lord," "of the
Nativity," as it is styled in later centuries—although it was so late as 816,
that, by the Council of Chelsea, it was decreed that all bishops should date
their acts from the year of the incarnation of our Saviour.[2] Although the
Church had, from the middle of the fourth century, apparently thought of
rivalling the Calends of January by its newly-fixed birthday of Christ on

---

itself, or even the whole time from December 25 to January 6, was a festive and gay time,
at which, even for sinners, fasting was suspended. Ecgbert's Confessional and Penitential
ordains this expressly (Thorpe's *Ancient Laws*, II., 135: "Secundo anno licebit homini
[poenitentiam agenti] levare poenitentiam suam a Nativitate Domini ad Epiphaniam, et a
Paschate ad Pentecosten; On tham odhrum geare man môt lihtan his dædbôte fram Drihtnes
gebyrd-tîde odh twelftan dæg. and fram Eastron odh Pentecosten"). Haddan and Stubbs,
Councils and Ecclesiastical Documents, Oxford, 1871, Vol. III., p. 429, Egbert's Penitential,
A.D. 732-766, xiii., 11: "De natale Domini usque in Epiphaniam et illos praedictos dies,
qui supra scripti sunt, in penitenia non computantur." Even so late as about A.D. 1000,
in the Canons of Aelfric, the time from Christ's Nativity till a week after Christ's Epiphany
is excepted from Friday fasting, just as the time between Easter and Pentecost (Thorpe,
Ancient Laws, II., 362: "And fæste ælc man twelf monadh ælcne Frige-dæg. buton fram
Eastron odh Pentecosten. and eft fram middan-wintra odh seofon niht ofer twelftan dæg ").

[1] "Regnante in perpetuum ac gubernante Domino nostro Salvatore secula universa,
Anno recapitulationis Dionisi, id est ab Incarnatione Christi sexcentesimo octuagesimo.
Indictione sexta revoluta, etc. Quapropter ego Oshere Rex, etc." (Sir Harris Nicolas, *The
Chronology of History*, London, 1838, p. 3, obs.). Sir Harris gives some more instances
from the eighth century, from the charter of Ethelbert, King of the West Saxons: "Scripta
est hoc charta anno Dominicae Incarnationis, DCCXC."; from a charter of Offa, King of
Mercia: "Actum anno Dominicae Incarnationis, DCCLXXXVIII."; from a charter of Ethelbert,
the second King of Kent: "Actum [anno] Dominicae Incarnationis, DCCLXXXI."; and from
the charter of Egbert, King of Kent: "Actum anno Dominicae Incarnationis, DCCCLXV."
(*Textus Roffensis*, pp. 134, 132, 131, 127). As to the introduction of the Dionysian
computation, see *Notes and Queries*, Eighth Series, xii., 421; Ninth Series, i., 10, etc.

[2] Sir Harris Nicolas, *The Chronology of History*, p. 4.

December 25, the struggle was by no means fought through energetically or even consistently. The popular customs connected with the Calends of January in Italy, Gaul, and the West of Germany gave the Church ample grounds of objection to the whole institution of that Pagan beginning of the year. The Council of Tours (569),[1] Bishop Caesarius of Arles (+542),[2] and Bonifacius (+755)[3] fought against it.[4]   But in the seventh century the Church made the very same day a church festival—a commemoration day of the *circumcisio domini.* (As the economic year began at Martinmas the civic year commenced on January 1 all through the Middle Ages,[5] although the Church, in its documents and accounts, letters and publications, purposely ignored that style, and, having in its hand almost all the secular offices of princes, excluded it from documents relative to them likewise. The Papal Office used the beginning of the year at Christmas up till the middle of the tenth century, then taking March 25 instead.   Under Bonifacius VIII. (1294-1303) December 25 was introduced again, and maintained through the whole of the fourteenth century.   In the fifteenth a new change set in, March 25 competing with January 1.[6]

The earliest documentary evidence of the beginning of the year at Christmas has been stated to be of A.D. 1027.[7]   But even centuries later the Roman

---

[1] Mansi, *Coll. Conc.*, IX., c. 803.

[2] *Opera Augustini*, ed. Benedict., V., app. 233.

[3] *Epistula*, xlii, Jaffé, *Bibl.*, III., 111.

[4] Grotefend, *Zeitrechnung des deutschen Mittelalters*, 1891, I., 22.

[5] Grotefend, *Zeitrechnung*, I., 22 ; Bernold, in his *Chronicon* (*Monumenta Germaniae, Scriptores*, V., 395), says : "Civilis sive vulgaris et lunaris annus in calendis Ianuarii . . . innovatur"; Burchard of Worms (+1025), in his *Decretalia*: "Fecisti quod quidam faciunt in calendis Ianuarii id est in octava natalis domini, qui ea sancta nocte filant, nent, consuunt et omne opus quodcumque incipere possunt, diabolo instigante propter novum annum incipiunt"; and an addition to a Canon of Pope Zacharias of 743 about the same subject runs: "Vel aliquid plus novi facere propter novum annum."

[6] Grotefend, *Zeitrechnung*, I., 205. Germany is the country which laid most stress on Christmas as the beginning of the year, and it is quite in keeping with that fact that even now in Germany a great number of customs are connected with Christmas, which in France and Great Britain belong to New Year.

[7] *Monumenta Germaniae, Scriptores*, XI., 265, in the writing of Wipo, the biographer of King Conrad II. (+1039): "Inchoante anno Nativitatis Christi, 1027, Rex Chuonradus iu Iporegia civitate natalem Domini celebravit." Brinkmeier, *Praktisches Handbuch der historischen Chronologie*, p. 89.

Church used that Roman beginning of the year for secular business.[1] If the Church was not successful in achieving its purpose, it was because its endeavours were soon divided. The 25th December of the year o having been made the beginning of a new era, it was by no means strange that that date also should begin the several years. But soon the consideration came in that the incarnation of Christ had really begun with His conception, which was dated on March 25th of the year o, and that style won considerable ground under the name of the Annunciation style,[2] so that within the Church two styles rivalled each other: the Annunciation style and the Nativity style, for both of which the name of Incarnation style can be proved to have been used.[3] The confusion thus arising was detrimental to Church purposes, and at last fatal to both styles, which in the course of the sixteenth century were completely beaten by January 1.[4] Nevertheless through the whole Middle Ages, for almost all matters in any way connected with the Church, December 25 was—however numerous may be the exceptions—the beginning of the year in Great Britain as well as on the Continent. In the British Isles it was not before the twelfth century that March 25 was taken as the commencement of the ecclesiastical year, which practice was not followed by civilians earlier than the fourteenth century.[5] Perhaps even Bishop Liberius, who created the festival of the Nativity of Christ, had not thought of replacing altogether by it the Calends of January. But when, two hundred years later, Dionysius Exiguus founded a new era on the year of Christ's birth, and the festival of the annual recurrence of the date of that fact grew a more and more important ecclesiastical institution, it was only the logical con-

---

[1] Grotefend, *Zeitrechnung*, I., 22, *Minutes of the Synod of Gnesen of* 1297: "Annum autem a tempore circumcisionis domini, prout tenet ecclesia, intelligimus computandum"; Gervasius of Canterbury (+1208): "Annus solaris secundum Romanorum traditionem et ecclesiae dei consuetudinem a calendis Ianuarii sumit initium."

[2] Grotefend, *Zeitrechnung*, I., 7.   [3] Grotefend, *Zeitrechnung*, I., 7.

[4] For the details, see in Grotefend's *Zeitrechnung*, I., 23.

[5] Sir Harris Nicolas, *The Chronology of History*, London, 1838, p. 41, from which day the opening of the year was transferred to January 1 as late as 1753. It had been so transferred in Scotland in 1600 (*Ibid.*, p. 43).

sequence that the year should come to be reckoned to begin with December 25 instead of January 1, a fact by which Christ's Nativity again rose in importance, so that, for the clergyman of the seventh and eighth centuries, it became the most prominent day of the whole year, and soon it could no longer be imagined that there had ever been a time when it was equally unknown to the Roman calendar, to the Christian religion, and to Germanic popular tradition.

CHAPTER XI.

A CENTURY after Roman Christianity had come to Britain, the largest part of it was christianized; and in one of its monasteries there lived and studied a youth of not yet twenty, the greatest genius of the early Anglic Church, Beda, whose life, probably, extended from A.D. 673 to 735, and to whom we owe some most important statements about the ancient Germanic calendar and ancient Germanic religion, to the extinction of which his life was devoted. Although he lived all his life in a Northern English monastery, he was in almost as close contact with Greco-Roman learning as any Goth had ever been, and was as good a Christian believer as any Roman could have been who spent his whole life in the immediate neighbourhood of the holy See. Put into a monastery at the age of seven, and brought up under the special care of Abbot Benedict, who was famous for his learning and the wide circle of his interests, he was estranged from the popular belief and customs of his home early enough to know comparatively little about them, and to care for them the less, the more he was taught to regard them as the relics of a creed which led its followers unmistakably to eternal damnation.

The passage bearing on our question is chapter xv. in his work *De Temporum Ratione*, a book consisting, with the exception of that one chapter, solely of facts gathered from various Latin and Greek treatises on similar subjects, and showing an amount of classical and astronomical learning which is astounding. The chapter is headed *De Mensibus Anglorum*, and runs thus :—

"But the peoples of the ancient Angles (for it does not seem to me

suitable to relate the yearly custom of other nations and to be silent about
that of my own nation) counted their months after the moon's course;
whence the latter, according to the habit of the Hebrews and Greeks, receive their name from the moon, the moon being called by them *Mona*,
and the month *Monath*. And their first month, which the Latins call
January, is called *Giuli*: then February, *Sol-monath*; March, *Rhed-monath*;
April, *Eostur-monath*; May, *Thri-mylchi*; June, *Lida*; July, in the same
way, *Lida*; August, *Vueod-monath*; September, *Haleg-monath*; October,
Vinter-fylleth; November, *Blot-monath*; December, *Giuli*, with the same
name by which January is called. They began their year from the eighth
day before the Calends of January [Dec. 25], on which we now celebrate
the birthday of the Lord. And they then called that night, which is now
sacrosanct to us, by a native word *Modranicht, i.e.*, night of mothers, as I
suppose, because of the ceremonies which they performed in it, keeping
watch all night. And when there was a common year, they gave to each
of the single seasons three months. But when there occurred an Embolism,
i.e., a year of thirteen lunar months, they affixed the supernumerary month
to the summer, so that then three months were called at the same time by
the name of *Lida*, and on that account that year was called *Thri-lidi*, having
four summer months, but the usual three months in each of the other
seasons. Again, they divided, in the main, the whole year into two seasons,
namely, into that of winter and that of summer; those six months in which
the days are longer than the nights to be given to summer, the other
six to winter. Hence, among other things, they called the month, with
which the winter times began, *Vuinter-fylleth*, this name being composed of
winter and full moon, of course, because from the full moon of that month
winter took its beginning. Neither is it out of the way, if I take the trouble
to interpret what is the meaning of the names of the other months of the
Angles. The months *Giuli* get their names from the turning round of the
sun towards the increasing of the day, because one of them precedes and
the other follows it. *Sol-monath* can be called the month of cakes, which
in it they offered to their gods; *Rhed-monath* is called after their goddess
Rheda, to whom they sacrificed in it; *Eostur-monath*, which is now interpreted as the month of Pasch, was once called from their goddess named

Eostre, to whom in it they celebrated festivals. After it we now name the time of Pasch, calling the joys of a new festivity by the wonted name of an ancient observance. *Thri-milchi* was thus called, because the domestic animals were in it milked three times a day. For such was, once upon a time, the fertility of Britain, or of Germany from which the nation of Angles entered Britain. *Lida* is called calm or navigable, because in each of the two months there is a genial serenity of the air and the sea is usually navigated. *Veod-monath* is month of tares, because these abound very much at that time. *Haleg-monath* is the month of worship. *Vuinter-fylleth* may be called by a newly-made name winter-full-moon. *Blot-monath* is the month of immolation, because in it they devoted to their gods their cattle which they intended to kill. Thanks to Thee, good Jesus, who, turning us away from these vanities, hast granted unto us to bring Thee the sacrifices of praise!"[1]

---

[1] Giles's edition of *The Complete Works of the Venerable Bede*, VI., *Scientific Tracts and Appendix*, London, 1843, but with the addition of the deviations from it in Grimm's text, from Jacob Grimm's *Geschichte der deutschen Sprache*, Vol. I., Sec. Ed., Leipzig, 1853, pp. 56, 57, who says expressly that he used several texts for forming his own. The deviations or additions are given in brackets. The italics are mine :—

" De Mensibus Anglorum. Antiqui autem Anglorum populi (neque enim mihi congruum videtur, aliarum gentium annalem observantiam dicere, et meae reticere) juxta cursum lunæ suos menses computavere : unde et a luna Hebræorum et Græcorum more nomen accipiunt. Si quidem apud eos luna *Mona*, mensis *Monath* appellatur [apellatur *Monath*]. Primusque eorum mensis, quem Latini Januarium vocant, dicitur *Giuli*. Deinde Februarius, *Sol-monath* : Martius, *Rhed-monath* [*Hredmonath*] : Aprilis, *Eostur-monath* : Maius, *Thri-mylchi* [*Thrimilci*] : Junius, *Lida* : Julius similiter *Lida* : Augustus, *Vueod-monath* [*Veodmonath*] : September, *Haleg-monath* : October, *Vuinter-fylleth* [*Vintirfyllith*] : November, *Blod-monath* [*Blotmonath*] : December, *Giuli*, eodem quo Januarius nomine vocatur. Incipiebant autem annum ab octavo Calendarum Januariarum die, ubi nunc natale Dominicum celebramus. Et ipsam noctem nunc nobis sacrosanctam, tunc gentili vocabulo *Modranicht* [*Modranecht*], id est, matrum noctem appellabant : [ ] ob causam ut suspicamur ceremoniarum, quas in ea pervigiles agebant. Et quotiescunque communis esset annus, ternos menses lunares singulis anni temporibus dabant. Cum vero Embolismus, hoc est, XIII. mensium lunarium annus occurreret, superfluum mensem æstati apponebant, ita ut tunc tres menses simul *Lida* nomine vocarentur, et ob id annus ille [ ] *Thri-lidi* [*thrilidus*] cognominabatur, habens IV. menses æstatis, ternes ut semper temporum cæterorum. Item [Iterum] principaliter annum totum in duo tempora, hyemis videlicet, et æstatis dis-partiebant : sex illos menses quibus longiores noctibus dies sunt æstati tribuendo, sex reliquos hyemi. Unde et mensem, quo hyemalia tempora incipiebant, *Vuinter-fylleth* [*Vintirfyllith*]

This is a very strange record indeed, and it is not easy to take up the proper attitude towards it. There is no doubt that, coming from so distinguished a scholar as Beda, it deserves most careful consideration and examination. One thing, however, is clear at first sight. When Beda speaks of the ancient Angles, there is no reason to doubt that he believed them to have had the views and customs he ascribes to them. But, on the other hand, it is quite plain that he could not have any direct information about their beliefs and rites, but simply inferred their views from what he knew about the Angles of his own time, either from direct observation or from hearsay. So all the allowance that can be made is that he heard the things he relates in his early childhood from people who were considerably older than he was, whilst some things he may have seen himself. Another feature of his report is remarkable: he divides his statement into two parts. In the first he simply gives what he regards as plain facts; in the second he gives explanations or speculations of his own, which certainly have their value as the opinions of so great a mind as Beda's, but cannot in any case count for more. He opens that part with the remark: "Neither is it out of the way if I take the trouble to interpret what is the meaning of the names of the other months of the Angles."

---

appellabant, composito nomine ab hyeme et plenilunio, quia videlicet a plenilunio ejusdem mensis hyems sortiretur initium. Nec ab re est, si et cætera mensium eorum quid significent nomina [eorum nomina quid significent] interpretari curemus. Menses *Giuli* a conversione solis in auctum diei, quia unus eorum præcedit, alius subsequitur, nomina accipiunt. *Sol-monath* dici potest mensis placentarum, quas in eo Diis suis offerebant : *Rhed-monath* [*Hred-monath*] a Dea illorum *Rheda* [*Hreda*], cui in illo sacrificabant, nominatur : *Eostur-monath*, qui nunc Paschalis mensis interpretatur, quondam a Dea illorum quæ *Eostre* vocabatur, et cui in illo festa celebrabant, nomen habuit : a cujus nomine nunc Paschale tempus cognominant, consueto antiquæ observationis vocabulo gaudia novæ solemnitatis vocantes. *Tri-milchi* [*trimilci*] dicebatur quod tribus vicibus in eo per diem pecora mulgebantur. Talis enim erat quondam ubertas Britanniæ, vel Germaniæ de qua in Britanniam natio intravit Anglorum. *Lida* dicitur blandus, sive navigabilis [navigabilis eo quod] quod in utroque [utroque illo mense] mense et blanda sit serenitas aurarum, et navigari soleant æquora. *Vueod-monath* [*Veodmonath*] mensis zizaniorum quod ea tempestate maxime abundent. *Haleg-monath* mensis sacrorum. *Vuinter-fylleth* [*Vintirfyllith*] potest dici composito novo nomine hyemeplenilunium [hiemiplenium]. *Blot-monath* mensis immolationum, quia [quod] in ea pecora quæ occisuri erant, Diis suis vovebant. Gratias [gratia] tibi, bone Jesu, qui nos ab his vanis avertens, tibi sacrificia laudis offerre donasti."

There is no doubt that Beda's record contains facts of great antiquity. The most striking thing in it is certainly the assertion that the Angles, even about his time, had a common name for December and January, and one for June and July, namely, *Giuli* and *Lida*, which means that they had still to some extent preserved the old three-score-day tides of Oriental extraction, which they had used before they came into contact with the Roman pre-Julian calendar, the basis of which was the moon and months. *Giuli* we know to have been in use two hundred years earlier among the Goths, *i.e.*, an Eastern Germanic tribe living as far distant as Italy from the Western Germanic Angles, though, according to the Gothic calendar of the Bobbio MS., *Iuleis* then meant November and December, and not December and January. This latter difficulty we have solved already by showing that the old Germanic three-score-day tides began about the middle of the Roman months, so that *Iuleis* covered approximately the time from November 15 to January 15, and was, among the Goths, shifted a fortnight backwards so as to correspond to Roman November and December, and among the Angles a fortnight forwards, so as to cover December and January. *Lida*, the name for the middle of summer, is new to us, and we ought to be grateful to Beda for preserving it. That exactly four months are between *Giuli* and *Lida* shows that no confusion has taken place, but that two other three-score-day tides have to stand between them. When Beda, however, tells us that in a leap year, as in the pre-Julian calendar, a whole month was inserted, and that the leap year therefore was called *Thrilidi* and the thirteenth month the third *Lida*, this state of things cannot be old, but must be the consequence of the intro-duction of the pre-Julian calendar. For *Lida* was not at all the name of a month among the ancient Angles, but of a three-score-day tide, so that thirty days added would have meant only half a *Lida*, and there would have been one *Lida* and a half, and not three *Lidas*. Besides, the Angles having no months, but only three-score-day tides, could not insert a month in a leap year, but, had they inserted anything at all, would have inserted a whole three-score-day tide every sixth year, just as the later Scandinavians objected to the insertion of a single leap day, but waited till the past leap days amounted to a week, then inserting a whole week at a time, so that the year always began with the same week-day, *i.e.*, Thursday.

However much we owe Beda for the preservation of those two ancient names of three-score-day tides, *Giuli* and *Lida*, we cannot conceal from ourselves the fact that the very names of those two tides amount to a complete proof that the other eight month-names which Beda mentions *are not old*. So we have a right to express our regret that Beda was not, by the existence of two names for three-score-day tides, put upon the right track towards an understanding of the ancient Germanic year, and that he did not take all possible trouble to find out the names of the other four three-score-day tides, which, together with *Giuli* and *Lida*, formed a complete Germanic year of, probably, three hundred and sixty or three hundred and sixty-six days. In his time it should have been possible to ascertain something about them. Perhaps even all of them were still in use among the country population of the north of England, and some ingenuity and perseverance might have sufficed to gather them.

The eight month-names which Beda mentions, beside *Giuli* and *Lida*, are not old. It is, indeed, not too difficult to see that. One of them is called *Thrimilci*, a name which shows a very suspicious parallelism to *Thrilidi*. However important a fact it must be for a tribe consisting of herdsmen and hunters that the cattle can be milked three times a day, we have Beda's own word for it that, in his time, it was not a fact at all, but only a legend, a legend of a golden age in the far-away past, when such was "the fertility of Britain, or of Germany from which the nation of Angles entered Britain." A second month is said to bear the ingenious name of *Winter-fylleth*, or winter full moon, which is not a month-name at all, but merely the name of a date from which the beginning of winter was supposed to be reckoned. Besides, this looks rather like a counterpart to the calculation of the Christian Easter-festival, and would amount to the fact that the winter, the beginning of which was, in common Germanic times, at the same time the beginning of the year, began in the middle of the month! The remaining six month-names are compounds of *mânôth*, and thus characterize themselves as being late formations. No scholar now would ascribe any considerable age to the Germanic month-

names, since even Professor Weinhold, who has overlooked the fact that
the Germanics received the institution of months from the Romans, pro-
fesses that there were no month-names in common Germanic times.
Besides, they can only be taken as representative of a purely local
denomination of months. Neither *Rugern* (August ?), which we know
from an even older source,[1] nor *hlȳd-mônath*, or *hlyda* for March;[2] *seár-
mônadh, midsumor* for June; *mædmônath* for July; or *hearfestmônath* for
September, which occur in almost contemporaneous literature, are amongst
them. Nay, they contain scarcely a single month-name which appears a
second time in Anglo-Saxon.[3] Of the six month-names composed with
mânôth Beda apparently knows the right etymology of only two, these
being *Blôtmânôth* (November), the month of immolation, or, as he says, the
month in which the Angles "devoted to their gods their cattle which
they intended to kill," and *Haleg-mânôth* (September), holy-month, or month
of worship, a name probably resting on a Christian foundation. As regards
the etymology of the other four, he makes vague guesses. That August
should be called *Veod-manoth*, *i.e.*, "month of tares, because these abound
very much at that time," is very doubtful, and a very poor explanation
indeed. How *Sol-manoth* (February) should come to mean month of cakes
nobody can say, there being no such word meaning anything like cake in
any Germanic language. When he has exhausted all resources, he takes
refuge in the assumption that the names he cannot explain are names of
imaginary goddesses. *Eostre* comes from a root *auzrô*, which is cognate
to Latin *aurora* and Greek ἠώς, and means something like spring.
Professor Weinhold says: "I explain *eôsturmônad* simply as spring-month,
notwithstanding Beda's *dea Eostre*, in whom I do not believe, so long as
it has not been proved that the principal feast of the Church could be
called after a heathen goddess. Doubts I also entertain as regards his
dea Hreda, who is said to have given a name to March. That Beda's

---

[1] King Vihtraed's Laws, A.D. 696.   [2] Martius *rêdhe, Hlȳda* heálic Menologium, 37.

[3] *Hlȳda* for March comes dangerously near to *Lîda* for June-July. If February and
March, or originally January 15 to March 15, were *Lîda*, the insertion of a leap month
would almost take place on the same date as it did in the pre-Julian calendar, where it
was inserted into February, which, of course, was impracticable in the highest degree.

strength did not lie in etymology is shown by his explanation of *solmônad* as the month of offering cakes, and his remark on *Giuli*";[1] and at another place he states,[2] "I, at least, regard Beda's explanation of *Hredmônad* and *Eôstre-mônad* as bad guesses, and do not believe in any goddesses *Hreda* and *Eôstre* (which doubts have, as I observe, been uttered before by Leo, *Rectitudines*, p. 206)." I should not wonder, if in *Hreda* and *Eostre* names of two old three-score-day tides were preserved, which had in Beda's time become limited to the time of a month. They can be as little explained as *Giuli* or *Lida* (*Hlyda*).

Whilst Beda knows of a dual division of the Anglic year, which was bound to be familiar to him on the ground of the existence of the two terms *winter* and *summer* together covering the whole course of a year, he knows nothing whatever of a tri-partition and the legal institutions resting on it, although that tri-partition is a fact warranted as well as any from the early history of the Germanic tribes. Instead, he gives us a description of the Roman year of the Julian calendar, which is quartered by solstices and equinoxes, a statement which is the more extraordinary, as, from what he said before, it is quite plain that he thought the Angles had a lunar year of 354 days, into which now and then (presumably every third year) a whole intercalary month had to be inserted, just as under the reign of the Roman pre-Julian calendar. His words practically amount to the following proposition : Whilst the Anglic year, according to his own description, was a lunar year, it yet began at the winter solstice. This, of course, means that it was not a lunar year, which is quite out of the question, since we not only know that the Germanics began their year with the beginning of winter and not at the winter solstice, but that, in addition, the common Germanic language possessed not even a term for solstice; nay, that, when the Western Germanics had got the term and meaning of solstice from the Romans, they never used it for the winter solstice, but solely for June 24, all through the Middle Ages. Nor is this all. According to Beda's description, the Anglic year did not begin at the real solstice (which A.D. 701 fell at four o'clock in the morning of December

---

[1] *Die deutschen Monatnamen*, Halle, 1869, p. 4. [2] *Ibid.*, p. 24.

K

18),[1] but on December 25, the date which Julius Caesar had erroneously fixed for the solstice. When he comes to speculations confessedly his own, the value of his statements becomes still more doubtful. He says that the Angles called December and January *Giuli*, after "the turning round of the sun towards the increasing of the day, because one of them precedes and the other follows." This can only mean that the Anglic *Giuli* extended from about November 25 to January 24, so that the first *Giuli* ended at December 25, a statement contradictory to the other statement that the Anglic months were identical with the Roman months. Further, we know that the Gothic *Iuleis* tide extended from November 1 to December 31, and that the common Germanic *Iuleis* tide probably extended from November 15 to January 15, and that, consequently, December 25 was by no means the middle of it. So if Beda means to say, that *Giuli* was originally the name of the winter solstice, and that from it December and January received their names (a statement, however, which he himself gives merely as his own supposition, or interpretation, as he chooses to call it, and by no means as a warranted fact), he may without any hesitation be said to be wrong—the more so, as he goes on to say that the day of the alleged solstice (to which he ascribes in one sentence the name *Giuli*) was called *modraniht*, *i.e.*, night of mothers, so that we may conclude from this that it was not called *Giuli*.

Such a mass of mutually contradictory facts cannot be explained by being ascribed to Beda's inaccurate observation and expression, though he may not have understood absolutely all he was told, and not have expressed things as carefully as he might have done on a Christian dogmatic subject. That the names he gives, or at least names similar to them, were used within the neighbourhood of Beda's home in his own or his parents' time nobody will dispute. But he apparently received from those sources merely facts, and no theory with them. The theory he must have formed out of what he thought the bearing of the facts. And he was bound to misunderstand the bulk of his facts, because he mistook them for ancient Anglic customs, whilst, in reality, they were the product of a strange shifting of old elements under the influence of the pre-Julian Roman

---

[1] I owe all calculations about the real dates of solstices to Prof. Hermann Jacobi of Bonn.

calendar, followed by the Julian calendar, and by the attempts of the Church to make the supposed night of the winter solstice, which had been made Christ's birthday, the beginning of the year as well. So in Beda's time there were four distinct layers, one above the other, in the popular notions about the course of the year, and if we bear this in mind all the seeming difficulties are elucidated. Whilst the observation of new moons and full moons among the Germanics had nothing to do with their theory of the course of the year, Beda thought it had. Whilst they owed to the Romans their leap month and the conception of months altogether, he mistook these things for a genuine Anglic growth. Whilst the Germanic year began at the beginning of winter, he made the Angles begin their year in the middle of it. Whilst the Germanics knew nothing of solstices and equinoxes, Beda based his theory of the Germanic year on them, and put into the centre of all his theory the 25th day of December, which was bound to be dear to him, both as the alleged day of the solstice according to the Julian calendar, and as the day of Christ's birth, venturing even the suggestion that originally that day was called *Giuli*, and that December and January had got their common name from it.

That in this suggestion he was wrong, appears from the fact that, except in the Anglo-Saxon version of Beda himself, there is no case known in which December 25 is called Yule in the three centuries which followed Beda's life, *i.e.*, up to the eleventh century. And even then there are few cases which are not doubtful for one reason or another. Either the MSS. are of too late date, or the original is not preserved, or interpolations are suspected. This state of things is the more strange, as December 25 is frequently referred to, *e.g.*, in the *Saxon Chronicle*. But it invariably is called by the calendar term *midwinter, midwinter's mass,* or *to Nativited,* neither the Parker MS. nor the Laud MS. of the *Saxon Chronicle* containing a single *Yule*. *Geôhel, geôhhel-dæg, geôhol, geôhhol, gebl, giûl, iûl* are the forms appearing in the eleventh and twelfth centuries. When towards the end of the eleventh century *Jôl*,[1] with the popular meaning of December 25,

---

[1] There is no doubt that Old Northern *jôl*, Original Northern *jul*, Gothic *Jiuleis* is not identical, and has absolutely nothing to do with A.S. *hveol*, Old Northern *hvel*, English

sets in, it is apparently due to Scandinavian influence, where that word had
come to mean Christmas through Hakon, King of Norway, who reigned
from 940 to 963, and had shifted to December 25 the date of an old
February festival, which in the course of time had come to be celebrated
between January 9 and 14, with the view of celebrating it on the same

---

wheel; for the Anglo-Saxon word corresponding to Old Northern *jól* is *Geola, gehhol,
geohhol* (Kluge, *Englische Studien*, IX., p. 311 ss.). Deriving with Kluge (*Englische
Studien*, IX., 311) and Bugge (*Arkiv for Nordisk Filologi*, IV., 135), *jól*, A.S. *gehhol*,
from an original Germanic **jehwela*, and declaring with Bugge the latter as identical with
Latin *joculus*, Professor Mogk (Paul's *Grundriss der germanischen Philologie*, Strassburg,
1891, Vol. I., p. 1125) finds this denomination as the "gay festival" appropriate, because
masquerades, especially in the shape of animals, are the custom then. But, apart from
the fact that I regard the establishment of a relation between *joculus* and **jehwela* as a
very bold etymological attempt : the mummery and masquerade at the beginning of January
are missing just where that time is called Yule. These usages were a Roman Calends-of-
January custom, and were on Germanic soil limited to Gaul and to the extreme west of
Germany, where the Roman influence was strongest. Professor Weinhold adduces the
Cyprian term 'Ιούλιος, which is assumed to have covered the time from December 22 to
January 23, and which he, as Grimm's follower, boldly derives from the month of July,
maintaining that the name of the month of the summer solstice (which, however, is June!)
was transferred to the time of the winter solstice ! He assumes that the Germanics did
the same, but fails to perceive that, as the name is found among Goths, Northern Germanics, and Anglo-Saxons, we should in this case have to assume that it had been
received at a time when Goths, Scandinavians, and Anglo-Frisians spoke one language.
He further overlooks the fact that, in the Germanic languages, it is not a month-name
at all, but the name of an Oriental three-score-day tide, so that the alleged analogy
with the Cyprian name—which is by no means proved to have had anything to do with
the Roman month of July—does not even hold good, though the whole argument is based
upon it (Weinhold, *Deutsche Monatnamen*, Halle, 1869, p. 4; *Deutsche Jahrteilung*,
1862, p. 15; K. Fr. Hermann, *Über griechische Monatskunde*, Göttingen, 1844, p. 64;
Grimm, *Geschichte der deutschen Sprache*, 1848, I., pp. 78 and 106, 107). The form of
the Greek name varies considerably, as was shown above. In some cases it is not clear
which month is meant. Perhaps, we have, as I suggested before, to do there with a
relic of the same Oriental six-fold division of the year as among the Germanics, and,
consequently, with the same name for November and December. Perhaps that institution,
like the whole sexagesimal system of notation, is of Babylonian origin, the sixty minutes
of the hour and the sixty seconds of the minute being perfect parallels to the sixty days
of the tide. The *sari* and *sossi* of ancient Babylon, which lived in the sixty shekels to
the *mina* and the sixty *minas* to the talent, and elsewhere, are contained in them. The *saros*,
or sixty, is at the basis of all. Compare *Notes and Queries*, Ninth Series, III., p. 136; and
Max Müller, *Chips from a German Workshop*, New Ed., Vol. I., London, 1894, pp. 202 ss., *Some*

day as that on which the Christians celebrated the birth of Christ. In England the new term for Christmas became popular in the twelfth century, but in Scotland not before the thirteenth and fourteenth centuries, so that it is only in the fifteenth, that mentions of it in Scotland become very frequent.

The laws of King Alfred, composed about 888, ordained that whoever stole on Sunday, or at Christmas, or at Easter, or on Holy Thursday, or on Rogation days, or during Lent-fast, should be fined twice as much as he who stole at other times.[1] Here *on Gehhol* apparently does not mean the day of Nativity, but the time about that day in so far as it was proclaimed holy by the Church, which would not be longer than twelve nights. So it shows a decided narrowing of the old term which once covered a three-score-day tide, and, later, apparently a single month, but it does

---

Lessons of Antiquity. Still more uncertain is the connection of *Giuli* with the name of a Greek Song or exclamation, Ἰουλος:

$$\text{Δενδαλίδας τευχοῦσα καλὰς ἤειδεν Ἰούλους}$$

(preparing the salted flour she sang the pleasant *Iuloi*). Jamieson, *Etymological Dictionary of the Scottish Language*, under "Yule" says: "Didymus and Athenaeus assert that the hymn was in honour of Ceres," and the same thing is intimated by Theodoret in his work, *De Materia et Mundo*, when he says: "Let us not sing the *Iiulos* to Ceres, nor the *Dithyrambos* to Bacchos."

[1] Thorpe's *Ancient Laws and Institutes of England*, London, 1840, Vol. I., p. 64, v.: "Sethe staladh ôn Sunnan niht. oththe on Gehhol. oththe on Eastron. oththe on thone Halgan Dunres dæg. on Gang-dagas. thara gehwelc we willadh sie twy-bote. swa on Lencten-fæsten." Thorpe's *Ancient Laws*, II., 450 (*Alfredi Legum Versio Antiqua*) v.: "Qui furatur die Dominica, vel in sancto Natali, vel in Pascha, vel in Sancto die Iovis, in Ascensione Domini, in quolibet eorum volumus dupliciter emendandum sit, sicut in quadragesimali jejunio." Christmas was to be held for twelve festival days (*freols*), whilst Easter was held for fourteen, and in the harvest, a whole week before St. Mary-mass was celebrated. Thorpe's *Ancient Laws*, Vol. I., p. 92, xliii.: "Be Mæsse Daga Freolse: Eallum frioum monnum thas dagas sien forgifene butan theowum mannum ond esne-wyrhtum. XII. dagas on Gehhol. ond thone dæg the Crist thone deofol oferswidhde. ond Scs Gregorius gemynd-dæg. ond. VII. dagas to Eastron ond. VII. ofer ond an dæg æt Sce Petres tíde and Sce Paules. ond on hærfeste tha fullan wican ær Scta Marian mæssan. ond æt Eallra haligra weordhunge anne dæg. ond. IIII. Wodnesdagas on. IIII. Ymbren-wican. Dheowum monnum eallum sien forgifen tham the him leofost sie to sellanne. æghwæt thæs the him ænig mon for Godes noman geselle. Oththe hie on ænegum hiora hwilsticcum geearnian mægen."

not yet mean December 25 alone, a sense which it does not seem to have
reached before the eleventh century.[1]

It is the same thing with the first documentary evidence of *Iól*.   In it the
term also means the holy tide about *Natale Domini*.   It occurs in Edward
the Confessor's writ of privileges to the Abbey of Ramsey, co. Huntingdon,[2]

---

[1] Unfortunately of the four manuscripts which contain Aelfred's laws, three are of the
tenth century and one is of the twelfth century, the MS. British Museum, Nero EI
belonging to the end of the tenth century, and the Textus Roffensis to the twelfth century
(Wülker, *Grundriss zur Geschichte der angelsächsischen Literatur*, Leipzig, 1885, p. 399).
How cautious one has to be in order not to take later expressions for older ones, the
following example may show, in which later manuscripts replace *middan-wintra* by *geolum*
and *fires Dryhtnes gebyrd-tide*. A note added to Theodore's *Book of Penitence* (*Liber
Poenitentialis Theodori Archiepiscopi Cantuariensis Ecclesiae*), ed. in Thorpe's *Ancient Laws
and Institutes of England*, London, 1840, Vol. II., p. 46, cap. xxxviii., § 14 : " In illa
die ante Natale Domini hora nona expleta missa, id est vigilia Domini, manducant Romani ;
Græci vero dicta vespere missa cœnant," mentions the different customs of the Roman
and Greek churches as regards fasting on Christmas eve, without giving any particulars
about what is to be done. Whilst the Greeks eat not before six p.m., the Romans take
food after three p.m. ; and Ecbert's *Confessional and Penitential* (*Confessionale et Poeni-
tentiale Ecberti, Archiepiscopi Eboracensis*) ed. in Thorpe's *Ancient Laws and Institutes
of England*, London, 1840, Vol. II., pp. 162, 163, gives details about the fast time before
Christmas : " Legitima jejunia tria sunt in anno ; unum pro omni populo, ut illud XL.
diebus ante Pascha, cum decimam partem annuam solvimus ; et illud XL. diebus ante
Natale Domini, cum totus populus pro se orant, et orationes legunt ; et illud XL. diebus
post Pentecosten ; Dhreo æfæstenu syndon on geare . ân ofer eall folc . swa that XL. njhta
foran to Eastron . thonne we thone teodhan sceat thæs gearces lysad . and that XL. nihta ær
geolum . thonne gebiddedh hine eall that werod fore . and orationes rædadh . and that XL.
nihta ofer Pentecosten." Instead of "geolum," which is the reading of O, Y has
" middan-wintra," and Bx has " fires Dryhtnes zebyrd-tide," while X and Y add the
following : " On tham ærran dæge æt geolum [Y, middan-wintra] æt nône sidhdhan mæsse
bydh gesungen . heo gereordiadh Romane.   Grecas to æfenne . thonne æfen bidh gesungen and
mæsse . thonne fôdh hi to mete." Of these O is a small folio MS. of *Corpus Christi*, C.C.
190 (L XII.) ; Y is a small narrow volume of the eleventh century, *Bodleiana*, Laud, F
17 ; B is a tenth century octavo MS., *Corpus Christi*, 265 (K 2) ; X is a MS. of about 1000
A.D. belonging to the Bibliothèque des Ducs de Bourgogne ; O, which Thorpe, contrary
to his custom, has wisely abstained from dating, belongs to the twelfth century, and is
said to have been given to Exeter Cathedral by Bishop Leofric.

[2] John Earle, *A Hand-Book to the Land-charters and other Saxonic Documents*, Oxford,
1888, pp. 344, 345.

to be dated between 1042 and 1066, but preserved only in a twelfth
century manuscript.[1]

---

[1] *Cottoniana*, Otho. *B.*, XIV., f.˜257 : "inne Iol and inne Easterne and inne dha hâli
wuca æt Gangdagas.," "in natali dominico, in pascha, et in sancta hebdomada rogationum."
In the *Exchequer Rolls of Scotland* for the years 1264 till 1359 (*Rotuli Scaccarii Regum
Scotorum*, ed. by J. Stuart and G. Burnett, Vol. I., 1264-1359, Edinburgh, 1878), the
word "Yule" never occurs; while in the *Accounts of the Lord High Treasurer of Scotland* from 1473 to 1498 (*Compota Thesaurariorum Regum Scotorum*, ed. by Th. Dickson,
Vol. I., 1473-1498, Edinburgh, 1877), it is mentioned many times. Even very much
later, Yule by no means referred to Christmas day exclusively, but to the whole season.
The History and Chronicles of Scotland, written in Latin by Hector Boece, and translated
by John Bellenden, Edinburgh, 1821, Vol. II., p. 340, Lib. XIII., chap. xiv. (under
King Alexander II., A.D. 1222): "In the third yeir eftir, the Erle of Caithnes come to
king Alexander, quhen he wes sittand with his modir, on the Epiphany day, at his yuill,
and desirit grace." Hollinshead, in his *Scottish Chronicle*, in which he followed Bellenden,
even says (under A.D. 1222): "As King Alexander with his mother Ermingard were
sitting at their banket, on the 12th day in Christmas, otherwise called Yule," etc.
Instances from the fourteenth and fifteenth centuries, of Yule as identical with Christmas,
are :

> "Till Auld Meldrum thai yeid thair way,
> And thar with thair men logyt thai,
> Before Vhule ewyn a nycht but mar :
> A thowsand, trow I, weile thai war."
>
> Barbour, IX., 204, MS. (+ A.D. 1375).

> "A-pon a Vhule-ewyn alsua
> Wyttalis, that to the Kyng suld ga
> Of Ingland, that at Melros lay,
> He met rycht stowtly in the way."
>
> Wyntown, VIII., 36, 39 (+ circa A.D. 1430).

The spelling in the last quarter of the fifteenth century is Yule, Ywle, Yole, and Yowle
(*Compota Thesaurariorum Regum Scotorum*, *Accounts of the Lord High Treasurer of Scot-
land*, ed. by Thomas Dickson, Vol. I., 1473-1498, Edinburgh, 1877 : Yule, p. 17 ;
Ywle, p. 99; Yole, p. 239; Yowle, p. 245), and the term was used as identical with
Christmas. P. 17, "fra Pasche to Yule," from Easter to Christmas ; p. 99, again Ywle, a
short time before Christmas ; p. 239 gives quite a number of points of time, from "the
VIII. day of November" and "Sanct Martinis day" to "Sanct Nicholas day" (on which
also "tua Sanct Nicholas bischoppis" appear who receive "XXXVI. s."), "Sanct Androis day,"
and "Yole," the festival at which day is called "the Kingis Yole." We find there the
terms used : "upone Yole day"; "Sonday eftir Yole," and (p. 240) simply "eftir Yole."
On p. 240 also occur "vpone Newger daye" and "on Vphaliday"; while p. 241 has
"on Candilmess day," "on Sanct Patrikis day," "agane Pasche," "before Pasche,"
"on Pasche day" (twice); and p. 242, "vpone Sanct James daye," "vpone Sanct

Beda's report contains another item which must be touched upon. He says, the ancient Angles "began their year from the eighth day before the Calends of January, on which we now celebrate the birthday of the Lord. And they then called that night, which is now sacrosanct to us, by a native word, *Modranicht*, *i.e.*, night of mothers, as I suppose because of the ceremonies which they performed in it, keeping watch all night." However critical the attitude one may take up towards Beda's etymologies and theories about the course of the year, there is no getting over the fact of the word *modranicht* being applied in his time to December 25, a word which admits of one translation only, that translation being: night of mothers. This word has been the centre of much discussion, and the object of a number of very divergent explanations. Jacob Grimm thought of the mothers of *Heimdallr*, of whom Scandinavian poetry tells us; others thought of the mother of gods worshipped by a Germanic tribe, according to Tacitus;[1] others of a Germanic belief in a newly-born sun. But all these suggestions have lately been driven into the background by another theory started by Professor Eugen Mogk of Leipzig. He supposed Beda's word to refer to the *Matronae* of Romano-Germanic inscriptions,

Michaelis day," and "the VI. day of Nouember." As a family name Yule (Yole) appears in the *Exchequer Rolls of Scotland*, Vol. IV., 1406-1436, pp. 411, 621, 675 and elsewhere. In 1494 at the Royal Court of Scotland some timber was bought from Jonete Gule. Item, for III.** burdis fra Jonete Gule III. li. XV. s. (*Compota Thesaurariorum Regum Scotorum, Accounts of the Lord High Treasurer of Scotland*, ed. by Thomas Dickson, Edinburgh, 1877, p. 252).   As late as 1636 datings occur like "decimo tertio die mensis Januarii nuncupato *lie twentie day of Yule*" (*Charters and other Documents relating to the City of Glasgow*, A.D. 1175-1649, Part II., edited by Sir James D. Marwick, Glasgow, 1894, p. 386, "Charter by King Charles I."). The cases in which Yule unmistakably means December 25 to the exclusion of any adjoining days are very rare and very late. A case from A.D. 1535 is, *e.g.*, the following taken from *Extracts from the Records of The Burgh of Edinburgh* (A.D. 1528-1557), Edinburgh, 1871, p. 71: "It is statute and ordanit [be] the provest baillies and counsale that all nichtboures within this towne, merchandis and craftismen, as thai ar of power, till furnis cortise till pas and convoy the provest fra the kirk till his awin hows after evin sang in the haly dayes of Yule, New Yeir day, and Vphaly day, vnder the payne of xviii. shillingis to be tane of thame that wanttis cortise, and at every deykin haif power till poynd his craft for the samyn."

[1] "Matrem deûm venerantur Aestii; insigne superstitiorum formas aprorum gestant" (*Germania*, chap. xlv.).

whom he identifies with Old Scandinavian *dísar*, and to a cult of the dead about that time of the year.[1] He, besides, takes Beda's name *modra-nicht* as a collective singular denoting a number of nights, a whole holy tide, devoted to the dead, the female genii of protection, the souls of the deceased, whilst Beda decidedly speaks of a single night only. But if one goes so far, one may go further. In classical literature even there is a mention of deities called *the Mothers*. Plutarch tells us[2] that the town of Engyon, of Sicily, was celebrated for the appearance of goddesses who were called the *Mothers*. Such *Mothers*, mostly three in number, appear rather frequently in inscriptions in Germanic countries which had come into close contact with the Romans, while they are lacking entirely in Scandinavia and Iceland.[3] Professor Mogk's opinion is untenable, because

---

[1] In his *Mythologie* in Paul's *Grundriss der germanischen Philologie*, Strassburg, 1891, I., p. 1126.

[2] In his *Marcellus*, chap. xx.

[3] Dr. Collingwood Bruce, in his *Handbook to the Roman Wall: a Guide to Tourists traversing the Barrier of the Lower Isthmus*, 3rd edition, London, Longmans, 1885, says p. 155 s.: "It may be well also to mention that the worship of the *Deae Matres*—the good mothers—whose name it was not lucky to mention, was much in vogue with the Romans of a later age, especially with the Gothic portion of the Roman community. Several statues of them have been found here; two of these, shown in the woodcuts on the previous page (155), are now preserved in the Museum of the Newcastle Society of Antiquaries. These figures usually occur in triplets." On p. 201 another statue of one of the *Deae Matres* is mentioned, which was found at Birdoswald, the Amboglanna of the Romans, the twelfth station of the Roman Wall of England. It is represented by Dr. Bruce in a woodcut on p. 202. The body of the figure was, in 1885, kept in a farmhouse, while the head was preserved in the Museum of Newcastle. Other examples are contained in the *Corpus Inscriptionum Britannicarum*, Vol. VII., *Additamenta quarta*, p. 282, No. 844, a stone of Camulodunum now kept in the Museum there. It has the inscription: "Matribus Sulevis Similis Atti f(ilius) ci(vis) Cant(ius) v(otum) l(ibens) s(olvit)." Another inscription (927) is devoted to the Domestic Mothers: "Civliv Crescesi Matribus Domesticis vs m. l." (found in St. Mary's Convent, Eburacum). Nos. 980 and 992, 993, seem to belong to the same group, and perhaps even 1017: "(Mat?)ribus com-(munibus?) (p)ro salute de(curiae?) (A)ur(elii) Severi," because there is another stone devoted, "Matribus Com(munibus)" (1032); 1054, "Matribus . . . ntius," 1081; a part of an altar having the inscription, "Matribus tr(a)mar(inis)," 1091, which shows the syllables "Ma," "SA" may be attributed to *Mars* as well as to the *Matres*. Perhaps the most important inscription is 1186: "I(ovi) O(ptimo) M(aximo) Tarami Belatucabro

it rests on the assumption that there once was a Germanic dead festival about the middle of winter. But it was shown above that the facts which seem to support such an opinion do not in reality support it. For at their basis is the Egyptio-Roman "Table of Fortune," and no sacrifice to the dead. He who dares to put that interpretation upon Beda's words may assume that in it these deities are referred to. But it is certain that he has not properly read Beda's words.

Beda himself says that he does not know why the Angles called that night *modranicht*, and expressly gives his explanation as a supposition of his own, introduced by the words "as I suppose" (*ut suspicamur*). The allusion he makes by way of explanation is not to goddesses called *The Mothers*, as he speaks of a goddess *Hreda* or a goddess *Eostre* in the same chapter; but just as he derives the name *Solmanoth* from the *cake* baked, or the name *Blotmanoth* from the *immolation* made, so he ascribes the name *modranicht* to the *ceremonies* which were performed, and by no means to the object of veneration, a certain deity. Whilst he elsewhere clearly states the *tertium comparationis*, he in this case refrains from it, simply remarking that the name *modranicht* is probably due to certain ceremonies of which he knows, but does not care to inform the reader. There is only one explanation tenable: these ceremonies were of a maternal character, being either exercised by human mothers, or having as their chief constituent something maternal or referring to the natural functions of motherhood. Customs of that kind are certainly found in the Roman *Matronalia* and in the Calends-of-January customs on the banks of the Rhine.

The Romans celebrated, on the first of March, the *Calendae Feminarum*, the so-called *Matronalia*, at which the married ladies of Rome went to the Esquiline Hill to the temple of Lucina—celebrating the festival of matrimony.[1] If that festival had been brought to Britain by Roman legions, it could, when the beginning of the year was, by the Julian calendar, shifted

---

Mogvnto . . . Movno . . . Deabus Matribus Deae Svriae Fortunae ceterisq(ue) Britannorum Dis Deabusq(ue) C(um) verius Fortis(simis) Trib(us) Coh(ortibus) I(ulius) Ael(ianus), Britonn(icus) V(otum) S(olvit)."

[1] Ovid, *Fasti*, III., 179 ss.

from March 1 to January 1, have been removed with it to the Calends of January, and, when the Christian birthday of Christ, on December 25, began to compete with the Calends of January, have been transferred to that day. Something similar, indeed, seems to have taken place on the banks of the Rhine in Germany, where on the Calends of January, men went about in women's dresses, using that disguise as a means for all kinds of sexual transgressions, or women went about in hides of hinds, whilst men wore hides of stags, licentiousness of every description prevailing.[1] But I do not think that Beda thought of things like these. Had he done so, he would probably have used stronger language, mentioning the abominable disgrace of heathendom. And there certainly is something decidedly Christian in the report, the *keeping watch all night*, a peculiarity of the early Church which again and again occurs at Christmas eve and at Pasch eve, and about which elaborate rules existed. If the custom he referred to was Christian, or might be considered as Christian, or as happening even in a Christian Anglic community, by those who might read his record, the reserve Beda uses in this case would be explained only too well. And there were indeed such usages in the early Church, ceremonies which had evolved out of the Roman Calends usage of preparing and eating cakes with certain observances. These had got into very close connection to motherhood, producing a kind of obscene cult, in which the motherhood of the Virgin Mary and the peculiarities of Christ's birth were not only made the object of veneration, but were expressed in visible symbols in the shape of cakes. In such celebrations human mothers no doubt took the leading part. From the night of birth to the night of motherhood and the night of mothers there are only two small steps. That the night of the birth of a child should be dedicated to all mothers or to motherhood is only natural. But over and above, we can prove the existence of such a cult, exactly contemporaneous with Beda, because it was forbidden by the Council of Trullus, A.D. 706. The development of a

---

[1] *Homilia De Sacrilegiis*, ed. by Caspari, Christiania, 1886: "Et illud quid turpe est! Viri tunicis mulierum induentes se feminas videri volunt." See the list of cases quoted in the above chapter headed the "Calends of January."

cult of the Virgin Mary instead of that of her divine son, is clearly traceable in the Councils of the early Church. Seeking for ever-new objects of veneration and supplying the "eternal feminine," which was found lacking in the new religion, orientals and occidentals gave visible expression to all kinds of wild fancies about the act of Christ's birth, so that the Church had again and again to declare that he was born quite unlike human babies,[1] and above all, without an afterbirth, so that it was quite senseless of people to bake, divide, and eat a cake in honour of the afterbirth of the immaculate Virgin. Later, even the confinement of the Virgin seems to have been made the subject of imitation.[2] Beda was bound to know that custom as a heathen and abominable custom, it having been interdicted and having been alluded to in the Decrees of Pope Hormisdas (514-523), and in the canons of the Lateran Council of A.D. 649 under Pope Martin I., which had been brought to Great Britain by John the Precentor and adopted by the Council of Hatfield, A.D. 680. During Beda's own life-time the whole matter had been thoroughly treated in Canon LXXIX. of the Council of Trullus, A.D. 706. But, of course, he could know customs of that kind only from hearsay, or from his own experience, at any rate only as being contemporaneous. That in a thing so wicked, which to his pure mind was so unsympathetic, he did not see a growth upon the soil of the Church, but

---

[1] *Acta Conciliorum*, Parisiis, 1714, Vol. III., col. 1690, *Concilium Quinisextum sive in Trullo*, A.D. 706, Canon lxxix.: "Absque ullis secundis ex Virgine partum esse confitentes ut qui sine semine constitutus sit, idque toti gregi annuntiantes, eos, qui propter ignorantiam aliquid faciunt quod non decet, correctioni subiicimus. Quare quoniam aliqui post sanctae Christi Dei nostri nativitatis diem similam coquere ostenduntur, et eam sibi invicem impertiri, honoris scilicet praetextu secundinarum impollutae Virginis matris . . ." *Ibid.*, Vol. II., col. 1014, *Decrees of Pope Hormisdas* (A.D. 514-523), iii.; Haddan and Stubbs, *Councils and Ecclesiastical Documents relating to Great Britain and Ireland*, Oxford, 1871, Vol. III., p. 146, *De Beata Virgine.*

[2] It is a strange chance that we are able to show that this custom of representing in some way the confinement of the Virgin spread also over Great Britain, taking there even a more characteristic form. As late as 1800 it prevailed in Scotland (Jamieson, *An Etymological Dictionary of the Scottish Language*, under "Yule," VII.), where on the morning of the twenty-fifth of December one got up before the rest of the family and prepared food for them, which had to be eaten in bed. This frequently consisted of cakes baken with eggs, called Care-cakes.

a relic of heathendom, we cannot wonder. And he was not wrong therein. He erred only in so far as he did not ascribe it to the Roman Calends of January, at which the *Strenae* were in vogue, but to an imaginary cult exercised by the Angles in the very night on which the Church had fixed Christ's birthday.

Although in Germany—here and there at least—similar terms are found,[1] *e.g.*, *to myddewynter*, on the whole, quite different denominations prevail. The Germans formed for a number of Christian holy tides compounds with their word *wich*, holy. As they had for popular festivals the word *hôgetîdi* (Old-Saxon) or *hôchgezît* (Middle-High-German), *i.e.*, high tide, so they had the word *wîhtîdi* (Old-Saxon), *i.e.*, holy tide. With a derivation from *wîch* they called the Ember-days (Quatembers) *wîchfasten*, or later, *weichfasten*, which nobody will deny to be a purely ecclesiastical invention. And the same word they used to create a term for the ecclesiastical bearing of December 25. To denote an individual day they used the word *naht*, night, thus forming *Kristisnaht*[2] and *wîchnaht*, or for the plurality of four days *wîhnahten*.[3]

After the year 800, when the Pope on that date crowned Charlemagne Roman Emperor, Christ's birthday was a day frequently chosen for state ceremonies. And this apparently was the reason why William the Conqueror, who won the battle of Hastings late in autumn 1066, chose it

---

foran to midden wintra." Thorpe's *Ancient Laws*, I., p. 220, iv.: "Ædhelstan cyng cydh that ic hæbbe geahsod that ure fridh is wyrse gehealden thonne me lyste. oththe hit æt Greatanlea gecweden waere. ond mine witan secgadh that ic hit to lange forboren hæbbe. Nu hæbbe ic gefunden mid thæm witum the mid me wæron æt Exan-ceastre to middan-wintre," etc. The term *Chrystismess* lived on for at least four centuries, it still being found about 1460 in "Blind Harry's" *The Wallace*, v. 561 :

> "This Chrystismess Wallace ramaynyt thar ;
> In Laynrik oft till sport he maid repayr."

[1] Kempen, Town-Archive, D. i, No. 1, about 1442: "Hefft in myn hant ghetastet gheloeffiyke myn gelt to gheven in den ver hylghen daghen to myddewynter."

[2] "An der Kristisnacht dô begunde he zu gêne" (*Myst.*, 48, 1); "an der heiligen Christisnacht, *Jeroschin*" Pf. 58 d, Müller und Zarncke, *Mittelhochdeutsches Wörterbuch*, I., 301.

[3] "Gegen disen wînnahten *Tanhûser*," MS. H 2, 93 a ; "zu nêhest bî wînachten," *Pass.* K, 46, 47 ; "swer zu wînachten singet vor den hûsern," *Saalfelder Stadtrecht*, Wackernagel, *Literaturgeschichte*, I., p. 259, note 9 ; "zu weinachten," *Münchner Stadtrecht*, VII., 94 ; "nâch einen wînachten tagen," *Biterolf*, 478 ; "an dem zwelften tag nâch wichen nächten," *Züricher Jahrbuch*, 69, 5 ; "uf den hailgen tag zuo Wîchen-nächten," *Ibid.*, 80, 33 ; "zuo Wîchennächten ûf den ziestag," *Ibid.*, 92, 13 ; "an der kindlî tag zuo wichen nächten," *Ibid.*, 94, 33.

for his coronation at Westminster[1] a Christmas Day which opened a new chapter in the history of Britain. He apparently introduced a court festival on December 25, for from 1085 the Laud MS. of the *Saxon Chronicle* begins to state regularly where the king kept that festive time. In 1085, when he held court for several days at Gloucester, he knighted his son Henry.[2] In 1165 the Scottish king, William the Lion, was crowned on the same day.[3] The coronation ceremonies and courts at Christmas were other steps towards something like a popularising of the English Church festival among the wider circles of the people. Florence of Worcester (+A.D. 1108) also mentions the first court held by an English king, at Nativity, under the year 1065, which has to be regarded as the first secular celebration of Christ's birthday in Great Britain.[4]

---

[1] Florence of Worcester, under 1066 : "Willielmus . . . ipsa Nativitatis die, quae illo anno evenit, ab Aldredo Eboracensium archiepiscopo in Westmonasterio consecratus est honorifice."

[2] The *Saxon Chronicle* tells, under the year 1087, of William the Conqueror : "Thrice he wore his crown every year, as often as he was in England; at Easter he wore it at Winchester; at Whitsuntide at Westminster; at Midwinter at Gloucester; and then were with him all the rich men over all England, archbishops and suffragan bishops, abbots and earls, thegns and knights" (William Stubbs, *Select Charters and Other Illustrations of English Constitutional History*, Oxford, 1884, p. 81).

[3] There is a great number of other cases : *The Historians of Scotland*, Vol. I., Johannis de Fordun, *Chronica Gentis Scotorum*, Edinburgh, 1871, p. 259 (ad annum 1165) : "Igitur in vigilia natalis Domini, die videlicet XV. post regis mortem, idem Willelmus, amicus Dei, leo justiciae, princeps pacis, a Ricardo episcopo Sancti Andreae, et aliis episcopis coadjuvantibus, in regem benedicitur, atque regali cathedra sublimatur."

[4] He has, in his Chronicle, the following dates according to the Saints' Calendar (*Monumenta Historica Britannica*, I.) :

"696 Dies natalis beatissimae Caeciliae virginis (November 22).
917 Ante Nativitatem S. Johannis Baptistae (June 24).
918 Post Nativitatem S. Johannis Baptistae (June 24).
1021 Ante festivitatem S. Martini (November 11).
1029 Post festivitatem S. Martini (November 11).
1043 Ante festivitatem S. Andreae (November 30).
1052 In nocte festivitatis S. Thomae (December 18).
1053 In festivitate S. Kenelmi martiris (July 17).
1065 Post festivitatem Omnium Sanctorum (November 1).
In nativitate Domini (December 25).
Die sanctorum Innocentium (December 28).

At royal courts the *Natale Domini* had soon become a great day for royal pomp and splendour. On that day, in consequence, any humiliation was felt twice as much as on any other. That was apparently the reason why King Magnus of Norway, the son of Olav and grandson of Harald Harfagr, in 1098 sent to King Murecard of Ireland his shoes, with the order to carry them on that day through his palace in the presence of his ambassadors, in order to show that he confessed himself to be a subject of King Magnus.[1] From the end of the tenth century, Nativity banqueting must have become somewhat commoner, as legal regulations begin to refer to it.[2]   In Wales

---

1065 Epiphaniae Domini vigilia (January 5).
   Post haec rex Eadwardus paulatim aegrotare coepit. In Nativitate vero Domini curiam suam, ut potuit, Lundoniae tenuit.
1066 Willielmus . . . ipsa Nativitatis die, quae illo anno feria secunda evenit, ab Aldredo Eboracensium archiepiscopo in Westmonasterio consecratus est honorifice."

[1] King Murecard carried the shoes, at the same time declaring that he would rather eat King Magnus's shoes in addition, than allow him to conquer a single province of Ireland. *Chronica Regum Manniae et Insularum, The Chronicle of Man and the Sudreys*, edited from the Manuscript Codex in the British Museum, and with historical notes by P. A. Munch, Christiania, 1860, p. 6, under Anno MXCVIII.: "Murecardo regi Yberniae misit calceamenta sua, praecipiens ei ut ea super humeros suos in die natalis Domini per medium domus suae portaret in conspectu nunciorum ejus, quatinus intelligeret se subjectum esse Magno regi. Quod audientes Ybernenses, aegre ferebant, et indignati sunt nimis. Sed rex saniori consilio usus, non solum, inquit, calceamenta ejus portare, verum etiam manducare mallem, quam Magnus rex unam provinciam in Ybernia destrueret. Itaque complevit praeceptum et nuncios honoravit. Multa quoque munera per eos Magno regi transmisit, et foedus composuit. Nuncii vero redeuntes ad dominum suum narraverunt ei de situ Yberniae et amoenitate, de frugum fertilitate et aeris salubritate. Magnus vero haec audiens, nihil cogitabat quam totam Yberniam sibi subjugare. Itaque praecepit classem congregare, ipse vero cum sexdecim navibus procedens, explorare volens terram, cum incaute a navibus discessisset, subito ab Ybernensibus circumvallatus, interiit cum omnibus fere qui secum erant."

[2] *De Institutis Lundoniae, et primum quae portae observabantur* (under King Ethelred, 991-1016), in Thorpe's *Ancient Laws*, I., p. 300: "Et homines Imperatoris, qui veniebant in navibus suis, bonarum legum digni tenebantur, sicut et nos. Praeter discarcatam lanam, et diss[ol]utum unctum et tres porcos vivos licebat eis emere in naves suas; et non licebat eis aliquod forceapum facere burhmannis, et dare telonium suum; et in sancto Natali Domini duos grisengos pannos, et unum brunum, et decem libras piperis, et cirotecas quinque hominum, et duos caballinos tonellos aceto plenos, et totidem in Pascha; de

the first Nativity feasting occurs between 1056 and 1064,[1] in Ireland in 1171.[2]

On German ground the first great historical Nativity feasting appears about the middle of the eleventh century in the far-away North. At that festival Archbishop[3] Adalbert of Bremen, who died in 1072, was present,

dosseris cum gallinis I. gallina teloñ, et de uno dossero cum ovis v. ova telonei, si veniant ad mercatum. Smeremangestre, que mangonant in caseo et butiro, XIIII. diebus ante Natale Domini, unum denarium, et septem diebus post Natale, unum alium."

[1] Haddan and Stubbs, *Councils and Ecclesiastical Documents*, Oxford, 1869, Vol. I., p. 294: "Et firmata missis manibus super quatuor euangelia, et in manu Heruualdi Episcopi consolidata, et coram omni populo suo, in die Natiuitatis Domini apud Ystumguy"; *Ibid.*, I., 295 (A.D. 1056-1087): "Liber Landav. Familia Catgucauni Regis Morcannuc, filii Mourici, in die Nativitatis Domini, visitavit Landauiam bono affectu, et (ut dicitur de virga Aaron versa in draconem) animus illius familiae tardus ad sperandum bonum, velox ad faciendum malum; et ditatus prae nimio gaudio tantae festivitatis, cepit baccare copia potationis, sequestrata discretione sobrietatis; in tantum quod imperfecti viri, amissa vi scientiae et pietatis, devastaverunt unum familiarem et nepotem Herguldi Episcopi, Berthutis nomine, virum iustum, et medicum totius patriae."

[2] *Rerum Anglicarum Scriptores post Baedam praecipui*, London, 1596, *Rogeri Hovedeni Annalium*, pars posterior, p. 302, under "Henricus II." in 1171: "Rex Angliae perrexit inde usque Diueline, et ibi moram fecit a festo S. Martini, usque ad caput ieiunii: ibique fecit sibi construi iuxta ecclesiam S. Andreae apostoli extra civitatem Diueliniae, palatium regium miro artificio, de virgis leuigatis ad modum patriae illius constructum. In quo ipse cum regibus et principibus Hyberniae festum solemne tenuit die natalis Domini." The same is told by Giraldus Cambrensis, who, however, adds some details. *Anglica, Normannica, Hibernica, Cambrica, a Veteribus Scripta*, Francofurti, 1603. *Giraldi Cambrensis Expugnatio Hiberniae*, chap. xxxii., p. 776, under A.D. 1171: [Henricus II.] "Imminente vero Dominici Natalis solemnitate, Dubliniam terrae illius Principes ad Curiam videndam accessere quam plurimi. Ubi et lautam Anglicanae mensae copiam vetustissimam quoque vernarum obsequium plurimum admirantes; carne gruina, quam hactenus abhorruerant regia voluntate passim per aulam, vesci ceperunt."

[3] *Erpoldi Lindenbrogii Scriptores Rerum Germanicarum Septentrionalium, Vicinorumque Populorum Veteres diversi*, etc., ed. Jo. Albertus Fabricius, Hamburgi, 1706, M. Adami Bremensis *Historia Ecclesiastica* (Adam became *Canonicus Bremensis* in 1077), Lib. IV., chap. xxxix., p. 53: "In die itaque natalis Domini, cum *Magnus* Dux praesens adesset, magnaque recumbentium multitudo, hilares convivæ pro sua consuetudine finitis epulis plausum cum voce levaverunt. Quod tamen non parum displicuit Archiepiscopo [Adalberto + 1072]. Itaque innuens fratribus nostris, qui simul aderant, praecepit Cantori, ut imponeret Antiphonam, *Hymnum cantate nobis*. At vero laicis denuo perstrepentibus, inchoari fecit: *Sustinuimus pacem et non venit Domine*. Tertio vero cum adhuc in poculis ululrent, iratus valde, levari mensam praecepit, magna voce pronuncians: *Converte·Domine captivi-*

while the banquet was also attended by Duke Magnus, and a great crowd of others. The dinner being over, the duke and his people began to sing or shout songs or exclamations, which displeased the archbishop. He therefore ordered the clerical members of the feast to sing some clerical song, which they did without being able to defy their secular opponents. In high dudgeon, Adalbert therefore ordered in a loud voice the table to be lifted, asking God to free him from such captivity. Then, with his followers, he retired into the oratory, weeping bitterly.

The festive time about December 25 and January 6 evolves before our eyes, and receives one characteristic after another. Work on festival days is suppressed as early as in the Laws of Edward and Guthrum. Through it a freeman forfeits his freedom, or pays *wite* or *lah-slit*. And if a lord oblige his *theow* to work on a festival day, he has to pay *lah-slit* within the Danish law, and *wite* among the English.[1] Ordeal and oaths are forbidden on festival days.[2]

Under King Ethelred (991-1016), the older inhibition of ordeals and oaths on festival-days was repeated, and this inhibition extended to the regular Ember-days, and from Advent till the octaves of Epiphany; and from Septuagesima till fifteen days after Easter; and at those holy tides there was to be with all Christian men general peace and concord, even strife being appeased.[3] If any one owed another *borh* or *bōt* on

---

tatem nostram ; respondente choro ; *sicut torrens in austro.* Ita ille nobis pone sequentibus, in oratorium reclusus, flevit amare. *Non cessabo,* ait, *a fletu, donec justus judex fortis et patiens liberet Ecclesiam meam: vel potius suam ; quam Pastore contempto videt miserabiliter a lupis discerpi. Impletum est enim desiderium eorum, qui dixerunt: Hæreditate possideamus sanctuarium Dei, et quiescere faciamus omnes dies festos Dei a terra, et disperdamus eos de gente, et non memoretur nomen Israel ultra. Exsurge: quare obdormis, Domine, et ne repellas in finem. Quia superbia eorum qui te aderunt, ascendit semper. Miserere nostri, quoniam multum repleti sumus despectione. Quoniam quem tu percussisti, persequuti sunt, et super dolorem vulnerum meorum addiderunt."*

[1] Thorpe's *Ancient Laws*, I., p. 172, 7 ; the A.S. term is *freols-dæge.*

[2] *Ibid.*, p. 172, No. ix. : "Ordel ond adhas syndan tocwedene freols-dagum ond riht fæsten-dagum."

[3] Thorpe's *Ancient Laws*, I., p. 309, xviii. : "And ordâl and âdhar sindon tocweden freôls-dagum. and riht Ymbren-dagum. and fram Adventum Domini odh octabas Epiphanie. and fram Septuagesimam odh xv. niht ofer Eastran." xix. "And beo tham hâlgum tîdan eal swa hit riht is. eallum cristenum mannum sib and sôm gemæne. and ælc sacu getwæmed,"

account of secular matters, he was to fulfil it willingly before or after, but not within the festive tide.[1] In Germany the same habits can be proved to have existed about 1400.[2]

Edward the Confessor ordained again that strict peace was to be kept from Christ's Nativity till a week after Epiphany, i.e., the entire holy tide, which in previous centuries, as has been shown above in the chapter on the Nativity of Christ, had been exempt from Friday fasting, and later had been called *Gehhol*.[3] With little alterations these prohibitions appeared again in the so-called Laws of King Cnut, which were manufactured in the beginning of the twelfth century.[4] The same holds

---

[1] Thorpe's *Ancient Laws*, p. 308, xx.: "And gif hwâ odhrum scyle borh oththon bôte æt woroldlican thingan. gelæste hit georne. ær oththon æften." The same regulations are repeated in the resolutions passed at the Council of Enam, *Ibid.*, I., p. 320, xxii.-xxv.

[2] Rees, Rhine-country, Town-Archive, Bürgerbuch, fol. 6ᵇ: "Item desselben gelijck sall et oick vry wesen in den twaelff nachten ende in onsen jair marckten ende kirmissen ende als men onse vrouwe dreghet"; (*vry wesen*, i.e., there shall be no law courts).

[3] Thorpe's *Ancient Laws*, I., 443, *Leges Edwardi Confessoris* (1042-1066): "Quibus temporibus pax servanda est." ii. "Ab adventu Domini usque ad octavas Epiphaniae pax Dei et sanctae ecclesiae per omne regnum. Similiter a Septuagesima usque ad octavas Paschae. Item ab Ascensione Domini usque ad octavas Pentecostes. Item omnibus diebus IIII, temporum. Item omnibus Sabatis totius anni, ab hora nona, et totum diem sequentem. Item vigilia Sanctae Mariae, Sancti Michaelis, Sancti Iohannis Baptistae, sanctorum omnium Apostolorum, et Sanctorum illorum quorum festivitates a sacerdotibus in ecclesia diebus Dominicis annunciabuntur, et Omnium Sanctorum kalendis Novembris, semper ab hora nona vigiliarum et totum diem sequentem. Item in festivitatum celebrationibus Sanctorum quicumque fuerint in parochiis ubi sunt ecclesiae eorum." The king's peace, however, was different. *Ibid.*, I. p. 447: "Pax regis multiplex est. Alia data manu sua, quam Anglici vocant kinges hand-sealde gridh. Alia die qua primum coronatus est; ipsa habet VIII. dies. In Natali Domini, VIII. dies; et VIII. dies Paschae, et VIII. dies Pentecostes," etc.

[4] Thorpe's *Ancient Laws*, I., p. 368: "De Iciuniis." xvi. "And that man ælc beboden fæsten healde. sî hit Ymbren-fæsten. sî hit Lengcten-fæsten. sî hit elles odher fæsten. mid ealre geornfulnesse. and to Sanctam Mariam mæssan ælcere. and to ælces apostoles mæssan fæste man. butan to Philippi and Iacobi mæssan we ne beôdadh nân fæsten. for tham Easterlican freôlse. and ælces Frige-dæger fæsten. buton hit freols sŷ. And ne thearf man na fæsten fram Eastran odh Pentecosten. buton hwâ gescrîfen sig. oththe he elles fæsten wylle. And of middan-wintre odh octabas Epiphanie. that is seofen niht ofer twelftan mæsse-dæge." This last sentence forms one of the few conclusive

good of those laws which hold themselves out as written under Henry I.
(1100-1135).[1]

At the end of the eleventh century the time of Christ's Nativity seems
to have passed from a mere ecclesiastical and state celebration into popularity
so far, that it became general to keep it by feasting and banqueting.
This is to be seen from the change of the attitude of the Church towards
that festive tide. So far it had proclaimed it to be a joyous time, during
which all fasting was suspended—not only regular Friday fasting, but also
the stricter fasting for grave offenders, who had to do penance for a
number of years. But by that time Nativity banqueting seems to have
become too gay, so that now the Church made attempts to check it.
This is evident from the so-called Laws of King Cnut, (1016-1028), which
in reality, as before mentioned, were fabricated in England under

---

proofs that, in the beginning of the twelfth century, the term midwinter meant December
25. *Ibid.*, I., p. 370, *Laws of King Cnut*: "De Temporibus Iustitiae." xvii. "And we
forbeôdadh ôrdâl and âdhar freols-dagum. and ymbren-dagum. and lengclen dagum. and
riht fæsten dagum. and fram Adventum Domini [this term does not mean the Advent-
tide, but December 25] odh se eahtodha dæg âgân sig ofer twelftan mæsse-dæge. and
fram Septuagesima odh xv. nihton ofer Eastron. And sancte Eadweardes mæsse-dæg
witan habbadh gecoren that man freôlsian sceal ofer eall Engla-land on xv. kl. April.
And Sancte Dûnstânes mæsse-dæg on xiiii. kl. Iunii. And beo tham hâlgum tîdum.
eal swa hit riht is. eallum cristenum mannum sib and sôm genæne. and ælc sacu
tôtwæmed. And gyf hwâ odhrum sceole borh oththe bôte. æt woruldlicum thingum.
gelæste hit him georne. ær oththe æfter." About the general observance of festival
days, compare *Ibid.*, I., 402, xlv., xlvii. and xlviii. of the *Laws of King Cnut* from
the beginning of the twelfth century.

[1] Thorpe's *Ancient Laws*, I., 562-63, lxii.: "De Observatione temporis leges faciendi.
§ 1. Ab Adventu Domini [*i.e.*, December 25] usque ad Epiphaniae octabas, et a lxx.
usque ad xv. dies post Pascha, et festis diebus, et quatuor temporum, et diebus
Quadragesimalibus, et aliis legitimis jejuniis, et in diebus Veneris, et vigiliis sanctorum
Apostolorum, non est tempus leges faciendi, idem vel jusjurandum pro fidelitate domini,
vel concordiam, vel bellum, vel ferri, vel aquae, vel alias legis examinationes tractari ;
sed sit in omnibus vera pax, beata caritas, ad honorem Omnipotentis Dei, cujus
sapientia conditi sumus, nativitate provecti, a morte redempti, consolatione securi. § 2.
Et qui debitor est, ante persolvat vel induciet, donec dies isti transeant, gaudiis et
honestis voluptatibus instituti. § 3. Et si quis malefactum inter manus habens alicubi
retinetur, ibi purgetur vel sordidetur. Si solum inculpatio sit, plegiis, si opus est, datis,
ubi justum fuerit terminanda, revertatur."

Henry I. about A.D. 1110,[1] and which ordain the time of strict peace, from midwinter to the octave of Epiphany, to be also a time of strict fasting.[2] This, however, was so little carried through, that in the thirteenth century the Church itself was most seriously involved in gaieties, which were shifted from the Calends of January to a date dangerously near Christmas.[3] In thirteenth and fourteenth century stories, Christmas is presupposed as the time when everybody shows himself in his best dress, and whoever does not follow the fashion in that respect is ridiculed.[4] When the giving of presents at Christmas had become more general,

---

[1] Liebermann, *On the Instituta Cnuti Aliorumque Regum Anglorum*, pp. 83, 85; Thorpe's *Ancient Laws*, II., 521, *Leges Regis Cnuti*: "Haec sunt instituta Cnuti, regis Anglorum, Danorum, et Norwegarum, venerando sapientum ejus consilio, ad laudem Dei, et suam regalitatem, et commune commodum habita, in sancto Natali Domini, apud Wintoniam," etc.

[2] Thorpe, *Ancient Laws and Institutes of England*, London, 1840, Vol. I., p. 368, *Ecclesiastical Laws of King Cnut*, No. XVI: "De Jeiuniis: And that man ælc beboden fæsten healde . . . mid ealre geornfulnesse. . . . And of middan-wintre odh octabas Epiphanie. that is seofen niht ofer twelftan mæsse dæge."

[3] Compare the note on p. 100. Ducange, *Glossarium*, under *Kalendae*, *Concilium Copriniacense*, A.D. 1260, c. ii.: "Rursus cum in balleatione, quae in festo S.S. Inno-centium in quibusdam Ecclesiis fieri inolevit, multae rixae, contentiones, et turbationes, tam in divinis Officiis, quam aliis consueverunt provenire, praedictas balleationes alterius sub intimatione anathematis fieri prohibemus." He also refers to *Statuta Joannis Archi-episcopi Cantuarensis*, A.D. 1279, and mentions from the *Necrologium Ecclesiae Parisiensis*, vii. : "Idus Januarii obiit Hugo Clemens Decanus noster et Sacerdos" [frater Henrici Clementis Franciae Marescalli]. "Procuravit etiam salubriter et devote, quod Festum B. Joannis Evangelistae post Nativitatem Domini, quod prius negligenter et joculariter agebatur, solenniter et devote celebraretur in Ecclesia nostra," etc.

[4] "Rex quidam misit cuidam militi bacones, ut ipsos venderet et vestes contra festum Natale sibi compararet. Sed stultus miles in festo bacones a dextris et a sinistris circa se suspendit, et alii milites egregie induti apparentes, ille cum baconibus apparuit vestitus. Cui cum requireretur, cui hoc fecisset, dixit quod talem induit qualem sibi misit dominus, nec illam voluit mutare" (Thomas Wright, *A Selection of Latin Stories*, London, 1842, p. 112, No. CXXII. *De Milite Stulto*, from the MS. Harleana, No. 3244, of the thirteenth or fourteenth century). So in the German epic of Meier Helmbrecht, v., 1158-1160, the lines appear:

> "Daz hilfet mir daz ich sol tragen
> gewant ze wihnahten
> swie ich daz mac betrachten."

Christmas fairs were instituted at various places,[1] and family gatherings were held about the same time.[2]

In addition to the usages enumerated in former chapters which can be directly derived from Roman Calends-of-January customs, there now evolved a number of beliefs and habits, legends and usages, springing from a purely Christian soil, and showing how deep root Christianity had, in the course of time, taken in Germanic minds. The song *Rorate Coeli* had not been sung in vain for so many centuries.[3] Founded upon it, the folk-belief had sprung up that at Christmas the heavens really gave a special and beneficial dew, which blessed everything that came in contact with it. The Church added to this automatic benediction, which every year took place in commemoration of the birth of God, another more express one, which took the form of a benediction spoken by the priest from the altar. Out of this both Great Britain and Germany evolved popular customs.[4] According to Franz Wessel's description of the Roman Catholic service at

---

[1] So in A.D. 1461, in Kempen, Rhine-country; Town-Archive, Document No. 367, April 18, 1461, *Annalen des historischen Vereins für den Niederrhein*, Vol. LXV., p. 42. Archbishop Dietrich of Cologne allowed the town a fair of six days at St. Jacob (July 25), and St. Thomas (December 21). Compare also Document No. 387 of March 10, 1465; St. Jacob is one of the days which frequently divide the summer into two parts, previous to the introduction of the summer solstice of June 24.

[2] Johannis de Fordun, *Scotichronicon cum Supplementis et Continuatione Walteri Boweri*, Edinburgh, 1759, Vol. II., p. 59, Lib. IX., chap. xlviii., under the years 1231 to 1233: "Patricius comes de Dumbar, aeger corpore, convocavit filios et filias, cognatos et vicinos, ut festa Dominicae nativitatis secum celebrarent. Peractis quatuor diebus vocat Adam abbatem de Melros, et ab eo extremam unctionem accepit ac habitum religionis, induit se monachum, et ultimum valedicens omnibus, diem clausit extremum." Bower having written in the first half of the fifteenth century, and there being no earlier evidence for this statement, the habit of celebrating Christmas in the family circle cannot be set down as of the first half of the thirteenth century.

[3] "Rorate coeli desuper et nubes pluant justum" was sung on Wednesday after the third Advent, and later on the fourth Advent, Grotefend, *Zeitrechnung des deutschen Mittelalters*, I., 169.

[4] Gervasius of Tilbury wrote about 1200: "Apud antiquos Britanniae inolevit, quod in nocte natalis Domini ponunt manipulum avenae sub dio, aut vasculum aliquod plenum avenae vel hordei, ut, si fortassis, ut assolet evenire, pestis mortifera coeperit alia tangere, ex illo vel hordeo vel avena, super quam asserunt rorem coelestem nutu divino quotannis hora nativitatis Dei descendere." Liebrecht, *Gervasius von Tilbury*, s. 2, chap. xii.

Stralsund before the year 1523, a similar ceremony took place there, which was even named after Christ's birth. When a child was born, its brothers and sisters used to receive little presents which were called "child's-foot," *Kindsfuss*. By that name also was called the gift which all the domestic animals got on the occasion of Christ's birth.[1] That the same custom was still existing about the end of the sixteenth century is witnessed by Nicolaus Gryse's *Spegel des antichristlichen Pawestdoms*.[2]

When Charlemagne forbade[3] drunkenness in general; the conjurations by St. Stephan, himself, or his sons; and the participation in banquets of bishops and abbots,—this applied to the habit of men drinking on St. Stephan's day, as on other saints' days, to the memory of the saint of the day, a habit called later *Stephan's minne, Johannes minne, Martin's minne*. In the same way they had, in pre-Christian times, drunk to the memory of their gods. To speak, however, on the basis of this passage, of *Stephan's minne* as a special custom, as, *e.g.*, Ulrich Jahn does,[4] is out of place—for such a custom cannot be proved to have existed before the second half of the sixteenth century, or 800 years after Charlemagne, and even then it appears not as a popular, but as a purely

---

[1] When the peasants there had fasted on Christmas eve till they saw the stars appear in the sky—"so drogen se garuen in de koppele efte sus in de lucht, dadt se de windt, sne, rip efte sus de lucht beschinen konde. Dadt hetede men des morgens kindesvodt; dadt deelde men des morgen allem vth, schloch eine garue ₂ efte 3 vth vndt gaf den swinen, koyen, enten, gensen, dad se alle des kindesvothes geneten scholdenn."

[2] Rostock, 1593, *De I. Beal*, where we are told the following: "An S. Steffens dage wyhet men nicht alleine dat water, sonderen ock den Hauer vnd allerley Korn, mit etlyken auergelöuischen gebeden vnd affgödischen Crüttzslegen in, vnd sprickt, dat solckes an dissem dage ingesegendes korn, dem vehe krefftige stercke geue, mehr alse dat vngewyhede, vnd wenn ydt geseyet, sehr vele fruchte bringe, ock den Minschen de daruan ethen, Lyues vnd der Seelen gesundtheit mitdele." Ulrich Jahn, *Deutsche Opfergebräuche*, pp. 277, 278, where a great number of cases are given in which that custom still survives.

[3] *Acta Conciliorum*, Parisiis, 1714, Vol. IV., col. 846, *Caroli Magni Regis Capitula alia*, x. ; Schannat, *Concilia Germanica*, I., p. 286, chap. iii., anni 789: "Omnino prohibendum est omnibus ebrietatis malum: et istas conjurationes, quas faciunt per sanctum Stephanum, aut per nos, aut per filios nostros, prohibemus; et praecipimus ut episcopi vel abbates non vadant per casam miscendo."

[4] In his book, *Die deutschen Opfergebräuche bei Ackerbau und Viehzucht*, Breslau, 1884, p. 273.

ecclesiastical custom.[1]　So it is with *Johannes minne*, which was drunk to the memory of John the Evangelist on December 25.　From the fifteenth century onwards, the Church, in its commemoration of the legend that John the Apostle destroyed the poison contained in a cup by making the sign of the cross over it, adopted that custom by the repetition of that benediction as part of the service.　The blessed cup was regarded by the people as a means useful for all kinds of things, and wine blessed at that opportunity enjoyed a great reputation.[2]　*Johannes liebe* and *Johannis trunk* appear for it.[3]

In the marvellous night on which the Saviour was born, the most extraordinary things happened, according to the Christian legend.　The animals rejoiced in the salvation that was bestowed on the world, in the rivers there ran wine instead of water, and the trees in the forest began to bud and bloom all in one night in spite of the ice and snow by which the fields were covered.　Ecclesiastical fancy had played with these things for some time, eloquent preachers had with them adorned, and lent impressiveness to, their sermons, so that at last it became a popular belief that every year, at the hour when Christ was born, the same miracles happened again.[4]

---

[1] Fischart, *Bienenkorb*, I., chap. ii., p. 63: "Zu Freuburg in Preiszgau bey den Johanniten an einem silbernen Kettlin ein Stein, darmit S. Stephan gesteiniget ward: denselben legt man jährlich an S. Stephanstag in einen Kelch, geusst Wein darüber, gibt dem opferenden Volck darab zu trincken, das heisst für S. Johanns-Segen S. Stephanswein, soll für die Baermutter gut seyn."

[2] A large part of the more important literature for this item is quoted by Ulrich Jahn, *Die deutschen Opfergebräuche bei Ackerbau und Viehzucht*, Breslau, 1844, p. 269 ss. : "Seb. Franck, 1567; Thomas Naogeorgus, 1553; Burckhardt Waldis; Strigenitius; Nicolaus Gryse, 1593; Matthesius; Petrus Mosellanus; Fibiger, 1675."

[3] *Städtechroniken*, X., 375; III., 149; XI., 673.　Rarely is it transferred to June 24. *Wiener Sitzungsberichte*, XL., 180; Grotefend, *Zeitrechnung*, I., 99; Spiess, *Archivalische Nebenarbeiten*, mentions a foundation from the year 1484: "Daz man davon alle jar schike und bestell wein doselhst zum goczhausz an sandt Johannstag zu weynachten so man dem volck pfligt ausz dem kelch sandt Johanns mynn zu geben;" Grotefend, *Ibid.*, I., 100; Birlinger, *Aus Schwaben*, II., 158, and II., 122.

[4] A fine example for the evolution of a Christmas legend into a popular belief is contained in *Die Pilgerfahrt des Ritters Arnold von Harff*, ed. by Dr. G. v. Groote, Köln, 1860 (a description of a journey to the Orient, A.D. 1496-99), p. 26, where a church at Rome is mentioned: "Item beneven deser kirchen is ein pallais zo broecken den der keyser Octavianus lies bouwen. He vragde die affgoede ind de bouwelude wie lange

An Arabian geographer of the tenth century[1] is the first to tell the story that, in the night between December 24 and 25, the trees of the forest actually stand in full blossom, and this belief is carried through Spain and France to Germany and Great Britain.[2]   On German ground it appears first in a saint's life, the life of St. Hadwigis, who was born about 1180 in Franken.   The story tells of her: "Once, when she was young, on Christmas day somebody entered the room, saying, while she was sitting on the table, that a cherry tree in the garden stood in full blossom.   She, on hearing this, sent him back in order to see whether the buds sprang from the lower or from the upper part of the tree.   He went, and on his return reported that the tree blossomed at its lower branches.   But she said: 'That is a sign of the coming mortality.   Many poor will die this year.' And as she foretold, so it happened."[3]

---

der pallais waell stayn moechte.   Do spraich ein stimme van dem hemell, he seulde stain also lange bis dat ein maget in junferlicher reinicheit ein kint geberet.   Doe spraich der keiser Octavianus : soe wirt he ewich stain, want sulch is neit moegelich.   Darumb lies er in des tempels muire hauwen : *Templum eternitatis*, ein tempel der ewicheit.   Doe nu Cristus unser herre van Maria der reiner maget geboren waert, doe veil des tempels vil dar neder ind noch all jairs zo cristmissen veldt ein stuck der muyren van dem tempel."

[1] Georg Jacob, *Studien in arabischen Geographen*, Heft I., 5, pp. 8, 9, and Heft IV., 5, pp. 171, 172.

[2] Christ Himself as a child sitting on a tree covered all over with candles appears in the Old French epic, "Durmars le galois," of the thirteenth century, 151, 2 ss.; 155, 60 ss.; 158, 17 ss. (Alwin Schulz, *Das höfische Leben zur Zeit der Minnesinger*, Leipzig, 1889, I., p. 364; Simrock, *Handbuch der deutschen Mythologie*, 5th ed., Bonn, 1878, p. 572 : "Durmars sees a tree whose branches are covered from top to bottom with lit candles, of which some stand properly and some upside down.   But still more shining than these, a resplendent child is sitting on the top.   Terrified and wondering what this means, Durmars asks the Pope, and receives the answer : 'The lit tree is humanity, the upright lights are the good men, the reversed lights the bad men, the child is the Saviour.'"

[3] Aufsess und Mone, *Anzeiger für Kunde des deutschen Mittelalters*, III., Nürnberg, 1834, col. 10, probably of the thirteenth century : "Quoniam eo tempore, dum adhuc iuvenis esset, in die natalis domini venit qui diceret coram ea sedente in mensa, quod arbor una cerasus stans in horto recentibus esset floribus decorata.   Quod audiens misit ad considerandum, si praedicti flores in inferiori aut in superiori parte arboris pulularent.   Qui missus fuerat, renunciavit arborem in ramis inferioribus florescentem.   At illa, signum est, inquit, mortalitatis futurae.   Multi enim pauperes morientur isto anno.   Et sic, ut praedixerat omnino evenit."

This is a legend. But a century later we find the same thing as a belief purposely furthered by the Church.[1]   A bishop tells, in a letter to a friend, of two apple trees which on Christmas night blossomed and ripened. A nobleman testifies to the truth of the affair, describing the colour of the apples, and stating that he had held them in his own hands. About 1430 the same story is told of the neighbourhood of Nürnberg,[2] by a theologian, Johannes Nider. He reports: "Not far from Nürnberg there stood a miraculous tree. . . . Every year in the wildest and most disagreeable time of the year, invariably and only on the night of Christ's birth, when the Virgin of Virgins . . . gave birth to the son of God, it bore blooming apples the size of a thumb. . . . Therefore every year, trustworthy people go there from Nürnberg and the neighbouring regions and keep watch all night at that place to test the truth of the thing. A tree similar to this one in every respect is found in the diocese of Bamberg." From the beginning of the fifteenth century, the belief spread over all Germany, being attested again and again in various popular books and chronicles of the sixteenth, seventeenth, and eighteenth centuries, so that it became one of the most popular parts of the German Christmas creed of modern times.[3]   In England the story appears somewhat later, but has got a peculiar form. Legend tells that after Christ's death Joseph of Arimathea came to England and settled at Glastonbury. There he was, therefore, specially revered, there his grave was said to be, and there in the crypt his coffin was shown. Although the legend bears the stamp of learned origin, and was perhaps invented by William of Malmesbury, yet from the beginning of the twelfth century

---

[1] Letter of the Bishop of Bamberg to Nicolaus von Dinkelsbühl of January 16, 1426, in the Court Library of Vienna, No. 4899, fol. 312; von Perger, *Deutsche Pflanzensagen*, Stuttgart und Oehringen, 1864, p. 57.

[2] F. A. Reuss, *Kleine Beitraege* in the *Jahresbericht für den historischen Verein für Mittelfranken*, 1859, p. 95.

[3] An extensive sketch of the further development of that belief is found in my *Geschichte der deutschen Weihnacht*, Leipzig, 1893, pp. 219-255, chap. viii., *Die blühenden Bäume der Weihnacht*.

Joseph was regarded in England as a kind of national saint.[1] He was said to have brought with him his walking-stick, which he planted in the ground of his new home. Like Aaron's rod, or like Tanhûser's staff in the thirteenth century legend (from a mixture with which the story of Joseph of Arimathea has arisen), it put forth leaves; further it took to the habit of blossoming every year on the eve of Christ's Nativity. Whilst in reality the thorn from which the staff was cut, the *Crataegus praecox*, blossoms in November when the weather is mild, the Christian legend connects it firmly with the night of Christ's birth. An old report on it[2] gives the following account: "Mr. Anthony Hinton, one of the officers of the Earle of Pembroke, did inoculate, not long before the late civill warres (ten yeares or more), a bud of Glastonbury Thorne, on a thorne, at his farm house, at Wilton, which blossoms at Christmas, as the other did. My mother has had branches of them for a flower-pott, several Christmasses, which I have seen. Elias Ashmole, Esq., in his notes upon Theatrum Chymicum, saies that in the churchyard of Glastonbury grew a walnutt tree that did putt out young leaves at Christmas, as doth the King's Oak in the New Forest. In Parham Park, in Suffolk (Mr. Boutele's), is a pretty ancient thorne, that blossomes like that at Glastonbury; the people flock hither to see it on Christmas Day. But in the rode that leades from Worcester to Droitwiche is a black thorne hedge at Clayes, half a mile long or more, that blossoms about Christmas-day, for a week or more together. Dr. Ezerel Tong sayd that about Rumly-Marsh, in Kent, are thornes naturally like that near Glastonbury. The Soldiers did cutt downe that near Glastonbury; the stump remaines."[3] When, in 1752, September 2 was by law turned into September 14, Christmas was held twelve days earlier than the year before. This afforded a good opportunity of watching the qualities of these legendary thorns, and this was made use of at various places. Records of it are preserved in

---

[1] *The Legend of Joseph of Arimathea* (709 verses) has been edited by Prof. W. W. Skeat; and by Frederick Furnivall, 1862, for the Roxburgh Club.

[2] Aubrey, *Natural History of Wiltshire.*

[3] Ashton, *A Righte Merrie Christmasse,* pp. 105-106.

the Historical Chronicle (for January) of the *Gentleman's Magazine* for 1753, which contains a striking report, dated : "*Quainton in Buckinghamshire*, December 24. Above 2000 people came here this night, with lanthorns and candles, to view a black thorn which grows in the neighbourhood, and which was remembered (this year only) to be a slip from the famous *Glastonbury* Thorne, that it always budded on the 24th, was full blown the next day, and went all off at night; but the people, finding no appearance of a bud, 'twas agreed by all, that December 25, N.S., could not be the right *Christmas Day*, and, accordingly, refused going to Church and treating their friends on that day, as usual: at length the affair became so serious that the ministers of the neighbouring villages, in order to appease the people, thought it prudent to give notice that the old *Christmas Day* should be kept holy as before.

"*Glastonbury*. A vast concourse of people attended the noted thorns on *Christmas Eve*, New Stile; but, to their great disappointment, there was no appearance of its blowing, which made them watch it narrowly the 5th of Jan., the *Christmas day*, Old Style, when it blow'd as usual."

From Roman times the adorning of the houses with laurel and green trees at the Calends of January had been known to the Germanics; and when Christmas finally took the place of the Roman beginning of the year, the usage, like so many others, was transferred to that date. Beside the conifers, laurel and evergreen, bay and box, holly and mistletoe were used for that purpose.[1] Then the legend of the blossoming trees of the Christmas night reached the Germanics, and before long turned into a popular belief, which ascribed that wonder to every night between December 24 and December 25. Out of the union of these two elements the usage of the Christmas tree seems to have sprung, which, fully developed, appears for the first time in 1604 at Strassburg, the same town in which the adorning of. houses with fir branches at New Year is witnessed at the end of the fifteenth and the beginning of the sixteenth centuries.[2] Fir trees

---

[1] Compare pp. 103 to 106.

[2] *Memorabilia quaedam Argentorati observata*, which I edited in the *Jahrbuch für Geschichte, Sprache und Literatur Elsass-Lothringens*, VI., 1890, p. 62, ss.: "Auff

were put up in the rooms, adorned with roses cut out of many-coloured papers, apples, leaf-gold, sweets, etc., and fixed in a rectangular frame.[1] These trees, with their artificial flowers and fruits, remind the reader too clearly of the legendary blossoming and fruit-bearing apple trees of Christmas eve to admit of the connection with them being overlooked.   And even the direct link between the two is supplied by popular custom.

Whilst, on the one hand, evergreens were applied, and by preference such as bore fruits of a colour different from that of the leaves, like holly with its red berries, and mistletoe with its white ones; on the other hand, since the sixteenth century at least, boughs of cherry trees and hawthorn were, a fortnight before New Year, put into water in a warm place, so that they had a chance to bud and bloom at New Year, or later on at Christmas. The blossoms were used as an oracle.   Were they numerous and beautiful they meant luck; were they scarce and crippled, or not apparent at all, they were considered unlucky.   In all probability something similar was done with the green trees at the Roman Calends of January.   Nay, this was the natural consequence, when cherry trees, hawthorn, or similar early-blooming bushes were put into water in order to be kept fresh for some time.   The blossom oracle looks very much like the Roman cake oracle with the *Strenae*; and had not special heathen ideas and practices been connected with them, the Church would scarcely have taken the trouble to forbid their application to festive purposes.   A Salzburg regulation about forests, of 1755, forbids the taking from the forests of *Bächlboschen* or *Weihnachtsboschen, i.e.*, bushes— not trees—so that the custom of putting up bushes at Christmas must then have prevailed.[2]   In an etching by Joseph Kellner, *Das Christbescherens oder der fröhliche Morgen*, which, according to the costumes, has to be dated about 1790, the presentation of Christmas gifts is shown.   In the

---

Weihenachten richtett man Dannenbäum zu Strasburg in den Stuben auff, daran hencket man rossen auss vielfarbigem papier geschnitten, Aepfel, Zischgolt, Zucker, etc.   Man pflegt darum ein viereckent ramen zu machen."

[1] The further evolution and spreading of the Christmas tree is elaborately treated in my book, *Die Geschichte der deutschen Weihnacht*, chap. ix., pp. 256-278, and pp. 351-355.

[2] Schmeller, *Bayrisches Wörterbuch*, I., p. 271.   The probable etymological connection between "*Bächl*boschen" and the "*baculus* episcopalis" was pointed out on pp. 100 and 110.

corner of the room stands a fresh green tree in foliage, which bears three lit candles and other adornments,[1] and the autobiography of the painter, Albrecht Adam, who was born in 1786 at Nördlingen, tells that, in his youth at Nördlingen, not the dark fir tree was in use at Christmas eve, but months before Christmas, a cherry or agriot tree was put into a big pot in the corner of the room, so that at Christmas it stood in full bloom and extended along the ceiling. That was regarded as a great ornament, and indeed added much to the festive joy. One family competed with the other to have the finest tree, and the members of that house which had the most beautiful were very proud.[2] The same was done as late as 1858 with cherry boughs, elder boughs, and lime boughs, near Coburg.[3] So there is no doubt the modern Christmas tree is simply an artificial substitute for these trees and bushes in bloom.

The Roman Calends-of-January customs had in themselves not the power of transforming Germanic usage and belief. But inspired with a new life by the Christian religion and its legendary apparatus, they produced after the fourteenth century quite a new world of popular tradition, which has all too long been regarded as a relic of purely Germanic antiquity, but which we now, on the basis of historical evidence, are entitled to claim as a great product of the popularisation of the religion of the cross among the Christian Germanic nations.

---

[1] My *Geschichte der deutschen Weihnacht*, pp. 248-9.
[2] Albrecht Adam's *Selbstbiographie*, herausgegeben von Holland, p. 23.
[3] A. Schleicher, *Volkstümliches aus Sonneberg*, Weimar, 1858, pp. 91, 92.

CHAPTER XIII.

THE SCANDINAVIAN YEAR.

WHILE there is a continuous stream of literary tradition between the
Roman and the Germanic periods in the west of Europe, and while
we, by the medium of historical documents, can show not only how
political power passed over from the Romans to the Germanics in Gaul,
Germany, and Britain, but also how Roman civilisation and culture,
Roman habits and customs, Roman writing and learning, the Roman year,
and the Roman week, Roman months, and the names of Roman week-
days were gradually accepted by, and popularised among, the Western
Germanics—there exist no such connective literary links between the
Roman and the Scandinavian worlds. There we have no early records at
all that might compare with our Latin sources from the first to the eighth
century, dealing with Roman and Western Germanic relations. We have
no literary documents in the Scandinavian dialects of the eighth, ninth,
tenth, and eleventh centuries which could stand by the side of our oldest
Old-High-German, Old Saxon, and Anglo-Saxon poetry. Even the history
of the texts which were written down in Iceland, after the introduction
about A.D. 1150 of Roman characters, is in part very uncertain, very
few fragments having come down to us written before the year 1250—a
time when for many centuries Western civilisation had been influencing
Scandinavian tribes at home, a great number of Eastern stories and fairy-
tales had been communicated to them, and the Viking voyages of large
numbers of North-Eastern Germanics had on the coasts of Germany,
Britain, Gaul, Spain, Italy, and Asia Minor brought these men into

M

close contact and eye to eye with the whole world of Roman, Romance, and even partly of Greek and Eastern civilisation. Yet we possess, from the pen of a Greek, one sixth century report on a Scandinavian festival, though on one which, under all circumstances, must have been partial only. When in the sixth century the inhabitants of northern Scandinavia had been thirty-five days without sunlight, they used to send messengers to the summits of the highest mountains to look out whether now the sun would soon return. When he had been seen, it was announced everywhere that in five days the light would reach the ground of the valleys. Then a great rejoicing arose, and the highest festival of the year was celebrated. For although the same event took place every year, the inhabitants of the Norwegian islands were perhaps afraid it might happen that the sun would not return.[1] In the sixth century, the day of the

---

[1] Procopius, *Bellum Gothicum*, II., 15: Μεθ' οὓς δὴ Δανῶν τὰ ἔθνη παρέδραμον οὐ βιαζομένων σφᾶς τῶν τῇδε βαρβάρων. ἐνθένδε ἐς ὠκεανὸν ἀφικόμενοι ἐναυτίλλοντο, Θούλῃ τε προσχόντες τῇ νήσῳ αὐτοῦ ἔμειναν. ἔστι δὲ ἡ Θούλη μεγίστη ἐς ἄγαν. Βρεττανίας γὰρ αὐτὴν πλέον ἢ δεκαπλασίαν ξυμβαίνει εἶναι. κεῖται δὲ αὐτῆς πολλῷ ἄποθεν πρὸς βορρᾶν ἄνεμον. ἐν ταύτῃ τῇ νήσῳ γῆ μὲν ἔρημος ἐκ τοῦ ἐπὶ πλεῖστον τυγχάνει οὖσα, ἐν χώρᾳ δὲ τῇ οἰκουμένῃ τριακαίδεκα ἔθνη πολυανθρωπότατα ἵδρυνται· βασιλεῖς τέ εἰσι κατὰ ἔθνος ἕκαστον. ἐνταῦθα γίνεται ἀνὰ πᾶν ἔτος θαυμάσιον. ὁ γὰρ ἥλιος ἀμφὶ θερινὰς μὲν τροπὰς μάλιστα ἐς ἡμέρας τεσσαράκοντα οὐδαμῆ δύει, ἀλλὰ διηνεκῶς ἐς πάντα τοῦτον τὸν χρόνον ὑπὲρ γῆς φαίνεται. μησὶ δὲ οὐχ ἧσσον ἢ ἓξ ὕστερον ἀμφὶ τὰς χειμερινὰς τροπὰς ἥλιος μὲν ἐς ἡμέρας τεσσαράκοντα τῆς νήσου ταύτης οὐδαμῆ φαίνεται, νὺξ δὲ αὐτῆς ἀπέραντος κατακέχυται· κατήφειά τε ἀπ' αὐτοῦ ἔχει πάντα τοῦτον τὸν χρόνον τοὺς τῇδε ἀνθρώπους, ἐπεὶ ἀλλήλοις ἐπιμίγνυσθαι μεταξὺ οὐδεμιᾷ μηχανῇ ἔχουσιν. ἐμοὶ μὲν οὖν ἐς ταύτην ἰέναι τὴν νῆσον τῶν τε εἰρημένων αὐτόπτῃ γενέσθαι, καίπερ γλιχομένῳ, τρόπῳ οὐδενὶ ξυνηνέχθη. τῶν μέντοι ἐς ἡμᾶς ἐνθένδε ἀφικομένων ἐπυνθανόμην ὅπη ποτὲ οἷοί τε * * ἀνίσχοντος εἴτε δύοντος τοῖς καθήκουσι χρόνοις ἐνταῦθα ἥλιον. οἴπερ ἐμοὶ λόγον ἀληθῆ τε καὶ πιστὸν ἔφρασαν. τὸν γὰρ ἥλιόν φασι τεσσαράκοντα ἡμέρας ἐκείνας οὐ δύειν μὲν, ὥσπερ εἴρηται, φῶς δὲ τοῖς ταύτῃ ἀνθρώποις φαίνεσθαι πῆ μὲν πρὸς ἕω, πῆ δὲ πρὸς ἑσπέραν. ἐπειδὰν οὖν ἐπανιὼν αὖθις ἀμφὶ τὸν ὁρίζοντά τε γινόμενος ἐς τὸν αὐτὸν ἀφίκηται χῶρον, οὗπερ αὐτὸν ἀνίσχοντα τὰ πρῶτα ἑώρων, ἡμέραν οὕτω καὶ νύκτα μίαν παρῳχηκέναι διαριθμοῦνται. καὶ ἡνίκα μέντοι ὁ τῶν νυκτῶν χρόνος ἀφίκηται, τῆς γε σελήνης τῷ δρᾶσθαι ἀεὶ τοῖς δρόμοις τεκμηριούμενοι τὸ τῶν ἡμέρων λογίζονται μέτρον. ὀπηνίκα δὲ πέντε καὶ τριάκοντα ἡμερῶν χρόνος τῇ μακρᾷ ταύτῃ διαδράμοι νυκτί, στέλλονταί τινες ἐς τῶν ὁρῶν τὰς ὑπερβολάς, εἰθισμένον αὐτοῖς τοῦτό γε, τόν τε δὴ ἥλιον ἀμηγέπη ἐνθένδε ὁρῶντες ἀπαγγέλλουσι τοῖς κάτω ἀνθρώποις, ὅτι δὴ πέντε ἡμερῶν ἥλιος αὐτοὺς καταλάμψοι. οἱ δὲ πανδημεὶ πανηγυρίζουσιν εὐαγγέλια καὶ ταῦτα ἐν σκότῳ. αὕτη τε Θουλίταις ἡ μεγίστη τῶν ἑορτῶν ἐστι. δοκοῦσι γάρ μοι περιδεεῖς ἀεὶ γίνεσθαι οἱ νησιῶται οὗτοι, καίπερ ταὐτὸ ξυμβαῖνον σφίσιν ἀνὰ πᾶν ἔτος, μή ποτε αὐτοὺς ἐπιλείποι τὸ παράπαν ὁ ἥλιος.

winter solstice was the 19th of December, and towards the end of it, the 18th of that month. A period of forty days of the sun remaining below the horizon would, therefore, have extended from November 29 till January 8. The festival at the end of it was accordingly the earlier, the more southerly people lived, and the later, the more northerly. That in a region of such northerly expanse such a custom should evolve is almost as natural as it is impossible that it should arise in a region in which the sun never stays for forty-eight hours below the horizon. Therefore it can scarcely be said to contribute anything to our general knowledge of the Germanic division of the year, and we have rather to regard it as a singular curiosity than as a fact connected by the link of tradition with the common stock of Germanic lore, which was at one time believed to be purest among the Northern Germanics. But probably it was only the peculiar charm and genuineness of the marvellously clear and beautiful prose attained by the inhabitants of Iceland in the twelfth and thirteenth centuries, that explained why the literature of the North-Eastern Germanics, from its first becoming known to wider circles, especially in Denmark and Germany, was regarded by so many scholars as the true and genuine expression of ancient Germanicism. There was a time, and it is not so very distant, when the products of late Norwegian and Icelandic poetic fiction which we are wont to call by the name of the *Older Edda* (although that collection of songs is not an outline of the art of composing poetry as is the *Edda* of Snorri Sturluson) were thought to be the stock of poetry which originally had been common to all Germanic nations, and, therefore, had to be taken as the basis of Germanic mythology. No serious scholar will now-a-days maintain this any longer, though in minor questions some minds have by no means been freed from that prejudice. So Professor Karl Weinhold still prefers to base his conceptions of the Germanic year of ancient times on a singular statement made by Snorri Sturluson in the first half of the thirteenth century in Iceland, instead of taking as his basis for such a reconstruction of the ancient conceptions on the course of the year, the huge pile of solidly warranted historical facts that can be gathered from contemporaneous and principally Latin sources, from the first to the tenth century in Gaul, Germany, and Britain. He makes his task very easy of fulfilment, by declaring that the report given by Snorri Sturluson in chapter viii. of the *Ynglingasaga*, to the effect that the Northern Germanics about the middle of January made great offerings to their gods· for fertility, guarantees this as a genuine and ancient heathen custom —the very proposition which has to be proved.[1]   He fails, however, to state in what he thinks the guarantee to consist.   Three times over he has elaborately dealt with the problems connected with the Germanic year— in his pamphlets on the German division of the year, and on the German names of months, and in a chapter of his *Old North Life*.[2]   Whilst the first of these writings rests on the assumption that the Germanics divided their year according to solstices and equinoxes (of· which the early Germanic tribes in reality knew so little that they had not even words for them), the second starts from the few comparatively early attempts to use the same German names of months over a larger territory, and tries to show in what measure they were successful, instead of ascertaining first of all, the early popular tradition about months and their names among the various German tribes, and showing then how it determined the action of those early reformers of calendar-denominations.   In it he arrives at the conclusion that the ancient Germanics had had—by pure chance— the very same division of the year as that reached by the Romans through a long course of historical evolution, with the solitary distinction that the Germanics began their year a quarter of a year earlier than the Romans, viz., on October 1 instead of January 1.

In his book on old Scandinavian life,[3] Professor Weinhold has tried

---

[1] *Zeitschrift des Vereines für Volkskunde*, 1894, Heft I., p. 100: "Die Nordgermanen brachten zu dieser Zeit (Weinhold confuses here the winter solstice with the middle of January, on which the offerings previously to the time about 940 were made, according to *Heimskringla*, *Story of Hakon the Good*, chap. xv., Morris and Magnússon's *Translation*, Vol. I., p. 163) die grossen Opfer til gródhrar, d. i. für die Fruchtbarkeit (*Ynglingasaga*, c. viii.), eine Angabe, die, wenn auch erst im 13. Jahrhundert von einem Christen gemacht, dennoch Echt und Altheidnisches verbürgt."

[2] Karl Weinhold, *Über die deutsche Jahrteilung*, Kiel, 1862 ; *Die deutschen Monatnamen*, Halle, 1869, and *Altnordisches Leben*, Berlin, 1856, pp. 371-383.

[3] *Altnordisches Leben*, Berlin, 1856, pp. 371-383.

to give a theory of the ancient northern year. It is true he has learnt from Ideler[1] that the Runic almanacs of Scandinavia are, rather than of Germanic, of Roman and Christian origin; but he has failed to apply this knowledge to the divisions of time in use among Scandinavians, and identical with the institutions of the almanac of old Rome. He thinks it even probable that the Germanics, without foreign influence, hit upon the week of seven days,[2] although it is an established fact that that Phoenician week came to the Germanic tribes through the Romans, as is clearly shown by the names of the week-days, which exactly correspond to the Roman names. Grimm assigns to the fourth or fifth century A.D. the introduction of the Roman week among the Germanics, but I should rather be inclined to assign it to the first century before or after Christ's birth. Professor Weinhold's statements in that book can scarcely be taken seriously any longer. It is true that the Germanics of Caesar's time observed the new moon, the full moon, and so on; but it is not true that either Caesar[3] or Tacitus[4] says that decisive divisions of religious life were based upon them.[5] Weinhold infers from that supposition that in Caesar's time periods of fourteen days or of twenty-eight days must have existed, and he declares these periods of twenty-eight days to be identical with months of thirty days.[6] In one place[7] he says that Germanic heathendom is based on things very different from the observation of stars, and in another place[8] he ascribes to the heathen Germanics a whole "art" of astronomy, of which before their contact with Roman civilisation they apparently knew next to nothing. He speaks of a "popular astronomy" of the ancient Scandinavians,[9] though he adds that nothing is known of it. He further states that this astronomy (of which, according to himself, we know nothing) was at first confined to images and likenesses, and yet produced bye and bye observations at large, and chiefly the division of time.[10] He further maintains that the first thing the Germanics did was to fix "exactly"[11] the four regions of

---

[1] *Uber das Alter der Runenkalender*, Abhandlungen der Berliner Akademie der Wissenschaften, Philologisch-Historische Klasse, 1829-1832, pp. 49-66.

[2] P. 373.   [3] *Bellum Gallicum*, VI., xviii.   [4] *Germania*, chap. xi.
[5] P. 374.   [6] P. 375.   [7] P. 383.   [8] Pp. 371-372.
[9] P. 372.   [10] P. 372.   [11] P. 372.

the sky, and that the division of the day was based upon it, whilst in reality this is one of the latest things we find among them, and was certainly not arrived at without Roman influence.

There is no doubt that, among the Scandinavians, there existed a division of the year into two parts. As has been shown already, etymology proves this conclusively.[1] The names of *winter* and *summer* are common Germanic expressions, doubtless much older than any definite denomination such as spring and autumn, in regard to which Germanic tongues are much at variance with each other. As little true is it that the fourfold partition of the year never took root in Scandinavia,[2] an assertion which is not reconcilable with his other affirmation (in 1894) that the Germanic year was based on solstices and equinoxes. This statement, if it implies anything, implies a fourfold partition of the year. In reality that partition took root, though somewhat late. The very fact that the three later months of winter were given a common name, *útmânadir*,[3] mentioned by Professor Weinhold himself,[4] proves that in the thirteenth century people had learnt to count the year in quarters. If he goes on to declare that a tri-partition of the year never took root in Scandinavia either, he is as much at discord with himself as before. He admits that the Norwegian summer of six months is divided into three three-score-day tides— *Vaarmoaner*, *Sumarmoaner*, and *Haustmoaner*—a fact which, by its very existence, suggests a combination of two such periods into a long hundred of days. This suggestion has not failed to present itself to his mind, as four lines further down he makes the observation that 360 days are just three long hundreds. He maintains that the phases of the moon played a part in the religious life of the ancient Germanics (for which there is no evidence), and yet does not overlook the fact that the Scandinavians celebrated three great annual festivals. But he tries to explain that fact away. I quite agree with Professor Weinhold that the Germanic year began with the beginning of winter, and that the Scandinavian year of olden times began between October 9 and 14, and that consequently,[5] according to the dual division

---

[1] Compare pp. 5 and 6 of the present book. [2] P. 375. [3] *Vigastyrs saga*, chap. iii. [4] P. 378.
[5] Weinhold, *Altnordisches Leben*, p. 376; *Deutsche Monatnamen*, p. 22; *Edda Saemundar*, ed. Finn Magnussen, Havniae, 1828, III., 1013, 1015.

of the year, which in historical times came again ever more strongly into the foreground, summer began between April 9 and 14. But when he goes on to say that (while on the preceding page he had maintained that the quartering of the year never took root in Scandinavia) these two seasons of about 180 days each, were halved by solstices in midwinter and midsummer, putting the winter solstice on January 14 and the summer solstice on July 14, and calling January 14 *Jól*; when he maintains that these incisive days were strongly accentuated by religious festivals, and were the principal religious points in the course of the year; when he states that the Northern year was based entirely on the course of nature, whilst before[1] he had stated that it was based on astronomic observations,—he leaves entirely the basis of fact, and jumps into a world of unjustifiable speculation. And he quite fails to establish his theory that the Scandinavians knew of a division of the year into twelve months before they came into contact with the world of Roman civilisation. Nobody is able to point out twelve names of months which can, with any probability, be assumed to have been those of the twelve alleged Germanic months. In truth, even the later Scandinavians have not twelve names which, in a proper sense, could be called month-names, for *sådhtídh*, sowing-time (March); *eggtidh*, egg-time (April); *heyannir*, *heyant*, the first part of which is "*hay*," are not month-names. According to Professor Weinhold's own list of Scandinavian month-names,[2] we have the following denominations of the Roman months:

October: *gormånudhr*, called thus after *gor*, *excrementa intestinorum*, from the cleaning of the intestines of killed cattle (?);[3] New Icelandic *ylir*, after the howling of the storm (?); Danish, according to the milder climate of Denmark, which allows work on the field so late in the year, *Sädemaaned*, month of sowing, formerly, besides *Ridemaaned*, after the rutting time of stags. (Not of swine?)

November: *frermånudhr*, month of frost; New Northern, winter-month.

December: *hrútmånudhr*, month of rams (?); Modern Northic, 'Jul-' month; New Icelandic *mörsugr*, sucker or eater of bacon.

---

[1] On p. 372.   [2] Pp. 376-378.   [3] The interrogation and exclamation marks are mine.

January : *Thorri* ; Norwegian *Torre*, Swedish *Thoree*—unexplained name.

February : *Gôi* ; Norwegian *Gjö*, Swedish *Göja*, Danish *Göie*—unexplained name.

March : *sâdhtîdh*, sowing-time (!) ; *einmânudhr*, important month (?) ; New Icelandic, Odin's month ; Swedish *Tormaaned*, *Thurrmaaned*, month with dry weather (?) ; Norwegian *Krikla* or *Kvine*—unexplained.

April : *eggtîdh*, time of eggs ; *stecktîdh*, from putting up the hurdles for lambs ; Danish *Faaremaaned*, month of lambs ; New Icelandic, month of the cuckoo or harpa—unexplained ; Swedish *varant*, spring.

May : *sôlmânudhr*, sun-month ; New Icelandic *eggtîd*.

June : *selmânudhr*, from *sel*, arbour ; Swedish, midsummer ; Danish, summer-month, and *Skärsomar*, after the fleecing of the sheep.

July : *heyannir*, *höant*, hay-month ; Danish *Ormemaaned*, worm-month ; New Icelandic *selmânudhr*.

August : *kornkurdharmânudhr*, month of reaping ; Swedish *skördemaaned* or *skörtant*, the same ; Danish *Hömaaned*, hay-month, and *Höstmaaned*, harvest-month. The New Icelandic name *tvîmânudhr*, double-month, cannot, as Grimm supposed and Professor Weinhold holds, be explained by the fact "that August in many places shared its name with a neighbour month" (which feature August has in common with almost every other month of the year),[1] but is of the same origin as Anglo-Saxon *Thrilidi*. Its duplicate served as an intercalary month, or, in other words, August was the month that was doubled in Scandinavia in the leap years under the reign of the pre-Julian Roman calendar.

September : *haustmânudhr*, harvest-month ; Danish *Fiskemaaned*, fish-month.

Nobody will regard this conglomerate of mutually inconsistent and even contradictory names as having sprung from one root, and being genuinely Germanic. Most of the names are very vague attempts to give native names to the new periods of about thirty days taken over from the Romans. Even the Germanic denominations of the old three-score-day tides

---

[1] Compare pp. 13 to 15 of the present book.

have been made use of so little for that purpose that the common Germanic name for the time from November 11 till January 11, or in Scandinavia from December 14 to February 14, Gothic *Iuleis*, as a monthly name appears solely in Modern Northic, and there, of course, is of artificial growth.

We know little of the development of the Scandinavian year under Roman influence, but we know something about it. As long as the pre-Julian Roman calendar prevailed among Scandinavians, an intercalary month was put in every fourth year by the doubling of the month of August. When the Julian Calendar, however, was adopted, the year was taken as consisting of 52 weeks at 7 days each, or 364 days. It was between the years A.D. 950 and 970 that, in Iceland, it was noted that this was wrong, the beginning of summer, which people had learnt to observe according to Roman custom, slowly shifting backwards.[1] Thornstein Surt found an admirable means to meet this insufficiency. The Roman week of seven days had (as was remarked above) been introduced to the Germanics very early, and was in Scandinavia rooted much more deeply than the Roman year of 365 days and 12 months. Now the Northern year so far in use had comprised 52 full weeks, and it seemed to the people of Iceland most desirable not to interfere with the division of the year through the week without a fraction remaining behind. Thornstein found the proper way to escape the difficulty by keeping the year of 364 days and adding a leap week every seventh year, and in those periods of seven years which contained two leap years after the Roman fashion adding one every sixth year, that year being called leap year (*hlaupâr*). A tribe which, not so very long before, had had leap months, would naturally become more easily familiar with leap weeks than with leap days, especially when the congruity of 52 weeks and a year was preserved.

In the *Heimskringla* more than once the statement is repeated that the Scandinavians had three great festive tides. As regards the respective frequency of the festive tides mentioned, it appears that the most important

---

[1] *Islendingabók*, chapter iv.; Weinhold, *Altnordisches Leben*, 1856, p. 379. The *Islendingabók* was written by Ari after the year 1134.

was the festive tide at "winter-nights," *i.e.*, between October 9 and 14, a fact at which we cannot be astonished, because the very names of October (*gormânudhr, slagtmanad, blotmanad*) point to the fact that it was identical with the great cattle-killing time, and had, as its natural basis, an abundance of fresh meat unequalled in the whole course of the year. In the face of these facts Weinhold maintains: "Among all feasts of heathendom, the Yule-festival is the most important, it being the anticipation of the celebration of the winter solstice, and being named by a name primeval and obscure. It was held in the winter night[1] (December 14), and originally (how does Professor Weinhold know?) comprised three days. The preceding day[2] also was kept holy, being called *hökunôtt*, hook-night.[3] The principal offering of the year was celebrated at Yule. When Christianity was introduced, the familiarisation of its customs was very much facilitated by the fact that its holy tides were close to those of the heathen. The Yule festival had to be advanced only by a few days to agree with Christmas. King Hakon Adalsteinfostri, the son of Harald harfagrs, fixed by law at least for Norway this advance by ten days. Yule bye and bye received a duration of ten days. In Norway, Yule, in a wider sense, is understood to mean the time between December 21 and January 13."[4] From this passage it appears that Professor Weinhold, when he wrote it, did not remember that the Gothic word *Iuleis* and Anglo-Saxon *Geola* do not mean single days, but three-score-day tides in winter time. The same term (*Jôl*) must at one time have meant in Scandinavia the time from December 14 to February 12. For we know that the Scandinavian year began at October 14; and if we will not make the year begin in the middle of such a three-score-day tide, we must allow one to pass before we come to Yule-tide. I fail to see what induces Professor Weinhold to suppose a festival to have ever been

---

[1] In reality *at vetrnóttum* refers to the time about October 14.

[2] Weinhold apparently meant the eve of December 14.

[3] Other explanations given by Weinhold are *höggunôtt*, hewing-night (from *hoggva*, to hew), offering-night (a term, perhaps, identical with English *hog-maney*, December 31); *haukanôtt*, hawk-night. I should rather be inclined to derive the word from *hog*, swine.

[4] Page 380.

celebrated on December 14. It is in no way apparent from his text why the Scandinavians did not prefer to celebrate the winter solstice at its proper date, viz., December 17 (in 901 A.D.), but are alleged to have celebrated an "anticipation" of it on December 14. Assuming there had ever been a festival on December 14, where is the evidence that that festival was an "anticipation" of the solstice? His reference to *Olafsaga Tryggvasonar*, chap. xxi., and *Hâkonarsaga gôdha*, chap. xv., of the *Heimskringla* shows how that strange confusion was created. Professor Weinhold simply misunderstood the text of the *Heimskringla*. King Hakon did not move forward a festival to fix it on December 25; he moved one back. So the festival, the date of which he shifted, was not celebrated at all in the middle of December, but a considerable time after the date of Christian Christmas. It is not without reason that modern Norway counts Yule till January 13. Whilst the three-score-day tide *Jól* extended from December 14 to February 14, the thirty-day period *Jól*, which sprang out of the former, lasted from December 14 to January 13.

Professor Weinhold is of opinion that the two feasts at the beginning and at the end of winter were of less importance than the *Jól* festival[1]— the harvest festival *til árs*, and the spring festival of spring and victory.[2] As regards his saying that summer was without any more important celebration, it is entirely erroneous, few things being vouched so well as the feast *at sumri* (between June 9 and 14), which he, forgetting all about the Scandinavian climate, seems to assume to have been celebrated in March or April. Whilst during the Vikings' time of Norway it seems to have fallen somewhat into the background, it was preserved in Iceland in the shape of an *Allthing* till a very late time,[3] so that, in reality, it is *the* great *Thing* of Iceland in the time when history sets in. Now, Weinhold himself says: "The Scandinavian year began with the winter; in historical

---

[1] Page 380.

[2] The passages *Olafsaga helga*, chap. civ., "hit thridhja at sumri, thâ fâgna their sumari," etc., and *Ynglingasaga*, chap. viii., "til sigrs," etc., point in the very opposite direction.

[3] The sketch of the calendar of the Icelandic summer, according to the rules laid down in 999, given by Dahlmann, *Geschichte von Daenemark*, Vol. II., pp. 227-231, shows the same lack in historical insight.

times the beginning of winter was fixed on October 14."[1]   It apparently
never occurred to him that June 9 to 14 and October 9 to 14 are distant
exactly a third of a year, or a long hundred of days, so that, if a tri-partition
is to be assumed for the Scandinavian year as for the Western Germanic,
the third term must have fallen in the middle of February; whilst the dual
division line went from October 9 to 14 to April 9 to 14, and in the course
of time superseded the tri-partition, only very faint recollections of it being
preserved.

---

[1] Weinhold, *Deutsche Monatnamen*, p. 22.

CHAPTER XIV.

SCANDINAVIAN OFFERING TIDES.

IT is needless to say that the dual division and the tri-partition of the Scandinavian year, which are found alongside each other, are in the same way based upon an older partition of the year into six Aryan tides as among the Western Germanics, the six tides allowing a combination of two complexes of three tides, as well as of three complexes of two tides, though much less decisive traces of three-score-day tides are found in Scandinavia than in Germany and England. But whilst the fact that at one time there had been three seasons was remembered well in the Scandinavia of the thirteenth century, the three terms which divided them were no more remembered exactly, so that a number of mutually contradictory statements were made about them.

In the time when King Odin ruled on earth, Snorri Sturluson tells us about 1230 in the *Heimskringla* that "all over Sweden men paid Odin *scat*, to wit a penny for every head, but he was bound to ward their land from war, and to sacrifice for them for a good year:" "Folk were to hold sacrifice against the coming of winter, for a good year, in midwinter for the growth of the earth, and a third in the summer that was an offering for gain and victory." [1]

---

[1] *Heimskringla*, Vol. I., p. 20 (*Saga Library*, ed. by Morris and Magnússon, Vol. III.), *Ynglingasaga*, chap. viii. : "Thá skylldi blóta í móti vetri til árs, enn at midhjum vetri blóta til gródhrar ; hit thridhja at sumri, that var sigablót. Um alla Svithiód gulldu menn Odni skattpenning fyrir nef hvert ; enn hann skylldi veria land theirra fyrir úfridi, oc blóta theim til árs," which the Latin translation which is added, paraphrases this way ; "Sacrificia

When Snorri, later in the *Heimskringla*, in the *Story of Olaf the Holy* (1012-1030), again touches on that point, he gives a still fuller account, thus : " Later on in the winter, the king (Olaf the Holy) was told that the Up-Thrandheimers were gathered together in multitudes at Mere, and that great blood-offerings had been there at midwinter ; and that there they had made blood-offerings for peace and a good winter season. And when the king deemed he knew for sure the truth of this, he sent men and messages up into Thrandheim, and summoned the bonders down to the town, still naming by name such men as he deemed the wisest among them. So now the bonders had a parley and talked over this message between them ; and they were all the least willing to go this journey, who had fared the winter before. But at the prayer of all the bonders Olvir undertook the journey. And when he came down to the town, he went straightway to see the king, and then fell to talk. The king laid it on hand to the bonders that they had had a midwinter blood-offering. Olvir answered and said that the bonders were sackless of that guilt. 'We had,' said he, ' Yule-biddings and drink-bouts far and wide about the countrysides. The bonders are not minded so to pinch them in their cheer for the Yule-feast, as that a good deal be not left over ; and this it was, lord, that men were a-drinking of long after. At Mere there is a great chief-stead and big houses, and mickle dwelling round about, and there folk deem it good glee to drink together a many.' The king answered little, and was rather cross-grained, deeming that he wotted that other things were truer than that which was now set forth. The king bade the bonders go back. ' But yet,' says he, ' I shall get to know the truth, to wit, that ye hide the matter and do not face it ; but however things have gone hitherto, do no such things again.' So the bonders fared home again, and told of their journey that it had been none of the smoothest, and that the king was

---

prima sub hiemem (jussit Othinus) institui, pro felicis anni adventu ; his proxima, media in hieme, pro annonae felicitate et ubere glebae ; tertia, sub aestatem, pro victoria obtinenda. Per totam Sueciam, quodvis caput nummo censebatur, qui Othino solveretur, ut omnem hostilem vim ingruentem armis propulsaret, sacrificiaque pro annonae annique felicitate curaret " (*Heimskringla af Snorra Sturlusyni, Historia Regum Norwegicorum conscripta a Snorrio Sturlae filio*, Havniae, 1777, *Ynglingasaga*, i., 13).

something wroth."[1] The truth about the story is told to the king by
Thorald:[2] "This is the truth to tell, king, if I am to tell things as they
are, that throughout Upper Thrandheim, wellnigh all the folk are all-heathen
in their faith, though some men be there who are christened. Now it is
their wont to have a blood-offering in autumn to welcome the winter, and
another at midwinter, and the third at summer for the welcoming of summer.[3]
These are the ways of the Isle folk, the Sparebiders, the Verdale-folk, and
the Skaun-folk. There are twelve men who take upon themselves to carry
out the blood-feasts; and now next spring it is Olvir's turn to uphold
the feast, and now he is in much ado at Mere, and thither have been
brought all the goods which are needed for the feast." Olaf, consequently
sailing there, hindered the festival by means of force, slaying Olvir and
many others, taking other men's goods and fining the rest. Another
account is the following:[4] "But at home at his house Sigurd was in no
way a man of lesser state. While heathendom was, he was wont to have
three blood-offerings every year, one at winter-nights, another at midwinter,
the third against [should be *in*] summer.[5] And when he took christening,
he held the same wont in the matter of the feasts. In autumn, then, he
had mickle bidding of friends, and in winter a Yule-bidding, and bade yet
again many men to him; and a third feast he had at Easter, and had then
also a multitude. And to this wont he held as long as he lived. Sigurd
died of sickness. Then was Asbjorn of eighteen winters. He took the
heritage after his father; and he too held to the old wont, and had
three feasts every year, even as his father had had. Now it was but a
short while after Asbjorn took the heritage of his father, that the year's
increase took to worsening, and the sowings of folk failed. But Asbjorn

---

[1] *Saga Library*, by Morris and Magnússen, Vol. IV.; *Heimskringla*, Vol. II., p. 194,
The Story of Olaf the Holy, chap. cxiv.

[2] Chap. cxv., p. 196.

[3] "En that er sidhr theirra at hafa blót á haustum ok fagna thá vetri, annat blót hafa
their at midhjum vetri, en hit thridhja at sumri, thá fagna their sumari."

[4] *Ibid.*, chap. cxxiii., p. 214.

[5] "Sigurdhr var vanr, at hafa threnn blót hvern vetr, eitt at vetrnóttum, en annat at
midhjum vetri, thridhja at sumri."

held to the same wont as to his feasts, and in good stead it stood him then, that there was old corn and other old stores that were needed. But when this season wore and the next came round, the corn was no whit better than it had been afore. Then would Sigrid have the feasts done away with, some or all of them. But this Asbiorn would not have; so in harvest-time he went to see his friends, and bought corn whereso he might, and got it as gift from some. And so it came to pass that year, that he upheld all his feasts." When, in summer, he went aboard his ship and got corn sold to him in the south, he was robbed of it by Thorir, who, however, then invited him to the Yule-feast, with his mother and such of their men as they would take with them. But Asbiorn refused, and when Thorir after that slandered him, slew him before King Olaf's eyes.

These three annual offerings point clearly to the old tri-partition of the Germanic year; and, being in contradiction to the quartering of the year according to Roman custom, which was prevalent in Snorri's own time, may well be assumed to be historical truth, although every remark made by a Christian writer of the thirteenth century about the state of things four hundred years before that time, will naturally be liable to much doubt. A very critical attitude, however, has to be taken up as regards the dates of these three festive times adorned with blood-offerings, as Snorri contradicts himself about them at various places of his book. There can be no doubt about the autumn festival—the feast *at vetrnóttum*, "for a good year"— the feast of the year's beginning. For apart from the fact that the record of such a festival agrees with the statement of Tacitus of the first century of our era, it has been pointed out before [1] that the Germanics in olden times regarded the preceding night as part of a day, and the preceding winter part of a year's circle, so that they must needs begin their year with the beginning of winter. The Goths of the sixth century, too, began with November a new tide of sixty days, called *Ijuleis*. Snorri's story is quite consistent as regards this point. About the offerings "against the coming of winter," we learn not only from Snorri himself that they were

---

[1] Compare pp. 17, 18.

not merely brought to the gods for "a good year" in general, but also for the bettering of the "earth's increase," which—*til gródhrar*—he mentioned before as the peculiarity of the midwinter festival.[1]   It was apparently in autumn also, when King Olaf Traetelia of Sweden was offered up "for the plenty of the year" (640 A.D.).[2]   These autumn offerings were connected with great feasting.[3]

---

[1] "Domald took to him the heritage of Visbur, his father, and ruled the lands; and in his days there fell on the Swedes great hunger and famine.   Then the Swedes set up great blood-offerings at Upsala: the first autumn they offered up oxen, but none the more was the earth's increase bettered; the next autumn they offered up men, and the increase of the year was the same, or worse it might be; but the third autumn came the Swedes flockmeal to Upsala, whenas the sacrifices should be.   Then held the great men counsel together, and were of one accord that this scarcity was because of Domald, their king, and withal that they should sacrifice him for the plenty of the year; yea, that they should set on him and slay him, and redden the seats of the gods with the blood of him; and even so they did" (*Ibid.*, Vol. I., p. 29, *Ynglingasaga*, chap. xviii.).
"The next autumn fared King Granmar and King Hiorvard, his son-in-law, to guesting in the isle called Sili at their own manor therein" (*Ibid.*, Vol. I., p. 62, *Ynglingasaga*, chap. xliii.).

[2] "Now, King Olaf was a man but little given to blood-offering, and the Swedes were ill content therewith, and deemed that thence came the scarcity.   So they drew together a great host, and fell on King Olaf, and took the house over him and burned him therein, and gave him to Odin, offering him up for the plenty of the year" (*Ibid.*, Vol. I., p. 66, *Ynglingasaga*, chap. xlvii.).

[3] "But when Halfdan was one winter old, in the autumn-tide fared King Gudrod a-guesting, and lay on his ship in Stifla-sound, and great drinkings there were, and the king was very merry with drink " (A.D. 784), (*Ibid.*, Vol. I., p. 71, *Ynglingasaga*, chap. liii.);
"King Halfdan went in the autumn out to Vingulmark; and so on a night whenas King Halfdan was a-feasting, there came to him at midnight the man," etc. (*Ibid.*, Vol. I., p. 80, *Story of Halfdan the Black*, chap. iv.).   An exact description of the festivities of these blood-offerings is given in the *Story of Hakon the Great*, chap. xvi. (*Heimskringla*, Vol. I., p. 165 s.): "It was the olden custom that, when a blood-offering should be, all the bonders should come to the place where was the Temple, bringing with them all the victuals they had need of while the feast should last; and at that feast should all men have ale with them.   There also was slain cattle of every kind, and horses withal; and all the blood that came from them was called *hlaut*, but *hlaut*-bowls were they called wherein the blood stood, and the *hlaut*-tein a rod made in the fashion of a sprinkler.   With all the *hlaut* should the stalls of the gods be reddened, and the walls of the temple within and without, and the men-folk also besprinkled; but the flesh was to be sodden for the feasting of men.   Fires were to be made in the midst of the floor of the temple, with caldrons thereover,

N

All through the *Ynglingasaga*, which stands at the beginning of the *Heimskringla*, and tells the story of the oldest kings of Norway up to A.D. 825, the great festivities and banquets are held in *autumn*, and are frequently used by some enemy as opportunities to slay the men when drunk, and burn their houses.[1] Their date was *at vetrnóttum*, at the winter-nights, *i.e.*, at the beginning of winter, or October 9 to 14.[2] Up to the year 840 the autumn festival stands first among the three annual festive tides, and, while frequent reference is made to it, there is not a single mention of a Yule-feast up to that year. Then for some time, until, indeed, about A.D. 1000, both are mentioned with about equal frequency; whilst after that date the importance of the Yule-feast grows as rapidly as the autumn festivity decays, and finally is merged entirely in a simple Christian St. Michaelmas. If even Eugen Mogk, as late as 1891, calls the Yule festival "undoubtedly the highest festival of our ancestors,"[3] this can, among the

---

and the health-cups should be borne over the fire. But he who made the feast, and was the lord thereof, should sign the cups and all the meat; and first should be drunken Odin's cup for the victory and dominion of the king, and then the cup of Niord and the cup of Frey for plentiful seasons and peace. Thereafter were many men wont to drink the Bragi-cup; and men drank also a cup to their kinsmen dead who had been noble, and that was called the cup of Memory. Now, Earl Sigurd was the most bounteous of men, and he did a deed that was great of fame, whereas he made great feast of sacrifice at Ladir, and alone sustained all the costs thereof."

[1] Thus King Granmar and his son-in-law, King Hiorvard, were slaughtered in the eighth century. "The next autumn fared King Granmar and King Hiorvard, his son-in-law, to guesting in the isle called Sili at their own manor therein; and so while they were at this feasting, thither came King Ingiald with his army on a night, and took the house over them, and burned them therein with all their folk," *Ynglingasaga*, chap. xliii., *Heims-kringla*, Vol. I., 62. Thus King Pudrod was murdered about 784; thus King Halfdan was surprised and forced to flee into the woods about 830, *Ynglingasaga*, chap. liii., and *Story of Halfdan the Black*, chap. iv. ; thus Earl Sigurd was surprised during the autumn festival at Oglo, fire set to his house, and the stead burned and the earl therein, and all his folk with him, about A.D. 970, *Heimskringla*, Vol. I., p. 205, *Story of Harald Grey-cloak*, chap. v.

[2] Compare Eugen Mogk, *Mythologie*, in Paul's *Grundriss der germanischen Philologie*, Strassburg, 1891, I., p. 1127.

[3] *Mythologie*, in Hermann Paul's *Grundriss der germanischen Philologie*, Strassburg, 1891, Vol. I., p. 1125.

Scandinavians, apply only to the time after A.D. 1000. The autumn was the great slaughtering time among the Scandinavians, and the memory of this fact lived still in Iceland about the middle of the thirteenth century.[1] Somewhat later the autumn festival was even connected with Martinmas, though probably under German influence. A northern monk[2] told how, about the end of the tenth century, St. Martin had appeared to Olaf Tryggvison, King of Norway, in a dream, and bade him give up drinking in honour of the old gods and drink in his honour in future. This can only apply to the feast on St. Martin's day, which even in Scandinavia, where the year began about October 14, seems to have prevailed in later times.

Things are not quite so simple with the Summer Festival. In chapter viii. of the *Ynglingasaga*, Snorri states that it was celebrated in the summer—*at sumri*—and in the story of Olaf Tryggvison (995-1000),[3] it is referred to as "the midsummer feast of offering,"[4] and as clearly heathen

---

[1] This is the date of the *Eyrbyggjasaga*, the story of which is laid about the year 1000. *Saga Library*, II., p. 173: "So in the autumn Thorod was minded to slaughter the cow, but when men went after her, she was nowhere to be found. Thorod sent after her often that autumn, but found her not, and men deemed no otherwise than that the cow was dead or stolen away. But a little short of Yule, early on a morning at Karstead, as the herdsman went to the byre according to his wont, he saw a neat before the byre-door, and knew that thither was come the broken-legged cow which had been missing. So he led the cow into the boose and bound her, and then told Thorod. Thorod went to the byre and saw the cow, and laid his hand on her, and now finds that she is with calf, and thinks good not to kill her; and withal he had by then done all the slaughtering for his household whereof need was."

[2] Odo monachus in *Vita Olafi filii Tryggwii*, chap. xxiv., according to Keissler, *Antiquitates Septentrionales et Celticae*, p. 358; Schiller, *Kräuterbuch*, III., 12; Pfannenschmid, *Germanische Erntefeste*, p. 499: "Ex Eoo mari veniens Olaus ad insulam Norvegiae Mostur nominatam adplicuit. Hic noctu innotuit ipsi S. Martinus episcopus dicens illi: moris in his terris esse solet, cum convivia celebrentur, in memoriam Thoreri, Odini et aliorum asarum scyphos evacuare. Hunc ut mutes volo atque in mei memoriam in posterum bibatur, tua cura efficies. Vetus autem illa consuetudo ut deponatur conveniens est."

[3] *Heimskringla*, Vol. I., p. 317, *Story of Olaf Tryggvison*, chap. lxxii.

[4] "So whereas the king spake softly to the bonders, their fierce mind was appeased, and thereafter all the talk went hopefully and peacefully, and at the last it was determined that the midsummer feast of offering should be holden in at Mere, and thither should come all lords and mighty bonders, as the wont was; and King Olaf also should be there."

in opposition to the Christian tendencies of Olaf Tryggvison. Although midwinter meant in Snorri's thirteenth century language January 1, the midsummer festival was held *at sumri*, *i.e.*, approximately between June 9 and 14.[1]

The offering was made "for peace and the plenty of the year,"[2] and Professor Mogk admits that at that time of the year the great Thing assemblies were wont to be held.[3] He is of opinion that the offering tides in June and October, although mentioned at various places, were comparatively unimportant as compared with the great festive tide at midwinter. This is, again, in some degree to be admitted for the time after 1000 A.D., but before that time the very contrary was the case, as the simple enumeration of autumn offerings mentioned in the early parts of the *Heimskringla* shows.[4] It is not strange that the summer Thing should have lost its old consequence at a time when, every summer, more men were abroad on board their ships, so that sometimes even the whole arms-bearing host was far in the west, and scattered along the coasts of the Baltic and the German Ocean, up to the Orkneys and Iceland. It well

---

[1] Mogk, *Mythologie*, p. 1127, in Paul's *Grundriss der germanischen Philologie*, I., who believes in the quartering of the Germanic year, also puts it in June. So does Willibald Leo, in his notes to his translation of the *Hovard Isfjordingssaga*, Heilbronn, 1878, p. 129: "Ist kurzweg von 'Thing' die Rede, so ist dabei auf Island gewöhnlich das für das ganze Land geltende Allthing gemeint, welches alljährlich einmal in der elften Woche des Sommers (Auf Island wurde das Jahr nämlich in Sommer und Winter geteilt, und der Beginn des Sommers fiel auf den Donnerstag zwischen dem 9 und 15 April) ungefähr um die St. Johanniszeit (gegen Ende Juni) abgehalten wurde und 14 Tage währte." His note is explanatory of a passage of the *Hovardsaga* (p. 19 of his translation), which runs: "Thorbjörn, Thjodrek's son, rode every summer with his folk to the Thing;" p. 20: "In the same summer in which Hovard and his son went away, Thorbjörn rode to the Thing;" p. 21: "Thorbjörn rode home from the Thing with Gest to Bardastrand, where, in the very same summer, the wedding was held with a splendid dinner;" p. 32: "But in summer Thorbjörn rode to the Thing." The story of the *Hovardsaga* is laid in the tenth century.

[2] *Heimskringla*, Vol. I., p. 319, *Story of Olaf Tryggvison*, chap. lxxiv.

[3] *Mythologie*, p. 1127.

[4] Compare Maurer, *Bekehrung des norwegischen Stammes zum Christentum*, München, 1855-56, II., 233, 237.

accords therewith that the feast, and the Thing connected with it, are touched comparatively seldom by Snorri and other writers, although the existence of a midsummer festival is proved by the few existing mentions of it.

Beside the Summer Festival or feast *at sumri, i.e.,* June 9 to 14, there was, in the eighth century, a Spring Festival "at the coming of summer," also containing a blood-offering "for good peace."[1]

It is to Snorri himself that we owe the detailed knowledge of the further evolution of that festivity. "In Sweden," he tells us in the *Heimskringla*, "it was an ancient custom, while the land was heathen, that the chief blood-offering should be at Uppsala in the month of *Gói* (February); then should be done blood-offering for peace and victory to their king. Thither folk should seek from the whole realm of Sweden, and there at the same time withal should be the Thing of all the Swedes. A market and a fair was there also, which lasted for a week. But when Sweden was christened, the Law-Thing and the market were holden there none the less. But now, when Sweden was all christened, and the kings forbore to sit at Uppsala, the market was flitted, and held at Candlemas, and that has prevailed ever since, and now it is held for but three days. There is holden the Thing of the Swedes, and thither they seek from all parts of the land."[2] It is very strange that this *Góiblót* should not have been recognised as one of the three old offering tides, but that, ever since Maurer gave his opinion in that sense, it has been regarded as a feast of second rank.[3] Professor

---

[1] "The next spring went King Granmar to Uppsala to the blood-offering, as the wont was at the coming of summer, for good peace; and suchwise the lot fell to him thereat that he would not live long: so he went home to his realm" (*Heimskringla*, Vol. I., p. 62, *Ynglingasaga*, chap. xlii.). This festival must not be confused with the feast at Hadaland (*Heimskringla*, Vol. I., p. 86, *Story of Halfdan the Black*, chap. ix.), riding home from which King Halfdan the Black was, in A.D. 863, drowned in the river through the ice breaking under him, just as King Hring, when he drove with his queen, Ingibiörg, to a great guesting, was in danger of being drowned, because the ice of the lake broke over which he drove (*Fridhthjófssaga*, chap. xiii.).

[2] *Heimskringla*, Vol. II., p. 111, *The Story of Olaf the Holy*, chap. lxxvii.

[3] Maurer, *Bekehrung des norwegischen Stammes zum Christentum*, München, 1855-56, II., 236.

Mogk says, however, rightly enough, that at this chief-offering at Uppsala, before all, Freyr, the god of the sky, was revered, that in those days the Scandinavians began to feel the return of the sun, and that this feast was probably the feast of the sun returning.[1] When he continues— "About the same time it is that up till to-day the folk celebrate festivities. Then, at Shrove-tide, outside, in the open air fires are lit; on those days the wheel as a symbol of the sun plays a part, not at the time of the twelve nights"[2]—he is quite correct, with one reservation. The time when these customs are observed is not Shrove-Tuesday, but *Mittfasten*, *i.e.*, the Sunday *Laetare*, which is, as a rule, about one month later—about the tenth of March—although it varies with Easter within a considerable space. But Mogk is clearly right in putting the *Góiblót* beside the German sun-wheel-festivities, the characteristic of which is that a wooden wheel tied round about with ropes of straw, and set on fire, is rolled down from a hill-top to make the fields fertile. The corresponding Anglo-German spring festivity is bound to be one month later, since the Anglo-German winter begins one month later than the Scandinavian, *i.e.*, about Martinmas.

Snorri himself tells us[3] how this festive tide, which was connected with a Thing and a market, was shifted back from about the middle of February to the very beginning of the month (February 2), its eve being, of course, the evening of February 1. Thus the feast came into almost immediate touch with the Germanic three-score-day tide called *Jól*, which among Scandinavians must have meant, in the time after the Roman months had

---

[1] Mogk, *Mythologie*, in Paul's *Grundriss der germanischen Philologie*, I., 1126-27: "Neben diesem Hauptfeste (Jól) wurde ungefähr einen Monat später, im Februar im Norden das Góiblót gefeiert. . . . In diese Zeit fiel auch das Hauptopfer zu Uppsala, wo namentlich der Himmelsgott Freyr verehrt wurde. An diesen Tagen beginnen die Scandinavier eine Rückkehr der Sonne zu merken. Ich glaube daher, dass vielmehr dieses Fest das Fest der wiederkehrenden Sonne gewesen ist."

[2] "An diesen Tagen ist es auch, wo noch das Volk in Deutschland Feste feiert; an ihnen, zu Fastnachten, werden draussen im Freien Feuer entzündet, an diesen Tagen spielt das Wagenrad als Symbol der Sonne eine Rolle, nicht zur Zeit der zwölf Nächte."

[3] *Heimskringla*, Vol. II., p. 111, *Story of Olaf the Holy*, chap. lxxvii.

been accepted, December and January, ending with January 31. At the same time the middle of the three-score-day tide *Jól* received a significance it had never possessed before. While, formerly, the year had begun *at vetrnóttum*, or between October 9 and 14, the beginning of the year was now shifted over to mid-*Jól*, *i.e.*, January 1.

CHAPTER XV.

SCANDINAVIAN YULE.

The Autumn Festival, held between October 9 and 14; the Spring Festival, celebrated between February 9 and 14; and the Summer Festival, kept between June 9 and 14, are without doubt, according to Snorri's own report, the three great offering tides appearing up to the beginning of the ninth century. Even the dates of them can be fixed very exactly. It is true Eugen Mogk rejects the assumption of fixed Germanic festive days altogether, and is of opinion that there existed only festive tides, which were not dependent on the position of the sun, but rather on the influence of the sun upon the earth, *i.e.*, on the fundamental condition of economic existence;[1] and, of course, in olden times the fixing of these festive tides may have been a little different in various parts of the country. On the other hand, the division of the year into six three-score-day tides was taken over by the Germanics in prehistoric times. It is tantamount to a counting of three hundred and sixty days, or perhaps even of three hundred and sixty-six days, and nobody will deny that a tribe which counts the days of the year according to an established standard is absolutely in a position to fix its festive tides very exactly. It is no doubt strange that Snorri, in his general remark on Scandinavian

---

[1] He says: "Sun and day were, in the minds of our ancestors, things thoroughly different from each other. The Germanics cared little for the increasing of days. It was only when they noticed that the days grew warmer through the resplendent star of heaven that they felt the sun drawing nearer to them." Paul's *Grundriss der germanischen Philologie*, Strassburg, 1891, I., p. 1126.

festive tides in chapter viii. of the *Ynglingasaga*, does not mention these three, but only two of them, leaving out the Spring Festival, and mentioning instead a feast between January 9 and 14. This is the more strange, as

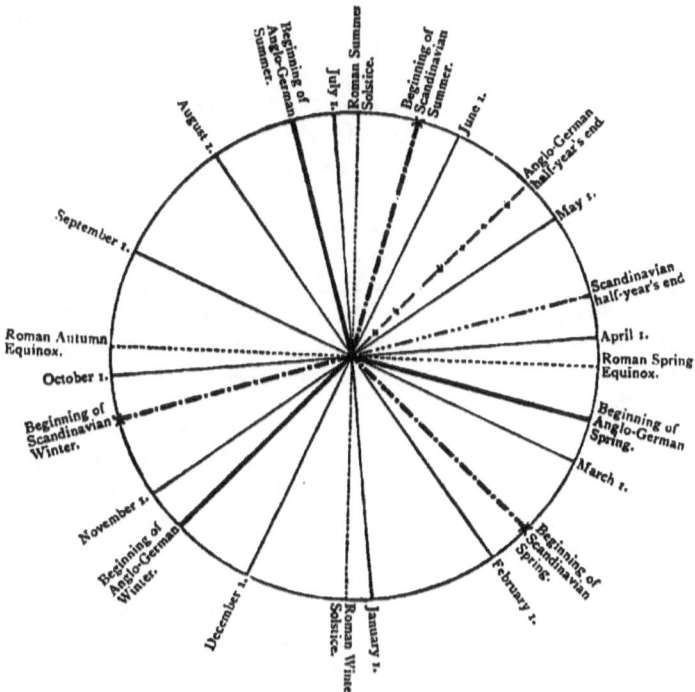

they fulfil all requirements of the three old Germanic beginnings of the single seasons, being each distant from the others by four months or two three-score-day tides. For the very same reason it is not well possible to assail Snorri's statement when he maintains that the old Scandinavians had *three* great offering tides only. He being not only acquainted

with and brought up in the Christian saints' days, but being also on
close terms with the Roman calendar, which at his time was the calendar
of his Icelandic compatriots, it would have been only natural for him to look
at all questions connected with the division of the year from the stand-
point of a quartering of the year according to solstices and equinoxes.[1]
Special weight has therefore to be attached to all statements of his in which
his mind appears to have been free from any prejudice to the effect
that conditions prevailing in his own time had obtained also in the far
away past of his ancestors.   Records of single outstanding events may
live unchanged for centuries in the memory of a nation, but as regards
customs and general conditions of life—such things as are gone through
year by year—every older status is almost completely wiped out of memory
as soon as it disappears from reality.   We ourselves find it difficult to
imagine that our own ancestors, a hundred years ago, should have lived
under conditions and forms of life different from ours, and historians have
always been only too much inclined to assume that the state of things
recorded by the oldest people living held good also for two centuries
prior to their own time.

Snorri has no knowledge of the fact that, four hundred years previous
to his own lifetime, *Jól* denoted a three-score-day tide extending approximately
over December and January; and although for him the word *Jól* never
means a single day, but in various places a shorter or longer festive period,
he apparently takes the festival about midwinter time for an old Germanic
festival.   On the other hand, a writer of the first half of the thirteenth
century cannot be regarded as an authority on the conditions of the
sixth or eighth century, more especially if his various reports are absolutely
irreconcilable.   And it apparently escaped his notice that, though he thought
that the festival about the middle of January was of ancient growth, he
was himself unable to give a historical instance of a Yule celebration
previous to 840, while his records of autumn festivals, spring festivals,

---

[1] King Olaf fell on Wednesday the fourth of the Calends of August (*Heimskringla*,
Vol. II., *Story of Olaf the Holy*); on the Nones of January (*Ibid.*, p. 157, *The Story of
Harald the Hard-redy*, chap. lxxix.); on the ninth of the Calends of January (*Ibid.*, p.
227, *The Story of Sigurd Jerusalem-farer*, chap. xxiii.).

and summer festivals were considerably older. Indeed, the spring festival had completely disappeared from his story when the Yule festival made its debut. These, however, are serious facts, and the only conclusion to be drawn from them is that, in his time, the old spring festival was merely preserved in a market in Sweden, having everywhere else been completely absorbed in the Yule festival which had arisen under the influence of the Roman calendar and won such an importance that it was regarded as genuine and old.

It is under King Granmar, in the eighth century,[1] that the last historical *Góiblót* is mentioned by Snorri to have been held, and it is about the middle of the ninth century that, for the first time, a Yule-tide is spoken of by him as having been celebrated by guesting. Is it too daring a supposition that, within the century which had elapsed between the two events, *Jólblót* had taken the place of *Góiblót*? And could *Góiblót*, which had its name from the month of *Gói*, have received with equal ease another name than *Jólblót*, according to the month in which it was now held?[2] In the tenth century the Yule-feast extended over some days,[3] and its celebration began between January 9 and 14.

It was Hakon the Good, King of Norway from 940 to 963, who changed, or tried to change, this state of affairs, ordering that the holy tide should in future begin with December 25 after the Christian fashion, and be kept in a festive and proper way. Snorri's report on this important episode

---

[1] *Heimskringla*, Vol. I., p. 62, *Ynglingasaga*, chap. xlii.

[2] The first instance of a particular *Jól* occurring in the *Heimskringla* is Vol. I., p. 82, *Story of Halfdan the Black*, chap. v.: "But at Yule-tide King Halfdan (840-863) was guesting in Heathmark, and had heard all these tidings." It is almost immediately followed by another which is connected with a story bearing a clearly legendary character, and telling how all the victuals vanished from the festive table (*Heimskringla*, Vol. I., p. 85, *Story of Halfdan the Black*, chap. viii.). The next Yule story is of the same kind (*Heimskringla*, Vol. I., p. 120, *Story of Harald Hairfair*, chap. xxv., about A.D. 880). It is, in fact, the German fairy tale of Schneewittchen, *i.e.*, Snow-white.

[3] King Hakon (940-963) held his Yule-feast at Thrandheim, which feast Earl Sigurd arrayed for him at Ladir. There, on the first night of Yule, Bergliot, the earl's wife, brought forth a man-child; and the next day King Hakon sprinkled the lad with water, etc. (*Ibid.*, Vol. I., p. 161, *Story of Hakon the Good*, chap xii.).

runs thus : " King Hakon was a well-christened man when he came to Norway ; but whereas all the land was heathen, and folk much given to sacrificing, and many great men in the land, and that he deemed he lacked men sorely and the love of all folk, he took such rede that he fared privily with his Christian faith. Sunday he held and the Friday fast, and he made a law that Yule should be holden the same time as Christian men hold it, and that every man at that tide should brew a meal of malt or pay money else, and keep holy tide while Yule lasted. But aforetime was Yule holden on *höku* night, that is to say, midwinter night, and Yule was holden for three nights." [1]

---

[1] *Heimskringla*, Vol. I., p. 163, *Story of Hakon the Good*, chap. xv. : " Hann setti that í lögum at hefja jólahald thann tíma sem kristnir menn, ok skyldi thá hverr madhr eiga mælis öl, en gjalda fé ella, en halda heilagt medhan jólin ynnist En ádr var jólahald hafit hökunótt, that var midhsvetrar nótt, ok haldin thriggja nátta jól," *Heimskringla eller Norges Kongesagaer af Snorre Sturlasson*, ed. by C. R. Unger, Christiania, 1868, p. 92. Morris and Magnússon translate *hökunótt* as Hogmanay, *i.e.*, December 31 ; but however well that would suit my own theory about the evolution of the Scandinavian year, in illustrating a stage at which, according to Roman Calends custom, Yule was kept on January 1, I do not think there is any reason to identify *hökunótt* with Hogmanay ; and the more caution is requisite since the etymology of both words is entirely uncertain. Hogmanay or Hogmenay was a Northumbrian name of December (John Jamieson, *An Etymological Dictionary of the Scottish Language*, under "Hogmanay"), while in Scotland it has denoted, at least since the beginning of the nineteenth century, the last day of that month only. Lambe (*Notes to the Battle of Floddon*, p. 67) derives it from ἄγια μήνη, holy month, the common Northumbrian form being at his time *Hagmana*, but he gives no proof that December was ever called ἄγια μήνη in Scotland. If, among the Scandinavian nations, a name slaughter-month for December could be shown to have existed, it would not be impossible to assume for the north country a name consisting of *hoggva*, to hew (*hogg* is stroke), and *month*. But an explanation would have to be given why the word was not formed of A.S. *heávan*, to hew, and *mondth*. For although there exists a word *hyge*, *hég*, hay, the A.S. verb has no more a *g*. Nevertheless *heávan* and *hoggva* must have been felt to be the same word. There remain two other possibilities of derivation, namely, from *hag*, witch, and from *hog*, pig. And until it has been shown what witches have to do with December, I should rather be inclined to take hogmanay as pig-month, *i.e.*, month in which pigs were killed. It is strange that the ultimate bearing of the name would thus be almost identical with what it would have been if it consisted of *hoggva* and *month*. But apart from all that, I do not see how, among a people which counts the winter from October 9 to 14 to April 9 to 14, as the Scandinavians always did in historical times, midwinter's night can mean anything but a night between January 9 and 14. When Eric Gustave Geijer, in his *History of the Swedes* (translated by Turner, London, without year,

However serious attempts were made by Hakon the Good to win his folk over to Christianity, he did not succeed. An earl of his called all his bonders together to a place called Ladir, and himself giving all the victuals and ale, arranged a huge blood-offering, at which the king appeared. His proposal to give up their old religion and customs was received with undivided disapproval, so that the king thought it wisest to take part in the offering in order not to lose his crown and kingdom. It is not quite plain from the record given by Snorri Sturluson [1] at which of the three great annual festivals this was; but it is certain that the next great event connected with Hakon's attempt to withhold himself from an all too public celebration of blood-offering festivities "took place in the autumn-tide at winter-nights," which at that time still outshone in splendour the January festivity. While so far the king had preferred to take his meal

---

p. 43), tells this according to Snorri, he adds a note which shows that that festival, in his opinion, was originally kept in February (between February 9 and 14), then about Candle-mas, then about midwinter (January 14), then about January 1, and finally on December 25. He only confuses February 9 to 14, and *midwintersnatten*. The time at the beginning or about the middle of February can never have been called midwinter, but was simply the end of the third of the year, beginning between October 9 and 14. Geijer's note is: "It is related of Sigurd Thorson, a rich Norwegian, that he had the custom, while heathenism existed, of keeping three sacrifices every year—one at the commencement of winter, the second in midwinter, and the third towards summer. But after he had embraced Christianity, he preserved the custom of giving entertainments. In harvest he kept with his friends a harvest-home, in winter a Christmas revel, and the third feast he held at Easter; and many guests were gathered at his board" (*Saga of St. Olave*, chap. cxxiii.). Hacon the Good of Norway had removed the Pagan Yule, formerly observed as midwinter's night (*midwintersnatten*), called also hawk's night (*hökenatten*), and kept at the beginning of February, according to the Harvarar Saga, to the Catholic Christmas (*Saga of Haco*, chap. xv.). Candlemas, celebrated at the time of the old winter sacrifice, is still called in some provinces Little Yule. In full accordance with this report Eugen Mogk says: "There is no foundation whatever for taking . . . the great winter festival, called Yule-festival by the Scandinavians, for the feast of the sun returning" (in Paul's *Grundriss der germanischen Philologie*, Strassburg, 1891, I., p. 1126). In conformity with that, Professor Kaufmann fixed its original date at the end of January, and Professor Elard Hugo Meyer at the beginning of February, but I do not see how we can help (according to the beginning of winter between October 9 and 14 and the beginning of summer between April 9 and 14) fixing it at February 9 to 14.

[1] *Heimskringla*, Vol. I., p. 166-168, *Story of Hakon the Good*, chap. xvii.

privately on such occasions, he was now compelled to take it publicly in the hall and to make many compromises, however much he might grudge them.   Snorri tells it thus: "In the autumn-tide at winter-nights was there a blood-offering held at Ladir, and the king went thereto. Heretofore he had ever been wont, if he were abiding at any place where was a feast of blood-offering going on, to eat his meat in a little house with but few folk, but now the bonders murmured at it, that he sat not in his own high-seat, where the feast of men was greatest; and the earl said to the king that so he would not do as now.   So it was therefore that the king sat in his high-seat.   But when the first cup was poured, then spake Earl Sigurd thereover, and signed the cup to Odin, and drank off the horn to the king.   Then the king took it, and made the sign of the cross thereover; and Karl of Griting spake and said: 'Why doeth the king thus, will he not do worship?'   Earl Sigurd answers: 'The king doth as they all do who trow in their own might and main, and he signeth the cup to Thor.   For he made the sign of the hammer over it before he drank.'   So all was quiet that eve.   But on the morrow, when men went to table, the bonders thronged the king, bidding him eat horse-flesh, and in no wise the king would.   Then they bade him drink the broth thereof, but this would he none the more.   Then would they have him eat of the dripping, but he would not; and it went nigh to their falling on him.   Then strove Earl Sigurd to appease them, and bade them lay the storm; but the king he bade gape over a kettle-bow, whereas the reek of seething had gone up from the horse-flesh, so that the kettle-bow was all greasy.   Then went the king thereto, and spread a linen cloth over the kettle-bow, and gaped thereover, and then went back to the high-seat; but neither side was well pleased thereat."[1]   This was not the end of the trouble caused by his Christian belief.   "The next winter was the Yule-feast arranged for the king in Mere.   But when time wore towards Yule, the eight lords who had most dealing in blood-offerings of all Thrandheim appointed a meeting" between themselves and "bound themselves to this, that the four of Outer Thrandheim should

---

[1] *Heimskringla*, Vol. I., p. 170, *Story of Hakon the Good*, chap. xviii.

make an end of the Christian faith in Norway, and the four of Inner Thrandheim should compel the king to blood-offering. So the Outer Thrandheim fared in four ships south to Mere, and there slew three priests, and burned three churches, and so gat them back again. But when King Hakon came to Mere with his court and Earl Sigurd, there were the bonders come in great throngs. The very first day of the feast the bonders pressed hard on the king, bidding him offer, and threatening him with all things ill if he would not. Earl Sigurd strove to make peace between them, and the end of it was that King Hakon ate some bits of horse-liver, and drank crossless all the cups of memory that the bonders poured for him. But so soon as the feast was ended, the king and the earl went out to Ladir. Of full little cheer was the king, and straightway he arrayed him for departing from Thrandheim with all his court, saying that he would come with more men another time and pay back the bonders for the enmity they had shown him. But Earl Sigurd prayed the king not to hold them of Thrandheim for his foes for this; and said that no good would come to the king of threatening or warring against the folk of his own land, and the very pith of his realm, as were the folk of Thrandheim. But the king was so wroth, that no speech might be held with him. He departed from Thrandheim, and went south to Mere, and abode there that winter and on into spring; and as it summered he drew together an host, and rumour ran that he would fall on the Thrandheimers therewith."[1] But when the king learned the news that the King of Denmark had invaded his country, he preferred to lead his army against him, and was supported therein by Earl Sigurd and the Thrandheimers (about 955 A.D.).[2] He died in 963, his attempts to establish Christianity in Norway having utterly failed. For some time to come the new belief could not root itself in Norway; and when the sons of King Eric of Denmark, who had been christened in England, came to Norway and broke down temples and abolished the offering festivals, they gained only hatred thereby. When Earl Hakon had hung up King

---

[1] *Heimskringla*, Vol. I., p. 170 f., *Story of Hakon the Good*, chap. xix.
[2] *Ibid.*, pp. 171, 172, chap. xx.

Harald on a gallows and subdued all the land, he bade restore the
temples and blood-offerings throughout all his dominions.[1]   And although
later some men took christening, they turned back to blood-offering;
and even when King Olaf I. Tryggvison established Christianity by
force and cruelty in Norway about 998, the country was by no means
Christian.[2] Just as, some centuries earlier, the Autumn Festival had been
the opportunity frequently chosen for surprising the enemy at feast and
drunk, now from the beginning of the eleventh century the Yule-tide

---

[1] *Heimskringla*, Vol. I., p. 242, *Story of Olaf Tryggvison*, chap. xvi.

[2] Under his reign the first Easter is recorded in the *Heimskringla*, I., p. 313, *Story
of Olaf Tryggvison* in 999 : "[he] came at Easter eve to Ogvaldsness in Kormt-isle. And
there was his Easter-feast arrayed for him," as well as the first Michaelmas, I., p. 336,
Story of Olaf Tryggvison, chap. lxxxix. : "And now was Michaelmas come, and the
king let hold high-tide, and sing mass full gloriously; and thither went the Icelanders,
and hearken the fair song, and the voice of the bells."   In the Stories that follow in
the *Heimskringla* the names of Christian festivals get ever more numerous: "It befell on
Ascension day that King Olaf went to high mass," *Heimskringla*, II., p. 131,
Story of Olaf the Holy, chap. lxxxv. ; "at Candlemas," *Ibid.*, p. 152, *Story
of Olaf the Holy*, chap. xciii. ; "King Olaf had a great feast at Easter, and had
many men of the town bidden and many bonders withal," *Ibid.*, p. 195, *Story of Olaf
the Holy*, chap. cxv. ; "After Candlemas," *Ibid.*, p. 221, *Story of King Olaf the Holy*,
chap. cxxiv. ; "The king says : 'Is it not a guilt unto death, Skialg, if a man break the
Easter peace?'" *Ibid.*, p. 223, chap. cxxv.; "the day before Michaelmas," *Ibid.*,
p. 325, chap. clxii.; "On Thomas-mass before Yule in the very first dawn," *Ibid.*,
p. 354, chap. clxxxvi. ; "The next day was Michaelmas Eve," *Ibid.*, III., p. 35,
The Story of Magnus the Good, chap. xxviii. ; "ere Michaelmas," *Ibid.*, p. 50,
chap. xxxvi. ; "the battle was on the Wednesday next before Matthewmass," *Ibid.*,
p. 168, chap. lxxxviii.; "about candlemas," *Ibid.*, p. 207, *The Story of King Magnus
Barefoot*, chap. ii. ; "the day before Bartholomewmas," *Ibid.*, p. 240, chap. xxvi.; "a high-
tide, Whitsunday to wit," *Ibid.*, p. 288, chap. xxx. ; "one night after Marymass in autumn,"
Ibid., p. 310, chap. xlii. ; "on Whitsunday," *Ibid.*, p. 325, *Story of Magnus the Blind and
Harald Gilli*, chap. ix.; "and this was Michaelmass," *Ibid.*, p. 458, *Story of King Magnus,
son of Erling*, chap. xviii. ; "when Lenten fast was wearing," *Ibid.*, p. 467, *Story of King
Magnus, son of Erling*, chap. xxv.; "to Rogation-days' Thing," *Ibid.*, p. 467; "on Tuesday
in Rogation-days," *Ibid.*, p. 468; "in the night before Ascension day," *Ibid.*, p. 468 ; "The
priest who sang at Rydiokul, which is on the water, bade the earl and his to a feast,
to come there at Candlemas," *Ibid.*, p. 475, *Story of King Magnus, son of Erling*,
chap. xxxii. ; "That was the latter Marymass," *Ibid.*, p. 481, *Story of King Magnus, son of
Erling*, chap. xxxix.

was used for the same purpose;[1] while among friends it became a custom to feast the first half of Yule-tide at the home of the one and the second half at the home of the other, the two parts being called the earlier and the latter Yule. "Thorod was with another man at Thorar's; and there was mickle Yule-feast and gild ale drinkings. There were many bonders living in that thorp, and they all drank together through the Yule-tide. Another thorp there was a little way thence; there dwelt a kinsman-in-law of Thorar, a mighty man and a wealthy. He had a son full grown. These kinsmen-in-law were to drink half Yule at each other's, beginning at Thorar's. The kinsmen-in-law drank against each other, and Thorod against the bonder's son. It was a champion drinking, and in the evening was mickle masterful talk and man-pairing betwixt the Norway men and the Swedes."[2] In the term "Little Yule," which provincially means Candlemas, and which presupposes a corresponding "Great Yule," and in the terms "earlier Yule" and "latter Yule," there are contained reminiscences of a halving of the older Yule-tide of three scores of days, which on A.S. ground was divided into *ærra Geola* and *æftera Geola*, and among the Goths in *fruma Iiuleis* and * *aftuma Iiuleis*.

The days of Yule are counted like the days of the month in the Roman calendar, and under our eyes, as it were, that festive tide grows and grows.

---

[1] *Heimskringla*, II., p. 48, *The Story of Olaf the Holy* (1012-1030), chap. xxxix. : "Earl Svein was then up Thrandheim at Steinker, and let array there a Yule feast; there was a cheaping-stead;" p. 53, chap. xlii. : "Even at that nick of time came the host of the earl into the town, and they took all the Yule victuals and burnt all the houses." The same is evident from the *Eyrbyggjasaga* written about 1250, but telling a story of the time about 1000 (*Saga Library*, II., p. 79), which contains the following: "That winter at Yultide had Thorolf a great drinking, and put the drink round briskly to his thralls; and when they were drunk, he egged them on to go up to Ulfar's-fell and burn Ulfar his house, and promised to give them there freedom therefore;" p. 125: "Then Steinthor and his men misdoubted them, that there would be going the sons of Thorbrand minded for the Yulefeast at Holyfell;" p. 147: "in the winter a little before Yule;" p. 148: "Kiartan and Thurid bade their neighbours to the arvale, and their Yule ale was taken and used for the arvale."

[2] *Heimskringla*, Vol. II., p. 296, *Story of Olaf the Holy*, chap. cli. : ". . . Now when mid-Yule was come, Thorar and all his freedmen with him went to his kinsman-in-law, and there he was to drink the latter Yule."

Snorri informs us that, so long as Yule was held in January, it was celebrated for three days;[1] but when it took its new date, for three-quarters of a century it became a celebration of at least eight days, the eighth day (January 1) being the day of giving gifts of friendship, according to Roman Calends-of-January custom.   Even King Olaf the Good stuck to that custom, however much stress he laid on Christian rites.[2]   King Olaf was expelled from his country by King Cnut of Denmark, who, at his death, was succeeded by King Svein.   As regards Yule-tide, Svein's reign is remarkable for the fact that he made it a legal term at which duties had to be paid, which it apparently had not been until then.[3]   By this act a new step was taken towards a complete overtaking of the Roman calendar, which made as quick and steady progress as the doctrine, feasts, and rites of Christianity.   Bye and bye the Christian customs obtained sway all over the land.   It became the habit to fast on Yule-eve, and begin the festivities not earlier than Yule-day, as the 25th of December was called in the twelfth century.   Neither was it any more the habit, as it had been, to have concubines on the night preceding Yule-day.[4]   The introduction of fasting also is vouched by another

---

[1] *Heimskringla*, Vol. I., p. 163, *Story of Hakon the Good*, chap. xv.

[2] "King Olaf had a great Yule-feast, at which there was gathered to him a many great men.   On the seventh day of Yule it fell that the king went a-walking, and a few men with him.   Sigvat followed the king day and night, and at this time he was with him.   So they went to a certain house, wherein were guarded the precious things of the king.   He had then had great store arrayed, as his wont was, and fetched together his precious things for this sake, to give gifts of friendship on the eighth eve of Yule" (*Heimskringla*, Vol. II., p. 337, *Story of Olaf the Holy*, chap. clxxii.).

[3] "King Svein (1030-1035) brought new laws into the land for many matters, which were framed after the manner of the laws of Denmark, but some mickle harder. . . . At Yule every man was to bring the king a measure of malt for every hearth, and a thigh of a three-winter ox, that was called pasture-tod, and a keg of butter withal ; and every housewife was to give housewife's-tow, that is to say, so much of undressed flax as might be spanned by the biggest finger and the longest " (*Heimskringla*, Vol. II., p. 450, *Story of Olaf the Holy*, chap. ccliii.).

[4] *Heimskringla*, III., p. 294, *The Story of Sigurd Jerusalem-farer, Eystein and Olaf*, chap. xxxiii. : "So befell on a time on Yule-eve, as the king (Sigurd Jerusalem-farer, 1103-1130) sat in the hall and the boards were set, that the King said : 'Fetch me flesh-meat.'   'Lord,' said they, 'it is not wont in Norway to eat flesh-meat on Yule-eve.'   He answered : 'If it be not the wont, then will I have it the wont.'   So they came and had in

Saga. The *Eyrbyggjasaga*, dating from about 1250, tells a story of about the year 1000. Its Yule is absolutely the Christian Christmas, preceded by an Advent-fast or Yule-fast,[1] and celebrated by a great drinking.[2] After another century people thought it no longer permissible to fight on Yule-day, and it became a specially memorable fact, when, in the case of necessary work, three days only were kept free from labour, though there were cases in which a fight would arise in a Yule company, and some men were killed.[3] The Yule-tide grew still further, so that in the twelfth century a celebration of fourteen days was reached.[4] From the beginning of the eleventh century the occasions on which Yule is mentioned in the Saga literature become ever more frequent.[5] So the *Bandamannasaga*, which has its origin no

---

porpoise. The king stuck his knife into it, but took not thereof. Then said the king : 'Fetch me a woman into the hall.' They came thither and had a woman with them, and she was coifed wide and side. The king laid his hand to her head, and looked on her, and said : 'An ill-favoured woman is this, yet not so that one may not endure her.' Then he looked at her hand and said : 'An ungodly hand and ill-waxen, yet one must endure it.' Then he bade her reach forth her foot ; he looked thereon, and said : 'A foot monstrous and mickle much ; but one may give no heed thereto ; such must be put up with.' Then he bade them lift up the kirtle, and now he saw the leg, and said : 'Fie on thy leg ! it is both blue and thick, and a mere whore must thou be.' And he bade them take her out, 'for I will not have her.'"

[1] William Morris and Eiríkr Magnússon, *The Story of the Ere-Dwellers*, London, 1892, p. 146: "And by then it was hard on the Yule-fast, though at that time there was no fasting in Iceland."

[2] *Ibid.*, p. 79.

[3] "King Harald came to Biorgvin on Yule-eve, and laid his host into Feoru-bights, and would not fight for its holiness' sake" (*Heimskringla*, III., p. 321, *Story of Magnus the Blind and Harald Gilli*); and III., p. 322: "Only three days in the Yule-tide were holden holy from smith's work. But on the out-going day of Yule, King Harald let blow the host to give way. In Yule-tide nine hundreds of men had gathered to King Harald." "King Hakon was in Cheaping through the Yule ; and one evening, early in the Yule-tide, his men got to blows in the Court Hall, and eight men came by their death, and many were wounded. But after the eighth day of Yule there fared into Elda these fellows of Hakon" (*Ibid.*, p. 415, *Story of Hakon Shoulder-Broad*, chap. xi.).

[4] "He went out of King's Rock on the latter part of Yule-tide with much folk, and they came to Force on the thirteenth day of Yule. He stayed there for the night, and went to matins there on the last day of Yule, and the gospel was read to him thereafter ; this was on a bath-day" (*Ibid.*, p. 420, *Story of Hakon Shoulder-Broad*, chap. xiv.).

[5] *Heimskringla*, Vol. II., p. 48, *Story of Olaf the Holy*, chap. xxxix. "may be that he will sit down in quiet at Steinker over Yule," *Ibid.*, p. 50, *Story of Olaf the Holy*, chap. xl.;

earlier than the second half of the thirteenth century, but the story of which is laid about 1050, mentions the Yule-tide in a general kind of way as a festive time.[1]

"and he let flit into the houses both the drink and the victuals, being minded to sit there Yule-tide over," *Ibid.*, p. 51; "The king had a great Yule-bidding, and bade to him many wealthy bonders from the countrysides," *Ibid.*, p. 79, *Story of Olaf the Holy*, chap. lix.; "This winter Eyvind was a Yule-guest of King Olaf, and took good gifts of him. There was also with the king at the time Bryniolf Camel, and he had for a Yule-gift from the king a gold-wrought sword and therewithal the manor called Vettland, the greatest of chiefsteads," *Ibid.*, p. 79, *Story of Olaf the Holy*, chap. lx.; "a little before Yule," *Ibid.*, p. 149, *Story of Olaf the Holy*, chap. xcii.; "After Yule," *Ibid.*, p. 151, *Story of Olaf the Holy*, chap. xciii.; "after Yule," *Ibid.*, p. 285, *Story of Olaf the Holy*, chap. cxlviii.; "after Yule," *Ibid.*, p. 296, chap. cli.; "after Yule," *Ibid.*, p. 337, chap. clxxii.; "Good store for Yule," *Ibid.*, p. 361, chap. clxxxvii.; "Forthwith on the back of Yule," *Ibid.*, p. 386, chap. cciii.; "after Yule," *Heimskringla*, Vol. III., p. 1, *Story of Magnus the Good*, chap. i.; "after Yule," *Ibid.*, p. 266; "When it drew towards Yule," *Ibid.*, p. 39, *Story of Magnus the Good*, chap. xxxi.; "A little ere the Yule-tide," *Ibid.*, p. 50, chap. xxxvi.; "Those cheapingsteads where ye, lord, are wont to sit and take Yule-feasts," *Ibid.*, p. 183, *Story of Harald the Hard-redy*, chap. cii.; "the earl should let set market for meat-cheaping for Sigurd all the winter, but this went on no longer than to Yule, and then meat grew hard to get, for the land is barren and an ill meat-land," *Ibid.*, p. 250, *Story of Sigurd Jerusalem-farer*, chap. iv.; "close after Yule," *Ibid.*, p. 349, *Story of Ingi, son of Harald*, chap. ii.; "this folk went on as if nothing was so needful as this Yule-drinking, and that might in no wise be given up," *Ibid.*, p. 422, *Story of Hakon Shoulder-Broad*, chap. xv.; "Erling arrayed there for a Yule-feast, but the Hising-dwellers had a guild-ale, and held their fellowship through Yule-tide. The night after the fifth day of Yule, Erling fared out," etc., *Ibid.*, p. 460, *Story of King Magnus, son of Erling*, chap. xix.; "But when Earl Erling had news of this flock, he fared with his host into the Wick, and kept to his ships through the summer, and was in harvest-tide in Oslo, and feasted there through Yule," *Ibid.*, p. 474, *Story of King Magnus, son of Erling*, chap. xxxi.; "and the King feasted there through the Yule-tide," *Ibid.*, p. 484, *Story of King Magnus, son of Erling*, chap. xlii.

[1] The *Saga Library*, edited by William Morris and Eiríkr Magnússon, Vol. I., London, 1891, p. 114: "Said Hermund: 'This is like the rest of thy lying, like as thou saidest in the winter-tide, Egil, when thou camest to me at my bidding from thy wreck of a house at Burg in Yule-tide: and right glad wert thou thereat, as was like to be; and when Yule was spent, thou grewest sad, as was like to be, thinking it hard to have to go home to that misery: but I, when I saw that, bade thee abide still, thou and another with thee; and thou tookest that, and wert fain thereof: but in spring-tide after Easter, when thou wert come home to Burg, thou saidst that thirty ice-horses had died, and had all been eaten by us.'"

There is no statement in the early parts of the *Heimskringla* about a Thing being held at Yule, a fact which alone proves that it was no old offering-tide; for both in Germany and Scandinavia the two things went together, being merely two different sides of the three annual assemblies of the men of the individual tribes. In the thirteenth century, however, Yule-tide seems to have been used for public announcements, for which it no doubt was fitted by the fact that men stayed either at home then or met in larger companies at the principal places of the country.[1]

The customs of Norway were transferred to Iceland and to Greenland; and in Greenland Yule was held, as in Europe, for a number of days, so that the *Völva* or prophetess could within the holy tide visit several farms, some of them more than a day's journey apart.[2] Christianity had at last conquered the Scandinavian tribes, as, half a millennium before, it had won over the Western Germanics. United to the world of Roman civilisation, it forced upon all its subjects a uniform system, not only of belief, but also of rite and custom. At the dawn of history an ancient, inherited unity of intellectual life had embraced all Germanic tribes, but amidst the various economic and mental environments into which the several tribes entered in the early Middle Ages that inheritance of the East was irrevocably lost. It was the destiny of Christianity to create a new mental unity for the Germanic world. A considerable part of the history of that nation is contained in the two words: *Yule* and *Christmas*.

---

[1] When, in 1262, King Hacon of Norway heard that the Scots committed all kinds of hostilities in the Hebrides, he resolved in council to issue in winter about Jól an edict through all Norway, and order out both what troops and provisions he thought his dominions could possibly supply for an expedition (*Bibliotheca Curiosa*: The Norwegian Account of King Haco's Expedition against Scotland, A.D. 1263. Literally translated from the original Icelandic of the Flateyan and Frisian MSS. By the Rev. James Johnstone, A.M., and edited with additional notes by Edmund Goldsmid, Edinburgh, 1885, p. 19).

[2] *Eirikssaga raudha*, ed. by G. Storm, p. 14 ss., Eugen Mogk, *Ueber Los, Zauber und Weissagung bei den Germanen* in *Kleinere Beiträge zur Geschichte, von Docenten der Leipziger Hochschule*, Leipzig, 1894, p. 86 ss.: "In a farm in Greenland, built and inhabited by Icelanders, there lived a woman named Thorbjörg. She was a prophetess, and was called Little Völva. She was wont in winter-tide to fare from one Yule banquet to another, and everywhere to ask for those men who wished to learn their future, and the course of the new year," etc.

CHAPTER XVI.

RESULTS.

I. Whilst early record and the history of institutions point to a tri-partition of THE GERMANIC YEAR, etymology is in favour of a dual division. This seeming contradiction is dissipated by the fact that, although, of old, the Aryans divided their year into two parts—winter and summer—only, they early took over a year of oriental origin, which consisted of six tides of three-score days each. Two such tides could be combined to form thirds of years, as three to form halves of years. Whilst there are no original Germanic month-names, there is ample evidence for these three-score-day tides. Yule was one of them. It originally extended from mid-November to mid-January; among the Goths of the sixth century it covered November and December; and among the Anglo-Saxons of the seventh century, December and January.

II. THE BEGINNING OF THE ANGLO-GERMAN YEAR doubtless was not wholly dependent on tradition, but was to some extent influenced by climatic conditions. Whilst all Germanic tribes began their year with the beginning of winter, the Western Germanics in Germany and Britain began their winter naturally somewhat later than the Northern Germanics did in Scandinavia and Iceland. The latter reckoned their annual circle as commencing towards the middle of October; the former began theirs towards the middle of November. Not only does the actual winter set in about that time both in Germany and Britain, but the coupling of November and December in Gothic to form one three-score-day tide, the usage attested by urbarial evidence, and the conditions of pasture life, all point likewise to a beginning of the Anglo-German year towards the 15th day of November.

III. There being evidence of a German festival in the first half of November as early as A.D. 14, we have good reason to regard THE FEAST OF MARTINMAS on November 11 as the successor of an ancient Germanic festive New Year, to which the Synod of Auxerre in 578, forbidding intemperance on that day, bears further testimony. The feasting about Martinmas even in the later Middle Ages possessed a higher popularity than belonged to any other similar annual feast.

IV. Martinmas being the successor of the ancient Germanic New Year, it is not strange that MARTINMAS AND THE TRI-PARTITION OF THE YEAR should be closely connected. Martinmas is the oldest legal term in the A.S. Laws, and appears as such very early on German soil also. Mid-Lent and Mid-July were the other two legal terms. The three constituted a division of the year into three equal parts, each of which consisted of a long hundred of days.

V. MARTINMAS AND THE DUAL DIVISION OF THE YEAR were no less closely connected. As late as the sixteenth century, Martinmas and Mid-May were German terms, and they are still the prevalent terms in Scotland. The Frankish May fields and the corresponding celebrations instituted by the Church as appropriate to the beginning of November and the Rogation days together point in the same direction. It was not before A.D. 755 that the latter two terms were superseded by March 1 and October 1.

VI. MARTINMAS AND MICHAELMAS were the two popular autumn festivities for which Germanic origin has been claimed. But in the matter of age, Michaelmas is far behind Martinmas. Whilst excessive Martinmas festivities were forbidden so early as A.D. 578, the ecclesiastical festival of St. Michael on September 29 was not instituted before A.D. 813; and prior to the seventeenth century the mentions of Martinmas are at least twice as frequent as those of Michaelmas—a fact which clearly shows the respective importance of the two terms. Michaelmas term owes its origin to the Roman quartering of the year. Even when agriculture grew in importance, and, consequently, the harvest festivals received an ever-increasing significance, Martinmas, as the centre of the slaughtering time of domestic animals, for ages outshone Michaelmas in popular splendour, till the stock of grain and potatoes under cultivation became in general so large that it ceased to matter very much when the cattle, sheep, and swine were killed.

VII. Whilst Martinmas, Mid-March, and Mid-July, on the one hand, and Martinmas and Mid-May, on the other, played the most important part as terms in the Germanic year, the Germanic tribes knew so little of SOLSTICES AND EQUINOXES that they had not even names for them. These conceptions they got from the Romans, and the different words which the various tribes formed to express these ideas are mere translations of the Roman denominations. There never was a Germanic solstice celebration, and December 25, the pseudo-winter-solstice of the Julian calendar, was no Germanic festive day until after the contact of the Germanic tribes with the Romans.

VIII. The first severe blow which the Germanic year received was from the Roman year. In course of time THE CALENDS OF JANUARY became the beginning of the year on Germanic soil as well as in the rest of the world. The Calends gifts, the Calends fires, the Calends mummery in the hides of animals, the Calends branches and trees are striking instances of the transference of customs which then took place and which came to form the centre of the later Germanic celebrations about the shortest day of the year.

IX. On the basis of a number of instances of sacrifices on tables occurring about the end of December and the beginning of January, it has been supposed that a Germanic dead festival was celebrated about that time. But these offerings were mere transformations of the TABULA FORTUNAE, a most important feature of the Calends-of-January celebration over the whole regions from Egypt to Rome in the early centuries of our era. The same holds for the New Year's cakes connected with that Egyptio-Roman custom.

X. THE NATIVITY OF CHRIST as an anniversary owed its origin to Rome and to the year 354, its evolution being clearly traceable. The *Dodeka-hemeron*, the time between Nativity and Epiphany, was one of its oldest products. In the sixth century a new era was begun with December 25 of the 753rd year of Rome, and the natural outgrowth of this was the moving of the New Year from the Calends of January to Christ's alleged birthday.

XI. One of the most important sources of our knowledge of the Germanic division of the year is the treatise of BEDA, DE MENSIBUS ANGLORUM, forming chapter xv. of his book *De Temporum Ratione*. It contains some facts of great antiquity, among them the names of two Germanic three-score-day tides, *Geola* and *Lida*. Some of Beda's other A.S. month-names were of comparatively late growth. Etymology was not his strong point, and no great weight can be attached to his interpretations of A.S. words. What he describes is not the Germanic year, but the Romano-Christian year, with which he was familiar. He was not aware of the numerous contradictions which his short statement contains. Notwithstanding his assertion that December 25 was originally called Yule, and that December and January from it received their names as the earlier and later Yulemonth, there is not a single case, prior to the eleventh century, in which December 25 was called Yule. His remark that the *ceremonies* practised in his time among the Christianised Angles on December 25 had given rise to its being called "the mothers' night," can only be explained as referring to human mothers who took part in an obscene but well-known cult in honour of the Virgin. It cannot denote any deities styled the mothers, for when he means to indicate that a celebration took its title from a deity, to which he supposed it to be devoted, he says so expressly.

XII. NATIVITY, CHRISTES MÆSS, AND CHRISTMAS are terms which show[7] the growth of a regular ecclesiastical celebration of December 25 in the centuries that followed Beda. Christ's birthday anniversary became from A.D. 800 the great day for state ceremonies. It was also observed as a strict Church holiday. Ordeals and oaths were forbidden from the end of the tenth century, and peace was ordained. Up to the end of the eleventh century the Church tried to make Christ's Nativity as joyous a time as possible. About the beginning of the twelfth century this goal seems to have been reached, for then the Church began a severe struggle against excessive gaiety at Christmas. Various peculiarly Christian conceptions and usages, evolved out of the hymn *Rorate Coeli*, generated the belief that the dew of the night between December 24 and 25 was specially beneficent. Out of the legend that in the actual night of Christ's birth all nature had rejoiced, all trees had budded, and all animals had talked sprang the fancy that on the holy anniversary apple trees and hawthorns bloomed. This combining with the Calends-of-January traditional usage of setting up trees and branches led at last to the Christmas tree.

XIII. In ancient historical times THE SCANDINAVIAN YEAR began between October 9 and 14, and was halved by a day between April 9 and 14. When the Roman quartering of the year gained the mastery, the dividing days lay between January 9 and 14 and June 9 and 14. These days alone, and under no circumstance December 25 and June 24, could properly have been called midwinter and midsummer.

XIV. The tri-partition of the early Scandinavian year, no longer recognisable in the oldest runic almanacs, was still visible in the SCANDINAVIAN OFFERING TIDES. The author of the *Heimskringla* remembered quite well that, originally, there were three of them, although he was not quite sure which they were. As, however, in the early parts of the *Heimskringla*, all great festivities recorded up to A.D. 840 were held in autumn at winter's beginning, there can be no doubt that this, held about October 9 to 14, was one of the three. The second, held between February 9 and 14, was called *Góiblót*, and the third, between June 9 and 14, coincided in later Iceland with the great annual assembly, the *Allthing*. After A.D. 840 a *Jól* festival began to appear, and was in the *Heimskringla* up to A.D. 1000 mentioned almost as often as the autumn festival. Subsequently it rapidly grew in importance, whilst the autumn festival was merged in a simple St. Michaelmas, and *Góiblót* disappeared altogether.

XV. The SCANDINAVIAN YULE festival was a product of the ninth-century. It arose out of the festivals *at vetrnóttum* and in the month of *Gói* (October 9 to 14 and February 9 to 14). For at least a century it was celebrated about the middle of January (a dividing-point in the Roman quartering of the Scandinavian year), and it was King Hakon the Good of Norway (A.D. 940-963) who first ordered its celebration on the same day as the Christian festival of the Nativity. By this act the Scandinavians joined, in an important point, the ritual world of Christian Western Europe, and recovered part of that intellectual unity with the other Germanic tribes which had been lost during their migration time in the early Middle Ages.

GLASGOW: PRINTED AT THE UNIVERSITY PRESS BY ROBERT MACLEHOSE AND CO.

www.ingramcontent.com/pod-product-compliance
Lightning Source LLC
Chambersburg PA
CBHW030122030726
47498CB00007B/2501